I0628741

Heart Like an Ocean

Christine Steendam

Hazelridge Press

Box 21 Group 37 RR3
Dugald, MB R0E 0K0
www.christinesteendam.com

ISBN 978-0-9939259-7-9
Heart Like an Ocean
Christine Steendam
Copyright Christine Steendam 2016
Published by Hazelridge Press

Photo Credit: AP Fuchs
Author Photo: Prairie and Pine Studio

Second Edition/First Printing March 2016

HAZELRIDGE PRESS.

The song *Spanish Ladies* is quoted in the text of this book. Credit to this song is first found in the log books of the *Nellie* 1796.

To Heather;
for being there from page 1 to 361
and everything in between.

CONTENTS

ACKNOWLEDGMENTS

This is the second time I'm sitting down to write acknowledgements for *Heart Like an Ocean*. It's a bit of a surreal experience to be proofreading, formatting, and revamping my very first book all over again. Wow, the journey life has taken me on is not one I expected.

Thank you to AP Fuchs for the *gorgeous* new cover. You worked with me to bring exactly what I envisioned to life and then made it even better.

Thank you to everyone who has read any of my writing, or is just now picking up one of my books for the very first time.

Thank you to everyone who encourages me every day to keep doing what I love. Thank you.

I'm including the original acknowledgements below because, well, all those people are still to thank and this book wouldn't be without them.

-Christine Steendam March 2016

Behind every author, there is a group of people who support, encourage, push and help get the book to the point of publication. I am no different.

Heart Like an Ocean began at Seasons ranch, so I'm going to start my thanks there. Thank you to Barb and George for the years of putting up with me, for teaching me about horses, and for providing me with a home away from home that fueled my creativity. To this day, your ranch is still my favorite place to write.

Thank you to my parents, who always encouraged my writing and always told me I would be published. Even when I thought it was a pipe dream, they told me it could be a reality.

Beta readers are an integral part of the novel writing process and without mine *Heart Like an Ocean* wouldn't be the book it is today. Thank you to Aunty Joanne, Aunty Theresa, and Andrew B for slugging through the first draft and giving kind but constructive criticisms. I know it's been a few years since I first started sending you those emails, chapter by chapter, but your contribution has not been forgotten.

I have one very special reader, who I would consider my Alpha reader. Thank you, Heather, for letting me bounce ideas off of you, always being the first in line to read what came out of my mind, and going through every single draft of *Heart Like an Ocean*. I know that was a lot of work on your part.

Of course, I also have to thank my husband, Kyle. Without you, I never would have moved forward and hired an editor or even considered publication. You pushed me to take the next step. I also owe you a huge amount of thanks for being willing to share me with my laptop.

Thank you to TJ, my copy editor. You were the person to polish *Heart Like an Ocean* and let it shine for submission. Not to mention your help with my query letter. Your support has been invaluable.

Thank you to Viola Estrella for some fantastic cover art.

Thank you to June, my 5 Prince Publishing editor, for seeing something in my story and bringing it into the 5 Prince family, and for your hard work and dedication to making it the best it can be. It was a pleasure to work with you and I hope to do so again in the future.

Thank you to the entire 5 Prince Publishing family: Bernadette, Marie, June, everyone behind the scenes, and all the authors that support each other. I could not ask for a better group of people to be part of my support network.

Without all of you, I wouldn't be sitting here writing these acknowledgements today. Thank you from the bottom of my heart.

-Christine Steendam, January 2013

HEART LIKE AN OCEAN

PROLOGUE

Spain-1666

Senona looked around the room full of swirling dresses of so many shapes and colors. It was like a dream and left her overwhelmed and unable to tear her eyes away. Tonight she was a princess in her new dress with her hair curled, cascading in loose waves down her back. Tonight she was perfect.

Browsing the room, this time in search of familiar faces, Senona spotted Caton Amador and Isidro Amato. The boys, although older, were her friends and a welcome relief to the overwhelming nature of her surroundings. She made her way around the perimeter of the room in their general direction.

Isidro was never very serious about anything and enjoyed teasing Senona, which annoyed her to no end. Caton was much more subdued and quiet, at least around her. Although they were not as close as they once had been, the families remained good friends, and the three of them spent many hours riding around the countryside or playing games in the garden. When they were younger, Isidro and Caton had been her constant companions, helping her sneak out of tea with their Madres or rescuing her from lessons with her tutor. Now they never voluntarily saw each other, but due to their families' relationship, they found themselves together often enough.

"Senona, my chica! You are a picture of beauty, as always," boomed Isidro's obnoxious and teasing voice.

Caton turned to look at the young girl. "Leave her alone, Isidro."

"Come on, Caton. She's glad to see us."

Caton frowned but said nothing, turning his attention back to the pretty girl standing next to him. Isidro seemed to accept that as permission to continue, and he smirked mockingly at Senona, beckoning her. The small flock of girls that surrounded the two boys giggled, causing her to blush and become hesitant and uncomfortable. She had never seen the boys in this environment, and she quickly questioned her decision that she belonged with them.

"It's okay, Isidro. I just wanted to say hello."

"Well then, run along. There must be some of your friends around."

Senona forced a smile and turned to Caton. "Hello, Caton."

He barely acknowledged her with a brief glance and nod in her direction, and then returned to ignoring her. Unsure of how to deal with Caton's rejection, she walked away, her eyes burning with angry tears that threatened to spill over. Why was he being so rude? Not even so much as a hello, as if he were embarrassed to be associated with her.

As she pushed her way through the crowd, she heard one of the girls laugh. "Caton, I do believe you hurt her feelings."

Caton's deep, unmistakable chuckle cut through the din and his voice was all she heard. "She's a silly, strange girl. I would rather not encourage her."

Senona expected this behavior from Isidro, but from Caton? She had always thought he was honest and simple, but his actions tonight had shown her otherwise. She had been a fool to think that these older boys were her friends.

Escaping into the shadows, she hid from the sneering glances and mocking laughter that seemed to follow her wherever she went. She had thought that tonight would be different, but nothing had changed. She was just a strange little girl.

The night was a blur, a blur of swirling skirts and obnoxious voices. To nearly everyone she was invisible. Even her madre and padre, who had never been overly affectionate towards their daughter, seemed to have completely forgotten her existence. But that wasn't so different from normal. They weren't very affectionate people ever, even towards each other.

At the end of the night, Senona lay in bed, her new dress hanging in her wardrobe, mocking her. She had realised tonight how far she fell from society's standards, her own parents' standards. Any illusion she had of being a princess, of being perfect for one night had been shattered. But that didn't really bother her. The truly odd thing was that she felt a weight lifted from her shoulders. Perhaps she didn't have to be that way. Perhaps now she had the freedom to do as she wanted. It wasn't as if anyone cared about her anyway. She was just a strange little girl.

CHAPTER ONE

Three years later
Spain-1669

Senona looked back hesitantly as she entered the dark stable where her father's horses were kept. It was the middle of the night; the countryside was quiet as slumber had overtaken everyone and everything around. She was confident that no one had witnessed her escape from the manor, nor would anyone know of her disappearance until morning. That was how she intended it; let them find out the bride had run the night before her wedding. She wouldn't allow herself to become the trophy wife of an arranged marriage.

She was young, though not so young that she shouldn't already be married. Nearing her twenties, she could have married anytime within the last three years, though she'd found no suitable match. Being the daughter of Don Marco Montez meant she would not marry just anyone, and her parents' final decision was with an older, rich, and influential doctor from Barcelona, Senor Flamez.

Senor Flamez was nearing fifty and widowed not five years earlier. She was to be his second wife, more to help him run his dilapidated household than anything else. Rumor had it that

Senor Flamez had allowed things to fall apart after Senora Flamez passed away in childbirth, losing the child along with her. It would be Senona's job to make the man happy again, provide him with an heir, and allow his life to become what it had been in previous years: rich, elegant, and prestigious. How he came to the conclusion that she would be suitable for that role she could not fathom.

Senona was not, by any definition, elegant or humble. She was quick to anger and didn't much enjoy doing the domestic duties expected of a good wife. Instead, she could be more often than not, found in a pasture or riding along the high cliffs bordering the coast of the Mediterranean Sea. Perhaps that was why her madre and padre were so pleased to have found her a husband; she would no longer be their problem or embarrassment.

This late at night the horses made very little noise. A few stamped their hooves or rustled the hay; otherwise, the only sound was their breathing. Senona's horse was a young stallion; a Spanish horse with the best pedigree money could buy. He had been a gift for her sixteenth birthday. Only a young colt then, she had trained him herself and preferred no other horse in her father's stable over Naldo.

Saddling him quickly and quietly, she shoved the small amount of clothes she had carried from her room into a saddlebag. She hid a bag of doubloons, which she had stolen from her father's safe, carefully among them. It was a small fortune and would surely have her father's hounds chasing her as soon as the red sun rose above the horizon. However, she did not plan to be on land by then. She would find a ship where she would be much harder to track. Perhaps, like the romantic stories, she would be able to disappear into the horizon never to be seen again. One could only hope. Yet, as she mounted Naldo and rode him down the road that led to Barcelona, Senona found herself looking back in sadness. Although she had not been happy here, it was her home, and this would be the last time she'd ever see it. No longer would she be living the life of comfort that she was accustomed to, no longer would she be secure in her future, and no longer would she be able to wake up every morning without fear or worry. Was she truly ready for this life? Looking forward again, she refused to allow herself another glance back. Whether she was ready for this change or not, she had made up her mind, and she would go through with it. As hard and as treacherous as it may be, wasn't freedom worth it?

* * *

Upon first entering Barcelona, the streets were quiet and abandoned. Rich homes and rich families resided here, and they were all in bed at this late hour. However, as she drew closer to the docks, she came across more and more people, none looking very reputable, many giving her looks that made her uneasy. There were still a few safe places near the docks, though. The merchant's quarter housed many rich men, friends of her parents, the Amadors being only one of them. Senona missed the years when she had been friends with Caton Amador. Age changed things and people, and as a result, friendships slipped away.

Not really knowing where to start, only knowing what her destination was to be, Senona dismounted and led Naldo to the docks in hope that a captain would be around from whom she could buy passage to Port Royale. There, in a British colony, she would be out of her parents' reach. She could start a new life.

While the rest of Barcelona was very much asleep, the docks were alive with activity. Music and raucous voices came from the many taverns that lined the docks, all dangerous places that Senor Amador had warned her about many times when taking her on tours of his ships. This was no place for a lady at any time of day, much less in the middle of the night. But desperate times called for desperate measures, and she was certain there would be more than a few captains in these taverns ready and willing to make some extra gold. Finding one who would willingly enter British waters would be a little harder. Pirates and privateers patrolled there, and it'd be even harder to find one who would allow a horse on board. The few who would have allowed Naldo held to the old sailor's superstition that having a woman aboard would bring bad luck. This made the task of finding passage more difficult than Senona had expected. Only one captain, an Englishman, Old Richard, seemed to hold no qualms.

"Port Royale ye say?"

"Si, Senor, are you making port there at all?"

"Just so happens I is. It will cost ye, though. It's bad luck for a woman to be on board, and I ain't too fond of livestock."

"How much?" It was never a question of the money to Senona. It was her Padre's, and its only purpose to her was to get her far away.

"Fifty pieces of eight."

Senona nodded. "And when do you leave?"

"First light."

"I'll give you thirty doubloons to cast off within the next two hours."

"Two hours, eh? I ain't barely supplied."

"Stop at the next port and get your supplies then. I can take my money elsewhere." Senona spoke with authority and confidence that she did not feel. She had seen her padre conduct business and knew that if she was to get her way, she had to appear in control. She carefully placed the bag of doubloons on the dirty wood table to illustrate she was able to provide what she promised. Old Richard's eyes gleamed greedily.

"Aye, two hours and the *Sea Vulture* shall cast off."

"I shall see you then, Captain." She got up and reached for the bag but Old Richard grabbed her wrist. Her eyes narrowed, but she held herself in check. She was in a strange place right now, and it wasn't a good idea to start any trouble.

"I'll be needing that pay in advance."

Senona smiled, gently pulling her hand from his grip and counted out the promised coins. "Two hours, Captain. I cannot wait longer than that."

Senona walked away, leaving the smoky, loud tavern behind a closed door, and breathed in the fresh sea air. Naldo was tied to a hitching post only a few feet away, nickering softly in greeting. There was something about that man that made her uneasy, but she was left with little choice. Therefore, as unpleasant as this voyage was going to be, she would have to make the best of it

* * *

In a far corner of the bar, hidden by shadows that the lanterns and candles didn't quite reach, a man got up and followed the girl out into the dark night. He was tall and moved smoothly from years of practice at walking on rolling ship decks. A brace of pistols and a cutlass were strapped to his belt.

He had not been blind to the transaction that had occurred between the girl and Old Richard, nor was he oblivious, as she seemed to be, of the danger she was in.

Following her at a safe distance, he waited to see what she would do. There were only a few short hours before she would find out that she had not bought passage but instead sold herself into the white slave market, of which there was plenty of demand and good return. Old Richard was no fool. He had seen how naïve this girl was, and he immediately saw the profit he could make. She had been sheltered, it was apparent by her trust in humanity. Stupid girl, foolish girl. It would serve her right if he just allowed her to continue on her self-destructive path. She thought her life was hard now? Just wait until she started her new life, the life Old Richard chose for her. He couldn't allow it, though. For all his questionable morals, Brant Foxton could not with clear conscience, allow this girl to fall into the hands of Old Richard.

The girl had led her horse down the docks a little way, but now she chose to stop. Looking around, she sat down, looking ready to wait for the next two hours. He studied her and sighed. He was sure he would not be able to trick her into coming onto his ship instead of Old Richard's, nor would she be so trusting as to accept passage for free. That would raise red flags in her mind. She was not stupid, merely sheltered.

Watching her a while, he became certain she wouldn't leave. He had less than two hours to get his crew together and leave town. Turning, he left the girl and her horse and walked the short distance to where his ship sat docked. Most of his crew would be away from the ship. He had promised them a two-day leave and they would be enjoying it. The only souls aboard the *BlackFox* would be Karl and Matt, taking care of tonight's watch, and James, the cabin boy, who was likely sleeping soundly below deck. But even with the four of them, that was not enough to sail a ship of the *BlackFox's* size, nor enough to successfully kidnap a girl at the same time.

Walking aboard, Matt, a young sailor who had been with him for the past three years, greeted him. He had proven himself honest, hardworking, and exceptionally skilled as a sailor, and had quickly worked his way through the ranks. Matt was the sailing master and a damn good one. If Karl ever decided to retire, which was unlikely, he was set to take his place as quartermaster. For now, Brant took advantage of Matt's exceptional navigation skills.

"Top of the evening to ye, Cap'n."

"That it is, Matthew. I need you to do something for me."

Matt, who was sitting near the mast playing a guitar, stopped and nodded. "Yes, Sir?"

"There's a bit of trouble brewing, and I need you to collect the crew. We need to set sail as soon as possible."

"Militia?"

"No, just some trouble with another captain. Tell anyone who won't come that he'll have to find a new billet. I wait for no man."

"Yessir." Matt took off without another word.

"Karl!"

An older man stood up by the railing of the upper deck. He stood unsteadily, visibly leaning on the railing for support.

"Brant, there'd better be a damned good reason why you're hollering at me at this time of night," he slurred.

"Karl, is there a reason you're yelling at your captain?"

The man slowly made his way down the stairs and approached him. Standing closer than was comfortable, Brant could smell the rum on his breath. "Brant Foxton, you may be captain but I raised ye from when ye were naught but knee high. I'll talk to ye however I wish when the crew ain't around to bear witness."

Brant laughed and took a slight step back. "We're leaving in a couple of hours. When the crew arrives, I need you to make sure things are ready to set sail. I have an errand to run."

"Aye, Brant. Trouble?"

"Nothing to be too worried about, I would just rather not be in port come morning. Go sober up; there's some coffee in the galley."

Karl walked off somewhat unsteadily to the galley.

Brant sighed. James would be asleep in the crew's quarters. He would rather he stayed asleep till morning, but someone had to get together a makeshift stall and collect enough water to make the next port. The rest of their supplies would be collected then. As for the crew, if he could find a handful sober enough to function, things might just work out.

* * *

The crew began to stagger in about twenty minutes later, all drunk and grumbling unhappily about their festivities being cut short. However, as unhappy as they were, they were all there within the hour. Not a man was missing. Walking among them, Brant instructed them all to get some hot coffee from the galley. Only Matt and the master gunner, Christopher, were sober enough to help him with the more delicate task of getting the girl aboard.

"You two, come with me," he instructed.

The girl still sat where Brant had left her only an hour earlier. Her horse stirred slightly but seemed content to stand watch near his mistress.

"Forgive me, Cap'n, but since when are we in the kidnapping business? This don't sit well with me," said Matt nervously.

"Matthew, we're immoral men. If you're choosing now to grow a conscience, perhaps you should find another line of work."

Neither man responded.

"I don't care if you two have to bind and gag the girl, just get her to the ship in one piece and preferably unharmed. I'll look after the horse."

"Yessir," they chorused.

Brant stood back as the two men approached the girl. It pained him to see the look of surprise and then terror cross over the girl's face as Christopher grabbed her from behind. She dropped the horse's lead rope as she struggled to break free, but Matt made quick work of tying her up, and then there was very little she could do. They were efficient; he could say that much. No scream managed to escape her lips, and although she struggled as Matt carried her over his shoulder, he never once faltered.

Brant went over to the startled horse that was dancing in confusion and picked up the forgotten lead rope. He followed behind them at a distance, being careful that the girl didn't see his face. He didn't need her recognizing him when morning came and explanations had to be made. Christopher fell into stride with Brant as they approached the ship.

"Where would ye like her, Cap'n?"

"Put her in my cabin for now. I don't imagine I'll need it tonight."

It would be a long night. With the majority of his crew drunk, he could only hope Old Richard didn't figure out who interfered until morning. All that aside, Brant would be happy if his stumbling, useless crew managed to get his ship out of the harbor unscathed.

* * *

A rough hand clamped over her mouth silenced Senona's scream. Her muffled protests brought no sympathy or release from either of the men. For only a brief second, his hand left her face, but he quickly replaced it with a musty, salty tasting gag. The other man picked her up easily, slinging her uncomfortably over his shoulder as if she were a sack of flour. Though she struggled against her captor, Senona couldn't see where she was going; only the retreating view of where she had been sitting a moment ago, and a dark figure followed with Naldo.

They walked up a long, wooden plank. So they were taking her aboard a ship. She had heard of young girls being kidnapped and sold as slaves. Was that to be her sad fate? However, much to her surprise, she heard the man who had been following instruct for her to be put in his cabin, not the brig as she had expected.

Upon entering the cabin, the man gently lowered her to the floor.

"I'm quite sorry, ma'am. I ain't in the business of kidnapping, but orders is orders."

He removed her gag slowly but replaced it with his rough hand, once again cutting off her screams. "Now I know you wanna scream and all, but no one here is gonna help. So it would be mightily appreciated if you'd just keep quiet and save up all that screaming for the cap'n. Lord knows he deserves it."

Senona wanted to ask what they would do with her and what they had done with Naldo, but she found herself too terrified to speak. Panic coursed through her body leaving her trembling against the man's hand. How did she manage to get herself into such a situation?

The man left her alone in the dark cabin. Closing the door behind him, she heard the distinct click of a lock.

Getting up slowly, she stumbled to the wall and felt her way around the room until she found a bed. She was exhausted and scared. All she wanted was to feel the warmth and comfort of a bed. She had an overwhelming urge to cry, but tears wouldn't fall. She was just too tired for tears, too tired to think about what had happened in the short time since she had left home, too tired to even function. Answers would have to wait until morning.

* * *

When Senona awoke the next morning, she was greeted by the sight of a young man with short blonde hair, sitting with an air of superiority. He was intently studying a map laid out on the ornate desk situated in the center of the room.

"Welcome to the land of the living," said the man, without so much as a glance up from his map.

"Senor, may I ask where the captain is?" she asked.

"Captain Brant Foxton at your service," he said with a smirk, this time rewarding her with his undivided attention.

Standing up, she drew herself to her full height. "So you are the man responsible for my abduction. What do you plan to do with me, Captain? Sell me as a slave? And where is my horse? You owe me an explanation for how I was treated last night."

She squared her five-foot-five body, waiting for his response. She could see him looking her over and his lips pressed together in a smirk. "Yes, yes you would bring me a tidy sum on the black market. I know a few men off Tortuga who would be more than willing to take you, but that is not what I have in mind. Old Richard, however, the 'oh so kind' captain whom you purchased passage from had just that in mind. He is most likely sitting in Barcelona right now very upset that the young Senorita did not show up. Though I am sure he has spent your doubloons quite frivolously already. Aside from that, I can assure you that your stallion is safe and content below deck."

"Captain Richard and I had a business deal. I don't know what made you think his intentions were anything less than pure when you are much more suspicious in my mind. Only the most diabolical man abducts and that is—"

Brant cut her off sharply. "Stop right there, Miss. I am a man of honor, which may be hard for you to believe seeing as what I put you through last night, but I will not have my character questioned by a girl who has barely seen eighteen years and hasn't sullied her ears with even the maid's gossip. Old Richard would never have brought you to Port Royale. I will. That is a fact and I urge you to accept it."

"I don't see what else I can do given the present circumstances. However, I cannot afford to pay you. I'm afraid you have brought any costs and trouble I bring upon your own head." She could afford to pay him, and she was certain he knew that, but since he had forcibly taken her aboard his ship, Senona had decided that it would be at his cost, not hers.

"Don't worry over the cost. We will hardly notice you. I can't guarantee a direct course to Port Royale, as I have other, paying business, to attend to. We can discuss this all later tonight, though. You will join me for dinner." There was no room for argument in his voice.

"Of course, Captain," she spat out snidely, knowing there was no use in protesting. The man seemed trustworthy enough—for someone that had just kidnapped her—and her energy was better spent elsewhere than fighting a useless battle.

"Wonderful. You are free to wander around the ship as you please, but try to stay out of the way. This is your cabin to use for the remainder of the voyage; however, I will have to make use of it from time to time as all my things are here. Now if you'll excuse me I have a lot of things to attend to. We left in such a great hurry last night, and I can't say any of my crew is overly pleased. We will likely be making port in the next few days to stock up. You have until then to decide if you wish to stay aboard the *BlackFox*. I assure you that you will not be kept here against your will." Bowing slightly, he left the cabin, giving her a brief glimpse of a clear, blue sky through the open door.

Senona sighed and fell back down on the bed, grimacing as her head hit harder than she'd expected. Sitting up again, she looked around. The cabin was bare except for the large desk and dresser. There were no portraits or items of sentiment. No clues as to who the young captain was. The only thing that gave Senona an insight into his character was the ornate woodwork that gave testimony to expensive and sophisticated taste. He was no simple captain, of that Senona was certain.

Straightening her dress and quickly braiding her long hair, Senona left the cabin to explore her surroundings and find Naldo. The ship wasn't large, obviously not meant for passengers, but instead for speed. Below deck, Naldo was calmly eating some hay. The fact that he was in a dark and smelly ship hold didn't seem to faze him at all. "Good morning, Naldo. I hope your night went better than mine." She stroked his muscled shoulder rhythmically as she spoke.

"He slept well, ma'am. I found him stretched right out on the floor when I came down to feed him this morning. Good thing I made the stall big so he could rest his legs," said a young version of the captain, as he came down the steps with a large pail of water in hand. He looked to be about sixteen.

"Yes, very thoughtful of you. How long do you suppose the supply of water and hay will last?"

"Only a few days. We'll make Port Gibraltar by the end of the week and get more. We left in a bit of a hurry last night."

"Thank you for looking after Naldo for me. What is your name?"

"James Foxton," he responded, not offering any further information. "Just doing my job, ma'am."

Senona smiled as she watched James walk away cheerfully. The captain was a mystery. She didn't understand how the same man who ordered her abduction could also have such a happy boy on his crew, a boy that she was certain was his younger brother. She picked some clean straw off the floor of Naldo's stall and gave him a quick brushing. Finding his halter and lead rope dumped unceremoniously on a crate, she put them on Naldo, who nuzzled her as she did so.

"Come, Naldo, let's get your legs stretched."

Senona didn't know why she always spoke to him. She knew he couldn't understand her, but somehow, it gave her an odd sort of comfort that someone was listening, even if it was only a horse. She led him out of his stall and up on deck. He followed her calmly, but his eyes showed his apprehension towards his new surroundings, and his ears twitched in constant attention. The sailors going about their various jobs and the surrounding water alarmed Naldo, but he stayed close to Senona, her reassuring words helping to calm him.

"That's a fine looking stallion ye got there."

Senona gave a start and turned around to face a grizzled, yet kind-faced old man. He wore a large smile that, she suspected, could put even her padre at ease. "Thank you."

"The name's Karl. I'm the quartermaster here."

"Senona Montez."

"Pleased to meet ye. If any of the crew gives ye any trouble, ye come see me. We ain't too used to guests."

"I'll try to stay out of the way."

"Don't ye worry your pretty little head about that. No one is gonna mind. I'm just makin' sure the men here treat ye right." Karl turned to walk away but Senona stopped him.

"Karl?"

"Yes, my pretty?"

"Why does the captain keep James aboard? How does he get his education?"

"We're naught but simple sailors. How would the cap'n accomplish that? Educations are for rich people, men much better than us."

"There is more to the captain and his brother than this life."

"Ye can keep those ideas if ye like, but I ain't gonna confirm them. The boy is happy here and, although this life is a hard one, even I can't say he'd be better off on shore. The cap'n does his best to do right by him."

"Are there no parents?"

"Begging your pardon, miss, but I can't be answering questions about the captain nor his brother. You're just gonna have to ask him yourself."

"Thank you, Karl."

"Aye."

Karl walked away, leaving Senona alone in the middle of a deck crawling with activity. Making her way over to the railing where she hoped to be out of the way, she leaned out to try and catch a glimpse of Barcelona. It was there; a dark line along the horizon. She could just make out the cliffs that she had ridden across so many times.

"You seem to have the young stallion's trust. Not many horses would be so calm at sea," said Brant as he approached her.

"Naldo has trust in me, and that was not easy to earn. But as calm as he looks, he is quite nervous."

"I wouldn't guess it."

"Not everything is as it seems. See, his eyes are wide and anxious, his ears are constantly moving in total attention, and if you touch him, you will feel that he is trembling. If not for his complete trust in me, Naldo would flee."

"I was raised in a lord's house and had riding instructors of the best caliber, but none ever taught me this," said Brant thoughtfully, as he studied Naldo more closely. "It's as if he's talking to you with every move he makes."

Senona smiled. So she had guessed right that he was a noble.

"That is exactly what he's doing. Teachers tell you how to handle a horse, how to tame it, and be master over it. They do not teach you how to communicate or form a partnership with one."

"You're different from other noblewomen I've known."

"I certainly hope so. If you hadn't been able to see any difference I would have been insulted."

Brant put her at ease. It was an uncommon feeling for her as she was used to constantly being on edge around people. What made it even stranger was that this man should terrify and anger her. He had taken her aboard his ship against her will, and now she found herself talking to him as if he were a friend, something she hadn't had in quite some time.

"I knew you were a noble from the moment I saw you, but there was something in your demeanor that made it apparent that you are different." Then he added, "Besides, what woman would leave a home such as the Montez estate?"

"Then you know who I am."

Brant's eyes sparkled in silent amusement. "Well, rumors do get around with the young women about 'that Montez girl.' I'm afraid I'd recognize you almost anywhere. Aren't you missing your wedding today?"

"I am. I'm sure I will be the scandal of the season after this exploit." She laughed. "I'll leave you to your work, though. I think Naldo has had quite enough fresh air."

After making sure Naldo was comfortable and had everything he needed, Senona went back on deck. Still unsure of what to make of the situation she found herself in, she figured the best thing to do was to keep busy and keep her mind off of things until a decision had to be made.

Due to the ship leaving in such a hurry, there was plenty that needed doing. Karl was walking around the deck giving orders to men or inspecting their work. He seemed to be a gentle taskmaster. Senona observed him dealing with a few younger sailors and was surprised to see him carefully explain what they had done incorrectly and proceed to show them how it was to be done. Not once did she hear an angry word cross his lips. As he passed near Senona, she called him over. "Karl, is there anything I can do?"

Karl stopped and looked at her, surprised. "Have ye ever been on a ship?"

"No, but I'm a fast learner."

He looked thoughtful. "Well, I ain't got time to show ye much now, but perhaps ye can take a climb up to the crow's nest. Take a good look around and let me know what ye see."

Senona glanced down at her skirt and was all the more thankful that she'd worn a simple dress without the layers of petticoats that would have impeded her climb. With a nod of her head and a shrug of her shoulders, Senona walked off towards the mast and was climbing quickly up the small ladder before Karl could get another word in. The thought of anyone being able to see up her skirts barely crossed her mind. She'd been climbing trees all her life and modesty was not something she had ever worried much about, plus it gave her a smug sense of satisfaction to imagine her mother's face if she could see her now.

Senona had never been so high in her life, and the view did not disappoint. It was breathtaking. She looked around and saw the thin lines that were the land masses of Spain and Africa on either side. However, out here in the middle of the Mediterranean Sea, they were completely alone with nothing but the wind and the waves for company, friends that could quickly turn on you out in open water. It was a daunting thought, being at the mercy of the waves and on a less-than-reputable ship. She had seen the Jolly Roger hanging idly below. Captain Foxton made no effort to hide his ship's purpose.

She could have climbed down then and reported to Karl, but instead she chose to enjoy the view.

"Breathtaking, ain't it?" asked a young man, standing on the spar directly below her.

Senona guessed he had just finished unfurling a sail, though she was too caught up in her own thoughts to notice. Reaching down, she held her skirts tightly against her legs, something she hadn't been able to do while climbing.

"It's amazing. I would almost be content to stay here forever."

"Almost, but not quite?" asked the man.

"Not quite. There is something about solid ground under your feet that you just can't replace. You're at the mercy of the wind and water here. At least on land you have more control. My name's Senona."

"Matt."

Senona smiled. She had yet to receive an introduction that included a last name from anyone besides the captain and his brother. "It's nice to meet you, Matt. If you don't mind me asking, what is life like on this ship?" It wouldn't hurt to try and get an idea of what the captain was like, and what better way to do so than to find out from the men who spent every day with him?

"Best life I ever had. The cap'n looks after his crew better than most cap'ns. Don't base what ye think of him by what happened last night. He's a good man."

"That's hard to believe."

"Ye aren't angry with me. I was the one that hauled ye here."

Senona grimaced. She had thought he sounded familiar but hadn't wanted to make any accusations. It wouldn't have gotten her anywhere to cause conflict. "On his orders."

"He was trying to help ye."

She said nothing. Could she really deny that? There had been no evidence to the contrary, and she had to admit they were treating her quite admirably so far, aside from the previous night.

Matt smiled a cocky sort of grin. He knew she had no argument. "I best be getting down. Karl will be hollering up at me soon to get down and back to work." He made his way over to a shroud and began to shimmy down.

Senona took one last look around and then she too climbed down to inform Karl of how alone they were. But with the threat of land all around her, Senona felt they weren't alone enough. She was still too close to home to be safe.

* * *

Senona walked into the captain's dining room that night wearing the same clothes she had worn the night before, and all day. It was very much against her upbringing, but she had a limited supply of clothing. She blushed briefly upon realizing she was late and had caused the captain, Karl, and James to wait. However, she quickly shook it off. After all, she was among pirates, not among the nobility of Spain.

"Good evening," she said with a forced smile.

Brant stood up and helped Senona to her seat, directly to the right of his.

"Thank you, Captain," she said, sitting quietly and placing a napkin on her lap.

The array of food was spectacular, considering they were on a ship, and one that had left in a hurry at that. Senona thought back to the days when she had been friends with Caton; he had told her horror stories about the food on ships and was somewhat relieved to see they weren't true.

"This all looks quite amazing, Captain."

"This is only the first day at sea. Just wait until we've been out here for a few weeks. Not much will look good then," said James.

Brant chuckled. "I'm afraid he's right. I would recommend enjoying it while the food is still fresh. We are fortunate that the cook had the good sense to get a few things when we had first docked."

At this, everyone started to eat. Those few words seemed to instill haste in everyone, as if the food may go stale as they sat there. However, after a few minutes of eating in silence, Senona spoke up, not entirely comfortable with the lack of conversation.

"How long do you expect to be at sea before we dock in Port Royale?" she asked between mouthfuls of potatoes.

Brant lifted an eyebrow in amusement. "You're staying with your kidnappers then?"

"I haven't decided yet, but I thought it best to make an informed decision."

"It all depends on the weather, how many enemy ships we come across, and how often we make port. I'd say maybe two or three months. I try to stay out the entire season if possible."

"Do you come across enemy ships often?" Senona asked, knowing very well they weren't enemy ships at all, just ships ripe for picking by pirates like Brant Foxton. This was no military vessel.

"Yes, ma'am, the French and Dutch have become quite bold, and the Spanish, well, we like them the best," informed James. Brant winced and kicked him under the table.

James gave Brant a glare that no cabin boy should get away with, while Senona studied the whole exchange in fascination. Smiling, she replied, "Let's not ignore the purpose of this ship. I'm not completely ignorant."

Karl smiled but remained silent as the other three spoke. He didn't seem to feel any need to speak while he was enjoying his food whole-heartedly.

Brant, however, did not seem comfortable with the subject they had breached and quickly changed it. "How do you think Naldo will do? Three months is a long time for a horse to be cooped up."

"I can't really say. If I find he's taking it badly, I suppose I'll just have to get off when we make port. If I stay, that is."

"The horse'll do fine," reassured Karl.

"You're sure?" asked Senona.

"Horses get transported by ship all the time in war or to the colonies. He'll do just fine after he's had some time to get used to everything."

"I hope you're right, Karl. Whether on this ship or another, I would like to get all the way to Port Royale."

Brant stood up then. His plate had been completely polished off. "If you will all excuse me, I believe I'm going to turn in for the night."

"G'night, Cap'n," said Karl.

"Lessons first thing in the morning, James," said Brant sternly.

James scowled a little but nodded his assent, and on that note, Brant left the room.

Karl followed Brant's example not much later. "My old age don't allow me many late nights anymore," he explained with a smile before he too took his leave to make one last round of the ship.

"Will you come with me to check on Naldo?" Senona asked James.

"Of course."

The two of them went below deck, laughing as they went, with James telling Senona some of the more amusing stories of things that had happened on the ship.

When she had woken up that morning, she had been scared, confused, and angry. She had been on a strange ship with strange people and in the span of a single day the crew had made her feel happy and at home. That was something Senona was only now experiencing for the first time in her life.

CHAPTER TWO

Senona watched Karl's hands as he wove the thick needle and thread through a sail that had torn earlier that day. Brant had asked her to repair it thinking she would know what to do. Karl, however, quickly discovered Senona was useless with a needle and thread and had taken over.

"Ye see? Simple. Now ye try it." He handed the needle and thread over with a reassuring smile.

Senona looked at it and grimaced. "I'm really not any good at sewing. What if I ruin it?"

"Ye won't; just try it."

Senona managed a few stitches before uttering a gasp of pain as the needle pricked her finger. She continued to sew, working painfully slow on every single stitch. Karl's frown continued to grow deeper as he watched her, shaking his head every time Senona would wince in pain. Finally, he had watched enough. "Stop. Let me see."

She handed the sail back, and he looked it over. With a sigh, he promptly pulled out his knife and cut the stitches that Senona had just made. "You're right." He chuckled. "You're terrible. These wouldn't hold together for five minutes up there."

Senona smiled sheepishly. "My madre always tried to teach me, but I just never had the patience."

"I can see that. Ah well, there be other things for ye to do." He worked quickly, redoing the few stitches Senona had managed to complete before he had cut them out.

"Karl, how long have you been a sailor?" she asked as she once again studied the movements of his nimble hands. It was hard to believe that a man with such big and rough hands could handle a needle so deftly.

Karl didn't look up from his sewing to answer. "Long time. Why do you ask?"

Senona shrugged. "Curiosity. Is it a good life?"

"For some. For others, it's just hard. I love the sea. There ain't nothing better, and I won't ever leave it. I'm gonna be buried out here, mark my words. My whole life has been for the sea—since I was naught but ten years old I've been serving on ships."

Senona's eyes widened in surprise. "Ten years old? Where was your childhood?"

He smiled softly. "Not everyone has the luxury of a childhood. Mine was given to the sea. I'm happy, though. These men, this crew, they're my family."

"You and Brant are close, aren't you?"

"Brant is like a son to me. The only regret I have is that I never had a family of my own."

Senona wasn't sure how to respond. Karl was confiding in her information that she doubted was common knowledge.

"Ye know, Senona, you're a good girl," he said suddenly with a grin. "Your parents may not realize it now, but someday they will."

She smiled half-heartedly. "I don't know about that, but thank you."

"I've been alone, Senona. It isn't a nice place to be. If ye ever need something, ye just ask, okay? I know it ain't easy being out here and experiencing new things."

"Okay," she responded with a grin before getting up. "Karl, I'm glad we met. You're so kind."

"As am I, lass."

* * *

Brant walked around the deck, watching as his crew worked at their various jobs. Senona sat with James at the bow of the ship, deep in conversation. He liked seeing James with someone to talk to, someone he could relate to, but he worried about the affect Senona was having on the voyage. They had been sailing peacefully, too peacefully. He didn't trust Senona to obey his orders in the heat of battle and knew that she wouldn't be safe if she were in a position where he couldn't protect her. He wasn't quite sure why he felt inclined to care about this girl. First he kept her from the mistake of boarding Old Richard's ship, and now he felt responsible for her continued safety.

Brant sighed. He needed a raid or he would have an unhappy crew, there was no way around that. The only way things could work out was to be sure Senona was adequately equipped and trained to defend herself if needed.

Brant walked over to where Matt was looking at his compass. "How's our course?"

"Good, Cap'n."

"That's what I like to hear. I have a favor to ask of you."

Matt looked at Brant curiously. "Yes, sir?"

"I want you to work with Senona at sparring. I need her to be able to defend herself in case anything goes wrong in a fight, and you're the best man I've got when it comes to the blade."

Matt shrugged. "I'll get started right away."

Brant smiled. "Good man."

* * *

Matt pocketed his compass and sprinted off, retrieving his cutlass from where he kept it by his bunk. Making a quick stop at the spare arms' locker, he selected a cutlass for Senona to use for her duration on the ship.

Senona was still deep in conversation with James when he approached her. She was laughing at something James had said, and Matt couldn't help but smile when he heard her. It wasn't often the men on the ship had her kind of cheerfulness to brighten their day; it seemed to raise everyone's spirits.

He cleared his throat. "Excuse me, Senona, but the cap'n has requested that I work with ye at a little blade training."

Senona looked up, a dancing twinkle in her eye. "He has?"

"He thinks it will be good for ye."

Senona stood up, smoothing the pair of breeches James had given her. "Very well."

Matt handed her a cutlass, observing how she held it. Senona had had training in the past, which was evident to Matt in her perfect stance and firm but comfortable grip of the hilt. However, it quickly became apparent that she just wasn't as quick or as familiar with a heavy blade.

He took a step back, indicating a break in their sparring. "What did ye train in?"

"Fencing, with a rapier," she responded, breathless after nearly a half hour straight of drills and sparring.

"A light sword," he said as if it explained everything. "You'll get used to the extra weight. I find it adds more control." He was still moving rather effortlessly, even though he had broken into a heavy sweat and was out of breath. Senona refused to let him get the better of her, though. She fought hard and struggled to keep up, and even though he offered to stop a few times, she insisted on continuing. She had an eagerness to learn that Matt couldn't help but admire, but everyone had a limit, and he saw that Senona had reached it a while ago. Matt stopped. "That's enough."

Senona began to protest, but Matt shook his head. "Ye won't get the best of me today. We'll try again tomorrow."

Senona frowned but didn't protest. She was spent, anyone could see it.

* * *

Thoroughly parched from sparring, Senona went to get a drink of water. Brant approached her smirking, the ever-present twinkle that Senona had come to recognize as a mischievous glint was in his eyes. "Miss Montez, I'm greatly disappointed. The daughter of a Spanish Don and you don't even know how to handle a sword. I expected more."

"I was trained many years ago. It's a lot harder than I remember."

"Try harder. If you can best Matthew, I will be happy."

Senona gulped down the water and looked at Brant, raising an eyebrow in question. "Is it possible to not only make you happy but perhaps earn your respect, Captain Foxton?" She hadn't seen much evidence that it was a feasible goal.

"It's possible, but not easy to earn."

Senona scoffed. She suspected the only person on the ship that Brant truly respected was Karl. "Someday, Captain, I will best even you."

"If you can do that, you will have truly earned my respect. I look forward to that day." He took off his hat in a sweeping bow and then strode away, his shoulders shaking in laughter. He obviously thought it impossible for her, but Senona knew that day would come, and Brant Foxton would give his respect to a woman.

* * *

Karl watched Brant carefully for the next few days as he interacted with Senona. He had noticed a difference in Brant a couple of days after she had come aboard. He seemed to be happier, quick to joke and laugh with his crew and teasing with Senona. The last time Karl had seen him as happy was with Catherine, and that worried him. He clearly remembered the self-destructive and reckless attitude Brant had adopted after Catherine had left him. It had been a dark time for everyone on the *BlackFox*. How quickly one woman was able to destroy one of the strongest men Karl knew, and he worried Brant would fall into that same trap again. It had taken him so long to climb out of that first hole, would he be able to make it out a second time?

He watched quietly as Brant bantered back and forth with Senona during dinner. It had been only two weeks since they had left Spain. It had been two weeks of a beautiful, young, and enigmatic woman flitting about the ship, distracting much of the crew, including the captain. Karl didn't know whether to be relieved or disappointed that she hadn't left when they made port a week earlier, but he readily admitted that he liked Senona and would have been just as sad to see her go as anyone else on the ship. She had a good heart and a lovely spirit. He found himself smiling every time the sound of her laughter or the clip-clop of her horse's hooves on deck would draw everyone's attention. Nevertheless, they were all sailing in dangerous waters if she captured their captain's heart.

After dinner, Karl approached Brant. "Beautiful night," he said as he came up and leaned on the rail beside him.

"It's peaceful. I have a hard time understanding how anyone could want to live on land when they could enjoy this every day. The calm sea and stars overhead, it's creation in all its majesty."

Karl smiled. "It's why I could never leave."

They stood in silence for a time, Karl uncertain of how to approach a subject that Brant may very well feel as stepping over the line.

"Karl, what's troubling you?" Brant prompted.

"Ah, ye know me too well, Brant. It's about Senona." There was no point in beating around the bush, so he said it straight out.

Brant smirked. "What about her? She's fitting in well here and working hard. Have you ever seen the crew so cheerful? I think it's doing them good to have her around."

"That ain't what I want to talk about. It's more about ye. I'm concerned about your attachment to her."

Brant immediately lost the carefree attitude. Karl could see he was gearing up for a fight. "What do you mean?"

"I mean what I said. Don't go making any mistakes. Catherine wasn't that long ago, and I'm concerned you're gonna let history repeat itself."

"I don't feel anything for her, Karl."

"And ye keep it that way, Brant, or mark my words, you'll be asking for trouble. She's a good girl, but you are just too alike. It can only end badly."

Brant chuckled, visibly relaxing. "You don't have to worry, Karl. I won't let anything happen. I learned my lesson once, and although I had to learn it the hard way, once is quite enough, even for me."

Karl patted Brant on the back. "Good. Now these tired old bones are gonna go to bed. G'night."

"Good night, Karl."

* * *

Brant stood there a while longer. What Karl said had gotten him thinking. Would he ever find himself settling down, or was he to spend the rest of his life alone? He knew very well that the life he led was too dangerous to bring a woman into, but part of him still wondered if perhaps a woman was somewhere in the future for him.

* * *

Senona stood on a spar, helping Karl unfurl a sail. She struggled to keep her balance on the spar in the strong winds, but she felt safe enough with a rope tied around her waist.

"Careful now," he warned.

She wobbled uncertainly as an especially strong gust of wind battered them and the heavy canvas they were working with. Senona squealed a little and laughed as she regained her balance. It took them twice as long as it should have to get the sail unfurled, but the job did get done. When they made it back down, Senona found herself actually thinking that the constant rolling motion of the deck was stable.

"Ye did good, lass," said Karl as they walked along the deck towards their next chore, inspecting all the ropes for weaknesses.

"Thank you, Karl."

They sat down, side by side, on the deck, sliding the rope through their hands and looking it over carefully. Karl started to hum a tune as he worked.

"What song is that?"

"It's just a British sea chanty. Ain't nothing special."

"Will you teach it to me?"

Karl smiled. "Sure."

He began to sing the first verse; "Farewell and adieu to you Spanish ladies, farewell and adieu to you ladies of Spain; for we've received orders for to sail for old England, but we hope very soon we shall see you again.

"We'll rant and we'll roar like true British sailors, we'll rant and we'll roar all on the salt sea. Until we strike soundings in the channel of old England; from Ushant to Scilly is thirty-five leagues.

"We hove our ship to with the wind from sou'west, boys we hove our ship to, deep soundings to take; 'twas forty-five fathom, with a white sandy bottom, so we squared our main yard and up channel did make.

"The first land we sighted was called the Dodman, next Rame head off Plymouth, Start, Portland and Wight; we sailed by Beachy, by Fairlight and Dover, and then we bore up for the South Foreland light.

"Then the signal was made for the grand fleet to anchor, and all in the Downs that night for to lie; let go your shank painter, let go your cat stopper! Haul up your clewgarnets, let tacks and sheets fly!"

Senona listened intently, laughing occasionally in amusement.

"Now let ev'ry man drink off his full bumper, and let ev'ry man drink off his full glass; we'll drink and be jolly and drown melancholy, and here's to the health of each true-hearted lass. We will rant and we'll roar like true British sailors, we'll rant and we'll roar all on the salt sea. Until we strike soundings in the channel of old England; from Ushant to Scilly in thirty-five leagues." He sang the last few lines, Senona humming along.

"Ain't nothing special, but it be good for working."

"I like it," she said with a smile. "It suits this world; a little rough around the edges."

Karl chuckled. "Now ain't that the truth."

Karl sang the song again; this time, Senona joined in as much as she could. It continued to run through her head for the remainder of the day, and even as Senona lay in bed that night, she found herself humming. She wondered if Karl had been like the British sailors in the song when he had been younger. She hummed a few more lines and then rolled over in an attempt to fall asleep.

"Farewell and adieu to you Spanish ladies, farewell and adieu to you ladies of Spain…"

CHAPTER THREE

A week had passed, nearly a month since leaving Barcelona, and Senona found herself missing dry ground more and more every day. She took Naldo on deck every day in a feeble attempt to give him exercise, but it wasn't enough. Over the weeks, he had become quite comfortable with the surroundings that had once alarmed him, but like her, she could tell he wasn't entirely happy with the rolling deck beneath his hooves. Neither one was meant to be on a ship. Naldo needed to run and burn energy, and Senona just needed to ride him at a full out gallop. Oh, what she would do to feel that kind of freedom right now.

Senona watched the sailors go about their small tasks; cleaning guns and cannons, sharpening swords, repairing sails, and a few other odd jobs that helped everything run smoothly. She found Matt sitting on the bow of the ship repairing an old sail and enjoying the crisp air blowing through his hair, a small form of relief from the hot sun.

"Matt, are voyages usually this quiet?" she asked, as she walked up to him with Naldo.

"No. I think the cap'n has been avoiding trouble."

"Will it stay like this?"

"I don't think so. Even the quietest voyages have some gold to be made. No way the cap'n could keep a crew if he went a season without a raid. It's how we're paid."

"I see," said Senona thoughtfully. "I'm going to take Naldo back below deck. Will you spar with me? I have a good feeling about today."

Matt laughed. "Today gonna be the day?"

"Maybe."

Matt and Senona had been practicing every day, and although she had trained when she was younger, she was out of practice. However, the last few times she had given him quite a workout. Matt was the best swordsman aboard the *BlackFox*, not including Brant, and if Senona could best Matt, she knew she had a fighting chance against Brant, which was her final goal. Nothing would please her more than bringing the arrogant captain down a few notches.

Senona put Naldo in his stall and got the borrowed cutlass from her cabin.

"I'm ready," she said, walking up to Matt who had also gotten his sword.

Matt nodded in response and, giving no instruction, attacked. Senona calmly and with ease blocked every thrust, swipe, or slash he made. She knew Matt wouldn't want to admit it, but she was getting better, perhaps even better than him. He appeared to be giving it his all, but it didn't take long for Senona to find an opening and bring the session to an end.

"There ain't a whole lot I can teach ye anymore. Ye had good teachers back at home," said Matt, breathing heavily.

Slow clapping came from where Brant leaned against the deck rail, observing in silence up until now. "Actually, you have improved quite a bit under Matthew's tutelage. I wouldn't give credit to your previous instructors. Would you mind terribly if I tried my hand against you?"

"I would never turn down a chance to learn from the captain," she replied with a smirk.

Brant drew his cutlass and swung it around a few times experimentally. "Consider yourself privileged. I told you last week that if you bested Matthew, I would be happy with how your training had progressed. Now it's time for me to see how good you really are." He turned to face her. "Ladies first."

Senona raised her eyebrows, wondering if it was a trap, but took the invitation anyway, and started with an easy swipe to the left.

The clanging of metal on metal became faster and louder, and soon they were moving all over the deck, dancing around the working sailors. Senona's laughter filled the ship as she parried blow after blow. She grabbed a rope and stepped onto the rail, in a single move gaining the advantage of being on higher ground. Unfortunately, as she soon realized, that advantage was countered by the fact that she was trying to balance on a precarious perch and rebuttal blows at the same time.

Senona jumped down so that she could fight without worrying about falling into the ocean, and thrust her cutlass at Brant. Brant nimbly sidestepped to the right, and the blade went harmlessly past, leaving Senona in a vulnerable position. She back-peddled quickly to avoid being hit. Suddenly, Christopher, the master gunner, gave a shout from his position in the crow's nest.

"Cap'n! We got us some company!"

"What kind?" asked Brant, quickly forgetting about Senona.

"Spanish treasure galleon!"

"Gun count?"

"Limited cannons but full Militia!"

"Militia shouldn't be a problem," he muttered. "Run up the colors! Suit up, men! Get the guns ready!"

The once dead deck became alive with activity. Brant turned to Senona. "Go lock yourself in your cabin, and don't open it for anyone but me, Karl, or Matthew."

"What about James?" asked Senona, sheathing her blade.

"He's going to look after Naldo. Now go to your cabin. That's an order," said Brant, walking away and shouting more orders to his crew. "All hands! Run out those guns! We're going to get us some gold, boys!"

Cheering erupted all over the deck. The crew was ready for a little excitement and a little gold. Things had been much too slow and quiet these past few weeks.

"James! Take care of Naldo! I want him strapped up and keep an eye on him."

James nodded and ran below deck.

Karl walked up to Brant. "Everything's in order, Cap'n."

"Very good. You going to sit this one out, old man?"

Karl shook his head. "Nay. Ye know I can't do that. This is my job."

"You're getting too old for this, Karl. Be careful."

Karl nodded and patted Brant on the back. "See ye on the other side, Cap'n."

Brant smirked. "Don't let me down, old man.

* * *

Senona paced around her cabin, waiting anxiously for the first cannon blast. She didn't have to wait long. A tremor went through the ship causing her to cling to the desk to keep her balance. The two ships exchanged cannon fire for what seemed like an eternity before Senona heard Brant's orders to board. With every gunshot, she felt more and more useless. With every scream of pain, she shuddered. She continued to pace, her hand resting on the hilt of her cutlass for reassurance. She felt like a caged animal, unable to do anything besides wait. Standing up straight, she took a deep breath. Resolved, she ran out of her cabin. She was unwilling to hide helplessly while others fought.

Boarding the Spanish ship immediately thrust Senona into the fray.

"Senona! What are ye doing here? You're supposed to be in your cabin!" Matt shouted, surprised when Senona joined him in the fight.

"Helping. Don't worry about protecting me. Just fight," she said, running a Spanish Militia through. Senona grimaced at the feeling of her blade piercing flesh and bone. She had never

36

hurt anyone. The man's dying scream echoed in her mind, and she froze. She had just killed a man. The overwhelming urge to become reacquainted with breakfast took over, but Matt grabbed her arm and gave it a shake.

"Don't worry about protecting ye? Ye get back to your cabin right now!"

Senona nodded, thoroughly shaken. Somehow, she'd imagined it would be a bit more glamorous than all this gore. However, one does not move around easily in the middle of a battle, and Senona had to fight her way through, her movements erratic and unstable as she struggled to cope with the murder she was committing.

Karl came over and moved in front of her. "Ye stick with me, lass. Ye try and get back to the other side, you'll get gunned down."

Senona fought furiously but only killed when she had no choice; the whole situation made her sick. Karl was old, though, and getting slower. It took everything he had to look after himself and Senona.

Senona didn't know how much longer she could last. She could match these men in skill, but she wasn't hardened enough to this life to kill and maim with barely a second thought. A particularly young boy engaged her then, and she hesitated. She couldn't do it. She couldn't kill someone so young. Karl stepped in the way and took him on while Senona stood helpless. She watched Karl's moves become more and more sluggish against the robust youth. She helplessly watched the boy inflict injury upon her protector. And she helplessly watched the blade enter through Karl's front and protrude through his back. A scream escaped Senona's lips as she ran forward to catch Karl as he fell.

"No! No! Karl! You can't die! I'm sorry. I'm so sorry. I never should have come here."

Karl smiled calmly. "Aye, Lass, I told ye I was gonna be buried out here. Ye make sure Brant says nice things about me."

"I'm sorry, Karl," she sobbed.

"It's an honor to die protecting the likes of ye, my pretty. I hope ye find what you're looking for." And then, he went limp.

Senona sobbed and could do nothing but hold the old man. No one attacked her. It was apparent she was no threat.

It didn't take long for the crew of the *BlackFox* to overpower the Spanish Militia. Brant's men had better training, and the Militia never stood a chance. Brant was arrogant, as always, as he accepted the surrender and, a smirk plastered on his face, he called for Karl. Senona hadn't moved from her position, but she called out weakly, still choking back tears.

Brant looked over and his face visibly paled. "Karl?" he asked, all traces of arrogance gone.

Striding over, he knelt beside Karl and Senona. His face hard, he gently closed the man's eyes.

"Matthew! Christopher! Get the body to the *BlackFox*."

They came over quickly, removing Karl's body from her lap. Blood covered her. Brant stood beside her, saying nothing. Reaching down, he grabbed her by the arm and pulled her to her feet. Wincing, she cried out in pain, and he let go quickly.

"Are you hurt?"

Senona inspected her bloody, throbbing arm. "It's just a slice. Stings a little."

"Good. What were you thinking? You stupid, foolish girl!" he shouted. "How dare you disobey my orders?! Was Karl protecting you?"

Senona said nothing; her lips trembled in fear, and the need to cry paralyzed her.

"Was he protecting you?" he shouted again.

Senona nodded slowly, afraid of what Brant would do.

"You're to leave the *BlackFox* at the next port. I will not have someone who disregards my orders aboard."

Senona opened her mouth to argue, but nothing came out. She knew she had done wrong, and there was nothing she could say that would make the meaningless death of Karl okay.

* * *

With Senona safely back on the *BlackFox*, Brant gave orders to the various crewmembers to clean out the hold and to look after the injured. It was everything he could do to stay in control as his emotions battered him on all sides. Walking to the upper deck where he could be alone, Brant attempted to regain composure. Tears flooded his vision and sorrow crashed into him like a tidal wave, utterly demolishing everything that dared stand it its way. "Not Karl," he said quietly, a pleading prayer. He could already feel the emptiness filling the ship, or maybe that was just his heart.

* * *

Senona went to check on Naldo and help James get him down from the straps. The straps were a set of thickly padded canvas that anchored into the ceiling of the hold. They were then put under the horse's belly and hoisted a few inches off the floor. This prevented the horse from hurting itself, as it had limited movement.

"How was he?" she asked softly, tears still staining her face. She stroked Naldo rhythmically in small circles to help calm him—and herself.

"Fine. He was scared of the cannon fire, but he did good. What's wrong, Senona?" James asked as she continued to cry silently. "Where did all that blood come from?"

She sobbed, holding onto Naldo to keep upright. "Karl..."

She didn't have to finish. James knew. His eyes filled with tears, and he embraced Senona. Together, they cried and mourned for a man that they loved dearly.

* * *

The funeral had even the most hardened sailors in tears. Everyone on the ship liked Karl. His kind heart and listening ear had been available to anyone who needed it during the many years he had served on the *BlackFox*.

Brant was remarkably strong throughout the whole thing. He didn't so much as shed a tear as he read the allotted scriptures and said the few words that everyone got at a ship funeral. James was taking it hard and wept unashamedly the whole time. Senona put her hand on his shoulder to let him know that she was there, but she was no stronger than he was; tears flowed down her cheek unchecked.

At the end, the entire crew recited the Lord's Prayer together and then dropped Karl's body, wrapped in a sail with the British flag and Jolly Roger folded proudly on his chest, into the ocean, as was the sailor's custom.

Senona desperately wanted to follow James below deck, but instead she climbed to the crow's nest, sitting there until dark, thinking and crying, getting the sorrow out of her system. She couldn't shake the feeling of guilt, and Brant hadn't spoken a word to her since he had told her she was to leave the ship.

* * *

Brant fought tears as he finished the Lord's Prayer and watched the crew drop Karl into the ocean. Karl would have been proud of his funeral, remembered fondly and a sailor to the end. After the funeral, Brant stood there for a long time, just staring out into the open ocean that he called home. The same ocean Karl had called home and now made his final resting place. The sea was a cruel mistress. It captured your heart and never let you go.

Brant couldn't help but wonder if someday he would be the one slowly sinking in her murky depths to his eternal rest. Brant wanted to let the tears flow more than anything, but he had to be strong; he had a crew to lead. His father's words always came to him at times like this.

"A man doesn't cry, Brant. We have to be strong. Tears are for women."

His father had been a hard man, but a perfect gentleman. London society had looked up to him. However, his relationship with his oldest son had never been a good one. He had never supported Brant's dream to become a captain, so Brant had run away and joined the crew of the *BlackFox*. The Captain of the *BlackFox* at the time had been an older man by the name of Pierre Lafleur. Pierre took Brant under his wing and taught him everything he knew, and when he died he left Brant the ship. When news of his father's death during the great plague reached him, Brant sailed home to take custody of his younger brother, James. That was the first time he'd been home since he was sixteen years of age.

James had grown up without a mother. She had died in childbirth, leaving their father to raise them. Brant had barely known his younger brother before he brought him to the *BlackFox*. He had raised his eleven-year-old brother with the help of Karl. Brant had been twenty-one then, too young to be raising a young boy. He was now twenty-six and had lost his father figure. He had come to know his younger brother quite well over the years, but he wasn't sure how he was going to raise him now, without Karl.

Karl had been more of a father to Brant than his real father had ever been. He always gave kind advice and help, even when Brant's pride wouldn't allow him to ask. Karl's words came to him then as if he was standing right next to him, giving him advice as he always had in the past.

"It takes more of a man to cry than it does not to. Anyone can hide from his emotions. Not everyone can acknowledge them."

Brant smiled to himself. Leave it to Karl to make everything better, to make sense of everything.

Brant let the tears fall. Karl deserved mourning.

* * *

After a few days of mourning, the ship was on its way back to normal. Even Brant was doing better, coming to terms with the idea of Karl not being around. There would always be a hole in the *BlackFox* where Karl belonged, but life still went on. Brant was back to ordering the crew around and helping

Matt get used to his new job. But he avoided Senona, taking meals with the crew. Senona sat at the bow of the ship looking out. Brant glanced at her briefly, but the sight of her brought images of Karl's body to mind. He quickly looked away and returned to talking to Matt.

"Forgive me, Cap'n, but ye should go talk to her."

Brant glared at Matt. "And what would I say exactly? In about a week, we'll be making port, and she'll be leaving."

"You're gonna leave her?"

"She disobeyed an order. I can't have that on my ship."

"Karl didn't have to protect her. He chose to. He wouldn't want ye to kick her off on account of him."

Brant scowled but he knew Matt had a point. "I'll talk to her, but that doesn't mean she's staying."

He walked over to Senona. "How're you doing?"

She started and turned to face him. "Oh, Brant, I'm so sorry. I thought I could help, and I didn't realize—"

"You didn't realize that you couldn't kill a man."

She nodded mutely

Brant sighed and rubbed his hand through his hair. He couldn't continue to blame her. She had made a mistake, and Matt was right; Karl had chosen to protect her. "You don't have to leave. Karl wouldn't have wanted that. But if you ever disobey an order again—"

"I won't!"

He nodded and walked away. He still couldn't help but blame Senona just a little, but that would fade in time. Karl never did anything he didn't want to. Including die.

CHAPTER FOUR

After two and a half months of sailing and about three successful attacks, four fatalities, and two ports, they were finally docking in Port Royale.

"We're here for a week, and I expect everyone to be on their best behavior," instructed Brant. "If you don't want to be finding a new billet, I suggest you find yourself back aboard on Wednesday. See Matthew about guard schedules; everyone will take a turn watching the ship."

There was much good-natured groaning, but the men were all more than happy for a week leave, especially since they would be spending the storm season in England.

Senona gathered her few belongings and put them in a trunk that Brant had given to her from one of the ships they had attacked. After the first raid, and how it had turned out, Brant hadn't trusted Senona to follow orders and had kept her near his side. Every raid shook her up, but by the last one, she could hold her own, and the act of killing a man seemed to have less of an effect on her. She was already hardening to the lifestyle.

Senona went below deck, packing up the few brushes and tack that she had acquired for Naldo.

"You sure you want to leave?" asked Brant, as he came down to bring her to shore. "There's always room in my crew for one more. You're a hard worker and you're getting to be useful in raids."

Senona flushed with pride. "I'm quite sure. I can't part with Naldo just yet."

Brant nodded, his lips pressed together in a thin line. "If you ever change your mind, my crew is always in need of a good sword hand. Let's get Naldo onto dry land."

Senona saddled up Naldo and put the last of his tack into her trunk. She attempted to lift it, but Brant stopped her.

"Matthew will take it to the carriage."

"Carriage?"

"Oh, yes. I'm bringing you and your stuff to my estate."

"Estate?" Senona hadn't really considered the fact that Brant might have a life apart from the one he led on the *BlackFox*.

"Yes. What do you think I do with all that gold I get pirating?" He flashed a teasing smile.

"I didn't think you'd waste it on an estate you're never at."

"I do expect to retire from this life of crime eventually. Maybe get married and have some kids. James can take over the pirating side of business."

"Why here and not England?"

"England is, well,... England. It doesn't appeal to me. Port Royale is an ideal place for a pirate. It's surrounded by ocean, and a little breathing space is always nice."

"I learn something new about you every day." She smirked.

Brant walked with her to the carriage. "Will you be riding or taking the carriage with James and me?"

"Riding," she replied as if there really was no other option. "I'll follow the carriage." She swung up onto Naldo's back fluidly, relaxing into the saddle and feeling instantly at home.

"Matthew, you'll finish everything up here?" asked Brant as Matt loaded Senona's trunk onto the carriage roof.

"Yes, Sir."

"You're welcome to join us at my estate once you're done."

Matt smiled. "Thank you, but no."

Brant nodded understandingly. "Remember to assign watches."

James was already sitting in the carriage as he climbed in. The carriage pulled away, Senona following behind on Naldo.

It took an hour to get to Brant's large estate, which was located five miles outside town. After weeks spent cooped up on a ship, the five-mile ride felt amazing, like pure freedom.

"Welcome to my humble abode," said Brant, stepping out of the carriage and paying the driver.

James jumped out and immediately ran to the long building that Senona thought to be the stables.

"It's beautiful. Is that the stables?"

"Yes, it is, though it's nearly empty. You can find a stall for Naldo in there."

"James has his own horse?"

"Yes. Admiral, a large black Arabian gelding."

"And do you? Or do your skills lie only in sailing?" she teased.

"I have many skills, but riding is not one of them. I do, however, own two standardbreds; Jester and Phantom."

"We'll have to go riding before you leave."

Brant chuckled. "If you insist. You'll be fine without me for a little while?"

"Of course, and James is around if I need help."

"Then I shall see you later." Brant walked away, leaving Senona alone to explore.

* * *

The front entrance of the estate house had a huge vaulted ceiling and marble floors. Brant turned around and sighed, "Ah, luxury." It was always a nice change to spend a little time at home and relax. Here, he didn't have to worry about death, injury, storms, or any other dangers that faced a sailor. Brant took a minute to look around before bellowing into the large house: "Liza! I'm home!"

There was a crash, and Brant winced as a middle-aged woman ran down the stairs with a rag in hand.

"Oh, Mr. Foxton, sir!"

Brant chuckled and hugged her. "How are you, Liza?"

"Oh, well enough."

"And how are Sam and Sarah?"

Liza was a widow with two children, who were now quite grown up.

"Sarah turned nineteen last month and got herself a husband."

"And how old is Samuel now? Twenty? And hasn't found a girl?"

"Ach! No, Sir! Says he hasn't found the right one yet. There are so many nice girls, though," she lamented. "And here I go rambling. Did you bring James with you?"

"I did. I figured he would enjoy a visit before we continued on to England."

"I will have him all cleaned up for you before you leave, Mr. Foxton."

"Good, good. It wouldn't do for him to go to school looking like a common sailor. And, Liza, could you prepare an extra room? I've brought a guest."

"A guest?"

"Yes. Senorita Senona Montez"

"A lady guest?" She grinned. Liza wanted him to marry almost as badly as she wanted Sam to.

"Yes. She got passage here but has nowhere to go. I'm thinking of offering her a job. Do you need help?"

"Help is always welcome, but I don't know how much work I'll have for her in the house. Samuel hired a girl when Sarah got married. She's working in town as a seamstress now."

"That's okay. I was thinking outside work anyway."

Liza made a sound of indignation and muttered, "outside work," then ran back up the stairs to prepare the rooms.

Brant shook his head and chuckled; Liza was opinionated, but he couldn't help but love her.

Brant went back outside in search of Samuel, Liza's oldest and only son, and Brant's overseer. One of Brant's least favorite things about his visits home was going over the books and general business. He would feign interest, give Sam money, and head back out to sea. That was just the way it was with Brant.

He found Samuel in the sugarcane fields, riding by the men hard at work, offering a word of encouragement or approval. Brant didn't believe in slavery, and so he mainly employed men from the surrounding area and a few ex-cons—Brant found he could sympathize with them.

"Sam!" he called.

The young man on horseback looked up and rode over, a huge grin on his face. Dismounting, Sam gave Brant a firm handshake. "What brings you back?"

"Business, my dear friend, always business," Brant joked.

Sam chuckled. "I'm sure. What's the real reason?"

"Come with me to the stables; I'll explain on the way."

The two men walked side-by-side towards the stables, Sam leading his horse.

"A lady needed passage here, so I decided to bring her and let James come visit before going to school. Which is why I'm here early," Brant said, giving the simplest version he could.

Sam smiled. "A lady? Where is she? Who is she? Where is she from?" It all came out in a string of words that Brant attempted to sift through.

"Whoa! Slow down! Last I checked she was in the stables with James. Her name is Senona Montez, the only child of a Spanish Don. I'm bringing you to meet her now because I'd like to offer her a job."

"Senona Montez," Sam rolled it off his tongue. "If you're wondering if you can afford it, the answer is yes. What else can you tell me?"

"Nothing. You get to find that out for yourself."

They entered the stables and Brant headed straight to Senona, who was standing outside Jester's stall, stroking his neck. He was a beautiful light gray, almost white standardbred gelding.

"I see you've wasted no time in finding my favorite horse," said Brant, coming up behind her.

Senona smiled. "He is a beauty. Is this Phantom or Jester?"

"Jester. The black one is Phantom. Half-brothers from some of the best breeding lines."

"Only the best for Captain Brant Foxton," laughed Senona.

During their exchange, Sam had been putting his horse away. He walked up now. "Senona, I would like you to meet Sam. He runs everything from the finances to the stables. The only thing he doesn't look after is the actual house."

"Pleased to meet you, Sam. I'm Senona."

"The honor is all mine," he replied giving a slight bow. "Is that your horse?" he asked, motioning towards Naldo.

"Yes, that is Naldo," her voice filled with pride.

"He's a beautiful animal. Spanish blood?"

"Yes, my father bought him for me a few years ago. I trained him myself."

"Really? That is a useful talent."

Senona smiled but shook her head. "No one would hire a woman to train their horses." No one said anything, so she changed the subject, "James and I are going to go riding, he's going to show me around."

"When you're done here, you can go up to the house. Liza will show you your room," said Brant.

"Thank you"

Brant and Sam left the stables, walking along the gravel towards the house. As soon as Brant was sure Senona was out of earshot, he turned to Sam. "So, what do you think?"

"She seems nice enough. But how much experience could she have had with work?" Sam's tone was criticizing and immediately set Brant on edge. "It's not that I don't like her; it's just I don't want you wasting your money."

Brant frowned; his eyes were flat and hard, betraying his emotions. "She is a noble, but she's a hard worker and a fast learner. You heard her yourself; she trained that horse so she has some skill. If I could, I'd keep her on the crew, but she doesn't want to. Sam...you should see her with a sword."

Sam laughed. "Okay, you would know better than me. Why do you want to help her so badly, Brant?" He didn't say it, but both men knew Sam was really asking if there was something more between Brant and Senona.

"I just can't leave her alone in this cruel world. She wouldn't last a day."

"Well, I'm sure she'll work out. She could look after the stables, maybe fill them up for you."

"There's really no point in filling the stables. I'm never here except during storm season, so Phantom and Jester don't get enough attention as it is."

"Well, there you go, a job for Senona."

"What?"

"She can exercise your horses. Maybe get you a pair to pull that carriage you have rotting away at the back of the stables. Have everything set up for your retirement."

"Who said I was going to retire anytime soon?"

"No one. In fact, I'll give you another ten to twenty years of sailing before you settle down. Really, Brant, you're rolling in riches; you could buy your way out of the noose if you needed to. Do you think we could coat the floors in the house with all that extra gold you have?"

"You kidding? I need that money to buy my way out of those nooses. I can't go wasting it on pretty floors."

The two men entered the house to hear Liza yelling, or rather shrieking, at someone upstairs. "NO! Not like that! Can't you get it right?! This is a lady we're preparing a room for, not some doxy!"

"Sorry, Miss Liza, sorry," said a young girl timidly, sounding as if she was ready to cry.

"Just go make some tea for Mr. Foxton and Lady Montez," said Liza, sounding quite exasperated.

The girl scurried out of the room nearest the stairs and began running down, tripping when she saw Brant and Sam and falling right into Sam, who caught her and set her back on her feet. Brant stood there, his eyes twinkling with amusement as he attempted to hold a stern expression.

"I'm Brant Foxton. Who are you and what are you doing in my house?" he asked, his face a mask of seriousness.

"Oh! I'm sorry, Mr. Foxton, sir. I'm Julie. Mr. Samuel hired me, Sir." She stood there at the base of the stairs, trembling and looking from man to man with wide eyes shiny from unshed tears.

"Then welcome to my household, Julie. Don't mind Liza; she's just grumpy with me because I brought a lady guest here to move in on her turf."

Julie laughed uneasily. "Liza is awful protective of this house."

"Yes, she is. Now, would you be so kind as to get Sam and me some coffee? No tea, please—terrible stuff."

"Of course, Sir," said Julie, curtsying as she turned and rushed to the kitchen to escape the ones responsible for her terrified state.

"Flighty little one, isn't she?" asked Brant.

"Yes, but despite what you just heard, she helps my mother out plenty."

"You've done well for this place. Let's get this unpleasant business part done and over with," he said, walking into the study. "You can give me a financial report, and tell me how the crops are."

"My favorite."

* * *

Senona spent the afternoon riding the grounds with James. When they finally made it to the house, teatime was long over, and the smell of dinner cooking filled the house.

Liza met her at the door and curtsied. James hurried away in search of Brant before Liza could stop him.

"Lady Montez, I'll show you to your room."

Senona smiled. "Please, call me Senona. Formalities are not necessary here."

"Senona then," she said kindly. "I'm Liza. I run Mr. Foxton's house, and my son, Samuel, runs everything else."

"I had the pleasure of meeting Samuel this afternoon. You and your son have done a fine job for Brant."

Liza smiled, her head tilted ever so slightly up and her eyes shining with pride, and led Senona into a beautiful room. She looked around at the rich decor and deep colors.

"Is the room satisfactory?"

"More than satisfactory. Thank you, Liza."

"Just doing my job."

Senona fell onto the bed, reveling in the softness and comfort of it.

"Something funny, Miss Senona?"

"Oh no. It's just, I forgot how nice a soft bed was! Those sea beds don't do much for sleep."

"I imagine that's so. Now you'll please excuse me; I have to look after dinner."

"Of course. Thank you again."

Liza curtsied and left the room at a brisk walk, her heels clicking loudly through the spacious house.

Senona continued to lie on her bed, her eyes closed as she relaxed.

"I see you've found your bed," said Brant from just outside the open door.

Senona's eyes shot open in surprise. She quickly sat up and smoothed her breeches and tugged at her shirt. "Um, yes. I forgot how soft they can be," she replied.

"That they are. You aren't planning on sleeping so soon, are you?"

He had been teasing Senona more and more often lately and it was beginning to wear on her. She almost preferred it when he had been angry and ignoring her. "No, I wouldn't want to miss dinner. Real food will be a nice change."

"Are you suggesting that the spread on the *BlackFox* is less than satisfactory?"

"Never! It's the most delectable food I've ever had."

Brant laughed. "Make sure you hear the dinner bell."

He left the room then called in as an afterthought, "Liza doesn't take too kindly to people being late. I may be lenient about it on the ship, but Liza will never forgive you."

Senona lay back down and sighed, blowing stray strands of hair out of her face. Sometimes Brant could be so infuriating. He always teased her, and when he wasn't teasing, he was maddeningly arrogant. He reminded her a bit of her childhood friend Isidro, only less mocking.

The bell woke her about an hour later. She sat up in a panic, realizing she was going to be late, but she could do nothing about it; it was inexcusable to arrive at the meal all dirty and wearing the same clothes as she had worn all day, or so her mother had raised her to think. It might have been acceptable on the *Blackfox*, but here she had to keep some semblance of propriety.

Senona hurriedly changed into a skirt and blouse, washed her hands and face, and quickly ran a comb through her hair. She ran down the stairs and into the dining room, attempting to slow down at the last second and, at least, give a show of being lady-like.

Everyone sat and talked though the food had yet to arrive. Senona knew Brant had noticed her the second she stepped in. His face had adopted a teasing look that seemed reserved just for her.

"I'm sorry to keep everyone waiting. I must have dozed off."

She caught Brant's eyes with her own, glaring at him in a warning. She wasn't in the mood. His reply was silent amusement, made known only by the twinkle in his eyes and a slight shaking of his shoulders. He was in too good of a mood to behave. Senona caught Liza's obvious look of disapproval, but Brant quickly apologized before she could say anything.

"It's okay, Liza, Senona is new here and doesn't know the rules. As you can imagine, dining rules on the *BlackFox* are much more relaxed."

"I can imagine," she replied, and then added under her breath, just loud enough for everyone to hear, "poor girl."

Brant scraped back his chair and stood. Walking over to Senona, he offered his arm. Lifting her chin, she brushed by him to the chair beside his and pulled it out herself, noisily shuffling it into place under the table. She could see the laughter in his eyes, which only resulted in her annoyance growing.

"Sam, would you say grace?" asked Brant once he settled back in his seat.

Samuel responded with a nod and everyone bowed their heads.

Samuel's prayer was short but sincere. Senona had never heard anything so holy from any of the priests at the church back in Spain, and it impressed her. After the prayer, Liza got up, and along with a young woman, who Senona had yet to meet, brought dinner out.

The large oak table was soon covered with plates full of food; mashed potatoes, corn, peas, beef, chicken, and rice. Senona's mouth watered. She hadn't eaten real food in a while. It would have been quite the stretch to call the ship's fare food.

The instant everyone was sitting, James dug into his food with such relish that you would have thought he hadn't eaten for weeks, and Brant tackled his meal with nearly the same ferocity.

Senona ate slowly, using small bites, just like how she had been told to eat all her life.

"Are you looking forward to school, James?" asked Liza halfway through dinner.

She obviously cared about Brant and James, and so naturally, she was interested in James' education.

"Yes, ma'am," James said between gulps.

Liza took what James had said as the truth, that much Senona could tell. She assumed he didn't want to disappoint Liza and appear ungrateful for the chance of an education that Liza could only dream of giving her own children.

"Good. I wish I could have given Sam that kind of schooling."

"Mother," warned Sam.

"What? Sam, we've had it good here because of Sir Foxton and Mr. Foxton, but we haven't ever had the chance to get you an education."

Senona felt ashamed. She had left a life filled with privilege, and she had thrown it away like it meant nothing, all for a little freedom and understanding. Liza could only dream of a life like the one she had left. She ate silently, with a look on her face that showed something troubled her, but no one seemed to notice, except maybe Brant—he seemed attuned to all.

Concern flickered in his eyes, and his hand strayed to rest on her arm in a reassuring manner. Senona flinched away, her eyes darting to him in surprise. He quickly took his hand back and continued to eat, their small exchange going unnoticed by everyone else.

Senona smiled at something James said and left her thoughts alone. It wasn't the time or place.

* * *

When everyone had finished their supper, they retired to the parlor. Liza and Julie brewed some tea. Brant requested that a pot of coffee be made for him and Senona. He called tea a nasty potion, which had Liza muttering things in disapproval.

Brant watched Senona carefully and was relieved to see she was no longer preoccupied with her thoughts. Whatever had been bothering her earlier had obviously been forgotten as she laughed and joked with everyone else. Brant worried that this new life she had chosen was suddenly becoming all too real for her. Any doubts or concerns she may have been ignoring could very well be forcing their way up now, and it concerned Brant. He too had made a similar choice ten years ago, and he knew it wasn't easy.

"I'm going to retire for the evening," came Senona's voice cutting into Brant's thoughts.

Brant and Samuel both stood as Senona did.

"Please, Brant, Sam, we don't need formalities."

Brant sat, respecting Senona's wish, but Sam continued to stand. Although Brant knew Sam had been raised that there was never a proper time to put aside propriety or respect for a woman, he figured that respecting someone's wishes was more polite than sticking to unwanted formalities, especially in Senona's case, but Liza obviously didn't agree.

Liza glared at Brant when he sat and gave an approving nod towards her son.

Brant nearly chuckled but managed to keep a straight face, though he was certain that Senona had noticed his amusement when she directed an appreciative glance at him. He only hoped she didn't think he was amused with her; he wasn't sure she would have taken that well.

Senona thanked Liza and Julie for dinner and coffee and left in a soft rustle of skirts and clicking of heels on the tile floor.

When Senona left, Liza spoke up, ready to give her opinion to anyone who would listen. Brant wondered what could have possessed him to have all the women in his life opinionated, hard-headed, and not afraid to express themselves. It was madness, really.

"Mr. Foxton, you may be my employer but I feel I must speak my mind."

"Then speak it, Liza. I can't stop you," said Brant with a sigh.

Sam smirked at Brant, the tirade to follow was nothing new to them.

"You of all people should know how to act around a lady. Teasing her at dinner and now this—"

"Liza, Senona requested that I ignore formalities. I was merely respecting her wishes."

"Mr. Foxton, I would have thought you had been raised better. To throw away formalities like that is unforgivable. The lady was just trying to be polite when asking you not to stand on her account, and you insulted her by agreeing that she wasn't worth it."

"Liza, please," he said, exasperated. "I sailed with Senona for over two months, and I know when she says to ignore formalities, she is not just trying to be polite."

Liza opened her mouth to speak again, but Brant cut her off. "I am going to turn in as well. James, another hour?"

James nodded, only briefly looking up from the book he was reading.

Brant smiled to himself as he walked out of the parlor. He would be glad to set sail in a week. As nice as it was visiting the estate, he was already going land crazy, and he hadn't even been here a full day. He made a mental note to stay away from the house as much as possible in the days to come.

Brant turned the corner at the top of the stairs and walked towards a large balcony instead of his room. He didn't even realize that he was going there until he found himself stepping out into the cool, yet muggy night air. A storm was coming; it would most likely hit tomorrow morning at some point. So much for staying out of the house. Brant closed his eyes and imagined he was back on his ship until the echoing click of heels on hardwood met his ears.

CHAPTER FIVE

Senona hadn't been troubled about her decision to leave home until now. The excitement and novelty of the voyage had kept second guesses and doubts far from her mind. She had been running forward into the unknown and not looking back, but that short moment of questioning, that brief glimpse back when Liza made her realize what she had left behind was now plaguing her with doubt.

She had thought that with things going so smoothly, with Brant looking out for her, she had nothing to worry about. Why should she second guess when she was living comfortably?

Karl's death had distracted her for some time, as well as the hard work that had occupied her every day. At times, she had wondered what she had gotten herself into when she was in the middle of a raid, the thrill and adrenaline fueled by fear forcing her to live in the bloody and gory moment. It scared her. The various ports had also kept her busy as James dragged her around towns, and she had gotten her much-craved rides on Naldo. A third raid had also been successful and a night of celebrating had left her in no condition to think. Then there was the bustle of finally docking in Port Royale. She hadn't had much time for reflection.

She had made it to her destination; she was on an island held by the British, far from her parents' reach. It was protected by privateers who were paid to attack any Spanish vessel that dared to venture near. Well, they weren't paid in the strictest sense of the word. They attacked the Spanish, kept them away from the island, gave a percentage of the gold they collected to the crown, and in exchange, England turned a blind eye to any not-so-legal activities the privateers might be involved in. Some pirates jumped at the opportunity and gladly gave up the small amount of gold for a little security. Others weren't so eager to pay for their safety or fight under the flag of the king, but they were just as eager to attack any Spanish vessel they came across.

Senona was as far from her parents' reach as she possibly could be, but not from her thoughts.

She tried to sleep, but her nagging doubts kept her awake. She gave up tossing and turning and got up. Pulling on her breeches and a shirt, she slipped her feet into the heels she had been wearing earlier instead of her boots. Wandering around the house aimlessly in search of some form of relief, she came across a set of doors that were open to a balcony. She saw Brant standing by the rail, his back to her and looking out over the dark estate.

"I'm not disturbing you, am I?" she asked.

He turned slowly to face her, a smile on his face. "Not at all. I'd be glad for some company."

"No you don't," said Senona, seeing through his lie.

"What?"

"You don't want company."

"Here I thought I was something of a mystery, and then you come along, and after only two months you can tell when I'm lying."

Senona walked up beside him, leaning on the railing. "There are plenty of things I haven't figured out about you, Brant Foxton, but you're a terrible liar. You have a tell."

"What's that?" asked Brant, leaning back on the rail, opposite of Senona.

She looked out at the landscape, thinking. "You can't make eye contact when you're lying, and you always make eye contact when you are talking to someone. It's why it's so easy to trust you."

"You seem to have me figured out."

"Not at all. That was merely an observation."

"I'm sure you didn't come out here to talk to me about my lies. I'm pretty certain you didn't even come out here to talk to me. So, Senona, why did you come out here? I thought you were sleeping."

"I was, or trying at least," she said, her attention riveted on a gently swaying palm tree in the yard.

"Does that lack of sleep have something to do with how distracted you were acting during dinner?"

"Not at all. I'm merely not used to sleeping without the rock of a ship and the sound of the waves."

"Ah," said Brant.

"What?" she responded defensively.

"Nothing. It just amuses me that you, a lover of dry and solid land, would miss my ship."

"It was a sanctuary of sorts."

* * *

Brant was sure she was telling the truth, but she was holding something back. He couldn't force her to talk, especially when he'd been less than serious with her for the majority of the time he'd known her. "The *BlackFox* is something of a sanctuary for me as well. I suppose for you, she took you away from your parents and to a new life; for me, she *is* my life."

"And yet I can't help but second guess this new life I chose." There. It was out. What he knew she had needed to say, to tell someone, and what Brant had suspected all evening.

"Every decision we ever make we second guess."

"Maybe, but when I was on the *BlackFox*, I was confident. Even when I was scared, sickened, or fighting, even when I was terrified or challenged in ways I had never been before, I loved it. Why do I feel this now that my journey is over?"

"You may have made it to your destination, but now you have to create a new life. The journey was the easy part. Finding your place in the world, that's the hard part. It's enough to scare anyone. It scared me too."

"It's not that. Everywhere I turn, I seem caught up by the same falseness, the same empty formalities, the same lies, and the same spoiled attitude, all the things I ran from. If there truly is no escape, I could have stayed there."

"Is that why you asked Sam and me to ignore formalities?"

"Yes. I couldn't bear to see any more of it. The play acting."

"I got a lecture from Liza for listening to you. She said I shouldn't have respected your wishes, that ignoring formalities was unforgivable."

"So I suppose she didn't mention how I asked her to not call me by any title, and she complied with that wish."

"It must have slipped her mind."

They stood there in silence for a time, listening to the night noises that floated gently on the breeze.

"You'll do fine, Senona. You'll constantly turn and find yourself trapped by the very things you ran from, but then you'll see a weakness and break through. Nothing is holding you back. Not your parents, society, no human on earth, but yourself."

Senona smiled appreciatively and quickly wiped away a few escaped tears.

"I suppose life is never easy, no matter which path you walk."

Brant nodded. "You think you'll be able to sleep now?"

"Yes, thank you. I know you didn't come out here to listen to me. I'm sure you have enough troubles of your own without adding mine to that pile."

"It's okay. I've been in your place once upon a time."

Senona touched his arm briefly as she turned and left to attempt sleep again.

Brant sighed and took a deep breath of the muggy night air, then headed back to his room. He could pretend all he liked, but he could never make this house feel like a home.

* * *

James was out in the stables grooming Admiral when Senona came out to check on Naldo the next morning. She had slept late, and the sun now beat down with a cruel heat, the thick air offering no relief.

Senona wore a simple white dress made of a light, cool material. Her hair was pinned back in an elegant twist, keeping it off her neck. "Good morning, James," she said cheerfully. It felt good to be on land for more than twelve hours.

"Morning, Senona. You sleep well?"

"Yes, thank you. Though I'll admit I miss the rocking of the ship," Senona said as she walked into the tack room and selected a brush to groom Naldo.

"I never sleep well on the first night back," offered James when she returned.

Senona slipped into Naldo's stall and began doing long, brisk strokes down his back with the brush. "What's the plan for today?"

"I'm going to ride Admiral around the grounds, maybe see the fields with Sam."

"Is Brant out there now?" A quick look around proved Jester, Brant's favorite horse, was missing.

"Yes, which reminds me, he wants you to meet him there when you can."

"I'll head out right away."

"Keep an eye on the weather. Brant says rain is coming, and he's rarely wrong."

Senona smiled as she stepped out of Naldo's stall. "Thank you. I really don't relish the idea of getting sick the second day here just because I didn't see a storm coming."

James didn't reply but continued to brush Admiral. Senona disappeared momentarily into the tack room, coming back out with Naldo's saddle and halter.

"If you aren't careful, Admiral won't have any hair left to brush," teased Senona.

James blushed. "It's soothing for me, and he really doesn't get the care he deserves when I'm gone."

Senona led Naldo out of his stall and mounted, positioning herself side-saddle. "I'll see you later, James," she said with a wave of her hand as she nudged Naldo into a walk out of the stables.

After riding a couple of minutes at a walk, Senona nudged Naldo into a trot, then cantered down the road that led to the fields. "Come on, Naldo, let's go!" she urged. As he stretched out into a gallop she laughed in exhilaration.

They arrived at the fields all too soon for Senona's liking, and she reined Naldo into a slow, controlled jog, directing him to a well-worn path in the field and headed towards the two distant figures on horseback. Five minutes later, she rode up beside Brant.

"Good morning, Senona," said Brant with a smile.

"Good morning to you as well, and Sam."

Sam nodded acknowledgment and turned to Brant. "If you don't need me any longer, I'm going to ride ahead and check on the other fields."

"Of course, Sam."

Sam kicked his horse into a gallop and was swallowed by a cloud of dust as he rode away.

"James told me you wanted to see me."

"I'm heading to town and I was wondering if you would like to come along."

"Of course. Will we be seeing Matt at all?"

"We'll stop by the ship and see how things are. Matthew should be there looking after things."

"When do we leave?"

"Now. Sam was just explaining some things to me, but now that we're done, I'm ready. Your timing, for once, was spot on."

Senona smiled, Brant just couldn't give a straight compliment.

"I'll race you to the road," she challenged.

"You think your little Spaniard can beat Jester?"

"I guess the results of our race will answer that question."

Brant reined Jester to a halt, and Senona turned Naldo to face him.

"I really don't think it would be a fair race. You're riding side saddle, and Jester is bred for speed."

"Brant Foxton, are you afraid of losing?" taunted Senona.

"Not at all," came his cool reply. "I just don't like racing under unfair conditions."

"I am a better rider than you, so riding side saddle should even the odds. And Naldo is built for speed. You can breed all you want, but if the horse doesn't have the build, it won't have the speed. So are you going to race me or not?"

"Okay. Line up."

Senona maneuvered Naldo so that he was even with Jester. "Call it." Mentally, she tensed herself, giving Naldo the feeling of urgency.

"On your mark," said Brant. "Get set."

Brant and Senona positioned themselves low against their mounts' necks. "Go!"

Senona barely pressed her heel into Naldo's side before he took off, Jester and Brant not a second behind. They galloped neck and neck towards the road. Brant was urging Jester on with his heels while Senona did nothing but whisper encouragement into Naldo's ears. Naldo may not have understood her words, but he heard her tone and responded accordingly.

With less than a quarter of a mile to go, Senona decided it was time to pull ahead. "Come on, Naldo! I know this isn't your fastest. Let's wrap this up and prove you're the best."

Naldo's ears pricked forward, and Senona nudged him. "Let's go, boy!"

Naldo stretched out into a full out run, pulling ahead of Jester. Brant attempted to keep up, but Jester was already running full out and had nothing left to give his rider.

Senona made it to the road and reined Naldo in. Turning, she expected to see Brant and Jester right on her tail. However, she was surprised to see them just approaching the road. "I do believe you lost," said Senona with a laugh as Brant reined Jester in beside Naldo.

"So I did. I really didn't think Naldo could have beaten Jester."

"Never underestimate your foe. I thought you would have known that."

"I should; though in my defense, you are hardly my foe," said Brant, turning Jester down the road towards town.

Senona followed suit, the two of them trotting down the dusty road.

* * *

Senona laughed as she walked with Brant down the dock towards the *BlackFox*. "So you were arrested after having command only a month? And were heading to the gallows?" she asked, disbelievingly.

"Yes. It was quite horrible, really."

"How is it you're still alive and not swaying in the sea breeze as a warning to all pirates?"

"I apologized," he answered, completely serious.

"Ah, yes. Apologies are generally accepted when you are charged with piracy," she answered sarcastically.

"No, I did. Governor Modyford recognized my name and came to talk to me. I convinced him that I was only serving the crown, and I apologized for not realizing that the previous Captain's letter of Marque was non-transferable. Governor Modyford and I had a nice long discussion, and in the end, the charges were all dropped and a letter of Marque was commissioned."

"That's a bit of a ridiculous story. Are you sure you aren't making it up?"

"Of course. Ask Governor Modyford."

"No, that's alright. I believe you." He never ceased to surprise her, but somehow she felt inclined to believe his tales.

"Ah, here we are. My Lady, allow me to assist you up the ramp," said Brant, offering Senona the crook of his arm as they stood at the base of the ramp leading up to the deck of the *BlackFox*.

Senona smiled and took his arm. "Why thank you, Captain."

They walked onto the deck together. Matt approached them instantly. "Cap'n. Senona," he said with a smile, nodding once to each of them.

"Matthew, how is my ship?"

"She's fine. Got a round-the-clock watch going."

"Good. Keep an eye on her tonight; a storm is on its way."

"Aye. That mugginess in the air."

"Mugginess?" questioned Senona.

"Aye. Can you feel it?"

"No. Feels quite nice out. Getting a little cool actually."

Brant and Matt looked to the sky.

"Aye it is cooler, and look at the clouds. Your storm be moving in faster than we thought, Cap'n."

Brant frowned. "It looks like a bad one too. We won't beat it home."

"No, ye won't. Perhaps ye should stay on the ship tonight?"

"No. Senona will go to an inn. I don't want her on the ship with a storm, she could get tossed about. I'll come back to the ship and help once she's settled in a room."

"I can help," argued Senona as he took her arm and led her off the ship.

"No. You're a fine sailor in clear weather, and even in slightly choppy seas, but I don't want you on the boat with a storm. Looks like a bad one, and we have to keep the ship from getting banged around too much on this dock. I'll get you a room here tonight."

Brant led Senona into a shabby but warm inn and purchased a room for her. He led her through the many sailors and poorer residents of Port Royale who used the inn as a place to visit, gamble, and drink. "Here's your room. Don't leave it or open it for any reason," he warned. "The people here are of the disreputable sort, and not all pirates are as honorable as I am. I would take you somewhere better, but I don't have the time."

Senona started to argue, but Brant shut the door, leaving no one to listen but the walls.

She watched out the window and watched him walk down the street in the direction of his ship. The winds howled outside the window, sounding like a loosed banshee, and the sky grew dark. It didn't take long until the rain came. Thunder rolled and lightning lit up the sky and Senona found herself praying for Brant and the crew fighting the storm.

Senona sat on the smelly mattress and sighed. The room had so far proven to have three leaks, but she was sure more would appear as the rain came down heavier. And to top things off, she was starting to get hungry. She hadn't eaten since that morning, and it was nearing dinnertime.

Knowing Brant didn't want her to leave, Senona convinced herself that food was a necessity, and what he didn't know wouldn't hurt him. Resolved, she stood up and left the room.

The common room was loud and full of smoke, but Senona walked confidently down the stairs and found a seat at an abandoned table deep in the shadows of a corner. It wasn't long before a barmaid came and asked if she wanted something to eat.

Senona smiled. "Yes, please, and a glass of rum."

Senona had taken a liking to rum during her time on the *BlackFox*. It was the drink of choice among the crew.

Five minutes later, the barmaid brought out a plate of food, if you could really call it that—it looked as if the food Senona had eaten after weeks of being at sea—and a glass of amber liquid.

"Thank you," said Senona. The girl nodded and continued her rounds.

Senona finished her food quickly and then sat back, watching the goings on around her as she slowly drank her rum. It burned down her throat and settled in her stomach, the warmth spreading throughout her entire body. She loved the feeling.

"Ye look lonely, sweetheart," came a voice from across the table.

Senona startled slightly and turned to look at the scarred face of a sailor who had taken the seat across from her. "If I'm lonely, I'm not looking for company from the likes of you," said Senona, sitting up a little straighter and looking straight at him, her gaze unwavering, "Now will you please vacate the chair and leave me alone."

The sailor grunted and muttered something about high and mighty girls and how much trouble they were before getting up and leaving in search of more pleasant company.

Senona smirked in amusement and looked out once again. She watched a card game going on intently, trying to figure out what the point of the game was.

"I thought I recognized ye when ye first came in with Cap'n Foxton, but I told myself no one like ye would be in a place like this."

Senona turned smoothly to face the voice, ready to send off yet another sailor who thought she needed company but was surprised to see Old Richard, the captain she had almost gotten passage with. There was no doubt in her mind anymore that it would have been a deadly mistake on her part if Brant hadn't abducted her.

"Captain Richard, we meet again. Have you come to return my money?"

"Ha," he said mockingly. "I don't have any of your money. We had ourselves an agreement, and ye went back on that there agreement, so I owe ye nothing."

"If you aren't here talking to me for some reason, then please leave so I can enjoy my drink."

"Girl like ye shouldn't be drinking rum," he said, plucking the glass from between her fingers and downing it in one gulp. "Now I do have myself a purpose in talking to ye. Ye see, I want to know why ye went with Cap'n Foxton and not me."

"I don't wish to discuss this with you."

"Well then, let's go ask Cap'n Foxton." Richard smiled, revealing his crooked, tobacco stained teeth. "Boys, let's take the lady for a walk. She needs some air.

A couple of well-muscled, scarred sailors walked up and grabbed Senona, roughly dragging her to her feet.

"Unhand me, Captain," she said angrily. She trembled but was too angry to allow that fear to convey in her voice.

"Now, now. We're just taking ye to your beloved Cap'n."

The two sailors dragged Senona through the inn behind Richard and out into the driving rain. No one in the inn gave the spectacle even a second glance. It was an unwritten rule that no one interfered in other people's business.

"Let me go, Captain. Brant won't stand for this. You'll pay."

Richard laughed. "First name basis with Cap'n Foxton, are we? I assure you no harm will come to me. Foxton is too peaceful, and so he'll do whatever I ask of him. Besides, he wouldn't want to see your pretty neck slit, now would he?"

Senona struggled in anger but it had no effect on the strong men dragging her along. They all piled into a longboat that pitched viciously next to the dock and rowed it out to where the *BlackFox* was anchored about a mile out.

"Foxton!" called Richard as he climbed up on deck.

They held Senona not far behind him, just out of sight, but the sailors of the *BlackFox* watched them warily, though they couldn't leave the job at hand. Old Richard and his men stood there for a few minutes in the pouring rain. Senona was soaked and freezing, and Brant hadn't shown himself. She found herself praying he would come before something worse happened.

"Foxton! I got something of yours, so come on out!"

Senona saw Brant walk out from his cabin, and her body immediately relaxed; she could deal with any anger he might have towards her later. Now she just wanted him to save her.

"What's the meaning of this, Richard?" he fumed. He hadn't yet caught sight of Senona. "Get your filthy, despicable self off of my ship."

"Happy to oblige, Foxton. But then ye won't be getting her back."

Richard motioned to his men to drag her forward for Brant to see.

Brant's face fell, and his hard glare turned to Senona. "I told you to stay in your room."

"I'm sorry, Brant," said Senona softly.

CHAPTER SIX

Brant could barely hear what Senona said over the noise of the storm, but any anger he had felt towards her washed away with the falling rain. He could see that she was terrified and felt horrible for disobeying. He suspected that she would be a little more inclined to follow orders from now on.

"You think she means anything to me? I gave her passage; I did not sign up to be her father. Do what you want." His face was a mask of apathy, his voice cold and uncaring.

Senona almost believed him, until she noticed his gaze was directed past Richard, instead of making eye contact. He was making a dangerous gamble by lying, and Senona hoped that Richard would buy it.

Richard's choking, raspy laugh cut through the noise of the storm. "Trying to bluff, Foxton? It won't work. Ye see, I saw ye escort the lady to her room and your hand was on her arm all possessive like. No, Foxton, I know she's something to ye. In fact, I got me a notion that there be more to this picture than either one of ye wants to admit. I'm not daft, and I can see when someone feels more than just fatherly or even friendly. Ye two are even on a first-name basis. So let's cut to the chase and talk business." Richard grinned; he knew that he was holding the upper hand.

Senona's eyes were opened to the far reach of pirating. It was a chilling thing, to know that piracy wasn't just on the high seas. Men like Richard were criminals all the way through, whether on land or sea. The fact that he would take advantage of Brant's upbringing was detestable. She knew Brant couldn't leave a woman helpless; it wasn't in his nature. It had nothing to do with any special relationship he may have with her. Sometimes she wondered if he liked her at all, or if he only helped her because of some misplaced sense of duty.

"Okay, Richard. Let's take this to my cabin and talk terms. No point in us standing out in this weather."

Richard grunted and led the way. He motioned for his men to follow with Senona.

They jerked her forward, causing her to slip on the wet, pitching deck and fall. A hiss of pain escaped her lips as her knees connected with the hard planks.

Brant rushed to her side, pushing away one of the men and helped her to her feet. The deck rocked unsteadily in the storm, making it more difficult for her to find her balance, her legs rubbery from fear and her fall.

"I'll assist the Lady," he stated. It wasn't a request.

The sailor nodded and motioned to his partner to flank Brant and Senona.

Brant put his arm around her shoulders and gently guided her along.

"Are you okay?" he whispered.

Tears ran down her face, but the rain made them invisible. "I'm fine," she said, her voice trembling from a mixture of emotions and cold.

* * *

They entered the cabin and the warmth and comfort hit them instantly, welcoming them in. Outside, the weather continued to batter the ship with driving wind and rain, and Brant couldn't help but think that the atmosphere outside was better suited to the situation.

Richard took the chair behind Brant's desk and propped his feet, still clad in dripping boots, on Brant's maps that covered the surface of the desk. Brant winced as he saw the ink run and bleed. Those maps were high quality, up to date, and very expensive.

"Nice li'l boat ye got yourself," said Richard as he slowly looked around.

"Don't make yourself comfortable," replied Brant, his teeth clenched. He tried to control himself, but men like Richard made it very hard.

He led Senona to the bed, forcing her to sit and wrapping one of his blankets around her shaking form. She looked so fragile, soaked through, her eyes wide in fright. It pained Brant to walk away; he wanted to make sure she had a handle on herself, but things had to be taken care of.

"How about we get straight to business? I don't want you on my ship longer than is absolutely necessary. I think it's starting to smell like you already."

Richard smiled, showing off his crooked, rotten teeth. "Very well. Ye stole my cargo, and I want payment."

Brant stared the man down, feeling nothing but disdain. "The way I heard things was that you got paid a fair amount for a passenger that didn't show up, and you got to keep that money, so don't come to me acting as though you've been robbed."

"Maybe so," said Richard thoughtfully, his hand scratching his stubbly chin. "Maybe so, but ye see, I got the girl and she'll bring me a tidy sum on the black market. Now I know she means something to ye, so either ye and I discuss business, or I take her back to my ship, put her to good use there, and then sell her."

Brant was disgusted. Richard was the kind of captain that gave privateers a bad name, albeit Richard was no privateer, but few distinguished between the more legal side of the business and flat out piracy. He saw how Senona paled when she heard what Richard had planned for her. He didn't wish the fate on anyone.

Brant carefully considered his options. He could command what few men he had on board to attack, he had enough to overpower Richard and his men, but that would leave Richard too much time to escape and take Senona with them. What other choice did he have other than to negotiate?

"Name your terms," he said grudgingly.

"Ye have a hull full of shiny treasure, no?"

"I did a little work on the voyage here," Brant answered vaguely, his face an unreadable mask. He didn't want Richard thinking his hull was bursting with "Shiny treasure."

"Good, good. Work is good for me. I also understand ye attacked a Spanish treasure galleon." His eyes shone greedily.

"You sure your sources have the right Captain Foxton?"

"Don't fool with me, Foxton. Ye did cause I saw it all. Now I doubt ye spent it all—"

Brant cut him off before he could continue. "I already divided it with my crew," he lied. He had divided the other two ships' treasure but hadn't touched the gold from that particular ship. It had been Karl's last raid, and Brant had wanted to use it for something Karl would have liked.

"No, ye didn't. Ye be lying to me. Now I'm being reasonable. I ain't asking for all your swag, just what ye got from that galleon."

Richard was after their best take, and the only one he hadn't divvied up. It was disconcerting how much he knew about what occurred on the *BlackFox*, but Brant suspected it was mostly guesswork. Richard likely thought Brant had kept the take from the Spanish galleon as his share and allotted the rest between his crew. Richard was that type of man, and he was counting on the fact that Brant was the same. His evaluation of Brant's character was incorrect, which would have resulted at any other time in him walking away empty handed. The bastard was greedy and lucky.

"Okay." He sighed. "The five chests I took from the Spanish galleon are yours." He didn't even know what to do with it anyway; he just wanted to honor Karl. Karl had died protecting Senona; maybe giving up the gold for the same cause would honor him.

"I knew ye would be reasonable. Now, I'm gonna keep the lady here with me until my boys finish the transfer. I need myself some insurance. I'm sure ye understand."

"I'm going to stay with you. I have to make sure you don't try anything. You understand." Brant smirked at Richard.

"Don't ye want to oversee the work?"

"My quartermaster will look after that."

Brant walked over to Senona and rested his hands on her shoulders. "There's a pistol under the blanket to your right. Use it if he tries to harm you, but only if he tries to harm you," he whispered as he brushed the wet hair that had escaped from its confinement away from her face.

Senona nodded slightly, still pale and trembling.

"I'll be right back."

If Richard were as intelligent as he seemed to think he was, he wouldn't have let Brant go or even suggested that Brant go anywhere. This alone proved to Brant that the man was uncomfortable around him, maybe even scared of him. Richard was on Brant's turf, and although he was holding the upper hand now, Brant could easily turn it in his favor. On top of it all, the fact that Senona was armed meant that Richard really didn't have any insurance at all. Instead, Richard just nodded and Brant left the room in search of Matt.

* * *

Senona listened silently as Brant and Richard came to terms on how much she was worth. She was somewhat flattered that Brant was willing to give up some of the money from the treasure galleon for her, but at the same time, insulted that the two men thought she was something to buy. It reminded her all too clearly of the way her father viewed marriage.

She wanted to tell Brant not to give up the gold for her. If she had just listened to him in the first place, they wouldn't be going through any of this. Once again she had let her pride take the lead, and it got her in a great deal of trouble, trouble that Brant shouldn't have to deal with. If she was in Brant's position, she would have left Richard to his own devices, but she knew Brant wouldn't do that. He was constantly making her problems his. At first, she knew he had been angry with her for disobeying, but he had forgiven her quickly, even showing concern for her and doing the best he could to get them out of the mess she had created.

Her hand wandered to the right, touching the cold, reassuring metal of the pistol. Would she have to use it? She hoped not. Senona knew she could kill Richard if she had to, but she was afraid. She had killed men on the raids, and Brant knew if needed she would defend herself, but killing made her sick, and guns were so messy and loud. Senona viewed them as a cowardly weapon, an easy way out. They made killing too detached and easy; it disturbed her. She hoped she would never find herself in a position where she had to use one.

Brant was only gone mere minutes, but to Senona, it felt like hours. Her eyes were riveted on Richard. She didn't trust him and needed to be prepared if he tried anything. Her steady gaze issued a challenge, daring Richard to find out how tough she was. How she wasn't a helpless woman. It was only a cover to hide her nerves.

Senona didn't break her gaze that Richard was so desperately trying to avoid when Brant walked back in. He was followed by a gust of wind that seemed to systematically rustle everything in the small cabin.

"Senona," he said lightly, adding the teasing flare that always managed to get right under her skin.

Her eyes tore away from Richard and bore into Brant. Richard visibly relaxed.

"Senona, relax."

Senona looked at Richard, forcing him to make eye contact, and glared at him in warning. Then, as if nothing in the world was wrong, she relaxed and looked around the cabin. Now that Brant was here, she obviously felt safe.

* * *

Matt silently watched Richard's men take the five huge chests off the *BlackFox* and load them onto their longboat. He didn't know all the specifics of why Richard was getting a large amount of treasure, but Brant had made it clear that his job was to keep an eye on the huge men to ensure they didn't take anything that hadn't been part of the agreement.

As they carried the last chest out, Matt turned to them. "You're done here. Ye can go tell your vile cap'n that."

One of the sailors stepped forward threateningly. He obviously didn't take kindly to being ordered around by someone other than the captain or quartermaster.

Another one of Richard's men drew his pistol on his crew mate. "Leave him and do what he says," he growled.

The sailor grunted but didn't look any less threatening. Matt looked him up and down, taking in his appearance. The big man was bald and covered in tattoos. He looked every bit the miscreant that he was.

Matt led the two sailors to Brant's cabin and entered, not even bothering to knock. He just wanted these degenerates off his home.

"It's all done," said Matt.

Richard turned to face his quartermaster from where he still sat. "Good."

He stood up and walked to Brant, extending his hand in a mocking fashion.

Brant looked at it and raised his eyebrow but made no move to accept the hand. It was the polite thing to do after business, shake hands, but this was not polite business, and there was no reason to pretend that it was.

Richard retracted his hand and laughed as he strode out of the cabin, limping from an old battle wound, his two men following.

Matt followed them and watched them climb down to their waiting longboat. When he was certain they wouldn't be coming back, he went to his cabin. It had been a long night. If Brant wanted him, he could come find him.

* * *

Brant breathed a sigh of relief. Everything had gone as smoothly as could be expected. No one had been hurt, and in his books that was a good day.

Senona didn't move from her position on the bed, her body shook violently with her hands clenched in her lap. Her knuckles were white and her fingernails dug into her palms. Now that it was over, her barriers had fallen, and the terror that she had been holding must have hit her full force.

Brant looked over at Senona and saw the fear in her eyes. "It's okay. They're gone," he reassured her.

"I know," she whispered. "But if it wasn't for me, they never would have come."

He quickly walked over and sat down next to her on the bed, pulling her against him in an attempt at giving comfort. "I'm not angry with you."

Tears streamed down Senona's face and soaked into Brant's already wet shirt. "How can you not be?" she asked with a sniffle. "I brought them here. It's my fault they took your gold. I should have listened to you; I never should have left home." Her voice was bitter, "It would have saved you a lot of trouble."

Brant's eyes flashed with anger. "Don't you ever talk like that," he said harshly, his eyes hard and dangerous. "You disobeyed me, that's true, but you meant no harm, and I'm sure you won't do that again," he spoke sternly, commanding Senona's attention.

She slipped out of his arms and met his gaze.

"The gold they took was Karl's. I wanted to do something with it to honor him, and I think he'd be happy that we used it to protect you. As for trouble—" Brant chuckled, "I really can't get angry with you over that when I'm exactly the same. We both learn the hard way. It doesn't bother me that I get stuck helping you through it. But if you ever, ever try and go back home, I won't let you. This is your home now."

Senona frowned; the tears had stopped. "What do you mean you wouldn't let me? You don't have any control over me."

"Maybe I have no right to keep you from doing what you want, but that won't stop me from trying. When I first brought you on my ship, I promised myself that I would never let harm come to you while I could protect you. You left home for a reason, and I will never let you go without making you look long and hard at why you left and why you want to go back. If you can do that and still want to leave, then I will wish you all the best, though I sincerely hope it never comes to that."

Senona looked at him in question. "What do you mean?"

"I mean, I don't think I could live without you, trouble and all."

There, he had said it. What he had been denying all along. He felt free, as if a great weight was lifted from his shoulders.

Fresh tears glistened in Senona's eyes, concerning Brant. "Senona, what's wrong?"

"Nothing. It's just that no one has ever said anything like that to me," she said, smiling through her tears.

Brant laughed, cupping her face in his rough, work beaten hands. "You silly girl." He leaned in and gently brushed her lips with his.

She was too surprised to respond and sat there stiff and wide-eyed in surprise.

Brant searched her eyes for an invitation, anything that would let him know that she was ready. She smiled a little and rubbed her lips together. Ever so slowly she raised her eyes to meet his.

That was all he needed.

He kissed her again and, this time, she responded, not even hesitating for a second.

"We best get some sleep," he whispered, breathless with exhilaration.

Senona sighed, not wanting it to end. "I suppose."

"You stay here. I'll go sleep in the crew bunks."

Brant took his hands from her face, rubbing his finger along her cheekbone, then standing up. "We'll go to the estate first thing in the morning."

Senona nodded as he left her alone in the cabin.

The wind and the rain still battered outside, but he slept soundly, regardless of the events that had occurred that day. He had forgotten everything, everything but the kiss they had shared.

Brant had entered a dangerous place that night. Karl had warned him against it, but he didn't care. At the moment, it felt right, and that was all that mattered; the moment.

CHAPTER SEVEN

Senona woke up feeling rested and ready to face the day. The familiar rock of the ship soothed her, the storm from the night before leaving glassy waters and a clean, cool breeze that she could smell and feel, even in the closed cabin.

She sat up on the edge of the bed and looked around, the events from last night poured back to her, causing her to shudder as she thought of Richard and how she had cost Brant so much. Yet, the memory of what Brant had said and done came to her, and she smiled gently to herself at the memory of his lips on hers. Her hand strayed to touch her lips and she blushed, though no one was there to see or hear her private thoughts.

Brant loved her for who she was. It was an incredible feeling to be accepted. She only wondered if what she felt in return was truly love or just a reciprocation of the unfamiliar feelings. Never the less, she did feel something, and it both excited and terrified her.

A knock sounded on the door.

"One moment!" she called, jumping off the bed and rushing to Brant's dresser, hurriedly pulling on a pair of his trousers and a shirt. Her dress, soaked the night before, lay in a wet pile on the floor.

The knock came again, more insistent. "Senona, if you're not dressed, I might just come in anyway," Brant teased.

She blushed and buttoned the last button. "Okay, come in."

Brant strode in, coming up behind her and wrapping his arms around Senona's waist, pulling her against his hard, muscled body.

Senona smiled and leaned into the embrace. Though she could not see him, she knew his touch, like a gentle whisper of wind, and the scent of cinnamon and nutmeg permeated the air. It was Brant's own personal scent, an identifying aspect of him.

"Good morning," she said.

"It certainly is. Are you ready to go back to the estate?"

"Of course. I'm eager to see Naldo."

Brant released his embrace and turned her to face him, looking serious. "Perhaps we should talk before we get to the estate."

"About what?"

"Last night. I think it needs to be discussed."

Senona nodded. "We can talk on the way back."

She didn't want him to see how terrified she was. What could he possibly want to talk about? Did he think he had made a mistake and needed to remedy it? Only a moment ago, she didn't know what she felt, but now she was terrified that she was going to lose it, whatever it was.

Brant smiled and offered Senona his arm as they left the cabin. She took it with a laugh, not allowing herself to dwell on her fears; instead, she decided to enjoy things while they lasted.

Matt was on deck, holding the first watch as he happily whittled at some wood.

"We're off, Matthew."

"Have a good day, Cap'n. Senona." He grinned, looking up momentarily from his project. Even Matt seemed to have forgotten the events of last night.

Senona smiled and waved with her free hand as she walked down the ramp with Brant.

They had stabled the horses not far from the docks, and a half hour later, they were trotting down the dusty road towards Brant's estate. It was amazing how quickly the ground dried up in the scorching Caribbean heat. However, the aftermath of the storm offered a clean air that granted some relief from the sun.

"Senona, I don't want you to think that when I say I want to talk about last night that I changed my mind about what I said, because I didn't," said Brant, breaking the silence and bringing up a discussion Senona wasn't keen on opening.

"The thought did cross my mind."

"I think we have to decide on whether or not to make this new relationship, if that's what it is, known to everyone else."

Senona looked at Brant, not quite sure she fully understood what he was trying to get at. "Are you saying we should keep our feelings a secret?" Her voice had an accusatory tone to it, causing Brant to visibly wince.

"I'm not saying we have to. I'm just saying it's something that we should consider."

* * *

Senona looked ahead as she rode Naldo, her lips pressed in a straight line that Brant recognized as a look of concentration. They rode in silence, and Brant started to worry that he had said something wrong.

Finally, she spoke. "Perhaps you're right. After all, we wouldn't want to announce something and then go back on it later. What if our actions were caused by the events that had transpired, and really we think nothing more of each other than just friends? Things would be simpler if we kept things just between ourselves for now," she agreed.

Brant looked at her, frowning. "Then it's agreed; we'll keep it a secret. But if you think what I said and did wasn't sincere…"

Senona stopped him. "I never doubted what you said, but I think we should keep things between us for some time. Just take things slowly."

Brant changed the subject, uncomfortable with where the discussion was going. "When I leave next Wednesday to bring James to London, I'm going to be gone for the summer months."

"I know."

"I want you to stay at Foxton Estate while I'm gone."

"Brant, I cannot rely on you to get me through life. I'm going to get a job in town, and if you absolutely insist I stay at your estate, I'll pay you board for both Naldo and me."

"I knew you would say something like that; that's why I arranged something both of us can agree on. A compromise."

Senona raised an eyebrow. "And what little arrangement would that be?"

Brant grinned. "You will work for me, covering both your board as well as Naldo's."

"I will work for you? That's still charity, Brant. You know I was raised as a noble; I have no experience in any type of work."

"No, you have plenty of experience. Don't sell yourself short. What about all the work you did on the *BlackFox*? I have full confidence in you and your work ethic."

"What exactly do you have in mind?" she sighed, giving up. "If it's cleaning house or needlework, I'll be of no use to you."

"Stablehand."

Senona laughed, looking incredulously at Brant. "Stablehand? You do realize my parents would have a fit if they knew you're offering me a job as a stablehand."

Brant nodded.

"Then they'd die right where they stood if they knew I was accepting."

Brant smirked. "Accepting? You don't even know the details."

"I'm sure I can trust you."

"Before we put any of this in writing, so to speak, I'll give you details."

Senona nodded for him to continue.

"You'll look after all the horses; exercise, grooming, feeding. You would be in charge of supplies, cleaning of the stalls and day pens, tack upkeep, anything and everything involving the horses."

"I like this arrangement." She grinned, clearly pleased that this was a job she had some experience in.

Brant's estate came into view, the large two-story mansion with its immaculately groomed yard and whitewashed stable yards off to the side. There were a couple of horses that were not in use in day pens, grazing lazily.

Brant saw a smile creep to her lips and knew that she could make his house her home, her new life.

* * *

"Senona!" James' excited exclamation rang from the second floor of the house.

Senona had barely walked in the front door when James had come running out of his room calling her name. He looked positively boyish, not at all like a youth who had been forced to grow up too quickly.

"Oh my! Did you miss me that much?"

James laughed, the same twinkle in his eye that Senona saw so often in Brant's. "Of course not."

Senona raised an eyebrow questioningly and walked up the stairs to meet James who engulfed her in a hug. It seemed as though he was growing more every day.

He smirked and looked around carefully. "Well, I missed you a little, but mostly I'm glad to see you because now you can rescue me from Liza."

"Whatever is she doing to you?" she teased, adopting a mock look of shock. She had no doubt the housekeeper could cook up no end of misery for a boy like James.

"She wants to cut my hair."

"What?" She wasn't sure whether or not James was being serious.

"She wants to cut my hair short like Brant's." James wrinkled his nose in distaste.

"Cut your hair?" she exclaimed in mock horror. "What kind of new torture is this? What is the world coming to? If your hair gets cut off, will you lose your strength?"

James frowned. "No, but I like my long hair. I'd look identical to Brant if I got it cut."

Senona held back the laughter that threatened to bubble over. "You already look identical. Come along to my room; we'll talk. We haven't had a good conversation since we docked."

"What about Liza?"

"If she comes looking for you, we'll tell her we're working on your studies." Senona winked mischievously.

"Genius! Liza will leave me alone for that while we come up with a diabolical plot to keep my hair."

Senona broke out into heartfelt, uncontrollable laughter, walking into her room with James close behind.

He flopped onto the large, plush bed and stared up at the ceiling.

Senona splashed cold water on her face from the basin sitting on the dresser. Liza had likely freshened it earlier that morning in preparation for her return.

"You know, it's funny, Brant could never consider this estate his home," contemplated James.

Senona wiped her face with a towel, not facing him but looking at him curiously in the reflection in her mirror as she picked up her brush and began to wrestle it through her tangled hair.

"Why do you say that?"

"Well," he started thoughtfully, playing with his shoulder length blond hair that he had left untied. "This used to be our father's estate, though, we never came here. Brant inherited it. But Brant and my father never got along, and all Brant really cares about is his freedom now."

Senona turned towards James, pausing her brushing. He sounded almost bitter, a little like how she sounded when she spoke of her parents.

"He cares about you, though."

"Sure, he cares about me, but the *BlackFox*, the money brought in by business, gives him freedom, and so that comes first. I'm second, and this estate is a bitter reminder. We could, should, have a proper family, but I'm either a part of his crew or just a responsibility holding him back. Why do you think he's sending me off to school?"

Senona walked over and sat on the edge of the bed next to where James lay.

"You're not second, James. Brant loves you very much. If he didn't, he wouldn't be concerned about your education. That's why he's sending you to school. Not to get rid of you."

James didn't seem to hear her; he just kept talking. "I wasn't always second, you know. When he first left all those years ago, I was the one he came back for. He told me all about his adventures and how great the sea was. It was a small comfort after father's death. I would dream of grand adventures we could have and how we could be a real family, not detached like my father. It did start out like that. Brant took responsibility, and he would talk to me. I got my brother back, a man I could barely remember aside from that last Christmas he had spent with us. And Karl was like a father. Those were the best times I can remember."

Senona smiled sadly. She had thought that James had a good life, but maybe even he had reasons for bitterness.

"What made that all change?"

"Then there was Catherine."

"Catherine?" Senona had never heard of Catherine, but the fact that she had changed things between Brant and James meant she had been something to Brant. She wasn't entirely sure she wanted to hear about her.

"Yes, Catherine. She was on a ship Brant found stranded. It had an odd look about it, so we boarded." James frowned.

"Dead bodies were everywhere. Catherine and Matt were the only survivors."

"Pirates?"

"Who else would have attacked a ship like that? Anyway, Brant found her hiding under a bed."

"Poor girl." Senona's voice was soft. She couldn't imagine the horror this Catherine had gone through.

James nodded and continued. "Brant took her to the *BlackFox*, gave her his cabin. He found out she had been en route to England when they had been attacked."

Senona got up and set the brush down on the dresser, no longer comfortable sitting. "So Brant took her home?" she asked while searching through her clothes for something to wear.

"Of course. But not before things got complicated. Brant was in love with her; everything about her fascinated him."

"Really? I never thought of Brant as the falling in love type." Senona felt a pang of jealousy as she pulled out a brown and green dress that she found in the wardrobe. She suddenly felt inadequate for the man who had confessed his love for her less than twenty-four hours earlier.

"No one did, but she was beautiful, tall and thin, blond hair and blue eyes and a wonderful sense of humor on top of that; society's picture of perfection. But she was delicate, too delicate for the life Brant had to offer. He asked her to stay with him."

Senona laughed in amusement as she changed behind the screen. She knew where this was going. Brant couldn't handle someone delicate. He needed an equal. "She turned him down." It wasn't a question; she was continuing the story.

"Yep. I think it broke her heart just as much, but she refused to be second in his life. She knew that the ocean owned Brant's heart. I did feel bad for Brant; he went to a dark place after that."

Senona stepped out from behind the screen. She knew how the little story would end, but she was morbidly curious about the details. "How so?"

"Brant drank a lot, and hid for a while, then poured everything into the *BlackFox*. I think he wanted to try and forget about Catherine, and so he poured his life into the reasons why she wouldn't stay with him. After Catherine, I became second in his life. I probably should have seen that sailing was more important, as she had, but I was young, and I had my own ideas as to how it should be."

"I guess he just couldn't let go."

James nodded in agreement.

This fact tore through Senona. Did Brant still love Catherine? Or had he found a new, deeper love with her?

Senona hurt, but she didn't know if she could confront Brant with something she wasn't even supposed to know, and with something from the past. It shouldn't affect them. She received one answer, though, she knew now that she truly did care about the noble pirate.

* * *

"Make sure that's secure!" called Brant after Oliver, a rough looking sailor in his mid-forties.

Senona smiled at Brant as he shouted orders, preparing to set sail for England. He was in his element, powerful and happy. Happier than Senona had seen him the whole week they had been on land.

Brant noticed Senona's smile and approached her; his long, even stride brought him to her quickly.

"What are you smiling at?" A teasing glint was in Brant's eyes, and Senona resisted the urge to step into his arms and feel his strong embrace. Why had she agreed to keep things secret? They went out on daily rides to be alone together, and then they'd get back and pretend they were nothing more than friends.

"You," was her simple reply.

"Do I look funny?" Brant stood up tall and crossed his arms.

"No, you don't look funny. You look…" After a brief moment of thought, trying to find the right descriptive word, "you look regal, in your element, commanding," she finished.

"Please, continue. I like your compliments."

Senona laughed but complied. "Handsome, roguish, conceited—"

"Whoa now! Conceited?" Brant looked at Senona questioningly, pouting a little.

"Yes, conceited. You are so full of yourself, Captain. Now, where was I?"

"Conceited," answered Brant with a scowl.

"Right. Intelligent, bold, brave, not a care in the world—"

"I care plenty."

"Oh, really?"

"Yes," said Brant, getting serious. "I care about my ship, my crew, the people I'm responsible for, the person I love."

"And who do you love, Brant Foxton?" Her voice was soft, a blush spreading across her cheeks.

Brant reached for her hand, stroking it gently. "There's only one person that could be."

"Catherine," whispered Senona. Pain etched across her face. She wasn't sure why she said Catherine's name, but ever since James had told her about Catherine, it had plagued her every thought. It ate away at her until she had no choice but to confront Brant.

"What?"

"James told me about her," she said, pain slowly growing in her chest. "Do you still have feelings for her?"

"I really don't think my past is any of your business."

Brant said it gently, but Senona felt the annoyance under the words. It would have hurt less if the metaphorical knife in her back was real. She only knew one way to react; in anger.

"So a woman who you loved is none of my business since when? Brant, you're courting me! It may be in secret, but you're still courting me and I think I have a right to know about a woman you may still be in love with." Senona's voice was full of venom but she spoke in hushed tones, not wanting to attract any attention.

She should have known better than to react like that with Brant, as his personality was so similar to her own. She could see the anger boiling inside him by the way his eyes hardened and jaw clenched.

Senona watched Brant's reaction, begging that he would deny her charges and put her heart at rest.

With no response from Brant other than his flaming eyes, she nodded. "You do still love her," she said, her voice flat, void of anger, void of any feeling it had previously had.

"No, I don't, Senona. I love you and only you." Brant put his hands on Senona's shoulders and looked her in the eye.

Senona laughed bitterly. Brant had answered what she had needed to know. He may have been able to look her straight in the eye, but she had seen something behind those eyes. Maybe Brant didn't even know of its existence, but it was there all the same. A hesitation.

"Brant, you're lying to me, and you don't even know it. Until you erase her rejection, the 'what ifs' and 'what could have been' from your heart and mind, I can't allow you to court me." Senona shrugged Brant's hands off her shoulders.

Confusion filled Brant's eyes. "Have things changed then?"

"No. But until you have the past sorted out, I'm nothing more than a friend and a stable hand. Come talk to me when you get back from England. I'll be waiting."

She spun on her heel—free hair fanning out—walked quickly off the ship and mounted Naldo, who was tied to a post near the ramp.

She felt Brant's eyes on her the whole time she was in sight of the *BlackFox*. Tears welled up in her eyes as Naldo trotted through town.

She had done the right thing. Hadn't she?

CHAPTER EIGHT

Brant stared after Senona as she rode away. Her words echoed in his mind as he attempted to process them. It had been so unexpected. The week they had spent together had been better than he ever could have imagined. Nothing had prepared him for Senona's actions. There had been no indication, no warning. Nothing in any conversation or action to show she had any doubts or worries. He couldn't understand why she had felt threatened by Catherine, a woman who had been out of his life for nearly three years.

"Women," Brant muttered as he turned back to the work at hand.

"Sir?" Christopher asked, who had heard Brant as he walked by.

"Nothing, Christopher. Continue on."

Christopher nodded and walked on, hefting a large crate further up in his arms as it began to slip from his fingers, and carried it below deck to the galley.

Brant sighed, walked across the deck, and stopped at the rail on the opposite side, facing the sea instead of the confining land. Seeing the open ocean was calming and helped clear his head. Looking out at the horizon, Brant thought about

Catherine. It had been three years. He had left her behind a long time ago and felt nothing.

Brant sighed again and ran his hand through his short hair, causing it all to stand up in a scruffy mess.

"Sir?"

Brant spun around in surprise, but he kept up the mask, so the crew wouldn't see his pain. "Yes, Matthew?"

"We're ready to cast off, Sir."

"Good. Give the orders."

"Yessir."

Matt walked away, yelling as he went, "haul up that gangway! Let us loose from the dock! Unfurl that sail! Tie down that rigging!"

Brant's crew rushed around to follow Matt's orders, eager to get under way. There wasn't a man on board who wasn't glad at the prospect of the open sea. It was their life and, although they appreciated the short reprieve, they were always happiest when they were surrounded by their unpredictable first love, the ocean.

Brant surveyed his crew as they worked quickly and efficiently. He found his eyes wandering towards the bow where Senona would often stand with Naldo as they left or sailed into a port. The only time she didn't help was when land was in sight.

"You're daft, thinking you can just look and there she'll be, right where she belongs. She left and even though she says she's waiting, she isn't," Brant scolded himself aloud, the wind snatching his words and carrying them away. He had needed to say it out loud, to be sure he wasn't dreaming.

The voyage would be hard, more emotionally than physically. This would be the first time in Brant's whole sailing career without Karl, and to make things worse, it would be without Senona.

Senona may have only been around for one trip, but she had made her mark, not only on Brant but on the whole crew. After all, they had cleaned up Naldo's manure. Not exactly the most pleasant job when out at sea and in a ship's hold.

Brant smiled at the thought. Sure, some of the crew would be glad for no manure, but they would miss Senona just the same, and perhaps even Naldo had found a spot in their hearts. The sound of his hooves and gentle nickers on deck had become a familiar presence.

Senona had brought new life to the ship, life that not many could bring. Brant had been able to, once upon a time. James had also been able to before he had lost his childish innocence and bright perspective of the world to the harsh life of a pirate. Karl had been the heart, the beat that kept the crew together and all loving their work. The guiding hand for Brant, the joy in everyday life, and then he had died and he had taken the joy with him.

Like Karl, Senona brought joy even after seeing Brant's men kill sailors and soldiers from her own country, even after killing them herself, even after leaving her family. She was optimistic and eager, beautiful, kind, and could bring a smile to even the most hardened sailors. She brought life and light to a crew who needed it, and now all sources of life for the crew were gone. The *BlackFox* was truly black, lost in the dark and dying without a source of happiness.

Brant knew things couldn't last long before it all began to end. More men would die in raids. Money would dwindle. With less and less money to go around, Brant would have increasingly unhappy sailors. Perhaps fighting would break out among each other, perhaps they would question Brant's position as captain, and eventually, Brant figured, his beloved ship would either be destroyed in a storm, or he would be forced to retire from pirating and pursue a legal way of life. Or worse yet, he would be charged as a pirate and hanged. It was important for a form of light-heartedness to find its way into such a depressing line of work. Without it, they were lost. Without a heart and light, a steadying beat, anything living will die.

* * *

Just under a month had gone by, and in that time, Brant hadn't stopped thinking about Senona. He knew he should. He was certain when he arrived back in Port Royale she would want nothing more than friendship with him. Why did he even bother hoping? He had thought she was different, but she was like every other woman he had ever known. Untrustworthy.

"Sir?" asked Matt as he entered Brant's cabin.

He had been interrupting Brant's thoughts a lot during the voyage, and it was starting to concern him. Brant looked up from the map that he appeared to be studying, though really he hadn't processed a thing that was illustrated there.

"Yes, Matthew?"

"It appears we are heading into a storm."

"Thank you. I'll be right out."

Brant rolled up the map and put it in its case. After Richard had ruined a few, he had taken to putting them away after use. Maps of the quality Brant collected were not easy, nor cheap, to come by, and he couldn't afford to have any more wrecked.

Brant walked out onto the deck and looked out to the open sea, shivering in the cool air. The sky was a dark gray, and the clouds held promise of rain.

"What do ye think? Should we ride it or try and get around it?" asked Matt from Brant's left.

"I think she can ride her out. We are running short on time to get to England before the storms start coming up, and if we try going around it, who knows how much longer it will take."

Matt nodded. "The girl is in good shape. She can take it."

"And hopefully, we'll be near enough to a port if any big repairs need to be done."

"We should be near Lisbon, Portugal."

"If the storm doesn't blow us too far off course."

Leaving Matt to his duties, Brant climbed up the stairs to the upper deck and looked back at the water they left in their wake. He leaned on the railing and sighed. Maybe the storm was just what he needed to get his mind on the here and now.

The storm came up quickly and without forgiveness.

"Tie down that sail! Get safety lines on!" shouted Brant as he walked around the tossing deck, struggling to keep his balance. "Don't let the sail rip! Keep that wheel steady!"

Wind whipped the rain around and grabbed at the sails. Waves tossed the ship about, threatening to send sailors from their perches high above as they attempted to tame the sails, wrestling with nature, a force much stronger than mere men. Brant took over at the helm and held it steady, bracing against the driving wind.

The night was exhausting, but as dawn broke, it brought relief for the men. They worked slowly, pulling down torn sails to be repaired, but fortunately, that was the extent of the damage.

Brant observed his crew as they tied down loose lines. "I know we're all tired but there is still some work to be done. Pull down the ripped sails, check on the cargo below, and put things back in place on deck. Then we can eat and get some much-needed sleep."

Brant only got tired, dejected mumbling in reply. His men respected him and appreciated the fact that he treated them fairly, but right now all they wanted to do was collapse.

One lone man didn't turn away to do the work at hand. Oliver stood rooted in place. "What are ye going to do? Read maps or stare out at the water?"

Brant winced. He had been neglecting his duties during this voyage, dealing with thoughts that continually bombarded him. Nevertheless, Brant couldn't stand for insubordination like that.

"Mr. Cornhill," he said, deathly calm, as he walked towards Oliver. Oliver met his gaze evenly. "I understand I have been a little distant of late, but that gives you no right to question my authority. I am the captain, and that means I am in charge. Not because I'm a better man, or because I have money, but because I am your employer. Your home is my home. I gave you this home, and I am in charge. My word is law out here, and when men stop following that law, people get hurt. I will not allow that."

Oliver Cornhill nodded, his face a blank mask.

Brant smiled and spoke loud enough for everyone to hear. "Don't any one of you forget that."

Brant started climbing up the rigging behind Oliver to help him pull down a sail. Oliver nodded his appreciation to his Captain, but Brant only smiled. He was merely proving a point.

The men made quick work of the tasks, and within an hour, nearly everything was done. Brant dismissed everyone for dinner as he looked over the sail that lay on his deck in a large pile. A few small tears from down below turned out to be a lot larger up close. They would repair this when there was time. Brant sighed, dropped the corner of the sail, and joined his men in the galley.

They ate breakfast in silence, everyone too exhausted to make conversation. Upon finishing their food, the men all went for some much-needed sleep.

Brant had been tempted to set a watch, but upon seeing his tired crew, ordered them to get some rest, and he stood watch himself. He strode the deck alone in the bright daylight. It was strange to have an abandoned deck at midday. It was at times like this that Brant missed Karl the most. Karl would often walk the deck with Brant and offer him counsel or a listening ear. He smiled sadly at the memories.

Brant shivered and looked at the ocean all around him. For the first time since he had stepped foot on this ship, his home, he felt utterly alone.

* * *

England, a land of civilization and wealth. Brant strode the deck as he watched his crew unloading cargo.

After just over a month of sailing, they were finally in England, docked in London, and already feeling closed in and claustrophobic.

Matt and Christopher were loading a carriage with Brant's and James' luggage. Everything was ready to go.

Brant let his gaze travel to the crow's nest where his brother was spending his last moments aboard. Climbing up the rigging, Brant joined him.

"James, it's time to go. Are you ready?"

James sighed and nodded. "As ready as I'll ever be."

Brant smiled and patted his younger brother on the shoulder. "Let's go."

He started down and James followed. On deck, James went around saying his goodbyes to the crew who had become his family. His last goodbye was to Matt.

Since Karl's death, it had been Matt and Senona who had been there for him. Matt was a friend and the closest in age to James.

"Ye get yourself some good schooling so that ye can come be a cap'n for us when Brant gets too old."

James nodded, his face hard as he held back tears. "I'll do that. And you look after my brother while I'm gone."

Matt nodded. "Someone has to," he said with a laugh. James smiled and then surprised Matt with a hug. Tears fought their way free and streamed down his face.

"Hey, I'll be fine. Not gonna disappear on ye," said Matt as James released his grip on his friend.

James nodded and smiled as he climbed into the carriage, which then slowly pulled away. His head stuck out of the window as he looked back at the ship he called home and the crew he called family. Was he ready for the next chapter of life?

CHAPTER NINE

The carriage pulled on to a large circular drive in front of a huge brick building in the heart of London.

"It looks nice," said Brant as he caught James' apprehensive look.

"It looks like a prison," James muttered in response.

Brant forced himself not to smirk. Sometimes James was so much like him. They climbed out of the carriage and the driver unloaded James' baggage.

"Thank you. Wait here for me." Brant tossed the driver a coin.

James sat on his trunk, arms folded, looking none-too-pleased with the situation. Brant made himself frown at his brother, trying to be an authoritative figure, but James only raised his eyebrow. He knew full well Brant hadn't loved his time here ten years ago and couldn't blame him for his lack of a good attitude.

Brant pulled on the bell rope, and not ten seconds later the door opened to reveal a woman in her mid-sixties dressed in a rich, but severe-looking black dress. Her silver hair was back in a tight twist that pulled at the skin on her forehead. Her face looked stretched and tired.

"Yes?" she asked in a nasally voice. She looked upset, as if life had dealt her a bad hand.

"I'm Brant Foxton." Brant made a slight bow. "And this is James Foxton. We're here to see Headmaster Mansfield."

"Come in."

The door opened wide to reveal a polished wood floor and brown painted walls. A snap of the woman's fingers brought two boys who she instructed to take James' things to his room.

"Right this way, Mr. Foxton," she said, leading the way through the dark halls. Her clipping heels echoed ominously in the empty corridors, and the short walk proved to be both uncomfortable and unnerving. The woman said nothing, only glared at the blank walls and abandoned halls.

"Where is everyone?" asked James.

The woman glared at him. "In class."

Brant couldn't help but feel relieved when they arrived outside a door labeled 'Headmaster'.

"Wait here."

The woman walked into the office and then, only a second later, opened the door again.

"Headmaster Mansfield will see you now."

Brant smiled and strode into the office, James close behind.

Headmaster Mansfield was a short, plump man with a tendency for high blood pressure. His hair was slicked back, his round glasses sat at the end of his nose, and he looked about ready to burst out of his expensive suit.

"Brant Foxton! It is such a pleasure to see you again!"

"The feeling is mutual, Headmaster. You still smoking in the parlor with delinquent students?" He grinned warmly.

"I have never done any such thing," he said with a wink. "You disappeared for a while there... And then your father's death." He clucked his tongue in sympathy. "But that's the past. What have you been up to?"

Brant took a seat, as did James who kept looking back and forth between Brant and the Headmaster, a look of confusion on his face. He had expected some amount of hostility between the headmaster and his former student, but instead, they conversed like old friends.

"I've been seeing the world. I have a ship and an estate in Port Royale."

"Ship, right. I've always thought that sailing would be a grand adventure. Although, if I remember correctly, your father called you a pirate."

Brant laughed. John Mansfield was the same as always; brilliant, well spoken, soft, and had the enthusiasm of a young boy.

"I prefer the term privateer. It's slightly more legal that way."

"Ah, yes, employed by the king. What's that like?"

"A bit of a nuisance, but it keeps my neck noose free."

"The noose is what always kept me from getting into that kind of thing."

Brant smirked. John Mansfield was a dreamer; he wasn't the type to be interested in danger. "I never really thought you were much of one for adventure anyway."

"I'm not. The idea is intriguing, but I don't think I would enjoy the real thing. Perhaps that's why I got into teaching."

"An admirable occupation. Are you ready to take my troublesome brother in?"

"I'm quite ready. A little pirate in my school, that will be a first." He laughed jovially.

James folded his arms across his chest, appearing petulant. "I'm just a cabin boy. Not a pirate."

"You're sure?"

"Quite."

"Yes, well, would you like to see the classrooms?"

"Perhaps James would. I really must be going."

"Of course, of course. I'm sure you are quite busy."

Both men stood and Brant bowed. He was looking forward to all the letters of complaint he was bound to get about James.

He stepped out of the quiet, dark building and breathed a sigh of relief. The wind had picked up, and the rain was coming down with a fury. Brant pulled his jacket around him tighter. He hated London.

The carriage stood waiting for him, a small army of royal guards standing at the ready, guns in hand.

"Brant Foxton?" asked the captain of the guard.

Brant smirked a little. "At your service."

"Brant Foxton, you are bound by law under the authority of his Royal Majesty King Charles II. Will you come peacefully?"

Brant pretended to weigh his options, drawing his cutlass and turning it over in his hands thoughtfully. He got amusement from the guards tensing up, but they didn't move against him. They wanted things to go as smoothly as possible. Brant walked up to the captain and, after a moment of staring him down, surrendered his cutlass.

"Peacefully. Might I inquire as to the charges?"

"Piracy and murder."

"How pleasant," he replied sarcastically.

The captain didn't bother with a response. His face was a hard mask behind his large mustache.

Brant climbed into the carriage along with two guards while the others formed an armed guard all around.

During the trip, Brant thought back to the last few months, trying to come up with a reason for his arrest. It just didn't add up. He hadn't attacked any English or allied ships, nor had he killed anyone, at least, no one that didn't have it coming.

As the carriage pulled to a stop, the guards who were riding inside with Brant opened the door and motioned him out. Brant got out of the carriage slowly and looked around. They were not at the palace; instead, they were on a street lined with large townhouses. He recognized the area; it had been about three years since he had been here last, and he had certainly not expected it to be his destination today.

"This way, Sir."

Brant followed, flanked by guards, as they entered the large townhouse. They marched him through the house and straight into a large and ornate study. Everything was rich mahogany; bookshelves lined the walls and maps filled the space on the desk.

"Brant Foxton, I'm quite disappointed in you."

"What is it that I have done to warrant such disappointment, Lord Marshall?"

"Well, I was informed you docked this morning, and you did not come to visit."

"So you called the captain of the guard to put me under arrest?"

"I thought it would amuse you."

"Consider me amused." Entertaining the notion that he was headed for the gallows for even a few minutes was not Brant's idea of a good laugh. But it was important to stay on the good side of powerful men, and Lord Marshall was a powerful man.

"Now, Brant, I'll get right down to business. You know I gave up my position as ambassador to Spain quite some time ago, but I still have connections. I received a letter not too long ago that Senona Montez, the daughter of a rich and powerful don has run away. They believe she took to sea and may have headed to Port Royale. Have you heard anything?"

Brant frowned. Senona, she just couldn't leave him be. "No, Sir. I've heard nothing. I spent very little time in Port Royale this winter, though. Perhaps she met with the wrong men? There is demand for white slaves on the black market."

"There are rumors, Brant, that a girl fitting her description was seen involved in a raid aboard a Spanish Galleon. You wouldn't know anything about that, would you?"

"There are many pirates eager to attack a Spanish Galleon. Why do you assume it's me?"

"The description of the ship fit the *BlackFox*."

"Ships are ships. A description of one could match half a dozen."

Lord Marshall nodded. "Very well. You will be spending the summer in London?"

"That is my intention."

"Then you will attend the ball here on Friday?"

Brant smiled. "It would be my pleasure."

He had known it would only be a matter of time before he saw Catherine again. He had hoped to put it off for longer; of course, her father would dash those hopes. Brant was a firm believer in the fact that there was never a good time to see a woman he had once loved.

* * *

James sighed as he lay on his bed, one of three in the room he shared. He had spent the day visiting classes and meeting teachers, but it had all been unfulfilling and discouraging.

The other boys had stared at him curiously, a few had whispered and snickered, but none had spoken to him. He had spent a very lonely dinner, eating in silence and staring at his plate. When it had been time for bed, one boy had spoken to him, but only to tell him to get out of his way.

James couldn't remember the last time he felt so alone. Why had Brant sent him here? He had been happy on the ship, and although he wanted an education, he didn't want to be all alone to get it.

* * *

Johnny Marshall sat slouched at his desk, his short blond hair a tousled mess that seemed only to add to his appearance and apathetic attitude. He looked around the room in disinterest, waiting for the teacher to arrive. The room was alive with activity but Johnny only sat. He was above all this, and he knew it. Everything about him; his name, his attitude, the way he held himself, radiated nobility. The younger boys looked up to him as a leader.

He looked up as another boy entered the room. He smirked a little. The new boy stood proudly in the doorway, looking around the room defiantly and daring anyone to meet his gaze. Johnny chuckled, accepting the challenge. His eyes met the boy's and held them in a silent battle of wills. The boy's stormy gray eyes held in them a knowledge that no sixteen-year-old boy should have, and yet there was an undeniable innocence about him. Johnny broke eye contact, uncomfortable with what he saw.

Standing, he approached the boy, offering his hand in friendship. They were about the same height and build, although Johnny was slightly less muscled.

"I'm Johnny Marshall."

"James Foxton," he said, smiling warmly.

Johnny had heard about Brant, who had been a student here himself. If James was anything like his brother, they would get along just fine. Another Foxton in the school was almost as good as Christmas.

"There's an extra desk in the back. You'll learn pretty quickly that you don't sit in the front. Only the truckles sit there."

He took seat to Johnny's left, eager to make a friend.

"Where do you come from?"

"Port Royale. My family is originally from London but my father died in the plague so my brother took me in. I've served on his ship until now."

"And now you find yourself here, society's prison for young men."

The teacher walked in, and the room immediately became silent. Boys found their seats quickly, most of them sitting in attentiveness. James was no exception.

Johnny rolled his eyes and kicked him in the shin. "Look less interested," he hissed. "You're new, so you have to find your place. As family of Brant Foxton, you have a reputation to uphold."

James looked at him in confusion, his brows furrowing in a frown, but he slouched down in his seat anyway. "How do you know who Brant is?"

Once again Johnny rolled his eyes and sighed. "Everyone here knows who he is."

CHAPTER TEN

Brant had arrived in London just as the social season was beginning. Every self-respecting family held a ball at one point, and nearly everyone came. Brant, being a Lord—he hadn't lost his father's title—was required to go to a few. It would be rude not to.

So, Brant found himself getting ready to go to a ball being hosted by the Marshalls. It was by invitation only, and Brant found himself in a situation that he couldn't turn down, not if he wished to remain in the good graces of the king, whom Lord Marshall had the ear of.

Matt was acting the part of his valet as he aided him in getting ready. In the past, Karl would have taken the job, but it now fell to Matt as the quartermaster.

"There. Ye look like a regular gentleman."

"Thank you, Matthew. Is the carriage waiting?"

"Yes, Cap'n."

"Good. Why don't you go get yourself a drink?"

"I'm next on watch duty at the ship. I'd rather not have a drink till after."

"Good man." Brant patted Matt on the back. It wasn't often he found a sailor as responsible as him.

Brant had never told anyone of his doubts on promoting Matt to quartermaster, but his fears had been quickly put to rest.

He strode out of the hotel room that he had made his summer residence and down to the luxurious lobby. The night air was crisp and clear, and a light mist seemed to hang in the air. It was beautiful to look at, if not enjoyable to experience. The carriage he had Matt call was waiting dutifully for him.

Brant gave the address to the driver, and the carriage lurched to a start and continued down the bumpy cobbled streets.

A half hour later, Brant entered the lavishly decorated ballroom. He silently laughed as he entered through the heavy wood double doors that opened into the large room full of people.

"Lord Brant Foxton, Privateer for his Majesty the King."

Oh yes, that would go over well. A pirate here, in the midst of proper lords and ladies, was the scandal of the season in the making. Everything got very quiet as he strode in. Fortunately, and much to Brant's relief, someone else entered and the focus was taken from him.

He made his way to the refreshments table, expertly avoiding conversation until he consumed some alcohol to make everything a little more bearable. He couldn't remember the last time he had been to a ball. He had left England when he was too young to accompany his father. In Port Royale, he had been to a few, but only as many as was absolutely necessary. And then there were a few in Spain he had attended. He had found those to be the most fun with their lively and exotic dancing. But he had become well known and unpopular among the Spaniards, despite them being at peace with Britain, and was now no longer able to safely attend public events.

Brant smirked as a group of young women cast admiring glances at him, older women sending disapproving glares. He felt like quite the novelty as even the young men wanted to hear stories while older men wanted to hear news of Spain or the British colonies.

Brant was quickly coming to realize why he hated these ordeals so much. Perhaps, judging by the many glares he received, this would be the only ball he would be required to attend.

He managed to make his retreat to a shadowed corner in the room where he was content to watch the goings on and avoid any dance requests from curious young women.

A light hand rested on his shoulder and Brant inwardly groaned; his escape had been short lived. He only hoped it wasn't someone who was going to pester him in any way, shape, or form.

"Captain Brant Foxton, It has been a long time," came the soft, all too familiar voice.

Brant turned with a teasing smile, his heart pounding wildly. He wasn't ready to see her; although, he had expected it. "Catherine Marshall. I must say you are a welcome sight."

She smiled gently with a light laugh that lacked any real amusement. "Are you overwhelmed by it all? It would appear that you are the highlight of the night."

"Yes, well, who can resist someone like me?"

Catherine could, and had. The barb reached home.

"Not all talk is good, you know."

"Yes, but I choose to ignore the less than flattering content. What are the women saying? I imagine I'm the most eligible bachelor around for miles."

This time, Catherine's smile was sincere and her laugh truly amused. "I do believe you are at least one step above soldiers in their eyes."

"You don't say? I always thought soldiers were the ones to go for."

"Of course. They present a sense of adventure but unfortunately not much in riches. But a privateer—"

"Like me, who is favored by the King, rich, young, handsome, a lord, and with more than just a sense of adventure. I dare say I'm nearly irresistible."

"I disagree, but every one of the single woman and a handful of married ones are desperately wishing for a dance with you."

"Should I grant some of those wishes? Or are you willing to dance with me?"

Brant didn't really want to dance with anyone, but Catherine was as enjoyable to spend time with as he'd remembered, and he almost wished she'd accept.

"Oh, it wouldn't be right to only dance with a few, think of the jealousy that would create. But I, on the other hand, you can dance with."

"How does that work exactly?"

"I've approached you. It would only be polite for you to ask me to dance."

"I have a slight problem with that."

"What is that?"

"After I dance with you because you approached me, wouldn't that have everyone who wants to dance with me approaching me?"

"Not if I dance with you the whole evening." Catherine wore a mischievous smile that made Brant wonder what exactly she was up to.

"That would seem a bit like favoritism, wouldn't it?"

"Maybe. But I have no attachments to anyone here and neither do you. Besides, you'll be leaving come October, so what's the harm?"

Senona quickly jumped into Brant's mind. Really, it should be her that he was dancing the night away with, not Catherine. But Senona wasn't here and Catherine was. Perhaps spending time with Catherine would help him smother any feelings he had kept alive in the past. "Well, when you put it that way... Shall we?"

Brant offered Catherine his hand and led her to the dance floor.

For the first two dances, they made small talk. Brant asked Catherine about her life, and Catherine inquired about Brant's. Brant was feeling quite relaxed. He had been worried that when he saw Catherine, she would address the fact that he was suspected to have helped Senona run away, no doubt she had heard from her father, but so far, it hadn't come up. Then the third dance came about, and it became time to talk about more than the weather.

"Is it true that you helped Senona Montez?"

And there it was. What he'd been waiting for. "Now why is it that everyone is accusing me of this?"

Catherine frowned. "I don't want to play games, Brant. This is a serious matter. A girl is missing."

"And everyone automatically thinks that every ship looks like mine."

"Brant, you attacked a Spanish Galleon, which hurts our delicate peace with Spain, and you are suspected to have helped the daughter of a very influential don run away. This is very serious. You could ruin everything we have worked towards."

"Really, Catherine, I'm not that powerful."

She sighed angrily. "It doesn't matter who you are. The peace we have with Spain could erupt at any moment for the smallest reason. If you helped Senona Montez, you need to let us know."

Brant smirked. "I helped her. I saw a bit of me in her and I had to give her a fighting chance to make it on her own."

"Did you tell my father?"

"I explained enough to make him happy, but I admitted to nothing."

"And explaining always gets you out of everything. I swear, Brant, you could talk your way out of anything."

"Well, that's because I'm so charming."

Catherine laughed. "I had forgotten why I enjoyed your company so much."

"The charm?"

"I was thinking more along the lines of amusing and a bit of a fool. A little like having a personal jester."

"I have always prided myself with a good sense of humor, but a fool? I resent that."

"That, and your arrogance and roguishness is often quite... interesting."

"I'm not arrogant," he protested. "I am a bit of a rogue, though; I am a pirate after all."

"Is the arrogance all an act then?"

"I suppose; though, I like to think of it as self-confidence."

"What about when you look down on someone?"

"Well, I can't help my height."

"I give up," she said, exasperated.

"Now that we are done examining my character, I have something to ask you."

Catherine nodded for him to continue.

"Would you accompany me to the next ball?" Brant was enjoying his time with Catherine and, quite frankly, he didn't want it to end.

"Well, I have no one better to act as an escort."

"Since you're making such a sacrifice, letting a lowly pirate escort you, I am very honored."

"As you should be. The next ball I plan on attending is the Hillshire ball next Friday. Do you think you could pick me up at six?"

"I'm sure I can make that work. It won't be easy with my busy pirate schedule."

"Oh yes, so busy. What do you have on that pirating schedule? There isn't any pillage to be had on your own land."

Brant gave her a stern look. "England isn't my land nor does it hold any sentimental value to me. The only reason I refrain from attacking British ships is because I don't care to find a noose around my neck, and I have James to think about."

"And now I remember why it is I couldn't stay with you." Catherine smiled sadly.

"Let's go for a walk. All this dancing is making me tired," suggested Brant. He wanted to talk to Catherine away from everyone else.

Catherine gave a slight nod and followed him out into the garden.

After walking for a time in silence, Brant spoke up. "You know, Catherine, I offered to give everything up for you last time."

He needed to know why she had refused him. He knew they got along fine, but as soon as anything got serious involving his choice of career, it got tense. He needed, for Senona's sake, to clear the air.

"You did, but you weren't ready. Taking that part of your life away may very well have killed everything I found attractive in you. To be quite honest, I'm not sure you'll ever be ready to give that up, and I know I can't be with you when that part of your life is so prevalent."

"You may be right, but that part of my life is slowly slipping away, and there's no amount of fighting that will help me keep it."

"What makes you say that?"

"The *BlackFox* has lost her life beat..." Brant breathed deep. "Ever since you left me, it hasn't been the same."

Catherine touched Brant's arm gently. Sadness filled her eyes.

"Really, what has my life meant? I've had nothing to live for since then." Brant surprised himself as he told Catherine what had been on his mind since the day she had left. He shouldn't be talking to her like this; she had ripped his heart to shreds. She had left him. And now, only hours after seeing her for the first time since then, he found himself telling her things he had never vocalized to anyone, not to Karl and definitely not to Senona.

"Brant, you know that's not true. You just didn't move on. What happened to living for James? For the *BlackFox*? For your crew?"

"None of that—"

Catherine cut him off. "I used to think you were strong. Before I met you those were things you cared the most about in life, and I was certain you would be able to go back to living your life like before I came along. But now I see that you didn't. I'm still sure you could have moved on, but you chose not to. You're more than this, Brant. You're only holding yourself back."

Silence filled the air as he tried to digest what Catherine had said. When she had spoken, she had stopped walking. Now they stood facing each other, Brant not knowing how to respond.

Brant sighed. "I thought I had moved on. I found someone to care about and then she left me. Do you want to know why?" His gaze was hard, unspoken blame and hurt reflected towards her. She had no right to lecture him on his life and what had gone on in the years since she had left him.

Catherine looked back defiantly, her eyes filled with pity. "I don't want to get involved in your personal life."

"Well, it's a little late for that. She left me because she heard about you, from God knows where, and came to the conclusion that I still loved you. And you know what? I'm not entirely sure she's wrong. But I loved her, and I would have moved on with her. You! You continue to haunt me."

"Brant, I'm sorry but you did this to yourself. You have to realize that."

Brant's glare flickered and then fell. Catherine was right, of course. He had set himself up all those times. He had decided life wasn't worth the effort without Catherine, and so everything had slowly fallen apart. "You're right."

Catherine smiled. "Of course I am. I'm always right."

Brant raised an eyebrow. He was at peace with the past, if only for the moment. "Is that so? Well, Miss Marshall, I think it would be useful to have someone who is always right around."

"What are you suggesting?"

"I am suggesting that we see more of each other."

"I thought that was the plan."

"Catherine," Brant's face turned serious. "I mean, I want to court you."

Catherine looked up at Brant. "I know. But what's to stop what happened last time from happening again?"

"Nothing. But I think I've grown and am able to handle it. Besides, I'd be the one leaving."

"Take me to the ball Friday and ask me again then," she offered.

"Fair enough."

CHAPTER ELEVEN

After being in England for a month, Brant had attended a record six balls with Catherine.

It had taken some persuasion, but Brant did manage to convince Catherine to accept his offer of courtship. He was certain she still worried about any consequences, but they were both willing to accept the risks and let come what may. They had a messy history, and he really couldn't blame her for her apprehension. He wasn't even certain if he was ready for this. Commitment had never been something he was good with. Or maybe he was the one who was good with it, seeing as the two women he had loved had both walked away.

Brant grimaced at the pouring rain. It wasn't so hard to remember why he had left here for Port Royale. London was anything but enjoyable. Why he had chosen to leave the comfort of his hotel room to visit James on this day, of all the days he could have gone, Brant didn't know.

Brant, being used to the tropical warmth of Port Royal, was cold. Yes, the open sea was frigid at times, but somehow Brant found that the damp air and being soaked through, while huddling in a carriage, with a coat pulled around himself tightly, was much colder than any cold he had felt at sea. Perhaps it was because he moved around a lot on deck, and moving around much in a carriage was inadvisable, and probably not very easy.

By the time the carriage had pulled up to the dark and dreary school, Brant was thoroughly chilled, and he welcomed the heat that emanated from the fireplace he sat near. The parlor was as dark and foreboding as every other room in the school, exactly as Brant had remembered it from ten years earlier, except he had never been the lucky recipient of a visit from his father.

James seemed to be getting along fine. He spoke excitedly about his studies and about the friends he had made, especially Johnny.

"How are you liking London?" asked James as he finished telling his stories.

"Well enough. It's wet, dreary, and closed in, but it's fine. I certainly won't be complaining about leaving come fall, though."

"I quite like it. The rain takes some getting used to, but it's all so exciting. It's really nice to have friends my own age."

Brant laughed. James had lacked companionship all his life, so school was something of a novelty. Now that James had gotten over his initial prejudices, he was able to embrace the experience and get more out of it than Brant ever had.

"I hope you aren't getting in trouble at all with these boys."

"Oh, no. The headmaster quite likes me, actually."

"Good. Keep it that way. It's never good to get on the headmaster's bad side."

"You aren't speaking from experience, are you?"

"Well, you know me." He shrugged sheepishly. "Rule breaker through and through."

"I'll take that as a yes."

"Just be good. I'm not much of a role model, and I don't want you turning out like me," Brant finished off quietly.

James looked at his brother, his eyes sad.

"You aren't all that bad. You have faults, as do all of us."

Brant frowned. "You've grown up way too fast. I should have given you a proper childhood."

James looked at his brother incredulously. "Don't say that. I love my life on the *BlackFox* and wouldn't trade it for anything."

"You say that now, but you don't know what you've missed, what you could have."

"Well, I'll let you know in about ten years what I really think about my childhood."

Brant laughed. At least his brother was optimistic. He hoped optimistic enough to accept the news of his relationship with Catherine.

"I met Catherine again."

James looked at Brant sharply, his eyes filled with a worry. "And?"

"And, I'm courting her."

"Brant, why? You know what happened last time."

Brant laughed. "You sound like Karl. Aren't you supposed to be the younger one?"

"Someone has to look after you."

"If it makes you feel better, I'm being careful this time. Catherine and I talked it over. Neither one of us wants a repeat of what happened last time."

James smile weakly in response.

Brant got up out of his chair and looked fondly at his younger brother. "I had better head back. Don't worry so much. Being young only happens once, don't throw that away."

James nodded and looked into the fire. He wasn't good with goodbyes.

Brant tried to think of something to say but nothing came to mind and so he strode out of the room while James continued to stare at the fire.

* * *

James remained in front of the fire for an hour, thoughts just rolling around in his head until the stern voice of his English teacher barged in.

"James Foxton, why were you absent from my class?"

James trembled slightly. English was not a good class to miss. Even Johnny didn't mess with Mr. Clove. He was not a forgiving teacher and seemed to enjoy punishing his students.

"I'm sorry, Sir. My brother was visiting, and I must have lost track of time." James didn't plead. His voice was strong, simply giving an explanation, and he met Clove's glare evenly.

Mr. Clove's eyebrows rose slightly and then settled back into his permanent scowl. "Nevertheless, there are consequences for your actions, intentional or not. No dinner for you, and I expect a sufficiently long essay on the evils of shirking responsibility on my desk first thing in the morning."

James wanted to argue, but he was too afraid that Mr. Clove would decide the rod would be a better choice of punishment. Instead, he just nodded and mumbled, "Yes, Sir," before making a hasty retreat from the parlor.

Yes, James loved being in school, and yes, he loved his studies, but he was still afraid of getting on the teachers' bad sides, no matter how much Johnny urged him to. James had a kind and soft heart; it wasn't in him to upset people.

James wandered around the halls until he came across Johnny and Fredrick. Johnny's parents had sent him to boarding school to try and straighten him out. His tutor refused to teach him after a while and so, after being expelled from nearly every other prestigious school in the country, he was sent here. Johnny was James' best friend and, incidentally, also Catherine's younger brother.

Fredrick was a quiet boy who the other boys either ignored or taunted until James and Johnny had accepted him as their friend. He was the last person anyone would have thought to fit in with the boys, but everyone accepted James' and Johnny's choice. All the younger boys looked up to James and Johnny, after all, most of these boys dreamed of adventure, and what was more adventurous than sailing the high seas on a pirate ship? And Johnny's stories of defying authority made him nearly as popular. The older boys thought James and Johnny were entertaining and were willing to do things with them but would leave Fredrick or any of the younger boys out.

"James, where were you? Clove was not happy that you missed his class."

Fredrick was always concerned about his two friends, as their stories were often full of rebellion and skipping class. Fredrick, who just wanted to be accepted and survive among the vicious coyotes that were London nobility, thought James and Johnny were throwing away a blessing. It was something he couldn't condone.

"I forgot. I had a visit from Brant, and I got lost in thought. So I won't be eating tonight, and I need to write a 'sufficiently long' essay on responsibility before tomorrow morning."

Johnny laughed and slapped his friend on the back. "Finally going to start living up to your name?"

"What?" asked James in confusion.

"Aw, come on. Your brother was practically a legend here. Half the boys are just waiting for you to go against the teachers."

"You want me to continue the Foxton legacy?"

Johnny rolled his eyes. "Do you know of any other Foxton to take the job?"

James sighed. "No, but it's really not my thing. My brother and I are quite different."

"You're good, though, and you have it in you to be great."

James smiled a little, starting to sway towards Johnny's way of thinking. Perhaps a distraction from his delinquent brother would be just the thing to get Brant's mind off Catherine.

"I guess Clove doesn't really need that essay, and can he really stop me from eating? After all, I have the headmaster on my side."

James grinned, and Johnny gave a whoop. "Here we go! This is great! James Foxton and Johnny Marshall will continue the Foxton legacy."

* * *

As the dinner hour drew near, James became nervous and doubting. He'd never done anything so blatantly against the rules. He paced the length of the small room he shared, fighting an inward battle when Johnny burst in.

"The bell will ring any second! You coming?"

"I don't know, Johnny. You sure this is such a great idea?"

"Yes! You were pretty excited about it earlier if I remember correctly."

"Yes, but I had my reasons."

"What's changed since then?"

"I'm not sure it will work."

"What does that matter? Do it for fun!"

"But Brant... I promised him."

"What? He left you here, and he's done a lot worse in his time. You don't owe him anything."

"But, Johnny, I promised Brant I wouldn't be like him. He wants me to be better."

"Fine then," Johnny said quietly, disappointed. "No one in this institution will ever look up to you, and you certainly will never be like Brant."

James watched his friend walk out and shook his head. He only hoped Johnny could get over his disappointment. He knew the rest of the boys would forget soon enough.

James took out his writing desk and settled down on the floor, leaning against the bed frame. He wrote down the first paragraph and then dropped his quill onto the parchment, splashing ink. He didn't need to do this. James smiled, the boys would be happy with an obvious, yet silent defiance of Clove.

He shoved his writing desk aside and rolled onto his bed, hands behind his head, and closed his eyes. This would work, Brant would be sure to hear about this. Maybe not right away, but a few incidents like this and it would all fall into place.

An hour later, Johnny entered the room, a plate of food in his hands. "Here. The cooks sent it up, don't let Clove find out."

James opened his eyes, and his stomach growled in appreciation. "Thanks, Johnny. Were the boys disappointed?"

"They'll get over it."

James nodded and hungrily dug into the plate of food. He didn't tell Johnny about not writing the essay; it would be more interesting for the boys to not expect anything, especially after tonight.

* * *

As James walked down the halls the next day with Johnny and Fredrick, he was surrounded by disappointed and scornful glances from the other boys. The older ones wouldn't even talk to him. Fredrick had given James his full approval when he arrived back from supper, but that didn't make James feel very good. Fredrick was looked down on by the other boys, and James liked being popular.

The morning went by uneventfully, and James wondered if Clove would react at all, or if maybe he had forgotten. It wasn't until around three o'clock that Clove approached James as he stood in the hall talking with Johnny and Fredrick.

"Mr. Foxton, may I see you in my office?"

James looked at Clove and smiled, a crowd of boys was beginning to form. "I'm sure it would save you time to just talk to me here, Sir."

Clove glared at James but spoke calmly. "Mr. Foxton, I don't quite understand your wish to create a scene; it isn't at all like you. I am also not pleased with the fact that a certain essay did not appear on my desk this morning."

"Oh, yeah, that essay. Well, Sir, skipping supper affected me so badly that I couldn't think enough to get it done, or even start." James mocked Clove openly and the nudges being passed around by the gaping boys did not go unnoticed.

Clove seemed to study James carefully, as if he were looking for a point to start dissection, and then, with a sigh, turned on his heel and walked away.

James visibly slouched and sighed. He didn't enjoy confrontation, but the boys around him patted him on the back or voiced their approval, which gave James the confidence that he had done well. James turned to look at his friends and Johnny's beaming face greeted him.

"That was bloody brilliant! This was way better than coming to dinner ever could have been."

James laughed, but upon noticing Fredrick's absence, his face fell. If Fredrick was so disappointed in him that he couldn't even be near him, then how would Brant react? Then again, he did want to get Brant's attention.

* * *

Brant stalked angrily through the school. He had just come from a meeting with Mr. Clove about James' behavior in the past month, and he was not pleased.

James had pulled a few more stunts since his first defiance of Clove. It was apparent that Clove was his favorite target, due to the fact that his reactions were quite satisfying.

Brant wasn't exactly sure what had come over his younger brother. James was so unlike Brant, so why was he now walking on the same path as Brant had so many years earlier? Especially after he had said he wouldn't. It's not like this kind of behavior came naturally to James. He thought he had always raised him to obey authority, not disrespect and rebel. On a ship, this kind of behavior risked lives. It just wasn't like him. Brant couldn't help but wonder what was bothering James.

Brant silently worried about his brother as he walked into a sitting room where James was waiting.

"James!" It came out harsher than Brant had intended, but it got James' attention.

James turned away from the roaring fire to look at his brother; he had a triumphant glint in his eye and a slight smirk on his lips. Brant was startled at how much James had changed in a month, how much James now resembled himself.

"James," Brant said again. "I just got out of a meeting with Mr. Clove."

James smirked. "Guess he's been telling you about my behavior?"

Brant raised his eyebrow at his younger brother's tone and silently wrestled with how to respond. How did he tell a younger version of himself to smarten up when he wouldn't even follow his own advice? James would only see him as a hypocrite.

"A month ago you never would have done any of this. I've raised you better than this."

"Not by example."

Brant cringed inwardly but his face remained expressionless and James took it as an invitation to keep going, to keep battering at his brother emotionally.

"I may not be perfect, but you don't try to change. You are so caught up in your rogue image and you hide behind it and the *BlackFox* as if bullets were flying all around you." James turned on his heel and strode calmly out of the room.

Brant sank into a large chair and sighed. Right now he felt like a failure. With the enormous task of raising James put on his shoulders, he had made many mistakes but never had he thought this would happen. Never had he thought James would turn out like him.

CHAPTER TWELVE

Brant paced in the extravagant parlor, his nervousness apparent through his clenched jaw and tightly closed fists.

The room was painted an elegant cream with a rich, dark brown border. Brant felt uncomfortable and, at the same time, strangely at home. The Marshall townhouse was very British, very much like Brant's childhood home, something he had always viewed as a prison.

He glanced around his surroundings uneasily, too much like the past. Too many memories.

"Mr. Foxton?" came a quiet voice from the doorway.

Brant stopped pacing and turned to face the source of the voice. A small, timid, almost mouse-like girl greeted his sight.

"Yes?"

"Lady Marshall asked me to inform you that she would be a few more minutes, and she sends her apologies. Is there anything I can bring you while you wait?"

"No, thank you."

The timid maid gave a slight curtsy and left Brant alone once again in the large room.

Brant looked around and sighed. He could be here awhile, he might as well try to relax. He walked to a large cream-colored sofa that looked more like an ornament than an actual piece of furniture and sat down, legs stretched out in front of him in an attempt to appear nonchalant.

Nearly twenty minutes later, Catherine appeared in the parlor.

"Brant! I am so sorry. You weren't waiting long, were you?"

"Not long at all. For you, I could wait forever, and I very nearly did." Catherine laughed at his comment and probably the wild look his eyes always took on when she was near.

"Well, you should know by now that you should always come at least fifteen minutes late."

"I'll remember that for next time."

Brant offered his arm and led her outside. It was a sunny day for once and so they walked. Brant would not confine himself to a carriage unless absolutely necessary, and since sunny days were rare enough, he was more than happy to take advantage of it.

"Where are you taking me?"

Brant smirked, unwilling to part with his surprise just yet. "You'll see."

He could tell by the way she frowned that she wasn't entirely comfortable with being kept in the dark. Likely, due to Brant's tendency for mischief; it was dangerous not to know what was going on.

* * *

As they walked they talked about the future. It worried Catherine that after only a few short months when she looked at how her future might turn out it always involved Brant. How had she let the privateer get so deep under her skin? It was preposterous to think that she could handle a life with him. He wouldn't give up pirating, and she enjoyed her life a little too much to be willing to give it up, nor was she willing to share him.

As they continued to walk, Catherine began to wonder if Brant even knew where he was going, or if he had planned to wander around all afternoon. It would be just like him.

An hour later they found themselves standing at the harbor.

"Here we are."

"Are we here to see the *BlackFox*?"

"See? I guess you could say that." Brant smiled, laughing at a joke only he understood. Catherine felt uneasy, but allowed herself to go along with Brant's little plan, it couldn't be that bad.

They took a small rowboat and boarded the ship, which had been moved out and away from the docks.

"Cap'n. Lady. Welcome aboard," greeted Matt with a large grin.

Brant nodded, tipping his hat slightly. "Matthew! How are you? How's she doing?"

"I'm fine, Sir. Keeping dry for once. Your girl here be in tip top shape for when we cast off."

"Good man. You know your orders. We'll be around."

"Yes, Sir."

Matt ran off to bring any orders he might have to what few members of the crew were not taking advantage of their shore leave.

Catherine smiled. "It's been a long time since I've been here. We had some good memories."

Brant looked at Catherine and put his arm around her. "But you'll never love her like I do." It was a statement, not a question, and she saw no need to reply.

"Come, let's go to the dining hall. It's warm in there and, as beautiful as it is today, after such a long walk, I'm feeling a bit chilled from this fall breeze."

Catherine nodded in agreement and allowed his arm to direct her down the well-known path to the simple, yet elegant room Brant liked to call the dining hall.

It was like being back in time. It scared her, and yet, it was oddly comforting. Her time with Brant, on this ship, had been some of the best days she could remember. She had been free and in love; something most people only dream of having. She wondered now what had made her throw it all away.

Catherine stood in front of the unlit fireplace as Brant paced the room behind her. It was then that she looked at the window and noticed the shoreline receding.

"Brant?"

"Hmmm?" Brant stopped his pacing to give her his full attention.

"Why are we moving?"

"We're in a ship on the ocean. Ships always move."

"That's not what I meant and you know it. The shore, it's getting further away."

"Oh. That kind of moving. We're just going for a small little cruise, so to speak. Don't worry; I'm not kidnapping you."

Catherine smiled and turned back to the fireplace. "I wouldn't put it past you."

"Don't give me any ideas you might regret," he teased.

Catherine smiled at the easy banter; however, she could tell something was bothering Brant. Sure he was teasing, and pacing—which he did quite a bit—but it was so unlike him to be restless here, on his ship, where he was the most at home. If he was relaxed anywhere, it was here.

Finally, she couldn't take it anymore. "Brant!"

"What?" he asked, slightly confused by her outburst.

"Stop pacing! What's bothering you?"

"Nothing. I always pace."

"Not on your ship you don't. You're always relaxed here so don't even try to lie to me."

"It's nothing much, just summer is almost over."

"Is that it? You can get back to the sea, where you're happiest. Why does this suddenly bother you?"

Brant walked up to her and looked deep into her eyes. "I'll have to leave you. I don't want to do that again."

Catherine looked at him, frozen in surprise. She wasn't quite sure how to handle someone caring for her like that. They both knew he had to leave sooner or later, she had assumed he was at peace with that.

"Brant, it'll all work out," Catherine tried to reassure him, but it sounded empty. She didn't know what to say. She didn't want him to leave any more than he did. It was all ending too soon for her, too soon to process or even realize when this had gone from simple friendship to something more serious.

The past few months with him had been amazing. He understood her like no one else and brought out traits in her that she didn't even know existed. To have him leave, again, was... torture. It had been heart wrenching the first time, this time would only be worse. The heart paid no regard to any deals they had made. She had fallen for him again, and this time, she couldn't let him sail out of her life.

"Marry me," she said suddenly.

"What?" he said, his tone shocked.

Catherine herself wasn't even sure what she had said, she was so surprised at what had escaped her lips.

"Uh," she said, very unladylike. "Marry me?"

Brant just stared at Catherine, at a loss for words.

"I know it's awfully odd, me asking you. But why not? You have an estate that I can run while you're at sea. I can come on some voyages. We can make it work."

"Catherine," Brant began slowly, carefully. "I thought you loved London."

"I do, but it's just a place. I can make Port Royale my home. If you don't want to do this, then just say so."

"No! Let's do it. But I want you to be completely certain. It's a huge decision. There's no going back, and I'm not ready to give sailing up. Don't get into this with any preconceived notions."

Catherine nodded and was silent as she carefully thought it over. It was a huge step and a huge change. Just an hour earlier she wasn't sure if she could marry him, not if he was going to continue piracy, and now she had proposed. Yet somehow it seemed right. Somehow, at this moment, she couldn't imagine not marrying him. She would learn to live with his less-than-reputable side. She knew that at one time she had actually enjoyed being on a voyage on this very ship. Perhaps they really could make a life of it.

She looked at Brant and slowly nodded. "I'm sure. We can do this." Her voice was steady, full of conviction.

Brant smiled. "You know, I didn't give all the spoils of the escapades to the crown and crew, shall we pick out a ring?"

Catherine laughed and shook her head, not in disagreement, but in amusement. "I really am marrying a pirate."

"My brother is going to hate me."

"Why?"

"He wasn't at all happy to learn I was seeing you, and then he started to act up at school. He's friends with your younger brother, you know."

"Oh, dear. Johnny is a little terror. I'm not going to sugar coat it; my parents sent him away so that they could forget about him and the embarrassment he is to the family."

"You say that almost bitterly."

"Johnny needs something to keep busy. My father wanted him to get into politics, but Johnny just didn't like it. He wants more freedom than this society has to offer."

"Apparently Johnny doesn't know everything involved in the affairs of state, since many are, well, free spirited."

"Johnny knows, but he doesn't want the intrigue and deception involved. He wants to join the navy."

"The navy?"

"Yes, but my father won't hear of it."

* * *

Brant shook his head in amazement. Johnny was so much like himself. James could act like this, but Johnny *was* this.

Brant could see how upset Catherine was getting thinking about her brother. Obviously she supported her brother in his wish to join the navy, and so Brant decided to change the subject and get her mind on happier things.

"Come, let's get you that ring."

Brant led Catherine to his cabin where he pulled out a chest. He slowly lifted the lid to reveal sparkling gold coins, necklaces, bracelets, rings and almost any form of jewelry you could think of.

Catherine gasped. "I may be rich, but this," she paused for a moment. "This is incredible."

"Marrying a pirate doesn't seem so bad now, huh?"

"Bad? This is the way to go! I must tell my friends."

"Ah yes, out with the soldiers. Their daring-do is very much last season."

Catherine laughed and Brant continued to rifle through the chest. He remembered setting a ring aside from the Spanish galleon. At the time he had set it aside with Senona in mind, but she had ended that quickly enough, and he had no feelings for her except, perhaps, the need to protect her.

Finally, he found the ring. It was made of the finest gold. The band was in the form of a vine and there were tiny emeralds set in each leaf. In the middle of the ring was a flower made of white gold, and in the very center of the flower was a diamond. It wasn't a large diamond, but the intricate design made up for it.

"I believe this will do nicely."

Brant held the ring up for Catherine's approval. Her eyes welled up with tears and she smiled.

"Brant, it's beautiful," she managed to get out between tears of joy.

Brant took her hand and gently slipped the ring onto her finger, brought it up to his lips, kissing it, as if sealing the promise he had made to her in giving her the ring. He would love and cherish her forever. It was a promise he did not take lightly.

Brant released her hand and slowly returned the contents to the chest. When he had finished, he walked over to the chair Catherine had sat down in and offered her his arm.

"Come, my dear, we must not let this beautiful day go to waste."

Catherine took his offered arm and walked with him out of the cabin. They walked the deck in silence for a time, just enjoying each other's company and the scenery around them. Neither felt the need to speak and ruin the serenity of the moment. The crew seemed to sense this and worked as quietly as possible.

After a time, they headed to the upper deck to watch the sunset.

"Do you have any intention of bringing me home at a decent hour, Captain Foxton?"

"Absolutely not," he said with a smile.

"What kind of gentleman are you?"

"A pirate, my dear. I'm no gentleman at all. I live by the sea and I make my own rules."

He gently took Catherine into his arms and held her as the sun slowly dipped below the horizon. He buried his face in her hair and breathed in; she smelled of the sea and roses. It was heavenly.

"Shall we have some dinner?" he whispered into her hair.

Catherine nodded and turned out of his embrace, walking with him back to the dining hall.

Brant's cook had been on shore leave but had returned to the ship to prepare his galley and the food stores for the fast approaching voyage home, and so he had been around to prepare what could only be described as a feast.

"Brant, this has been a truly incredible day," said Catherine after they had settled down for their dinner.

"I'm glad you enjoyed it. Unfortunately, we should be back to shore by the time our dinner is done."

"Then we should make it last. I suppose we should inform my parents of our engagement when we get back."

Brant nodded his agreement. "We'll have to make arrangements for the voyage home. Do you plan on coming with me now? Or do you wish to wait?"

"When do you plan on leaving?"

"Within two weeks. I want to spend some time at the estate before I head out to sea for the season."

Catherine looked disappointed at the thought of Brant going back to sea so soon after they would arrive in Port Royale, but she let it go. She would be busy with wedding preparations and once they were married she might even join him on some voyages. It was something she was beginning to consider quite seriously.

"I'll come with you now. No need to wait."

After dinner, they docked and Brant flagged down a carriage to take them home.

The evening went quickly, and all too soon Brant and Catherine found themselves at her front door. They walked in and the butler greeted them, relieving them of their coats.

"William, are my parents in this evening?"

"Yes, Ma'am, would you like me to request they join you for a nightcap?"

"Please, that would be wonderful."

William nodded his head slightly and walked away.

Brant smirked at his air of self-importance.

Brant and Catherine made themselves comfortable by the fireplace in the sitting room. It was a more comfortable room than the parlor.

"Catherine, darling!" sounded Lady Marshall's voice as she walked into the room, Lord Marshall following right on her heels.

"Mother, how was your day?"

"Quite good, though I had to sit through the most dull of visits at Lady Connors'."

"Dear, I'm not entirely sure Catherine and Brant asked us to join them just to discuss the latest gossip you heard at tea today."

"Father is right," Catherine started slowly, pausing, and deciding the best course of action was to just say it. "Brant and I are engaged to be married."

Lord and Lady Marshall were silent, in shock, trying to digest what their daughter had just told them. Finally, Lady Marshall spoke up. "Congratulations, my dear. May I see the ring?"

Catherine held her hand out for her mother to examine.

"This all seems so sudden, have you thought this over?" asked Lord Marshall, who was clearly concerned for his daughter.

"Sir, I assure you we have discussed this at great length and both have thought it over for quite some time."

"Very well. I hope you understand that I'm not fully satisfied, though. You have a good name, but can you provide for my daughter? Legitimately?"

"Father!" exclaimed Catherine, horrified that her father would broach such a subject.

"Catherine, let's not pretend that Brant has a clean record. Everyone in this room knows he is a privateer, and the only reason I stand for this is because he is favored by the king."

"I understand your concern, Sir. I realize I have a reputation, and I will not deny its truth. However, I do own a sugar estate in Port Royale that brings in a very good sum of money. Catherine can live no differently than she does here, even without my less legitimate business on the sea. Furthermore, as you already stated, I am employed by the king, so what I do is not illegal, and there is no danger of me hanging, nor ruining your daughter's reputation."

Lord Marshall nodded. "Let us drink in celebration of the union to come."

CHAPTER THIRTEEN

James sat at the back of the classroom looking bored as the teacher attempted to teach arithmetic.

Johnny was sitting, or rather, draped, over the desk to James' right, sleeping soundly. James glanced over at his friend when he let out a particularly loud snore and threw his quill at him. Johnny woke up with a snort and sleepily wiped away the drool that had slid onto his chin.

"Is class over?" whispered Johnny, looking slightly confused.

"No."

"Then why did you wake me up?"

"Your snoring was annoying me."

Johnny groaned and promptly draped himself back over his desk, attempting to fall back into a blissful oblivion, which didn't take long, thanks to the teacher's droning.

James slouched down and attempted to look about as attentive as Johnny, but he drank in every word coming from the teacher's mouth. He didn't want to fall behind in his education, but he had a reputation to uphold. Johnny knew he secretly did his assignments late at night, but no one else did.

The whole "getting Brant's attention" plan had worked, although James doubted very much that it had changed anything between Brant and Catherine. However, the whole rebellious rogue image had stuck. People expected things from James, and he grudgingly complied.

James spent the rest of his classes the same way as he did arithmetic; slouched down at a desk in the back of the room.

Johnny actually paid attention in English. He enjoyed the stories and learning the artful twist of the language. He was a smooth talker, much like Brant, and had a knack for the writing as well. James, on the other hand, had very little skill in flowery words and found the class dull, so he drifted off to sleep and depended on Johnny's superior English mind to get him through any assignments.

Clove was constantly getting after James, punishing him every chance he got. Sometimes James worried it wouldn't be long until Clove had his way and he got expelled, which was not something James wanted, even if he did deserve it. Yet he continued to make Clove the target of his mischief because he knew that he was the best way to get to Brant.

Life was complicated for James. He actually enjoyed school and learning, but he had to act as if he didn't to get Brant to worry more about his little brother than his personal life. The life Brant led was not one James wanted; even now he was getting tired of always causing trouble.

Suddenly, a jolt of pain went through James, starting in his hand and abruptly breaking his train of thought. He stared at his hand in shock. The wooden ruler had left a mark that was already rising into a welt.

"Mr. Foxton, so kind of you to join us again. You have a visitor waiting in the parlor."

James looked at Clove, his face hard, unrepentant and arrogant as he stared the teacher down. Clove was not a weak man and he held James' eye contact for quite some time before turning away. James smirked and strode out of the room.

James wasn't at all surprised to see Brant waiting for him. There was no one else to visit him.

Brant was sitting in a large leather chair looking out the window at London's overcast sky.

James didn't take a seat, not expecting the visit to take long. He stood in front of his brother and smirked, waiting for Brant to say what he had come to say.

"I see you haven't gone back to normal yet," stated Brant after he had looked his younger brother up and down.

"Yes, well, I learned from the best."

Brant was silent for a moment. "I thought you would like to know that Catherine and I are engaged. She'll be going back to Port Royale with me in a couple of weeks."

James stared at his brother in shock. He had to be joking. Hadn't he learned from the first time round with her?

"I wanted you to find out from me and not Johnny."

"Johnny?"

"Yes, your friend. Catherine's younger brother."

James had completely forgotten about that little fact.

"I hope you two are very happy together," said James in a tone that expressed anything but sincerity.

He left the room. He had to think; he had to end this relationship before Brant got in any deeper, and he only had a couple of weeks to do it.

James wandered the halls the rest of the day, slipping into little alcoves wherever a teacher walked by.

He ran endless scenarios through his head, but nothing he came up with would end Catherine and Brant. He wasn't good at manipulating, that was Brant's area of expertise. He needed someone that had experience and knew how to get things done. Someone like Johnny.

Why he hadn't thought of Johnny earlier was beyond him. The only hitch, of course, was that Johnny might actually like the idea of Brant being his brother-in-law.

James waited outside Johnny's classroom, ready to grab him as soon as he walked out.

Johnny was one of the first to exit the room, tripping as he laughed hysterically. James peered around the corner into the room in an attempt to see what amused Johnny so much. Sure enough, Miss Laurence, the science teacher, was crying at her desk. One of Johnny's favorite things was to abuse the science teacher, who took everything to heart. She was much too sensitive to be in this profession as far as James was concerned, but he did feel bad about his friend's behavior. He grabbed Johnny's arm and dragged him into an empty room.

"Whoa! What's wrong?"

"I need your help."

"Does this have anything to do with your brother's visit?"

"Everything. Brant is engaged."

"Really? To who?"

"Doesn't matter. I need you to help me find a way to end it, and I have two weeks to do it."

James wasn't too worried about Johnny finding out that Brant's fiancée was, in fact, his sister. He knew nothing of their history since he had been attending another school at the time, and James highly suspected the family did not talk about it. James had also seen no evidence that the Marshall's kept Johnny very well informed of the family occurrences, making using Johnny much easier.

"Why would you want to end his engagement?"

"He has a history with this woman; last time she nearly ruined him. I won't let that happen again."

Johnny nodded and looked thoughtful. "I guess that's the reason for you suddenly wanting to pretend like you don't care about anything."

"Yeah, but it didn't work out so well."

"You had the right idea, but you didn't take it far enough. Not paying attention or skipping class isn't going to do it. You need to bring attention to yourself. Be obvious and vocal. Your brother is worried, now make it impossible to ignore."

"How?"

"Don't just talk back to teachers; pick arguments, play pranks, and break rules but brag loudly about it."

"I can do that."

"And I'll do it with you. I've been needing some excitement. Making Miss Laurence cry just doesn't hold any satisfaction."

James laughed. "So, what's first?"

"We start with Clove. We already know he'll make a fuss."

"What do we do? It has to be big."

"We steal his books, of course. What does he love more?"

James stared at his friend incredulously. Sometimes Johnny's brilliant, diabolical mind surprised him.

Johnny smiled. His expression could only be described as mischievous in its purest form.

"We're going to need a calling card."

* * *

"James!" whispered Johnny as he shook his friend's shoulder. "James! Wake up!"

James rolled over and groaned. "What?" he asked sleepily.

"It's time."

James rubbed his eyes and racked his brain to remember what the reason was for Johnny waking him up at, he looked at the clock; three a.m.

Books... something to do with books... and Clove...

"Okay, I'll be ready in a second."

James jumped out of bed and grabbed a pair of breeches and a shirt from the wardrobe.

The two boys ran silently in their stockings down the dark, familiar halls towards Clove's classroom. James turned the handle and slowly pushed it open to try and avoid a squeak. If anything, the squeak was longer and louder. It sounded like a banshee screaming from the depths of hell. Or, at least, that's what James imagined it sounded like.

"Bloody hell. You think anyone heard?" asked James nervously.

"This school is huge. No one heard."

They stepped into the dark classroom. The moonlight illuminated dust, giving the room an eerie feel. James shivered a little and wondered if maybe this wasn't such a good idea.

"Okay, we're going to take as many books as we can carry and bring them to the empty classroom down the hall," instructed Johnny very matter-of-factly.

"Are we going to take all the books?"

"Absolutely."

James grinned as he imagined Clove's face when he walked in later that morning. That was enough to abolish any doubts.

James quickly started to empty the shelves, getting about ten books and walking quickly to the empty classroom and, after dumping the books in a pile at the back of the room, quickly ran back for another load.

Clove had a lot of books, but between James and Johnny they made quick work of it. After making what seemed like countless trips back and forth, they now stood together looking at the empty bookshelves.

"So how long do we leave the books there?"

"Until they find them," said Johnny, who then walked over to the bookshelf and placed a piece of parchment on the middle shelf so it would be easily spotted.

"What's that?"

"Our calling card. If we want to get attention we need to show confidence and show that everything is done by the same people."

"You actually made us a calling card?"

"Yep." Johnny grinned.

James walked over to take a look at Johnny's handiwork. There was a fox and a hat with swords drawn on the parchment.

"Marshall and Foxton, it's great."

* * *

A pathway cleared quickly, like the parting of the red sea, as Clove walked through the halls with a look in his eyes that could kill and a parchment clutched in his hand.

James and Johnny didn't even bother to go see what all the commotion was about. They already knew. Instead, they sat in their usual spots in the back of Philosophy class. It was only a matter of time before Headmaster Mansfield asked to see them.

Sure enough, not five minutes later, one of the younger boys—also known as Mansfield's carrier pigeon—ran into the room and handed Mr. Fairchild a note.

He studied it for a moment and then turned to the class.

"Mr. Foxton, and Mr. Marshall, the headmaster would like to see you."

James and Johnny casually walked out as the other boys shot them looks of pity. Everyone knew Clove was involved, and it would not end well for them.

As they walked down the hall, James began to laugh, albeit nervously. "It worked. I can't wait to see Clove."

"Me neither," said Johnny, the biggest grin on his face.

Just before they walked into the headmaster's office they composed themselves, wiping the silly grins off their faces.

Clove's face was a funny shade of purple that looked something like an unripe blueberry. Johnny couldn't help it, he snorted in an attempt to hold back laughter, which earned him a glare from the headmaster.

"Please, sit."

James and Johnny sat down and waited for someone to speak.

"It seems Mr. Clove's books have gone missing from his classroom and he believes you may know something about their disappearance."

"Us? Why us?" asked Johnny.

The headmaster opened his mouth to reply but was cut off by Clove.

"Because the thieves left this," he said angrily, brandishing the parchment that the boys had left in place of the books just hours earlier.

"Sir, how does a parchment with a drawing on it condemn us?" Johnny tried to protest, but everyone in the room knew that in the end, Johnny and James would rightfully take the blame.

"The drawing resembles a calling card, in which a fox, or Foxton, and a symbol of a Marshall are drawn on it. Who else would it point to?"

Clove was becoming more and more irritated, and the headmaster just sat back and allowed him to deal with it.

"Sir, we are quite popular with the boys. Any one of them could have used symbols that represent our names."

"True. The other boys admire you, but most of them don't have your history nor your stupidity."

Johnny shrugged. "You got me there."

Clove smiled, making James uneasy. Anything that could make Clove happy would, in no way, be good for the boys.

"My dear boys, this is the last straw. One more incident and you both will be expelled. And believe me, it doesn't have to be anything big."

Johnny just shrugged. "I don't want to be here anyway."

James was silent, trying to appear confident while his stomach churned in worry.

As the boys walked out, James dropped all pretenses. "Johnny, this isn't good."

"You wanted to make a scene. And right now we're actually ahead of schedule."

"I don't want to get expelled!"

"Do you want Brant's attention?"

James nodded.

"Then you're going to get expelled. There's no other way to do it. Nothing else will work. Besides, you love the sea."

"Yeah, but out there it's me, Brant, and a bunch of men. I love being around boys my age, boys that look up to me. And what about you? You know Clove won't take just me down."

"I meant what I said in the office. I don't want to be here."

"Why? This school could bring a great future in politics or business."

"I don't want that kind of future. I just want to join the navy. What's wrong with that?"

"Nothing. Nothing at all," James said softly.

James and Johnny walked in silence the rest of the way to their room. James couldn't help but think how similar Johnny was to Brant. He was the real thing; James was just a fraud.

James wanted to do something for his friend, something to help him get into the navy. In another life, Brant may have been able to help him with that, but not in this life. James was screwing things up too much for that.

"So, what will be the final act to bring about our expulsion?"

James looked at Johnny. "We really have to plan that out? It won't take much."

"Well sure, but why not make it dramatic?"

"We can top stealing Clove's books?"

"You make a very good point, my friend. We need to top that, and it needs to involve Clove."

Johnny sat, looking thoughtful. "We could make a bonfire with his books."

"We want to get expelled, not go to prison," muttered James.

"We won't go to prison for that."

"Maybe not, but I'd rather not take the chance."

Johnny looked puzzled as he thought it over and then smiled. "I've got it. It's perfect."

"What?"

"You know Clove's powdered wig?"

"Yes," James answered cautiously. James knew the wig all too well. It was Clove's pride and joy next to his books.

"I think the white is a little dull. Don't you?"

James laughed. This would work. This would work very well indeed.

CHAPTER FOURTEEN

James and Johnny lay low for about a week, wanting to catch Clove with his guard down. However, Clove watched them carefully, trying to find something, any reason to expel them. They gave him no opportunity, though; he couldn't very well expel them for not paying attention in class.

Finally, Johnny could wait no longer, and he woke James at three a.m. again and they ran down the empty halls, jars of red ink in hand.

They found the powdered wig on a stand, sitting on Clove's desk, where it always sat, in pristine condition. Yet, James couldn't help but think of an old white rat when he saw it.

"Why does he have this thing if he doesn't even wear it?" asked James.

"I think he wears it on special occasions."

James smiled and opened a jar of red ink, pouring it all over the wig.

"This is going to ruin his desk too," observed James, as he watched the ink drip from the wig and pool on the desk.

"Oh well. We're going to be expelled anyway. What does it matter if we ruin one or two things? The end result remains the same."

James still felt uneasy about all that, but it was too late to turn back now.

The two boys soaked the wig in red ink. The once grossly white tresses were stained and dripping scarlet. James watched and couldn't help but think it was a morbid image.

* * *

Whispers traveled quickly through the school about the wig and desk. Clove's reaction made the last incident look like a slap on the wrist. He stomped through the halls, fists clenched, and yelling at any student who was unfortunate enough to get in his way. Word around the school was that he walked into the headmaster's office with so much force that the door hit the wall and bounced back, interrupting the headmaster while he was in the middle of a meeting with the parents of a potential student.

Headmaster Mansfield pulled James and Johnny out of Philosophy class again. No one even glanced in their direction as they made the walk of shame, which to Johnny was practically a red carpet to freedom, or, at the very least, the next step.

"Boys, I must admit I'm quite surprised and disappointed by your actions. Even after a warning of expulsion, you still vandalized the property of a teacher. It may be hard to believe, but I take no joy in saying that I must stand by my decision. For each action, there is a reaction, a consequence. I dare say, Mr. Clove is pleased to see you leaving. Your parents and guardian have been requested to come here, and they will be informed of your actions leading up to this expulsion as well as informed of the costs of damages caused." Headmaster Mansfield rambled on and Johnny rewarded him by rolling his eyes. With every action, there is a reaction.

James paled at the thought of having to pay for damages; it had not been a part of the plan. Brant would be angry enough that they were expelling him; this would make him furious.

"I'm going to have to ask the both of you to return to your lodgings and pack up your things. Remain there until I call for you."

Johnny practically skipped out of the office, whooping as he ran down the halls. James couldn't understand why Johnny was so ecstatic. To be losing a great opportunity, like education, even for the good of his brother, made James feel ashamed.

A few teachers poked their heads out of their classrooms to glare at Johnny, who was either blissfully unaware of everything around him or just didn't care. James suspected it was the latter.

However, James too began to lighten up as he watched Johnny dance around the room, throwing his belongings into a large trunk.

"How do you think your parents will react?"

Johnny stopped his antics and shrugged. "Same way they always do. My father yells a bit and then they find another quick fix and forget about me until that fails."

"That doesn't sound so great. Why are you so happy about that?"

"It's great fun and eventually my parents will run out of options and let me join the navy. All it takes is time, my friend. Time and a lot of guts." He winked and threw a few books on top of the growing pile of clothes.

Just then a knock came and one of Mansfield's "carrier pigeons" walked in. "Headmaster wants to see you."

Johnny and James both grabbed their trunks and lugged them down to the entryway where they were met by Lord and Lady Marshall along with Catherine and Brant.

Johnny looked at James in confusion. "Why is Catherine here? It's practically a family reunion," he whispered.

James shrugged and pretended not to know. To be honest, he was surprised Johnny didn't already know of Brant and Catherine's engagement. He really wasn't joking when he said his parents sent him away and forgot about him.

"Boys, please take a seat," requested Headmaster Mansfield.

They complied and waited for the unpleasantness to begin. Even Johnny knew it was all fun and games until the parents and guardians got involved.

Mansfield sat at his large oak desk in silence. He sighed and placed both hands flat on the desk's surface.

"Lord and Lady Marshall, Brant, I regret the need to have to meet under such circumstances."

Brant nodded, and Mansfield continued. "Over the past month, there have been a series of incidents of rebellion, mischief, disrespect, and most recently, vandalism, which James and Johnny have been involved in. Just this morning they soaked a teacher's wig in red ink, and in doing so, ruined both the wig and his desk. This behavior has resulted in their expulsion."

Lord Marshall shook his head as if to say 'here we go again'.

The room was silent for a moment; no one knew what to say. Finally, Lord Marshall seemed to get his thoughts in order and spoke; "I suppose you want the damages paid for."

"The teacher did request that. We have yet to calculate the cost of the damages caused, but I will contact you when I know."

"How long do you suppose that will take? I'm leaving for Port Royale at the end of this week," said Brant, speaking for the first time since the meeting had begun.

"I cannot know for sure. We will need to get the desk acclaimed."

"I see. If I am no longer in London, I will have to send the money from my estate in Port Royale. You know how to contact me?"

"I will cover it," Lord Marshall stated matter-of-factly. There was no room for negotiation in his offer.

"No. I couldn't ask you to do that."

"Nonsense! You're family now, and I'm sure it was Johnny's idea anyway."

"If you are certain..."

"Absolutely."

Mansfield folded his hands on top of his desk. "I'm glad you have that all figured out. I do suppose that is all we needed to discuss unless you have any questions." He paused but silence greeted him. "Very good. I will be in contact with you, Lord Marshall."

Everyone stood up and the men shook hands as if they completed nothing more than a simple business transaction. The adults spoke among themselves as they made their way to the entryway.

"Mother, father, I believe Johnny should come with Brant and me in our carriage. Then you can discuss what is to be done," suggested Catherine.

Johnny rolled his eyes and sighed.

Lord Marshall nodded his approval. "We'll meet back at home and discuss things further."

The four adults split into their two carriages, James and Johnny accompanying Brant and Catherine.

Brant ignored James the whole way to the Marshall's. He would deal with him later. Instead, he spoke with Catherine on the final arrangements before they left.

"All my things that I don't need right now are already loaded on the ship. Matthew has been most helpful."

"Good. And the engagement ball is when?"

"The end of this week. We can leave as soon as the day after if you wish."

"Catherine? I hate to interrupt, but I can't help but notice how father mentioned that Brant was a part of the family and how you plan on going somewhere with him. Is there any particular reason for this?" asked Johnny, who didn't seem at all ashamed of what he had done, and appeared quite comfortable at the moment, unlike James. Sometimes James had a very hard time understanding his cavalier friend.

"Did no one tell you?" Catherine asked in surprise.

"Well, you know how it is... I was away at boarding school; out of sight, out of mind."

"I'm sorry. I just assumed Mother, at least, would have told you."

"I must have missed her mentioning that during one of her many and numerous visits. Now would you be so kind as to explain what it is no one has seen fit to inform me about?"

"Brant and I are engaged."

"Oi! Engaged to Brant Foxton! How did you get Father to agree to that?"

"I see my reputation precedes me. Well, I was on my best behavior and tried not to mention pirates," replied Brant with a chuckle.

"So, uh, James, how come you didn't tell me about their engagement?" questioned Johnny.

"I didn't think you'd agree to help," James mumbled, not really wanting to get into detail with Catherine sitting right there.

Brant raised his eyebrows and gave James a look that said they would discuss that later.

For James, the trip was excruciatingly long, although only twenty minutes, it seemed so much longer. Finally, the carriages pulled to a stop outside the luxurious townhouse. James imagined it was probably one of the nicer ones in London, definitely one of the nicest he had seen.

James and Johnny were sent upstairs to put their things away—James would be staying with the Marshall's until they left at the end of the week. There wasn't much room in Brant's lodgings for two and Catherine kindly thought of that and had offered James a guest room.

* * *

"Brant, it seems your younger brother is walking in your footsteps," said Lord Marshall as the adults sat down in the sitting room.

"I'm not entirely sure what happened. This behavior isn't like him at all."

"I wouldn't be surprised if Johnny dragged him into all this." It came out nearly as a sigh. Lord Marshall's exhaustion and aggravation with his son was all too apparent in his reply.

"I wouldn't be so sure. Now, to discuss what is to be done; Catherine and I have been talking, and we came up with an idea."

"I'm ready to hear any suggestions. I'm at a loss as to what to do with him and joining the navy is out of the question."

"Well, I'm not sure how much you'll like this idea. I do some safe, legitimate business sometimes, and I'd be happy to take Johnny along as a cabin boy. It's low work, but he'll learn respect. When he's not on my ship, he can get tutoring along with James."

"This is something to be considered, but I don't want Johnny involved in piracy."

"And rightly so, it's no life for him. The only voyages he would come along on would be strictly legal."

"It's not dangerous, is it?" asked Lady Marshall.

"Not at all."

"But there is a possibility of an attack by other pirates, especially since you'd be carrying goods."

"There is always that possibility for any ship, but I have a good crew that can fight their way out of any situation. It's probably safer than a ship designed to carry passengers. My sailors are at least trained to fight. James has sailed with me for a few years, and he has never been hurt due to a boarding."

"I take it you sent him out of the way."

"James knows the drill. If he ever wants to advance past cabin boy then he has to obey the captain, no matter what, and he knows that a standing order of mine is for him to stay in the hold until I personally come for him."

"Johnny doesn't follow orders very well," worried Lady Marshall.

"Mother, there is no need to worry. I've been on Brant's ship, and Johnny will learn very quickly to obey or pay the consequences," assured Catherine. "A ship is nothing like a boarding school. There is no expulsion and the only laws are those of the captain's. He would learn very quickly that to survive and thrive, he will have to follow orders. If there is anything Johnny is good at, it is surviving."

"Very well. We will try this. Anything that has a chance of turning Johnny around is worth a try. However, I do not want him to know just yet."

* * *

The rest of the week went quickly as they made preparations for the engagement ball. Catherine needed to have a new dress made and checked to be sure it fit correctly. She insisted on Brant getting a new suit for the evening. Being the evening's center of attention and gossip, it was only right to look their very best.

James and Johnny, nearly forgotten in all the hubbub, were left to their own mischief. James figured that the next few days were imperative to his plan, and so he and Johnny brought nothing but misery to everyone in the house. Small pranks played on the maids, Catherine, and even Lord and Lady Marshall brought the tension levels to a maximum height.

James wondered why Johnny continued to help him. He was obviously happy about his sister's engagement. Perhaps he had his own motives; perhaps it was just to push his parents over the edge. James didn't really care, as long as he was helping.

* * *

Before Brant knew it, Saturday had rolled around and what had been madness before had turned into a full out whirlwind of activity. Decorating, cooking, cleaning... It all had to be done.

Catherine spent the day running between the ballroom and kitchen to make sure everything was going according to plan. Brant had to laugh as her maids burst out of her room, running after her, mid comb because she had jumped up and ran out when she had suddenly remembered to tell the cook to pull out extra red wine.

At one point, Brant was literally chased away from Catherine's room when he had tried to talk to her. Apparently he was not to see her before she was ready. The maids had finally gotten her into her dress and were now doing her hair and make-up. Distraction was not something they wanted to deal with.

Lady Marshall dragged James and Johnny, complaining loudly, around the house. They were to be present at the ball, and so they needed to wash up and put on clean suits. James wrinkled his nose as a maid roughly brushed his shoulder length blond hair and tied it back. Johnny's short hair spared him the rough combing and the feeling of his hair being ripped out of his skull.

At around six o'clock, the guests began to arrive. Brant and Catherine waited at the door to greet them and receive well wishes.

Whispers went around about what a handsome couple they made and shock that Catherine Marshall, someone very high in society, was marrying a privateer. His family name was the only thing that made the pair even moderately acceptable.

James and Johnny were the youngest boys there, but a few girls close to their age latched onto them pretty quickly and insisted on hearing stories about their "daring escapades" which were largely exaggerated.

Brant was thoroughly sick of smiling and greeting people he didn't care about. He slipped his arm around Catherine and kissed her on the cheek. "Dance with me, my love," he whispered.

"We can't." She continued to smile and shake hands.

"Enough of this hostess duty. We're celebrating our engagement, so let's actually celebrate."

Catherine shook her head. "Later."

"Not later, now. I'm sick of waiting."

Brant took her hand and dragged her away from the doorway, whirling her into a dance. She let out a great peal of laughter, something quite out of character for her. She was always reserved. Always proper.

The whole evening was spectacular, comparing only to an evening hosted by King Charles II himself. Even though whispers of scandal went around, for the most part, the guests were surprisingly supportive of the couple. As the evening drew to a close, many gave fond farewells to Catherine. It would be a long time before most expected to see her again.

By the time the last guest left, Catherine was utterly exhausted and collapsed into bed after her maids helped her out of her dress, jewelry, and let down her hair. Tomorrow was going to be another busy day.

As she slipped into an exhausted sleep dreams overtook her. Dark gray waters and cold winds were her night companions.

CHAPTER FIFTEEN

Today, Catherine would be leaving England to start her new life. Today, Lord Marshall would set both his children free into the world, one to marry, the other to learn life lessons. Propriety called for Catherine to be married before she left with her betrothed but with the weather as a timeline and no bishop readily willing to unite the couple, the Marshalls allowed their daughter to leave.

Lord Marshall called Johnny into his study mid-morning. "Johnny, please sit."

Johnny took a seat, looking bored. He knew what was coming. This was when his father told him of the plans to send him who-knows-where and he was expected to behave and blah, blah, blah. Every time it was the same.

"Johnny, your mother and I have become very concerned about you and have decided that it is time to take some drastic measures."

Here it comes, thought Johnny.

"You will be going with Brant and Catherine as a cabin boy on the *BlackFox*. Hopefully after some long weeks at sea, you will learn some respect and responsibility."

Johnny rolled his eyes, only half-listening. However, as it slowly sank in, his eyes widened, bright in shock and excitement. He opened his mouth in an attempt to say something, anything. He was too afraid it had just been his imagination.

"Well, don't just sit there. Go pack!" barked Lord Marshall.

Johnny jumped up and ran out of the room shouting for James.

"What!" asked James, running out of his room.

"I'm going with you!"

James looked at his friend in confusion. "You're what?"

"I'm going with you! That's my parents' solution; sending me with you as a cabin boy."

Johnny laughed gleefully as James stared at his friend, dumbfounded. He couldn't quite believe it was happening.

"Your parents are sending you to work on a pirate ship? Have they lost their minds?"

"I guess so. Come on, help me pack!"

James helped Johnny go through his things and decide what to take, but all the while, he wondered if it was really such a great idea. James had seen Johnny in action; he was too much like Brant, and two wrongs don't make a right, they make trouble.

* * *

Brant paced the deck, waiting for Catherine to arrive with James and Johnny. He wanted to be out of port by noon, but it didn't look as if that was going to happen.

Normally, the change in schedule wouldn't have bothered him. He lived for spontaneity, adventure, uncertainty, but now he wanted nothing more than to be away from the busy, smelly city of London and back on the open sea. The months had been much too long, and he was restless, restless for a fight, for some exhilaration, for the open air, the moving deck, a storm, something other than the everyday dreariness of London's nobility. So many times over the summer he had considered attempting the voyage back to Port Royale, but was held back by the thought of leaving Catherine and the thought of losing more crew to the terrible storms. It would be wrong of him to put his crew in that kind of danger; it would be an abuse of his authority.

"Sir?"

Brant turned to face Matt. "Yes?"

"We'll be ready to cast off in an hour."

"Thank you, Matthew."

Catherine and the boys should be aboard by then. If not, it would only be a small delay. Brant calmed himself and walked the deck. It was a surprisingly sunny day. Not a cloud marred the perfect sky but the air was crisp. Winter was coming. Brant was thankful that there was no snow. He hated snow. Thank goodness he was heading towards tropical paradise. Thank goodness he could get work again. Thank goodness he could be free.

He spent the rest of the time until Catherine arrived with the boys, charting the course they would take. This early in the season he didn't want to take the straightest and fastest route as it would bring them into open waters where they would be far from aid if anything were to happen. Normally he wouldn't have cared, but with passengers, he had more to think about.

When Catherine arrived with the boys, they were nearly ready to cast off.

"Catherine," said Brant as she walked up to him. "Harold will stow away your things; whatever you don't need for the voyage can go down below with the rest. Everything you're going to need can be taken to my cabin. I'll be taking over Matt's quarters for the voyage."

* * *

Catherine smiled slightly. Brant was always business when it came to his command, which meant she was just a passenger. She had to remember that. She walked over to the sailor Brant had indicated to be Harold. "These trunks need to go below," she said, indicating about five large trunks.

Harold rolled his eyes and chuckled. "Is that everything?"

"The rest will need to be taken to my cabin," said Catherine, choosing to ignore the sailor's jab at her heavy packing.

"Of course, Ma'am."

Catherine watched as he hefted a trunk up onto his shoulder and took it below deck.

"Be careful, and please tie it down securely!" she called after him.

He waved his free hand in response and Catherine, satisfied that he was properly looking after things, went over to the rail to take one last look at the city she had lived in all her life. Would she ever return to these shores? The possibilities frightened her, but as the *BlackFox* slowly left the harbor and the shoreline grew more distant, a feeling of excitement filled her, and she realized that at the moment she couldn't care less if she ever returned.

* * *

Johnny loved being at sea. Brant watched him carefully at first but relaxed when he appeared to behave. He took to the sea instantly, never having a problem with seasickness or balance. Brant caught him many a time climbing the riggings and would laugh as Catherine yelled at him to get down before he hurt himself.

James was, thankfully, back to his old self; although, he acted hostile towards Catherine every chance he had, but Brant was confident that all he needed was time.

It was the second week of the voyage when they came across the lone Dutch ship. The sun was high in the sky, and it was a hot day. The sailors on the *BlackFox* were mostly lazing around, taking advantage of the clean air and warm weather; something they had missed in London.

Brant had decided to take advantage of Johnny's love of climbing and put him up in the crow's nest to keep watch. A few times, when Johnny was on watch duty before, he had called "Sail ho!" just to get a reaction. The first few times everyone had scrambled to the rail, straining their eyes for a sight of the sail. They spent ten minutes there just looking, full of anticipation. After spending the summer cooped up in London, everyone was eager for some excitement. After a while, the men heard Johnny's hysterical laughter, and with disappointed shakes of their heads, they went back to work. After the third time, they were ready to ring Johnny's neck, and after the sixth, they just started to ignore him. When Johnny let out the warning call, no one even lifted a head. So the entire crew, except for Johnny, was startled when the Dutch ship fired on them.

Johnny, who had seen the guns being prepared and the Jolly Roger raised, had shouted down warnings but to no avail.

When the first cannon blast came, the whole crew sprang to life. James calmly led a trembling Catherine below deck while Brant quickly climbed up to the crow's nest to see what exactly had happened.

"Johnny! Get below deck!" He didn't have time to deal with the boy now.

Brant assessed the situation and frowned. "Bloody hell. Johnny, you idiot," he said under his breath. He mumbled threats the whole way down and immediately began shouting orders. "Pull in that sail! Run out the guns! Raise the colors!"

The whole deck was alive with movement. The men were a mixture of panic and excitement. As the Dutch ship drew near, Brant gave the boarding orders.

The fight was quick and bloody, with no losses on Brant's end. The Dutch pirates were not skilled, more like fishermen with dreams of gold. They raided the stores for supplies, but other than that, there was nothing worth taking.

The men returned to the *BlackFox* exhausted from the fight, but in good spirits. A few of the men, with much cheering from the rest of the crew, bombarded the floundering Dutch ship with cannon blasts until it sank. It was a waste of ammunition, but Brant allowed the men to have their fun. The first raid of the season was always exciting.

Brant and Matt pulled out some bottles of rum to celebrate. It was tradition on the *BlackFox*.

* * *

Catherine silently watched from her place on the upper deck. She watched the merriment and how happy Brant seemed. It disgusted her how they could take such joy in murdering and stealing.

Silently put out that Brant had sent below deck instead of allowing him to help out, Johnny sat on the deck next to Catherine. What he wouldn't admit was that he was terrified once the cannon fire began.

The crew's festivities went on well into the night, and Catherine went to bed before they finished, leaving James and Johnny free to join in. James was angry that Catherine had made him stay with her and Johnny. She had said that it was no way for a boy of his standing to behave. James had just rolled his eyes and sat, refusing to answer her whenever she made an attempt at conversation. She had no right to tell him how to behave, especially since he'd lived on the ship for the past few years, and Brant had never kept him from anything but the fighting. Catherine bothered him in even the best situations, interfering in his life made his dislike boil towards hatred.

At around midnight, Brant approached the boys. "Where have you been all evening? I expected you boys to be joining right in."

James and Johnny made sour faces. "Catherine," they said in unison.

"What do you mean?"

"She said we had to stay out of it because it was 'no way for gentlemen to act,'" said James bitterly, who had taken it harder than Johnny.

"I see," said Brant calmly, but James knew he wasn't happy. Perhaps he didn't have to do anything at all to break Brant and Catherine up. Perhaps their differences would do it for him.

"I'll talk to her. You boys enjoy yourselves. I want to talk to you both tomorrow."

The boys nodded and walked off to join the rest of the crew.

Christopher handed James a bottle of rum. "Here boys, drink up. Ye share now."

James took a good long swig and then handed the bottle to Johnny, who attempted to do the same but ended up choking on it as it burned down his throat. The men laughed and clapped him on the back.

"Not used to drinking, eh?" chuckled Matt.

"I'm fine. Went down the wrong tube is all," Johnny protested, embarrassed. He wasn't used to being the bottom ranked.

The men laughed again. "Just keep drinking, you'll get used to it," assured Matt.

The crew made Johnny feel at ease and James at home as they joined in the drinking, card games, and dancing. It was a night Johnny would remember forever. The carefree spirit and the total disregard for what was socially acceptable brought Johnny a feeling of elation. No longer was he beating against the goads. For the first time in his life, Johnny felt as though he belonged.

* * *

Brant knocked and then walked into his cabin, trying to remain calm, but inside, annoyance at Catherine struggled to find its way to the surface.

She was lying on the bunk reading a book.

"Catherine, what's this I hear about you keeping the boys away from the celebration?"

Catherine looked up from her reading. "I thought it best they didn't join in. It wouldn't be proper."

"Proper?" asked Brant, an eyebrow lifted in speculation. "Catherine, you are on a pirate ship. Proper gets you killed. And even if it wasn't proper, you do not order around my crew."

"Excuse me? Johnny is my brother."

"He is my crew on my ship. My word is law. And Johnny aside, you had no right to order James around."

"But we're getting married—"

"And you will be his sister-in-law, not his mother. He is old enough to make his own decisions, and any other judgment is made by me, his guardian."

Catherine looked at Brant in disgust. "It isn't proper..."

Brant was exasperated. "Look at where we are! Proper doesn't matter! I am a pirate, for goodness sake! I live by a different set of rules than your society. If you can't accept that, then why are you marrying me? You knew what you were getting into."

"You murder and steal and then celebrate it. I cannot condone that," was all Catherine said before rolling over to face the wall. The conversation was over.

Over the next few days, the atmosphere was tense between Catherine and Brant. Brant even forgot that he had been planning on talking to Johnny about taking things more seriously and to James about what had taken place at school, and why.

* * *

Catherine began to feel alone and depressed. She withdrew into the cabin and rarely came out. She even had her food brought to her room. She constantly ran the events from the past few months over in her head. She couldn't help but wonder if she had made the right decision. It seemed as if she and Brant couldn't work. They were so different. He did whatever he wanted or needed to do, regardless of the consequences. He didn't put any stock in what was proper or even what the law allowed. When he had been in her world, he had seen the need to follow the unwritten rules. That had been the Brant she'd wanted. Out here, he only saw the need to live his own way; there was no law. It terrified her. She couldn't live like that. To live with reckless abandon was not something she even knew how to do.

It was a week before Catherine came to a decision and ventured from her cabin in search of Brant. She found him leaning against a rail, staring out at the ocean, deep in thought. She gently placed her hand on his shoulder and stood next to him. They both stood in complete silence for a time while Catherine searched for the words to express what needed to be said.

"What happened to us?" she asked.

Brant didn't even look at her, his eyes still looking far across the ocean. "The same thing as last time. We're just too different."

"I want to make this work. The shame if I went back home—"

"Shame? Is that all you think of? Your silly rules of society? Out here it means nothing, and it is not something our relationship should be based on."

Catherine shut her eyes. She should have known better than to say that to Brant. "You're right. I want to make this work because, despite our differences, I love you. But if we are to make it work we are going to have to learn to communicate."

Brant finally turned to face her. "Can you still respect me, despite the things I do?"

"Yes. Though I do not agree with it."

"That is all I ask. At the estate, you will run things your way. Johnny will be your charge there, but I cannot allow you to become James' mother. He doesn't need one, nor does he want one. Things are hard enough for him as it is."

"And on your ship?"

"I run everything. You are free to give advice but not orders. I cannot have a contest for authority arise, even if it is not your intention."

Catherine nodded. "I do ask that you actually consider my advice."

"Of course. I respect you, Catherine. I respect what you have to say."

They were silent for a moment. They broke their gaze only when James' called, "Land ho!"

It was the Island of Hispaniola, the last port they would make before Port Royale.

"Bring those sails in! Look lively men! Let's make port!" shouted Brant.

Matt relayed the orders and joined in as Brant took the helm. Catherine smiled; she didn't mind this Brant at all.

* * *

After making port on the Island of Hispaniola, port St. Dominique, Brant retreated to his cabin and wrote a letter to Senona. He hoped she had gotten around to getting a team of horses for the carriage. He wanted Catherine to have a form of transportation. He wanted the transition of lifestyles for her to go as smoothly as possible. She was already giving up so much.

He also instructed her to meet them at the docks on Thursday, midday. If no storms arose, they should stay on schedule. He didn't mention Catherine in the letter; he didn't know how Senona would react or how to approach the subject.

Brant put the letter in the care of a courier before they left port the next day. It would hopefully arrive on Wednesday.

The remainder of the voyage was, thankfully, uneventful, and by the time they docked, Catherine and Brant were acting as if nothing had ever happened.

CHAPTER SIXTEEN

After Brant left, Senona spent a lot of time in the stable grooming Jester, Brant's favorite horse. It helped her feel closer to him while he was away.

Her months at sea had taught her what hard work was, so cleaning five stalls a day was nothing. She also made a point to ride each and every horse, except Archie, whom Sam had out in the fields all day. She discovered that, for an Arabian, Admiral was a quiet, gentle horse, even to the point of being boring. He was a good mount for James, who didn't do much riding. She always saved Admiral for last so she could have her relaxing ride at the end when she was tired.

In the evenings, after dinner, Senona always took Naldo out and explored the island. She stayed out late to avoid Liza who, for some unknown reason, had taken a great disliking to her. Senona attributed it to her blatant disregard of social rules, but it could have had something to do with the fact that she spent her days in a barn instead of doing lady-like things.

After about a week of the evening rides, she discovered a path down to a sandy oceanfront. It was an hour's ride from the estate to the path and then another half hour to the beach. Once on the open shore, she would push Naldo into a full gallop.

They would fly, allowing sand and water to spray out behind them, and didn't stop until they ran out of sand. She loved doing this bareback. Feeling Naldo's every move was pure freedom.

After their run, Senona turned Naldo around and they walked to the middle of the beach to cool down. Sliding off, she would just lie in the sand, Naldo resting calmly beside her and just stare up at the sky. On occasion, she would fall asleep and not wake up till morning. Naldo never left her side. She would hear him throughout the night walk around and nibble at a bit of shrubbery or seaweed that had washed ashore, but he always returned and lay down beside his master.

Tonight ended up being one of those nights. Senona woke up and slowly realized where she was. The crashing surf and the sun high in the sky made her jump up. She did not intend to sleep so late; she needed to get all the stalls cleaned and horses ridden.

Senona mounted and they started out at a fast-paced walk. By the time they got to the main road, they were galloping at full speed. Senona was not looking forward to facing Liza for not being at breakfast, or lunch for that matter.

When she arrived back at the house, she went straight to the stables and began cleaning out the stalls; she figured she could avoid Liza until dinner, and afterward, she could escape and let Liza sleep off her anger.

An hour later, the barn was clean and Senona was just saddling up Phantom. Hunger gnawed at her stomach, but she refused to face Liza until absolutely necessary.

Sam walked in to get Archie and head back out to the fields. "Ride with me for a bit?" he asked as he took Archie out of his stall, still fully saddled from earlier that morning.

Sam only asked out of habit; Senona rode with him out to the fields every day after lunch.

"Sure."

They mounted and rode out of the barn at a slow walk. It was about five minutes before Sam spoke.

"Do you enjoy aggravating my mother?"

Senona looked over at Sam to see him smiling and laughed. "Not at all. She is just aggravated too easily."

Sam chuckled. "That is true. Poor Julie gets the brunt of it."

"I can't say I envy her. Was your mother terribly upset with me?"

"I'm not sure. She did nothing during lunch except speak of you. Something along the lines of 'spoiled rich girl, thinks we must bow to her every whim.'"

Sam said it jokingly, but Senona's face still fell. "Oh."

"It's just my mother. Don't take it to heart."

"Yes, but I don't want to act spoiled. I didn't think what I did mattered."

"It doesn't, and you don't. My mother just doesn't understand you. She thinks everything should have structure and everyone should follow the same rules. The fact that you don't live like that is hard for her to accept."

"But what about Brant? He is much more 'free' and 'rebellious' than I am."

Sam thought for a moment. "No, he's not. He is similar to you in many respects but rules still govern him as a Captain. You do not see, or feel, a need for man-made rules. You are governed only by your heart and the oldest laws around. Brant is like that too, but it's more for the want of an escape, for the sense of adventure and freedom that cannot be found in society, compared to your need to go wherever the wind takes you." Sam seemed to struggle a few times as he searched for the words to describe and contrast his two friends.

Senona nodded in understanding. "Thank you... I think," she said with a laugh. "How do you understand me so well?"

Sam smiled. "You intrigue me, and our daily rides and conversations reveal a lot about your character. If you know how to observe, you can learn a lot. Just the way you treat the horses tells me so much about you."

"Why are you a steward? These skills of yours would be useful in the career as a businessman or land owner."

"I am a businessman, and act as a land owner. Brant treats me as more than just a simple steward. We are like brothers, and with the amount of time he's gone, I run this place as if it were my own, and I'm treated accordingly."

"I stand corrected."

Sam smiled. "You're an open book, Senona Montez. Maybe it's time you allowed people to read it." He paused but got no response. "Here we are. I best be getting to work."

Senona turned Phantom in the direction of the stables and was about to ride off when Sam called after her, "A word of advice. If I were you, I'd steer clear of Liza as long as possible."

Senona laughed. "I'll try."

The rest of the day went by uneventfully. Senona rode Jester and Admiral and then pulled some tack out to clean. She managed to get everything done and keep away from Liza, who never set foot in the stables.

Senona snuck into the house early so she could be at dinner on time and be clean. Liza hated Senona being late, but she hated Senona smelling like a horse even more. She walked into the dining room just before Liza rang the bell.

Liza glared at her all dinner long, never directing any conversation to her other than to throw jabs or outright insults.

Sam constantly made small defenses for Senona, which did not go unnoticed or unappreciated. With Brant gone, Senona was thankful to have Sam around to look out for her.

Once dinner was done, Senona helped Julie and Liza clear the table. Liza said nothing to her, refusing to acknowledge her at all. Julie nervously told Senona there was no need to help, but Senona quietly insisted and continued, but when it came to the kitchen, Julie stood her ground, and the quiet maid quite literally chased Senona away.

Senona didn't join Sam and Liza in the den for tea but instead escaped to her room to change and then silently made her way down the stairs with the intention of going to the stables.

"Where do you think you're going?"

Senona stopped and grimaced. Caught. "To the stables. Is that a problem?"

"You cannot just go gallivanting all over the place. Lord Foxton keeps you and your animal here out of the kindness of his heart. Don't make him regret it."

Senona looked at Liza incredulously. "Gallivanting? I do not gallivant. I ride my horse, there is nothing strange about that. And as for keeping me and Naldo here, I work for our keep."

"Do you honestly think we need an extra hand just to run the stables?"

"Yes. Though you are never out there, so I wouldn't expect you to know, but Brant and Sam would and they're the ones that matter, not you."

"You think you are so smart and that you can get away with anything just because you are a noble, but you can't. You ride that animal all over the place like some sort of barbarian, no saddle or any proper riding equipment. You don't come back at night, doing God knows what. You are often late for dinner, don't even show up for breakfast, and do a small amount of work. You think you earn your keep, but you are just a rich girl used to getting your way. You don't care that you are slowly ruining Lord Foxton's reputation, and your own, I dare say."

Senona looked at Liza, staring her down. Liza met her gaze with equal strength. They fought a silent battle for a moment, Senona surrendering in the end. It wasn't worth fighting.

"I'm sorry you feel that way."

Liza's words cut deeper than they should have. She knew that she didn't act like a "spoiled rich girl" and that she worked hard, but hearing someone say to her face that she was everything she hated, made her wonder if they were right.

Not five minutes later, Sam walked in. Senona was grooming Naldo in preparation for her ride. Sam didn't speak, walking over to Archie and saddling him. He had never accompanied Senona on her night rides, but something told him she needed a friend tonight.

As they prepared, Senona ignored him. They both seemed comfortable with silence. When she finished grooming, she patiently waited for Sam. They silently mounted and Sam followed Senona as she directed Naldo down the road.

"I apologize for my mother's behavior. It was wrong."

"It's fine. She doesn't like me. Everyone has a right to an opinion."

"No, it's not fine. It's extremely rude of her to act like that."

"Well, to be completely honest, I prefer her outright dislike to the backstabbing that went on where I came from."

They rode in silence again for some time until they came to the path that led to the beach.

"Where are we going?"

"I'm going to the beach. You're following me."

"Beach?"

"You'll see. Are you ready?"

"Ready for wha—!" Archie sprung into a full gallop after Naldo, cutting Sam off. He lost his balance and held on for dear life. The trail had many sharp turns, giving Sam no chance to pull himself back into place. When they got to a straight stretch, Sam managed to re-position himself and relaxed as much as he could and settled in to "enjoy" the break-neck speeds and sharp turns. All the while going through his head was the thought that he wasn't going to make it out of this trail alive.

He looked at Senona to see how she was doing. He thought she would be holding on tightly, but was surprised to see her riding calmly, leaning forward and moving flawlessly with Naldo, her hands stretched forward and resting on his neck, but not grasping.

When they reached sand, Senona pulled Naldo down to a walk. Once Sam did the same with Archie, he noticed she was laughing, pure joy coming from deep within her. He looked at her in astonishment. It had been one of the most terrifying and tiring rides he had ever been on.

"How can you be laughing?" he asked breathlessly.

"How can I not be? Did you not feel the freedom?"

"I don't know what I felt, but I saw my life flash before my eyes."

Senona burst out laughing again. "I think you're going to need some rest. We can let the horses go."

"Go?"

"They won't wander far. Just take Archie's bridle off."

Sam shrugged and dismounted, nearly falling to his knees. His legs were jelly from fear and exhaustion. He released Archie and sank down into the warm sand. The sun was nearly set, and he took a deep breath, sighed, and let out all the tension that had accumulated.

Senona walked over and settled down beside Sam. Naldo followed closely. After a few minutes, he lay down on the sand next to her and Senona leaned back, resting against her horse's neck and closing her eyes.

"He's quite attached to you, isn't he?"

"Yes. I've had him since he was a yearling."

"I don't think I've ever seen a horse act quite like him."

"I suppose he's special. I got him for a birthday gift, and I spent every waking moment with him. He spent more time with me than the other horses in the herd, so I suppose he sees me as his herd."

"Is that why you went through the trouble of taking him with you?"

"I couldn't leave him. I'm everything to him, and he is, in a sense, my best friend. My padre could have used him for breeding, but I'm not sure he would have been happy with that life."

"I didn't understand why you would have taken him with you. All that trouble just to bring a horse, but I suppose you didn't really have a choice, did you?"

Senona smiled. "I'm a little strange, aren't I?"

"It makes you different. As I said earlier, intriguing. I can understand Brant's fascination."

"Fascination?" asked Senona with a laugh.

"Yes. It's obvious. I'm surprised you haven't noticed."

"I did," she said softly. "We were courting... but I never would have called it fascination."

Sam raised his eyebrows. "Were?"

"Yes. Difficulties arose, so I ended it before he left."

"You realize Catherine is in England, and he is sure to see her while he's there?"

"That is why I ended things. He may feel for me, but he needs to get rid of any feelings he may still have for her, without feeling any guilt."

Sam looked thoughtful. "Perhaps he needs a little guilt, something holding him back."

"No."

"He is going to take advantage of this. It's in his nature."

"Perhaps, but from what I've heard of Catherine, she will turn him down for that very reason. And if she doesn't, then he will get tired of her and come back to me. His nature is all I have going for me. From what James has told me, she is too proper. It's doomed to failure."

Sam laughed. "You may be right. In allowing him to grow tired of her, he will have closure. He'll be able to forget her."

"Exactly. I'm feeling a bit manipulative right now." She laughed slightly and Sam smiled.

"Yes, you are manipulative, like every woman."

"Samuel! I think we need to find you a woman to change your perspective of the opposite sex."

Sam blushed and looked down.

"Or have you already?"

"There is someone, but my mother would never approve. I have a good job. I can offer a good, stable future, and so she wants me to court someone from the middle class, not lower."

"Class is meaningless. This is your life, your choice, not your mother's. Court whom you wish; marry for love. Not for class!"

Sam sighed. "You make it sound like an easy thing, but it's not."

"Nothing in life is ever easy. It's full of hard choices that need to be made. You'll be able to make the right decision when you're ready. Don't rush things."

"What about you? You just up and ran away."

"I'd been considering leaving for a long time. It may not have been the most planned out escape, but there were preparations in place."

"So you were just waiting?"

"I had hoped my parents would begin to understand, but when they decided to marry me off to Senor Flamez, I had to leave. I realized there was no other way."

"You really think the right circumstances will come?"

"Something will enable you to make the right decision. I'm not sure what, but something."

They lay there for a few minutes in total silence, letting the peace and calmness wash over her.

"Well, I think we should head back. Maybe show up for breakfast."

Senona laughed. "That's probably a wise idea."

They rode back at a relaxed pace, neither seemed to be in a hurry.

It was well past midnight when they got back. They lit a single lamp and settled the horses in for the night. As they walked out of the stables, Senona turned to Sam. "Same time tomorrow?"

"Sure."

CHAPTER SEVENTEEN

The next couple of weeks were mundane and slow. Senona avoided Liza as much as possible, and Sam continued to join her on most of her evening rides. He claimed it was to keep her from sleeping on the beach, but she suspected he just enjoyed their conversations.

It was one of those slow days. Senona had finished cleaning stalls early and all the horses had behaved, so no schooling was needed on top of their daily rides. She wanted to avoid the house until dinner, and so she saddled up Naldo and went to town in search of a couple horses to pull the carriage.

The last time she had been to town was to say goodbye to Brant, and she had been avoiding it ever since. However, today she had a purpose. She rode to various liveries, but there wasn't an abundance of good horses. One livery, in particular, had her nearly in tears.

"They don't look like much, but they'll work hard and get what needs done."

Senona looked the two horses over, rubbing her hands up and down their legs and backs.

"These horses are lame," she said, trying to keep her voice calm, but it quivered slightly.

"Nonsense, they're as sound as the day they were born."

"Do not lie to me. Their knees and coronets are swollen and every bone in their body is showing. What have you done to these poor creatures?"

"I didn't do nothing. They did their job is all."

"Worked too hard with not enough care. This is pure cruelty."

"Someone will buy them, so if you're not interested, don't waste my time."

Senona looked at the horses and let a tear slip, no animal in God's kingdom should be subject to this kind of cruelty. The man cared nothing for them as long as they could serve their purpose and make him money.

"I'm interested, if only to get them out of this place and keep them from another life of hardship that will likely kill them before a year's time."

"You rich girls. These horses are not pets. It's not cruelty; it's just life."

"I don't care if I'm naïve if it means I can still hurt when I see such diabolical acts as this. I will be back tomorrow with my decision."

"Talk to the mister, eh?"

"No, the owner of the stables I work in. I'm no rich girl." With that, Senona walked out of the barn to where Naldo was tied. She untied him and was about to mount but instead fell against his shoulder and cried. It struck deep in her heart to see the cruelty those horses were subject to.

It's not as though she hadn't seen things like this before, but she had somehow always felt akin to their captivity, whereas now that she had felt freedom it hurt her to see these animals she had once felt so close to, be so cruelly treated and in captivity. They could do nothing about their plight either. She felt no shame in openly showing grief for this mistreatment, maybe people wouldn't turn their gaze the other way if more people showed concern.

Senona started as someone touched her shoulder and turned around in surprise.

"Are you okay?" asked a young girl, only a few years older than herself.

"I'm fine."

"Are you sure? You look upset."

"It's silly, really. I was looking at some horses and the state they were in just sickened me. I was overcome. As I said, silly."

The girl smiled. "It's not silly. It's good that you care."

Senona wiped away her tears. "Thank you. I'm Senona, by the way. Senona Montez."

"Sarah MacKenzie."

"Are you Scottish?"

"I'm not. My husband is. But what brings you, a Spaniard, to Port Royale?"

"It's a long story."

"I have the time if you care to tell it. Come to the market with me."

Senona smiled and shrugged. "Sure, why not?"

The two girls walked off, Naldo in tow, as Senona told her story.

Sarah listened in rapture as she heard of her running away, finding passage on a privateer ship, joining in on a raid and having Karl die in her arms, coming to Port Royale, being captured by a pirate, falling in love, letting him go, and working in a stables for that very man.

The girls stopped in various shops, picking up food and sewing supplies.

"That is quite the story. What estate are you at?"

"Foxton."

"Oh! My brother works there."

"He does? What a coincidence. Does he work in the fields?"

"No, he's the steward. Actually, my mother runs the house as well."

"My goodness, you're Sam's sister!"

"Yes."

"So that means Liza is your mother. Oh my goodness..." Senona broke down laughing.

"What's so funny?"

"I was just telling Liza's own daughter about how terrible her mother is to me."

"My mother is terrible to everyone."

"Everyone?"

"Well, not Brant. She adores Brant, although she definitely expresses her opinion. But even with Sam and me, she's very controlling. I don't know how Sam can stand to stay."

Senona shrugged and changed the subject. "What does your husband do?"

"Blake is a blacksmith. It's a good job, and we manage better than most.

"Here we are, my home."

It was nothing extravagant, but it was clean, which was more than could be said for many of the nearby houses. Inside was a large room full of sewing supplies.

"You're a seamstress?"

"It helps us live in relative comfort and keeps me busy."

"I admire you. You work and help support your household."

"It's fulfilling. Gives me security, a way to support myself if anything were to happen to Blake. My mother was hard off after my father died; I don't want to be put in the same situation."

Senona looked at Sarah thoughtfully; she had no idea that middle-class families had the same issues as upper class. "I suppose it's the same for everyone. There are always people who want money and respect."

Senona spent the rest of the afternoon with Sarah. They compared life as children from two different classes, which might as well have been two different worlds. They spoke of hopes and dreams for the future, confiding in each other their fears. She found a relief that she hadn't felt in a long time.

Senona even attempted to help Sarah with her sewing.

"You aren't very good at this," said Sarah, laughing.

"No, not at all. You'd think after years of this I'd be okay, but it seems I'm doomed to domestic failure."

"I'm sure that's not true. You must have different skills. All those hours you weren't practicing sewing you had to be doing something."

"I was with my horse."

"All your free time?"

"Every moment I could I was out there with him."

"My goodness. You are a strange girl."

Senona laughed. "Thanks?"

"I don't mean that in a bad way. It's just different."

"I suppose. But I have become quite skilled with horses."

"So you have a means of support, which makes you independent."

"That's always something." Senona put down her sewing and got up. "I really should be going, though. Your mother will have my head if I'm late for dinner."

"By all means. Please come visit me again."

"Of course."

Sarah walked Senona to the door and hugged her. "It's funny; I've only known you for a few short hours but it feels as if it's been forever."

"I'm honored you feel that way. It's nice to have a friend being so far from home."

Senona's ride home was pleasant. She felt happy and free. Being able to talk to another woman was refreshing, to say the least. She couldn't remember any moment in her life before now that she had been able to talk to another female. It was almost sad to realize what she had missed.

Senona arrived back with just enough time to get ready for dinner.

Dinner was quiet. Senona made some conversation with Sam, but it was only to keep things from being completely silent—they didn't need to ruffle Liza's feathers anymore by showing their close friendship.

Senona made a point of helping Julie clear the dishes after supper and then went out to the stables where Sam was already saddling Archie.

"So, how was town?" asked Sam once they were on the road.

"Good."

"You find any horses?"

"Plenty. But the pair I want to get are a bit questionable."

"Why is that?"

"Malnourished and lame."

"You want them?"

"I want to get them out of that place," she answered honestly.

"Senona, we can't just be taking in a couple of horses that are going to need double the care and feed and give nothing back."

"They will give back. It'll just take time."

"Time costs money."

"Brant has the money to spare."

"Doesn't mean he throws out money on useless investments."

"How is this useless?" Senona was growing frustrated with Sam's lack of sympathy.

"There is no guarantee they will amount to anything. You can't be certain they will ever be sound even after we spend a fortune on them."

"Does that matter? If you had seen them, you would see the need to get them out of that place."

"That's the reality of life. You're going to find horses like that everywhere, and we can't buy every one of them. To most people their horses are just a means of money to survive. They have to work those horses to the ground. They can't afford to treat them like pets. They are tools."

Senona's insides filled with sorrow at this brutal reality. She tried to come up with a response but couldn't; she just didn't understand. Instead, she nudged Naldo into a gallop. She didn't know if Sam was following, nor did she care, she just wanted to get away from it all; from the truth she refused to accept.

She arrived at the beach and jumped off Naldo, walking along the crashing surf for a time. Senona kicked at the sand as she attempted to think of a way to help the two horses.

Ten minutes later, Sam came trotting onto the beach.

Senona didn't approach him right away. She needed some time alone to think and process the situation and was thankful to see him dismount and sit on the sand, presumably waiting for when she was ready to talk.

Eventually, Senona made her way over to Sam. "I'm sorry, Sam."

"It's okay. It's not wrong that you care."

"I've been thinking. Even if this is an unpleasant fact, my conscience cannot rest if I leave them in that state. What if I was to buy them and all you'd have to do is pay for their keep?"

"There's still the issue that they are going to need extra care."

"I'll pay for it. Anything a healthy horse would not need I'll pay for."

"That all seems reasonable. If you're willing to put what little money you have left into this, then I won't stop you. And I'll make you a deal. If these horses turn out, then I'll buy them from you. But if they don't, they're your responsibility."

"Thank you!"

"For what? You're the one taking risks."

"For supporting me. For understanding my need to do this."

"It's good to have a little bit of idealism, as long as you realize that the rest of the world doesn't hold to those same beliefs."

"I think I might need a reminder of that every once in a while or I might go broke trying to save everything."

"One woman cannot change the world."

"No, but I can pull my own weight."

"I think the world would be better off if more people pulled their own weight."

Senona laughed. "But then life would be too easy."

"Oh, no! We can't have that, now can we?"

"And Brant would be out of a job."

"Now that would be strange; a responsible Brant," said Sam with a smile.

"I do believe if that happened the world would come to an end."

"He will have to settle down eventually."

"I think he might do this until he dies. He'd have a hard time letting all this go."

Sam nodded. "He is full of surprises, though."

Senona smiled sadly. She missed that man too much. "So, I met your sister today. We had a long visit. She told me about your lives. It was nice."

"Sarah is a gem. I'm glad she married Blake. He's really good for her, and he got her away from Mother."

"How come you don't leave?"

"Someone has to stay."

"Don't you think she has it coming?"

"No. She has her faults, but so does everyone. She's been through a lot with my father dying and then raising us all alone. She didn't always have it easy here. Brant's father gave her a job as the housekeeper, but life wasn't comfortable until Brant made me overseer. Through it all, it's never been easy for my mother, and I'm not about to repay her by leaving her alone."

"I admire you. I could not think of my mother in that way. Just everything she's done wrong comes to mind, never what she's done right."

"Maybe she never really cared for you, or maybe you're just unable to understand her."

Senona nodded and looked thoughtful but then her face went hard. "Or maybe she doesn't deserve understanding."

* * *

Senona rode into town again the next morning. She had a bag of money with her, the majority of what she had left.

At the stables, she found the manager.

"I would like those horses I came to see yesterday."

"Didn't think I'd see you again."

"How much do you want for them?

"Hundred shillings for the pair."

Senona pulled out her bag of money and started counting. She cringed at the lightness of her bag after she had finished. She didn't have much money left, and she only hoped it would get her everything she needed.

Senona waited patiently as the dirty man re-counted to be sure she wasn't ripping him off. She would have been insulted, but realized that this man had to be cautious; Port Royale was not an easy place to live. Many shady, dangerous and untrustworthy people made port here.

"They're all yours," he said upon finishing. The man seemed to be pleased that he had made the sale, and Senona even believed she heard him mutter under his breath something about "worthless nags". Senona nearly smiled, the man was a liar. He would say anything to make a pound or two.

Senona's progress out of the livery was slow. The two geldings were so stiff it nearly made Senona cry. How could this man ever claim they were sound?

"They'll loosen up by the time you get home. They've just been cooped up for a few days."

Senona nodded but knew that was an outright lie, but for once in her life, she decided to take the high road and not argue. The point was that she was getting the horses out. That was good enough.

As she mounted Naldo and slowly walked off, leading the other two horses behind, the man called after her, "Pleasure doing business with you."

She didn't respond, only continued riding and attempted to erase the memory of his face. He disgusted her.

CHAPTER EIGHTEEN

Senona had one of the geldings in cross ties as she spread some disgusting looking paste on his legs. A week of good feeding and brushing had them both looking much better. Their coats were shiny and their eyes were brighter, but they were still deathly thin and lame.

Senona had been taking them out for walks every day, helping build muscle and loosen stiff joints so that the poultice, which she was applying now, would be more effective.

"How's he doing?"

Senona looked up to see Sam standing at the entrance. "As good as can be expected. They're moving a little better, but it's a long road ahead."

"What's that you're doing?" asked Sam, referring to the greenish paste that Senona was slathering on the horse's knees and coronet bands.

"It's a poultice. It helps with the swelling and pain."

"You still have hope for these boys?"

"It'll take some time, but they'll pull through alright. They're much healthier already, and between the poultice and proper rest, they'll do fine. The hardest thing will be getting weight on them."

Sam ran his hands through the glossy bay coat of the gelding. "Do they have names yet?"

"This one is Ahorrado and the other one is Viaje."

"Spanish?"

"Yes."

Senona stood up from kneeling on the dirt floor, led Ahorrado back to his stall, and took out Viaje.

Sam leaned against the wall and watched her work. First she washed the legs down with warm water she had boiled in the kitchen and then began spreading the poultice.

"My Spanish is a little rough, to say the least. What do their names mean?"

"Ahorrado means saved and Viaje means journey."

"It's fitting."

"I like names with a story. These boys have been saved from death and now have a journey through life."

"You were right; they wouldn't have lasted the year."

Senona finished the poultice and settled Viaje back in his stall. She threw some hay to the two geldings and then Sam and Senona headed to the house for dinner.

"I recommend washing up before dinner. You have green goop all over you."

Senona rolled her eyes. "Thank you. I'm sure I look beautiful."

"As always. Don't take too long."

Senona ran up to her room and hurriedly scrubbed herself clean, brushed her hair, and threw on a clean dress. She arrived just in time for dinner.

After dinner, she went back to the stables and gave Viaje and Ahorrado another armful of hay and some grain. Sam was saddling Archie for their evening ride, a ritual that they still hadn't abandoned. The whole ride to the beach was in silence as they enjoyed the peaceful calm. Sam was now used to the gallop through the narrow, winding trail. He managed to keep his seat but looked as if he was on shaking knees when they finished.

Senona lay in the warm sand and sighed. She had worked hard all week and had come to appreciate her evenings even more.

"I'm going to do it," said Sam out of the blue.

"Do what?"

"Court Julie. I cannot allow my mother to control my entire life just because Julie is lower class."

"Good for you! And to tell you the truth, I don't think your mother will have any objections."

"Why is that?"

"I think she's under the impression you're courting me or, at the very least, thinking about it. If she finds out that isn't true and you're courting Julie... well she'll probably throw a good old fashioned ball."

Sam burst out laughing. "You know, I think you're right."

"Of course. I'm always right."

"No, only occasionally."

"Occasionally must happen quite often."

Sam laughed and shook his head but said nothing.

* * *

A couple of days went by and Sam still hadn't asked Julie, having yet to work up the nerve. He was waiting for the right moment, but every time he got her alone, his mother walked in. On Tuesday, an invite to the Johnson's annual ball came.

"You should ask Julie to go with you. It's perfect," insisted Senona as she accompanied Sam back out to the fields after lunch.

"Are you sure? What if she says no?"

"She won't. Trust me. You should have seen the way she was eying the invitations when we were reading them. She's probably never been to anything so extravagant. She'll jump at the chance."

"You're certain?"

"I have never been more certain in my life. Besides, what have you got to lose?"

"My dignity," he grumbled.

* * *

Sam walked into the kitchen on Thursday afternoon, hoping to find Julie without his mother hovering around. He figured if she wasn't in the kitchen, she would flit in sooner or later, and so he put on a kettle and made himself a cup of tea, settling down to wait.

He was about halfway through his cup of tea when Julie burst in. She didn't notice him at first as she searched through cupboards, banging and swearing under her breath. Sam tried not to laugh but couldn't help it and chuckled slightly; she had the mouth of a sailor. Julie turned with a start and looked at Sam in shock.

"Oh! I'm sorry, Sir, I didn't see you there," she apologized, turning a deep shade of red and curtsying.

"It's okay. I shouldn't have been hiding in the shadows. It's just as much my fault as yours."

"Can I get you anything?" she asked timidly.

"No, I have my tea so I'm fine."

"Okay, well then, I best get back to work." She turned to leave, and Sam swore under his breath.

"Actually, Julie, there is something you could do for me."

Julie turned to face him and waited expectantly. "Yes?"

"I was ... um... was wondering... Or sort of hoping... or um—" Sam trailed off nervously.

"Yes?" she prompted again.

"If you would maybe, perhaps, want to go to the ball with me?"

Julie looked stunned and Sam turned red. He knew it had been a bad idea. Maybe this was Senona's idea of a joke.

"If you don't want to that's fine," he quickly added, trying to cover his embarrassment.

"No! No, I would love to... but I have nothing appropriate to wear."

Sam breathed a sigh of relief and smiled. That he could fix. "That's not a problem. Talk to Senona; she is going to see my sister about a dress for herself, you should go with her."

"Oh, thank you!"

Julie turned and walked out of the room, a slight bounce in her step.

* * *

The next day, Senona and Julie rode into town. They were both in need of dresses and had very little time to get them. Senona had spoken with Sarah earlier in the week and she had been generous enough to offer a dress from previous orders that had been canceled. Sarah always had a couple of those lying around and often sold them pre-made. Neither Senona nor Julie had the money or time to have a new dress made, so Sarah said she would modify a couple dresses for them, and then she would sell them when they were done.

When they arrived, Sarah's house was a bustle of activity. All the ladies of middle and upper-class standing needed new dresses and, although they all had their dresses made months ago, they all needed last minute fittings. But it was good business for Sarah.

"Senona, I'll be with you in a minute. I just need to finish this off," said Sarah, sounding slightly stressed.

"Do you want me to help with anything?"

"No! Just sit down and don't touch anything. I've seen you with a needle and thread and I don't need you injuring any customers."

Senona laughed. "I'll just stand back then."

Julie stepped forward. "I can help. I haven't done anything too fancy, but I can do a good stitch and not prick anyone."

Sarah didn't once look up from her work. "Okay. That dress over in the corner needs to be brought in a bit, there are pins and such."

Julie got straight to work, and Senona sat, waiting and wishing she didn't feel so useless. Maybe those sewing lessons she had always tried to escape were important after all.

Finally, Sarah was done.

"Okay. I have three dresses you can fight over. Follow me."

The two girls followed Sarah into the main room of her house where three mannequins were set up. The dresses were gorgeous. Senona had worn dresses much more amazing than these, but somehow she appreciated these ones more. They were even more beautiful, perhaps, because she didn't take expensive clothes for granted anymore. There was a time when she'd ruin a dress running through the fields without a second thought, a dress that would cost Julie a year's wages. Now she considered those clothes a luxury, a luxury she could no longer afford.

Senona stroked one of them, running the fabric between her fingers. It had been so long since she'd had real silk in her fingers. "Sarah, they are beautiful."

"Thank you. I was thinking the black and white one for you. It has a bit of a Spanish style, and it would look beautiful on you."

Senona looked the dress over. "I do like it."

"Go try it on, and Julie and I will pin you up."

Senona, with Sarah's help, slipped the dress on and laced it up. It was a little bit big for Senona's slim build as well as too long, but not by much, so no major adjustments were needed.

"What do you think?" she asked, spinning in a circle.

"It's perfect. Absolutely stunning. Too bad Brant wasn't here to see you."

Senona blushed at Sarah's comment but quickly dismissed it.

"Come on, Julie, your turn. Which dress do you like?"

"Oh, I love both so much; I really can't choose."

Sarah and Senona dragged her to the dresses and made her stand between them while Senona and Sarah held fabric from each of the dresses up to Julie's face.

"I think the blue one," said Senona.

"Yes, I agree The green doesn't look very good with her complexion."

And with that, Julie was dragged away from the dresses and quickly helped into the blue one.

It was a truly beautiful dress; sky blue in color with pure white lace around the sleeves and neckline. It was a simple dress with no extravagant embroidery, but it was elegant.

"You look... rich," said Senona, she had no other word for it.

"No, I think she needs her nose a little higher in the air before she looks rich, but she certainly is beautiful. And the best part is the dress fits you like a glove. It's as if it was made for you."

"Imagine me, Julie O'Conner going to a ball and looking like a princess! Oh, Sarah, I cannot thank you enough."

"Don't. It is my pleasure. Anything to keep my brother happy."

The rest of afternoon, the girls worked on adjustments on all the dresses. Senona worked on hems; there wasn't much she could mess up. She could keep her stitching straight and tight, but anything fancy and she just destroyed it. Even on the hems, there were constant mutterings of foul language due to some self-inflicted pain. Sewing was definitely not her calling.

* * *

The night of the ball loomed just ahead of them. Senona worked all week on Ahorrado and Viaje, hoping they would be ready to pull a carriage.

Already, after only two weeks of exceptional care and work on their joints with the help of some salves, they were doing much better, but it wasn't enough, so Sam hired a coach for the evening.

Senona had gone to town earlier that day and picked up the dresses, carefully wrapped to protect them from the elements. Sarah insisted, multiple times, that she hang them as soon as she got back to avoid wrinkling them.

Liza was sitting the evening out, but Senona and Julie helped each other get dressed and do their hair. Senona spent hours carefully pinning up Julie's blond curls but decided to go simpler for herself with a twist and a clip holding it in place.

When Sam met them at the door, dressed-up and his hair combed neatly back, his jaw nearly dropped. He barely managed to get out, "You look amazing." He spent most of the carriage ride in silence, just getting used to how different Senona and Julie looked.

At the entrance, they were introduced. Julie nearly swooned when she heard them announce: "Samuel Graves and Lady Julie O'Connor."

And then it was Senona's turn. She was used to going to balls without being on anyone's arm, that wasn't what made it so daunting. It was the familiarity. A reminder of the life she had left behind. For a split second, she imagined her mother's voice as she chided her for not dancing or for not looking more attractive, and then, taking a deep breath, prepared to descend into the ballroom as she was announced.

"Lady Senona Montez of Barcelona."

All eyes turned to her. It wasn't every day that Spanish nobility, much less a Montez—a well-known name even in British circles—showed up at the Johnson's annual ball.

Senona was asked to dance almost constantly all night, and she turned very few offers down. However, she was bombarded with questions as to what brought her to Port Royale. With each story she got more and more creative, sometimes even shocking. It was the only way to keep the evening from becoming completely overwhelming.

Sam and Julie danced a lot but spent just as much time visiting and taking advantage of the extravagant refreshment table.

Julie didn't stop smiling all evening; she was living a dream and she was in no hurry for it to end. It was how Senona had expected her first ball to be.

During a slower dance, Sam pulled Julie back onto the dance floor and Senona watched the goings on between her two friends from across the room. Judging by the smile on Sam's face she guessed that he had told Julie of his intentions, and she had responded agreeably. She was glad for her friends, but she could not help but feel a twinge of sadness. It was unlikely she would ever make someone that happy.

CHAPTER NINETEEN

Senona lay in the cool, long grass, sleeping in the shade of a tree in an attempt to escape from the sun. Summer in Port Royale was brutally hot and the fall wasn't much better. At least summer had the storms for relief—if vicious winds and rain could be considered relief.

She had decided to take the day off from exercising the horses and took Naldo out for the day, found an empty field, and just relaxed, as she used to back home.

The past few weeks had been extremely stressful for everyone as Liza was in an especially bad mood due to finding out about Sam's courtship of Julie. Senona had been unfortunate enough to hear Liza's multiple rants directed towards Sam about his bad choices. Often Liza would yell and Julie would hear, then it fell to Senona to convince her that whatever she said was not true. Sam was always too busy taking his mother's abuse to notice the effect it was having on others.

Senona admired Sam for being able to take all that from his mother. She knew that if she were in Sam's place, she would have yelled and screamed right back at her mother and then would have done whatever she could to make her life miserable. But Sam took everything calmly. He always replied quietly and allowed his mother to use him as a verbal punching bag. After a while, Senona couldn't stomach it any longer, and so she found herself falling back onto an old escape: nature.

Its calmness allowed her to sleep peacefully for the first time since Sam and Julie had started courting. Lately, everything reminded her of home that she was having trouble sleeping, either from a restless mind or nightmares.

Naldo wandered over to where Senona was sleeping and blew in her face. She groaned and swatted at him in her sleep which caused him to snort in annoyance, then turn and walk away.

An hour later, Senona finally decided to wake up. Her dark Spanish skin was bronzed even darker by the sun. She sent out a single, long and piercing whistle and was greeted by the sound of Naldo's distant whinny and thundering hooves coming from across the field.

"Hey, hey," she said soothingly as she stroked his neck and face, and then vaulted onto his back in one smooth move. They took off at a gallop. The wind whistled through her hair and ears and then, slowly, she let go of his mane and stretched her arms out on either side. She laughed in excitement as the sheer magnificence of the feeling washed over her. Her heart pounded in her chest and the wind caressed her hair, face, arms, every inch of her body lovingly. If men could fly, she was sure this is what it would feel like. The greatest sense of freedom ever granted to creatures.

When she arrived back at the estate, Julie met her at the gate.

"Sam wants you to go to town and see if there is any news from Brant."

Sam had been sending her every day for the last two weeks to check for news from Brant. The summer storms had died down considerably, and it was only a matter of time now.

"Okay. I'll probably stop in to say hello to Sarah as well, so maybe you should tell Liza I'm not going to be here for dinner."

Julie nodded and ran back to the house.

In town, Senona went first to the harbor master's office but found nothing waiting. She sighed in disappointment. She hated to admit it, but she was looking forward to hearing news; she missed Brant and the possibility of him returning any day now had his teasing smile and twinkling eyes consuming her thoughts.

She found herself wandering the wharf, looking for the *BlackFox*'s familiar mast. She missed the sea but wondered if she could ever love it the way she did the dry and stable land. She and Brant were similar in many ways, but in this one way, they were completely opposite.

"Hey, don't I know ye, lass?"

Senona turned to face a large, mean looking sailor. He was tall and muscled, covered in vicious looking tattoos and scars. His face bore a permanent scowl, and his bald head only seemed to add to the terrifying image.

Senona tried to breathe steadily and keep her nervousness out of her voice. "No, I don't think so."

"I is sure I know ye from somewhere."

"Must be someone else you're thinking of."

Senona continued walking down the dock, and then she saw it; Old Richard's ship docked just off the coast. She knew where the man was from and how he recognized her. He was Richard's first mate. She had to get away from here. She didn't need another run in with Old Richard and his crew. Not when Brant wasn't around to save her.

"No, wait. You're that girl that runs with Foxton."

Senona turned around slowly. "No, I'm sorry, you must be mistaken. I've never even heard of anyone called Foxton."

"Are ye calling me a liar?"

The sailor was getting angry now and Senona began to tremble violently. Richard's crew had a reputation for violence; she needed to get away, but there was nowhere to go, nowhere to get help. Men and woman walked by, ignoring the scene. Senona knew no one would step in and help; it wasn't their business. Living in a place with such questionable characters, they did what was best and stayed out of trouble.

"No, not at all. I just think you are mistaken is all. Now if you'll excuse me, I have to be going."

The man stood there for a moment, thinking, and Senona waited for his response, he was blocking her path.

"Okay," he said finally. "Sorry to be bugging ye."

As he stepped aside for her to pass, Senona heard him mutter how he was sure he'd seen her with Foxton. She took off at a run. She had to get away from him as fast as possible.

Senona was still quite shaken when she arrived at Sarah's. Sarah took one look at her pale face and trembling hands and sat her down with a cup of tea.

"You just sit while I finish dinner."

She didn't pry into what had happened to shake up her friend, only made sure Senona was alright and then went about things normally, something Senona was thankful for.

Blake came in a half hour later, just as Sarah and Senona were setting the table.

"Dinner will be ready in five minutes," Sarah called after him as he went straight to the back to wash up.

Senona had not met Blake, and he proved to be as kind as Sarah made him out to be. He was a big man, clean cut and, aside from his ordinary clothing, could have passed for a gentleman.

"So, Senona, I've heard much about you. How do you like Foxton estate?" Blake spoke with a thick Scottish accent that Senona had to listen to carefully to understand. She was as fluent in English as if she had been born in an English-speaking country, but the accent made things significantly more difficult.

"Well enough," she responded after a brief second to work it all out. "It's certainly different from home, or what used to be home."

"Ye don't consider here home then?"

"No," she said softly. "Right now I have no place that I can truly call home."

"You'll be leaving Port Royale then?" asked Sarah, sounding slightly concerned.

"No, not anytime soon, if ever. Perhaps it will only take time before it begins to feel right. Not everything is instantaneous."

Blake nodded in agreement and Sarah smiled, relieved that her friend had no intentions of leaving. They had only known each other a short time, but in that time, they had become quite close.

"Ay. I know what ye mean. Took me a time to feel at home here."

"Do you know when Brant will be getting back?" asked Sarah.

"No news yet, but it should be soon. Sam has me looking out for news every day."

"Aye, t'will be good to have him back. Though he'll probably head back out soon after."

"Most likely." Senona hadn't really considered the fact that he would be leaving only weeks, maybe days after he made port here. It wasn't a pleasant thought.

"Senona, you sailed with him last season, why don't you do the same for a little while this year? He always makes port here a few times so you wouldn't be gone the whole time," suggested Sarah as she sensed her friend's sudden sadness.

"I never thought of that. That might be nice. I'll talk to him when he gets back."

Blake looked slightly concerned. "Ay, but the *BlackFox* ain't no passenger ship. She is a pirate vessel. No place for a woman. It could be dangerous."

Senona and Sarah burst out laughing, and Blake looked slightly confused.

"Senona came from Spain to here on the *BlackFox* and even took part in a few raids."

Blake frowned. "That ain't safe. I know ye got passage, but to be around during raids and to take part in them... Not safe at all."

Senona smiled. "Not when you've bested Brant a few times while sparring."

Sarah smiled slightly and Blake whistled. "I take it back; you'll be just fine on that pirate ship. There ain't many who can best Brant."

Senona blushed with pride and smiled but could think of no response. She knew not many bested Brant, but she hated the idea that she was somehow more capable than he.

"Senona, would you like to help me clear the table?"

Senona nodded and got up, grabbing her plate and Blake's and put them in the basin. Blake went outside to pump up some water from the well to use for washing.

"Just leave the dishes in the basin. Blake has to heat up the water and then let it cool down a bit before we can wash."

"But that won't take long."

"No, but Blake and I will do the dishes later. He always helps me."

"He seems like a good man."

"He is. He really is. I'm so fortunate to have someone like him."

Senona smiled softly, painfully, as Brant's image came to mind. His mischievous smirk and the teasing twinkle in his eyes; to Senona there was nothing more she'd rather see than that, even if the teasing was at her expense.

"Thank you so much for dinner, Sarah. I should probably be heading back before it gets too dark."

Sarah nodded understandingly. "Of course. And don't worry; Brant will be home soon."

The two girls hugged, and Senona said goodbye to Blake, then mounted Naldo and headed home.

She knew Sarah thought her uncharacteristic paleness today was due to worry about Brant, but who could she tell about the docks? She had never been more terrified in her life. Not even when she had killed men, or run headlong into a pirate raid. She hadn't even been truly frightened when Old Richard had kidnapped her; she had only been afraid of what Brant would think. But today, when she had no means of defense and no one to save her, she had been terrified. She knew there were no chivalrous men hiding in the shadows. No Brant. She had been completely on her own and she hadn't liked the feeling.

She had the whole ride home to silently reflect on the events of the day. She was tempted to not go back and, instead, head straight to the beach but as she thought about it, she realized she didn't want to be alone at all.

It was dark when she arrived at the estate, so she put Naldo in his stall and threw some hay to all the horses.

In the house, she found Sam and Julie sitting in the den by a roaring fire. Why they enjoyed sitting by a fire in this heat Senona did not understand. Nevertheless, she found a chair and curled up in it.

"Any news?" asked Sam.

"No, nothing yet, but Sarah sends her love."

Sam smiled. He actually looked at ease, for the first time since he had started courting Julie. Senona was happy to see her friend like this. She quickly realized the reason was probably due to the uncharacteristic absence of Liza. Where she was normally hovering around, she was strangely... not. The whole atmosphere was different. It wasn't just Sam and Julie's contented and relaxed state. The whole atmosphere was calm. Senona sighed in appreciation.

"This is nice."

"Yes. Liza went to bed immediately after dinner," stated Julie, explaining why it was so calm.

Senona looked to Sam and raised her eyebrow in question. What had occurred to bring this about? Sam just shrugged and smiled slightly. He obviously had something to do with his mother's absence but didn't want Julie to know. They sat together silently for a few hours, just enjoying the peace that was so rare of late. At around eleven, Julie excused herself and went off to bed.

"What happened with Liza?" asked Senona after Julie was out of ear shot.

"What?" responded Sam, innocently.

"You know what I'm talking about. Why is she hiding?"

Sam smiled slightly. "I stood up to her." He didn't look completely sure of himself, and Senona wondered if maybe he was feeling a little guilty.

Senona stared at him in shock. "You did what?" She had always thought he was just going to take the abuse.

"She got after me again before dinner. This time she didn't just attack me, she went after Julie. I couldn't stand it, so I stood up to her."

"My, my, Samuel, I'm proud of you. A knight in shining armor; who would have guessed?"

Sam blushed. "Don't let Julie know."

"Of course not."

They sat in silence for a time and then Senona broke it. "How long will Brant stay when he gets here?"

"Not long. Long enough to be sure everything is in order, any repairs that are needed are done, and to stock up."

Senona sighed. "Never very long."

"He'll be here soon and he comes back often. Don't worry."

Senona forced a smile; it seemed everyone was telling her not to worry lately. Could that mean there was something to worry about? "I'm not worried. I'm actually considering joining the crew for a time."

"An interesting thought, but I'm off to bed now."

"Good night, Sam."

Senona sat alone for about ten more minutes, and then she went to bed. Tomorrow was another day.

* * *

The next morning was gray and dreary. Fog settled in over the countryside, and yet the air was warm. Senona woke up to see nothing but white out the window.

Most people would have immediately felt a heaviness in their spirit, though they may not have consciously noticed it, but Senona felt suddenly awake and happy. Free. She rushed to the balcony and stood, leaning out against the rail and breathing in the air. The fog carried with it a salty smell from the nearby sea and for a moment, Senona felt as free as she had on the *BlackFox*.

The early morning fog and stillness that would take over the ship was always her favorite time of day. The fog was like a giant eraser, blotting out memories of her old life, hiding thoughts of what was to come. In the fog there was only the present. And then the sun would rise higher and dispel the fog and all the complications of life would come pouring back. But that short time of utter peace and serenity was worth it all.

This fog didn't dispel in a couple of hours. It lasted all throughout the morning as Senona cleaned the stables and worked with the horses. And all morning she was at ease, at peace with her thoughts for the first time in weeks.

"Senona!" called out Sam as he walked into the stable.

"In here!" she called from Viaje's stall.

Sam walked over and leaned on the stall door. "Do you feel comfortable going to town?"

"You want me to check for news from Brant?"

"Yes. Will you be home for dinner?"

"I should be. But if I'm late, it wouldn't be the first time."

Sam laughed. "I'll just tell mother it's my fault."

Senona rose to get out of the stall and Sam moved away. "I have some paperwork to do. I'll see you later."

Senona went about grooming and tacking Naldo. It wasn't often she used full tack, but when going to town, she did. Better to fit into a strange place than stand out, at least no more than she already did.

Senona met no one on the road to town. Everything was deserted. Occasionally she thought she heard a cart or carriage, but it always turned out to be her imagination. Naldo's ears constantly flicked back and forth as he listened to things that Senona's less sensitive ears couldn't pick up.

In town it was like entering a whole other world. The street lamps were lit and the usual bustle of activity went on. Senona tied Naldo to a post and went to the harbor master.

"Did anything come in heading to Foxton Estate?"

"Yep. I've been keeping an eye out for ye. Someone been here every day, so I figured ye been expecting something. I got it right here." The old grizzled man pulled out a letter and handed it to Senona. She glanced at it and was surprised to see it was addressed to her and not Sam, but it was definitely from Brant.

"Thank you," she said and walked out.

She sat on the wharf and slowly read the letter. There wasn't much, just a few instructions and messages for Sam. Nothing personal. It disappointed Senona slightly but the purpose of the letter overruled that feeling.

Brant was coming home.

CHAPTER TWENTY

Senona couldn't help but smile as she rode Naldo through town towards the docks. The *BlackFox* was docking today, which meant Brant was back and, along with him, a great many possibilities. At the docks, she dismounted and tied Naldo as well as Phantom and Jester, who she had ponied along, to a hitching post. She walked down the docks in hopes of catching a glimpse of the ship coming into port.

At first Brant's request for her to meet him with two horses had confused her, but she had dismissed it quickly, figuring that perhaps Matt, the quartermaster and Senona's good friend, would be joining them at the estate for a few days.

She didn't know when the *BlackFox* would be getting in, only that they were due in today. All she could do was wait and keep an eye on the horizon, but it wasn't hard to spot as it made its way into the harbor at around noon. Senona watched its steady progress with growing excitement. As it drew closer, she saw Brant standing on the deck giving orders to the sailors, who were running around getting the ship in its place at the docks. She smiled; Brant looked incredibly handsome when he was in his element. She watched him, smiling at the thought that she belonged to him. He had returned from London, and she would have him back.

A tall, beautiful blond woman made her way across the deck towards Brant. What was she doing there? She knew who the woman was, but it didn't seem possible. It didn't seem real. But the pain in her chest, a weight pushing down, clenching, left her gasping for air and the threatening tears let her know just how real it was.

Brant looked at the woman, and Senona imagined he smiled, but she couldn't know for sure. She gritted her teeth as she watched Brant put his arm possessively around the woman's waist and led her across the deck towards the lowered ramp. Senona could remember a time not so long ago when she had been the woman Brant's arm was around.

The ship docked, and it was close enough that she could now clearly see the affectionate smile on Brant directed to the other woman that she had only imagined was there seconds earlier.

"Senona!" exclaimed Brant happily as he caught sight of her waiting with the horses. His smile broadened from one of affection to one of pure joy. Senona's heart skipped a beat, but she kept her face calm. How could she show her happiness when the man she loved had his arm around another woman?

"Brant," she replied with a genuine smile, but when she glanced at the woman at his side, it became forced and cold. "I'm sorry, if I had known there was a lady coming I would have brought the carriage. I was under the impression that Matt would be joining us." Her words were cold and overly formal, not like a friend speaking to a friend, but of an employee to her employer.

"I asked you to bring Jester and Phantom, why would you think to bring the carriage?" Brant's trademark teasing grin and mischievous twinkle in his eyes took over his face.

The familiar action of Brant's infuriated Senona. He thought he could just come waltzing back with some other woman and pretend nothing had changed. It made her heart ache but she knew it was her own fault. She had been the one to send him away and that very fact made her even angrier. She had been so confident, perhaps overly confident, that Brant was more loyal than this.

"I just assumed the lady would prefer something more protected from the weather," she retorted, but immediately regretted it. She was furious with Brant, but this woman didn't deserve this. She was an innocent bystander caught in the middle of a messy battle.

Senona was surprised to see the blond woman didn't even blush or show any sign of anger. Instead, she smiled kindly.

"Thank you for thinking of me, Senona, was it? But after my time on the *BlackFox,* the last thing I have on my mind is the effects of the weather on my complexion."

Senona smiled slightly. "Yes, that's my name."

"Montez, right? I'm Catherine Marshall."

Senona's face grew dark. "In a past life, yes. That name means nothing to me now."

"Your parents are concerned about you."

"How would a British socialite know how my parents feel? Don't take this the wrong way, but you don't know anything about my life, nor is it your business."

"It becomes my business when you threaten Brant's livelihood."

"Threaten? I do no such thing."

"Oh, really? That's why there are reports of you being seen aboard his ship? If your parents find out and if they raise a fuss about it, I can guarantee Brant will lose his letter of Marque and be left to sway in the breeze."

"I hate to interrupt, ladies, but perhaps we should be on our way," Brant interjected, taking Catherine's hand and assisting her as she mounted Phantom.

Brant deftly mounted Jester and the three headed towards the estate that Senona was now terrified to think would never be her home, not with Catherine invading and carrying horrible accusations along with her.

Catherine was not about to let things go. She would fight to the end. "So tell me, do you plan on enjoying Brant's hospitality much longer?"

"Brant can ask me to leave, or turn me in, anytime he chooses, and I would never hold it against him," replied Senona, reading into the hidden accusation.

"I would never do that. Really, Catherine, that is enough. Senona is no threat to me, and I am pleased that I could help her. I would appreciate it if you ladies would let things well enough be and try to be friends," said Brant, attempting to referee the two women.

Senona scoffed. "Friends? Of course."

"I would quite enjoy being your friend, Senona. I was just concerned about Brant."

"He can look after himself."

"I have no doubt about that. But I am curious, Senona, why did you leave a life of comfort to come here and work, having a slim-to-none chance of marrying to your status and struggling through the rest of your life?"

The concept was obviously something Catherine could not even begin to comprehend, and yet she was here with a privateer.

"I didn't leave such a grand life," said Senona firmly. "I left a prison. It is a life that is said to be comfortable and secure, but no one talks about the duties to image, or how everything revolves around money and status, around what everyone thinks of you and not who you truly are! There is no such thing as individuality or freedom."

"But what could this life possibly offer that is better?"

"Hard work and money of my own. Money that means freedom, not chains. A hope of finding love instead of an arranged marriage. I don't have to live up to any preconceived notion of who I should be. An honest life." Her voice was filled with anger and conviction. It was the first time she really got to voice her reasons for leaving, her opinions of society, to someone that actually believed it was the better way of life.

"You have a compelling argument. It makes me wonder if you're right, or merely blind."

Brant chuckled in amusement. "Two different views. I wonder which one is correct."

"Brant, you were offered the same life as me, but you followed your heart. I believe the majority is in my favor." Senona smiled, her eyes holding a malicious glint in them.

Brant shrugged. "For me and you. But I think for different people there are different truths. Not every right is right and not every wrong is wrong."

Senona nodded her consent grudgingly. He was playing it safe, but Catherine rode in silence, a smile plastered on her face, and somehow Senona knew she had achieved her goal. She had proven to the impostor that Brant belonged with people like him, not with a woman who could never understand him.

* * *

"James!" Senona exclaimed as she ran out of the paddock to the fifteen-year-old boy.

He had been instructed to take a carriage with the luggage to the estate and was just now arriving, a few hours after Catherine and Brant.

James turned to her and his face broke out into a grin. He had grown tall over the summer, taller than Senona, and he easily wrapped her in a hug.

"James, my friend. You never told me you had this to come home to," came a voice from behind James.

Senona peered over his shoulder to see another boy about the same age. He was a bit taller and less muscled than James but had a handsome face and with blond hair like Catherine's, except cut short. His eyes were a deep blue that Senona easily lost herself in.

James released Senona from the embrace and turned to face the boy. "Senona, this is Johnny Marshall. Johnny, Senona Montez."

Johnny bowed low and swept off an invisible hat. "My lady."

Senona giggled at Johnny's mocking antics and knew instantly that she would like this light-hearted boy. "It's nice to meet you, Johnny. I assume you're Catherine's brother."

"The one and only. And what's your story, love?"

James rolled his eyes at Johnny's outrageous flirting and Senona laughed. "It's much too long and complicated to get into right now, so how about we just get to know each other the way we are now instead of based on who we were."

Johnny smiled. "An admirable idea. What is there to do around here?"

"Let's saddle up the horses. We'll show you around and you can decide for yourself what trouble to get into."

"Trouble? I don't know where you would get that idea from."

* * *

Catherine watched from the balcony as Senona and the two boys rode out. They were laughing and having fun while she wandered around the house like a proper lady.

The conversation from the ride here kept playing over and over in her mind and was beginning to make her uneasy. Why, she didn't know. Perhaps it had been Senona, the way she so clearly disdained the life of the privileged and how she was so sure she and Brant were in the right. Yet, Catherine felt strongly that there were sacrifices to make for her comfortable life. You don't slap privilege in the face. Yes, that had to be it, the reason for the uncertainty that Senona had planted in her heart, there was no other explanation for the uneasiness she felt.

Brant came up behind her and wrapped his arms around her stomach resting his chin on the top of her head. "Hello, darling," he said softly in his strong, rich voice.

Catherine smiled and leaned into him.

"How do you like your new home?"

"It's beautiful, Brant. So large. More than I ever thought it would be."

"Then you don't regret coming here?" His voice was worried and Catherine felt comforted by his concern.

"Absolutely not. I just don't know how you could ever leave this place."

Brant sighed. "This may be my house, but it is not my home; at least not right now."

"But someday, Brant. Someday this will be your home. I'll just have to wait for that day."

Catherine could see the slight cringe on Brant's face over the optimism she expressed. She knew that he wanted nothing more than to make her happy, but sometimes he made her sad without even trying. She wished she could change him, to turn him into the man she wanted him to be, but she knew what she was getting into when she agreed to marry him. He wasn't ready to change his life for her, but someday he would settle down, and all the years of pain would be worthwhile.

The rest of the afternoon Catherine spent wandering around the grounds while Brant went out to the fields to see the state of things and to talk to Sam. Catherine found a book in Brant's large library and settled down on the lawn to wait for him to come back. An hour before dinner, Catherine heard the unmistakable sound of laughter and thundering hooves, and then Senona and Brant came galloping into the yard at top speed. Senona looked positively barbaric with her long hair whipping out behind her, a leg on either side, her skirts flapping about and no saddle. She came in only a length ahead of Brant, who was in hot pursuit. When he came to a stop, Catherine walked over. It hurt her to see his eyes twinkling, so alive. Senona had given him that, not her. She felt threatened by the beautiful, enigmatic woman that seemed so similar to the man that she loved. Perhaps that was why she had attacked Senona with accusations when they had first met. She was scared. She was scared of what Senona was.

A few moments later, Johnny and James rode up at a much safer pace. Brant and Senona had already dismounted and had briefly acknowledged Catherine's presence but continued to talk animatedly together. The boys didn't even glance at her before heading off to the stables. Catherine, who had no wish to be in a dirty stable, sat back down on the lawn with her book.

"Senona, that was amazing! We never got to ride horses like that before," exclaimed Johnny excitedly.

Senona laughed. "I'm glad you enjoyed it. There is something thrilling about reckless abandon, is there not?"

James and Johnny walked on either side of her, filling her in on their escapades. Senona seemed to have all the right reactions for the boys. Catherine could feel jealousy rearing its ugly head. Why couldn't she be like that for her younger brother, or make James like her? She wondered if perhaps Senona was the reason for James' dislike of her, and now Johnny seemed to be enchanted by her after only knowing her for a few hours. A scowl marred Catherine's perfect features as Brant joined her. She couldn't help but think that Senona was a threat.

"Why so unhappy, love?" he asked as he offered his hand to help her to her feet.

Senona's look of displeasure, however brief, at the physical contact between Brant and Catherine did not go unnoticed, and it gave her a momentary feeling of triumph.

"The sun was in my eyes was all," she lied cheerfully.

The five of them made a happy group as they entered the house. Catherine forced herself to appear as such, not wanting to show Senona any weakness. But with Brant's attention riveted on Senona, it was no easy task. She couldn't help but wonder if she had made a huge mistake in coming here.

Johnny, on the other hand, appeared to be having the time of his life. Senona seemed to appreciate his disdain for all things proper and even had a story or two of her own to tell. Just the fact that she was a woman that had been in raids put her as high in his books as Brant, and that was quite something.

James was the happiest he'd been since Brant had told him about courting Catherine. It was apparent he had missed life at sea and this estate, but also Senona and Catherine's obvious unhappiness, no matter how much she tried to hide it, over Senona's presence, made James even happier.

Catherine wasn't sure whether or not to be happy over Brant's ignorance of the tension between everyone. She worried a storm was brewing, though, and she was the only one that could sense it coming.

CHAPTER TWENTY-ONE

Weeks had passed, and Brant still showed no sign of planning to leave, especially now that Catherine was planning their second engagement ball, this one for the plantation owners on the island.

Brant paid for Catherine, Senona, and Julie to get new dresses for the ball, and Sarah seemed to take much joy in the visits with the three women.

On the day of the ball, the day they took the gowns home, Sarah pulled her aside and hugged her. "I know how torturous this must be for you. It's hard enough that Brant has someone else, but to see it all the time... I feel for you."

Tears streamed down Senona's face as weeks of pent up emotions were set free.

Finally, Senona stopped crying. "I shouldn't keep them waiting. I'll be fine."

Sarah gave her one final hug and Senona joined Julie and Catherine in the carriage. Julie was babbling in excitement and, even though it was grating on Senona's frayed nerves, it kept her from having to make conversation with Catherine.

At the estate Julie took Senona's dress up to her room while Senona went in search of James and Johnny. She needed some sort of distraction, anything to take her mind off of the man she loved. Instead of finding sanctuary she found the very source of her pain.

"Running off somewhere?" asked Brant.

"Just looking for the boys."

"Under lock and key," he laughed. "Catherine and Liza won't let them out of their sight."

Senona smiled, determined to make the conversation less awkward. "So I don't suppose she would appreciate it if I stole the groom-to-be away for an afternoon ride?"

Brant's eyes twinkled. "Only hours before the party? I highly doubt it."

"What a shame. I've grown accustomed to having company." Having seen an opportunity to get Brant alone, and perhaps make him realize the mistake he was making, was too great a temptation to pass up.

Brant smiled and looked thoughtful. "How about I join you?"

"Won't Catherine be upset that you're not around to help?"

"She's been trying to get rid of me all day."

Senona silently rejoiced in her triumph. "Then hurry and saddle up. I'm not going to wait around for you."

Brant's eyes twinkled as they playfully ran to the stables. Their behavior was juvenile, and yet it came so easily when they were together.

They raced through open fields on horseback, and when the horses could run no longer, they stopped and let them free to graze. Senona and Brant lay in the long grass and let the warm afternoon breeze wash over them, relieving them, if only for a moment, from the sweltering winter heat.

"You know, Senona, I've missed you," said Brant suddenly.

Senona rolled over onto her stomach to look at Brant in surprise. She knew he had missed her, but she had never expected him to be so frank about it. "Oh really? You're just realizing this now?"

"Well, it's just that in England I had to behave; courting Catherine I had to be cautious not to scare her and dealing with James misbehaving. With you, I have no worries. There's nothing holding me back. It's nice."

Senona smiled softly. Could it be so simple? Was he having doubts already? "I've missed you too. Sam is a good friend, but it's just not the same. And now he's with Julie..." she trailed off. "But if you had to be so cautious around Catherine, why are you going to marry her?"

Brant looked taken aback. "Because I... Well... She proposed to me."

It was Senona's turn to be surprised, but she covered it well and kept working at Brant's doubt, chipping away inch by inch at his protective shell until he was open to a final attack. "You never answered my question. Why?"

Brant looked off into the distance as he thought of the answer. "I really don't know. When you really think about it, it doesn't really make sense. I love her, but we're so different. It makes me wonder if love is enough."

Senona's heart seemed to grow light, and she wanted to sing, or jump, or dance, or spin, anything to express her joy. "You know we had something good. We could be ourselves and we loved each other for it," she said softly, timidly, desperately hoping for a good response. Instead she found confusion in his eyes.

"But you didn't want it anymore."

"I never stopped loving you, but I saw that you were still struggling with what had happened with Catherine. I had to let you go so that you could figure things out or you would have never truly been mine."

Senona waited in fear and hope for Brant's response. All her cards were on the table, and she could only hope she had a better hand than Catherine.

Brant said nothing, only moved closer to Senona and put his arm around her, drawing her close. She rested her head on his shoulder.

"You are a strange girl." That was all he said, but he continued to hold her, and it assured her that his reaction was the one that she had wanted.

They sat there for a time, and then Brant gently nudged her up. "We best be getting back. We have an engagement ball to attend."

Senona mounted Naldo and rode back with Brant, but the ride was silent. Senona didn't know what he had meant. Could he possibly be thinking of going through with the marriage? Even after they knew where they stood?

As they untacked the horses, Senona finally asked the question, "Are you really planning on staying with her?"

Brant looked at Senona, his eyes were full of sorrow. It was a strange expression for him when she was so used to his light-heartedness.

"I have no choice. It's too late now."

Senona stared at him incredulously. "Too late? Are you already married? No! It's not too late. Not yet." Her voice held a hint of desperation. He was hers. He only needed the last shove to make him realize that. He had to realize that he belonged to her, he had to.

"No, I owe her. I can't send her back in shame."

Brant left the stables before Senona could get another word in.

Catherine would ruin him; turn him into someone he wasn't. It made Senona seethe with anger and sudden hatred towards her. Before she had felt bad for Catherine, thought she was just stuck in the middle. Now Senona saw that it was truly her that had been stuck in the middle and Catherine had known what she was doing all along. But it wasn't over yet. Not until he said "I do".

* * *

Senona watched smugly as Brant and Catherine greeted their guests. It amused her that he could put on such a show. Once upon a time, he had done all he could to leave this life behind, and he'd done a good job of it. Now he had digressed back into it without even realizing, and Catherine was holding him there. Senona knew she was his only escape from this prison, and he knew it too; she just had to make him realize how miserable he was.

Senona made her way across the room to Sarah and Blake.

"Senona, you look beautiful!" exclaimed Sarah upon seeing her in the red and black dress she wore and her straight hair that hung freely down her back.

"Thank you. It's all your handiwork, though, so you shouldn't be surprised."

"No one else could look quite like you do. The dress was made for you."

Senona blushed in pleasure.

"Aye, lass, you look very bonny. Would you do me the pleasure of this dance?" asked Blake.

"If your bonny wife can spare you."

"Of course. Go have some fun."

Blake led Senona onto the dance floor for a lively waltz. He was a remarkably good dancer for a blacksmith, and Senona couldn't help but wonder where he had learned to dance so well. At the end of the song, Blake bowed and Sam deftly cut in. He had no chance of really talking to her since he had started courting Julie.

"How're you holding up?"

Senona laughed. "Is that the first thing you're going to ask? I'm doing just fine."

"Even though your plan backfired?"

"I'm not so certain it did."

"In case you haven't noticed, we're dancing at Brant and Catherine's engagement ball, not yours. What makes you think it hasn't?"

"I just think it's taking a little longer than expected."

Sam looked a little concerned. "But what if it isn't? What if it's over?"

Senona got quiet. Despair took over and she answered softly, desperately, "It will work."

As she spoke, the dance came to an end, and Sam led her off the dance floor. He gave his friend one last sad look before leaving her to search for Julie.

The doubt Sam had planted in her haunted Senona. She tripped on the dance floor continuously and she listened absentmindedly when people tried to make conversation with her. And then Brant walked over to her, the focus of all her thoughts, and he rescued her like he had so many times before. He pulled her out of the crowd for a slow dance.

"Senona, are you okay?"

"No, not really. I don't belong in all of this." She wanted to tell him the truth, but couldn't. He knew what was bothering her, he'd be stupid not to, but she wasn't going to let him in again. Not after he turned her down because of some sense of duty towards Catherine. It was madness.

"Well, neither do I." Brant paused for a moment, and a smile slowly crept onto his face. "Do you want to have some fun?"

Senona looked at him questioningly. "I'm always up for fun. What do you have in mind?"

"A shock."

"What kind of shock?"

"You'll see."

He led her off the dance floor, whispered for her to wait there and walked over to the band. Senona recognized that they were nearly done the number and was curious to see what Brant had in mind that involved the band. A dance, that much was certain.

She didn't have to wait long. The band struck up some slow, sultry Spanish music that was led by a guitar. Senona immediately recognized it as the Fandango, a young Spanish dance and one she knew well. The dance floor began to clear when no one else recognized the music and Senona realized what Brant had in mind. She nearly burst out laughing as she imagined the whispers that would go around. And Catherine... Catherine would be furious.

Brant didn't move towards her, only bowed in her general direction and raised an eyebrow in a silent dare. It was more than Senona could refuse, and so it began. The dance was one of courtship and, although they never touched, the sensuality and heat were apparent. Their gazes held passion that screamed of unseen touches and desires—Senona reveled in it. Every clap of her hands. Every stamp of her feet. Every swirl of her skirt shouted out her triumph to Catherine. And then, all too soon, the dance was over. The passion dissipated, and

Senona left the dance floor to cool her head in the garden. She had not noticed Catherine angrily exit to the garden during the dance or she might have avoided it.

"Why?" was all she asked, but it was enough to get Senona to turn around and face her. "Why do you hate me so? I ask only to be free to love Brant. But you insist on planting doubt in my mind and embarrassing me at my own ball."

"I don't hate you… I'm just trying to win," was Senona's feeble excuse. She saw the look of agony in Catherine's eyes, and suddenly her cause seemed juvenile.

"Well, you've won. It's apparent who Brant loves, and I don't want to have to fight for it."

Catherine was a defeated woman, and it was in her voice. All Senona could do was stand there in shock as she walked back into the house. Brant, who was just walking into the garden, caught her arm as she tried to rush past him and she stopped, looking at him sadly. There was no fight in her, only brokenness.

"Go, be with her." It was all she said before Brant let go of her arm in shock.

"What?"

"I know you love her. I'll go back to England and get out of your way. I'm done making a fool of myself."

"No, I don't. I love *you*. Never, ever forget or doubt that."

"You sometimes make it very hard to believe that, Brant." Tears flowed freely down her cheeks.

"I'm a fool of a pirate who acts before he thinks, but never, ever doubt that I love you. If I make you think differently, fight it. Make me realize the mistake I'm making. Please don't give up on me." He drew her into an embrace and then gently kissed her forehead. "I love you, Catherine Marshall. Only you."

Senona stood in the shadows as Brant's profession of love washed over her, hitting her like a brick wall. She knew she had lost and now it was time to let them live their lives out in peace. She softly made her way through the ballroom towards Sam. She had no one else to turn to.

"Sam, I need to leave."

Sam looked at her, shock on his face. "Right now is hardly the time to talk about this."

"I know, and I'm sorry, but I need to leave."

"Don't leave like this. Tell Brant. You know he won't stop you. He'll help you make the proper arrangements."

"I can't face him right now, and the last thing I want is more help from him. He's given me enough. Please, Sam, I need your help. You're the only one I can turn to right now."

Sam sighed. "All right. I know someone who owes me a favor. He'll take you and Naldo for cheap, but you'll have work for your berth on his crew, and he'll be taking you back to Spain."

Senona was torn, but it only lasted mere seconds before she made her decision. If he wasn't going to allow her to keep running, then so be it. "Where can I find this captain?"

"At the docks. His name is Gaspar Santiago, a Spanish pirate. You're going to have to be careful. He allows women on board, but he will ask for... things. Don't be afraid to say no. I know you can defend yourself."

"Is he trustworthy?"

"As trustworthy as any pirate. He's no Brant. He's dangerous, not saying Brant isn't, but you're going to have to be strong. Don't let him take advantage of you."

"Thank you, I appreciate everything you've done for me. You've been there for me whenever I needed you in these past few months and that means a lot."

Sam smiled gently, but it was a sad smile. "You better leave before I change my mind and tell Brant."

Senona laughed and tears rolled down her face as she hugged Sam.

"I thought you wanted to remain inconspicuous," he whispered as he returned the hug.

"I have to say goodbye properly. I'll write. Don't forget to look after the horses for me. And please, please keep James and Johnny out of trouble. They're good boys."

"You know I will."

Sam had tears in his eyes now as he gave Senona one last squeeze and let her go. She turned around and, without looking back, left the room full of celebrating people behind.

She went to her room and threw clothes in a bag, slowly slipped out of her dress, gently laying it on her bed to leave behind and then changed into her trousers, shirt, and high boots. She strapped on her cutlass and looked in the mirror. She looked different from the last time she had run away. Older. Braver. More dangerous.

She was about to walk out when she changed her mind about the dress and carefully folded it and put it in her bag. All the work Sarah had put into it; she couldn't leave it behind.

She silently snuck out the servant's entrance in the back and made her way to the stables. Working quickly, she threw her brushes and halter in a second bag and saddled Naldo in silence until a voice she knew well spoke her name.

"James, go back to the party."

"You're leaving, aren't you?" His voice pleaded with her to deny it, and it broke her heart that she couldn't.

"Yes. It's time."

Johnny stepped forward. "It's because of Catherine." His voice was softly accusing.

Senona considered lying, but the sad eyes of the two boys who had come to be such good friends made it impossible. "That's part of it."

"She ruins everything. Take us with you," grumbled James.

"I can't do that. You know Brant would never forgive me."

"You ran away. Why can't we?" Johnny pushed insistently.

"It was a different situation. You have Sam and Brant who will stand up for you."

James made a face as if he had just taken a large bite of something rotten. "How do you expect to get passage?"

"I'll work for my keep and somehow pay for Naldo's."

Johnny took his hand out from behind his back and held out a heavy looking moneybag. "Sam says this is his end of the deal. Viaje and Ahorrado are doing well."

Senona smiled. She had forgotten about the deal, but now it was a lifesaver. She hugged the boys and kissed them on the cheeks. When she had said goodbye, she mounted Naldo and quickly disappeared into the inky black night, not once looking back for fear that she wouldn't be able to leave.

The boys stood side by side in the doorway for a time, just looking at where Senona had disappeared.

"Well, there goes the sanity around here," muttered Johnny.

"Brant is going to be furious when he finds out," was all James said before the boys headed back to the party.

CHAPTER TWENTY-TWO

"She went where? With who?" burst out Brant angrily. Sam stood in the doorway of Brant's study calmly taking Brant's angry explosion.

"She went back to Spain. I sent her to get passage with Gaspar Santiago."

Brant shook with rage at Sam's explanation. "Gaspar Santiago is a pig and a dangerous man. What were you thinking, Samuel?"

"I was thinking about how desperate she was to get away from you, and you and I know that she is perfectly capable of protecting herself. What could you possibly have done to make her willing to run back home?"

Brant's breathing slowed and his anger slowly simmered down. "Go find James and Johnny. Send them here," he said, his voice flat and emotionless.

Sam nodded and left the room.

As soon as he was alone, Brant dropped his head into his hands and moaned. "What did I do? You know I can't live without you."

Brant carefully composed a letter that would be sent to the *BlackFox* instructing Matt to be ready to set sail by early next week, mid-week at the latest. James and Johnny would deliver it, and by next week, he would be on his way to find Senona. He couldn't let her go. Not like this. Not yet.

* * *

Senona deftly climbed up the rigging of the *Vengador*, Captain Santiago's ship, and helped a Spanish boy, close to her age, tie down a sail. They had been sailing for a week, and although a few sailors had tried to force themselves on her, she had calmly fought for her honor and quickly earned the respect of the entire crew. Her superior skills with a cutlass and her ability and willingness to work as hard as any man on the crew made her quite the novelty for the captain. Every night he would extend an invitation for her to dine with him, but she always refused; she didn't want to be set apart as special in any way. She had enough attention drawn to her as it was.

There were a few younger sailors who had been drawn in by delusions of grandeur (and had been sorely disappointed). They stuck close by Senona, watching her back, but none of them had the closeness Senona had felt with Sam or even Matt.

She cringed slightly at the thought of Sam and Sarah; she could only imagine how upset Sarah had been that she had left without even saying goodbye. Once she was home, she would write a long and lengthy explanation to everyone she had left behind. She owed them that much at the very least.

Senona shook off the thoughts of Port Royale and concentrated on the job at hand. Far below, Captain Santiago was yelling at a sailor that had made a mistake. It made her smile to hear the smooth, rolling words of her native language all around her. She hadn't really realized how much she had missed it until now.

"Senona! Stop daydreaming!" exclaimed the sailor she was working with as a burst of strong wind nearly toppled her from her precarious perch. She caught herself just in time and started laughing to help counteract the fear the made her heart pound wildly. It was a long way down, and if she had fallen, it would not have been a pleasant end.

"Did I scare you, Chale?"

"You're a good sailor, Senona, but you daydream too much. It's going to get you killed."

Senona laughed again, carefree. "Well you'll just have to look out for me then, won't you?"

Chale relaxed and smiled. Job done, the two of them climbed down to the main deck.

"I'm going to check on Naldo. If the captain looks for me—"

"I'll cover," finished Chale.

Senona smiled and waved her hand in thanks as she walked off.

This voyage was taking a much greater toll on Naldo than the last one. He was cooped up in the stall as Captain Santiago would not allow her to take him out to stretch his legs. It was always dark, and Senona was beginning to feel guilty about subjecting him to this, but she snuck away as often as she could. Chale was usually willing to cover for her.

Out of all her friends on the ship, she was closest with Chale. They watched each other's backs and did all their work together. They were "mates." Her first night on the ship she had challenged a man to a duel and, without even knowing her or if she could fight, Chale had offered to be her second. Ever since then they had been inseparable, but he was no Sam. No Matt. No James or Johnny. She would walk off this ship thankful for his friendship but more than willing to leave it all behind.

Senona spent a few minutes making sure Naldo had fresh water, a precious commodity on long voyages, and brushed him, moving quickly. Before the captain noticed she was missing, she ran up on deck.

They spent the afternoon repairing sails, though Senona was still painfully bad at it, so she would entertain the men by telling stories while they worked.

The day moved torturously slow, and Senona was beginning to wish they would come across a ship. A raid would be just the thing to add excitement to the day, but there would be no such luck, and she found herself crawling into her uncomfortable hammock that night feeling exhausted, sore, and entirely unsatisfied with the day. Senona knew she needed her cut from a few raids for added security when they reached Barcelona, and so she fell asleep hoping the next day would bring more profit but that was not to be so. It was as if Captain Santiago was avoiding common routes. In the week they had been at sea, they had not come across one sail, which was highly unusual for a pirate ship. Senona was beginning to feel disheartened and so she approached the captain.

"Sir, why is it that we haven't had even a single raid yet?"

Gaspar Santiago looked at her and burst out laughing. Senona was well aware that she amused the captain, it wasn't the first time she had surprised him.

"I'm waiting," was all he said.

A look a disappointment crossed Senona's features. "For what?"

"For the crew. They need to be ready, they need to want it bad enough. It helps guarantee a victory."

"But no ships—"

"When I feel the men are ready I'll change my course. Now get back to work, you're far too curious for your own good."

Senona smiled. "I've been told that more than a few times; it hasn't changed a thing."

With a wave of her hand, she sauntered off to join Chale in the crow's nest.

* * *

Senona woke up the next morning to shouts and running feet. She heard the thunder all around that could only be the crew rolling out the heavy cannons. As it dawned on her still sleepy mind what that meant, she jumped out of her hammock eagerly, her heart pounding in excitement. She ran up on deck in search of Chale, who was running up the colors.

"Chale, I need your help!" she shouted over the noisy activity.

He looked at her and nodded. "Almost done."

He got the flag raised and together they ran below deck to strap Naldo up.

"Here, hook this on the other side and then we'll hoist him up," instructed Senona, as she passed two thick canvas straps, part of a huge harness, under Naldo's belly. There were a few more straps to help secure him, and then he was quite literally hoisted up off the floor.

"Why...do... we... have...to...do...this?" Chale asked between breaths as the two of them struggled to lift the 800-pound animal.

"So he doesn't tear the ship apart when the cannons go off," she replied breathlessly after they had finished.

The two of them headed back on deck just as they started shooting off cannons. The deafening din made her want to cover her ears. She had forgotten how loud it was.

They waited impatiently at the ropes as part of the boarding party, and only hoped that the cannons wouldn't finish off the job. But soon enough they got their chance. After bombarding the ship and steadily moving closer for about twenty minutes, they finally boarded. The fight was on instantly, no time to breathe, cutlass out and clashing. Senona's cutlass was out before she even hit the deck and flashing as it caught the sun and then plunged into another man's gut not fifteen seconds after she had landed.

The battle didn't last long. They were lucky enough to come across a merchant ship, meaning the sailors weren't fighters, and the rewards would be large.

Senona felt a twinge of guilt when a man, not much older than herself, ran up to her, sword drawn. He was shaky and Senona could see fear in his eyes. It only took a second for her to realize that he had no idea what he was doing; it was a miracle he had lasted long enough to even engage her. Senona could have finished him off quickly and with very little effort, but she couldn't bring herself to do it. She knew Chale would watch her back, so she parried and took the time to give him a chance.

"I don't want to kill you," she stated in English, as she easily blocked another blow and forced him back.

"Then why would you attack us?" he replied in perfect Spanish—it could only mean he was a native and had recognized her accent.

"I don't care about them, but you—you aren't ready to die. Your eyes haven't seen enough of the world." He looked oddly familiar, making her even more hesitant to take his life.

"And then there are those that have seen too much."

It was then that Senona noticed his more expensive clothes; he was no mere sailor. "Who are you?"

"Caton Amador."

Senona suppressed her shock. She knew this man all too well. "Lovely to meet you. You wouldn't happen to be the son of the wealthy merchant family Amador, would you?" Senona knew Caton, she could remember the day she had realized he wasn't the friend she thought he was like it was yesterday, but why he was out here made no sense.

"The one and only."

"Well then, I most definitely can't go about killing you; you're an old friend of the family. Surrender."

"No," he said in disgust.

Senona rolled her eyes. Men, they thought it was so shameful to surrender to a woman. "Why not? I'm offering you a chance to live!"

"By surrendering to a woman, a pirate no less."

Senona shook her head; she had been right.

In two quick moves, she disarmed him and pushed him up against the rail. "Listen, you chauvinistic pig. There is no shame in surrendering to a woman if she is better than you. Secondly, if you don't surrender, I'm taking you prisoner. Your choice." Senona spoke harshly, but there was an amusement in her eyes. She refused to kill the man whom she had grown up with, though he obviously didn't recognize her.

"What's the difference?"

"One is slightly easier, but they're both embarrassing."

"Then I suppose I should, at least, make things difficult for you."

"If you insist," and without another word she hit him over the head with the flat of her blade, instantly knocking him senseless.

She scoffed and left him there to rejoin the fight; he would be safe as long as he didn't come back around.

The fight was nearly over. In the end, a few men surrendered, and they were left with some provisions. Senona insisted Chale help her get Caton onto their ship, and through much grumbling, they managed to get him safely away in Senona's hammock without the captain noticing. Of course, it wouldn't be a secret for long. On a ship as small as the *Vengador* it was nearly impossible to hide an extra body.

"I'm not protecting you on this one. We're mates and all, but I can't watch your back. Cap'n doesn't like me enough to get away with this."

"That's fine, Chale. I didn't expect you to. I'll deal with the captain myself."

With the excitement and noise dying down, Chale and Senona lowered a terrified Naldo back down to the floor. Senona spent a good hour with him grooming and calming him down. This voyage was not good for him. To make things even better, Captain Santiago burst below deck just as Senona was putting the brushes away. She took one look at him and knew that this was not going to be a very enjoyable conversation. He was furious.

"Look, girl, I gave you a place on my ship and even took your horse. How do you repay me? You take a captive! And where is he? But wandering on deck!"

"Oh. He woke up, did he?" Senona asked calmly, hoping that the captain would stop shouting if he saw how unconcerned she was.

"Yes, and he seemed to know exactly what was going on. How is it that a stranger knows more about what's going on around my ship than I do?"

Senona was trying to keep from laughing at the captain's red face. "Well, sir, it's like this; he is the son of a wealthy merchant in Barcelona, the very owner of that merchant ship we just finished attacking. So I imagine they'll pay a handsome ransom for his safe return." Senona stumbled over what she was saying, making it up as she went and hoping against all odds the captain would accept, and perhaps even like it.

He looked thoughtful. "I imagine you're right."

"But I want half the ransom money," she threw in quickly.

"Excuse me?"

"I want half the ransom. It was my idea, and I did all the work. And think; you can keep your half for yourself, no need to cut in the crew."

A greedy glint was visible in Gaspar Santiago's eyes as he thought about it, and Senona knew she had won this one.

"He's your responsibility. Lock him in the brig."

"No," she said firmly.

Santiago looked at her, incredulity plastered on his face. "Excuse me?"

"There is no place he can go and he won't be any trouble. Let him do a bit of work."

He raised his eyebrows and nodded. "But if he acts up even once, he's in the brig. No second chances. Now go deal with him."

Senona smiled, feeling triumphant, and Santiago shook his head as she brushed past him. She had won this one, and he was likely relieved that none of his crew had witnessed their exchange.

It wasn't hard to find Caton. An unhappy Chale was guarding him by the mast.

"You deal with him, and don't you involve me," was all he said before stalking away.

"So I see you're awake, Caton Amador."

"And with a splitting headache, no thanks to you," he answered indignantly.

Senona smiled cheekily. "That's your own fault. If you had only surrendered—"

"Fine, I'll admit I could have made this easier on myself. Who are you anyway? I thought pirate ships didn't take on women. Bad luck or something superstitious like that."

"They do on occasion. If the woman can hold her own in a duel, it counters the bad luck. My name is Senona Montez, perhaps you remember me."

Caton looked at Senona slightly confused, slightly shocked. "No!"

Senona laughed. "The one and only. How have you been?"

"Uh, fine... Up until today, that is. But... how? Your parents said you ran away. There were rumors that you were spotted aboard a British pirates' ship, but this ship is most definitely not British."

Senona inwardly cringed at the thought of Brant. Up until now she had successfully pushed him out of her mind. "Yes, and I had found work in Port Royale, but it was time I went home, so I got a place with Captain Santiago."

Caton seemed incapable of speech as he continued to stare at her in shock. "I always knew you were a bit strange, but a pirate? I never would have imagined."

Senona burst out laughing. "Me neither! But what were you doing on one of your father's merchant ships? It seems that lately I'm not the only one in places I don't belong."

Caton grinned. "My father's idea of getting me out of the way."

"What did you do?"

"Nothing. Just expressed dislike for a woman they wanted me to marry."

Senona looked at him, not believing that was the whole truth for even a second.

"Actually, I was quite rude to her. To three of them to be precise."

Senona's eyes opened wide in amazement. Not Caton. When they had been quite young, they had gotten along well, but Caton grew up and decided that Senona was too strange to be friends with, and he found new companions. Normal boys. He and his friends had been particularly cruel over the years. Their snubs and comments had hurt Senona more than anyone else's. She accredited it to the fact that once upon a time Caton, and his friend Isidro, had been close with her, and there was too great an age difference to understand their actions at the time.

She used to watch them at the parties as they successfully wooed girls. Senona had always imagined Caton would marry a beautiful heiress, a daughter of a duke or don, someone with status and acceptability.

"That surprises you?" asked Caton when he received no response other than her shocked expression.

"A little. It's not exactly in your character."

"Senona Montez, we haven't spoken in years, so how would you know?" chided Caton teasingly.

"And whose fault is that?" she countered, slightly bitter. "Just because we never spoke doesn't mean I didn't observe."

"You of all people should know that in our circles every little thing people do is nothing but a façade."

"I chose to leave that."

"And I chose to keep it. But I absolutely refuse to have my home life be an act."

Senona found new admiration for this man. Not everything was as it appeared. The only difference between them was that she absolutely refused to put on an act.

* * *

Brant saddled Jester as he mentally went over the route they would take. James and Johnny had gone to the ship over an hour ago to help with last minute preparations while Brant stayed behind, going over a few things with Sam.

He looked up as the sound of footsteps approached him and was surprised to see Catherine dressed in her riding habit.

"Going out for a ride?"

"I'm coming with you," she said as she saddled Phantom.

Brant frowned, and his voice grew harsh. "No, you aren't," he responded firmly.

Catherine stopped and looked at him. "Yes, I am. You said something to me only a few weeks ago, and you've already made it necessary for me to follow up on it. Do you remember?"

Brant flushed guiltily but shook it off. He wasn't being unfaithful; he just needed Senona in his life. "I'm taking the fastest route. It won't be safe," he argued feebly.

Catherine looked visibly upset. "I don't care," she said, her voice trembling. Why couldn't she be strong, like Senona?

Brant sighed and mounted Jester, Catherine only two steps behind him. "You won't be getting any special treatment."

"I know."

Brant muttered under his breath, "You'll only get in the way." He was not referring to the voyage, he was thinking about when he found Senona.

CHAPTER TWENTY-THREE

Senona and Caton waited while the *Vengador* finished docking, in hopes that Senona could collect her share from the voyage. She had spent the last week convincing Gaspar Santiago not to ransom Caton and instead to just let him go, after all, he had been a good crewmember, and he had worked for free. In the end, Gaspar had agreed, but on his own terms. Senona had been required to give up half her share so that, in a sense, he still got a ransom. The arrangement hadn't fazed Senona as she had been half expecting to lose it all, but Gaspar Santiago was not a very good negotiator.

In the end, it all worked out and Senona, Naldo, and Caton were free to walk off the ship and back into their lives.

"Where to now, Senorita Montez?" asked Caton as they walked down the streets of Barcelona.

"It's time I went home, and I suppose you have a report to make."

"There's no hurry; I'm not expected back for weeks. Would you like me to go with you?"

Senona struggled. She didn't want to go home at all, but he had insisted, and so she had promised, though she wasn't planning on going through with it. "No, it's fine."

"You aren't planning on going, are you?"

"No," Senona admitted with a nervous laugh.

"You're going and I'm coming with you. You have to face them." He spoke calmly but left no room for argument.

Senona nodded. "Okay, let's get your horse then."

Caton kept his horse at a local livery. His family was rich, but they lived near the docks for the sake of their business, and they had no personal stables, so they boarded all their horses at a high-end livery right next door.

He saddled his black Andalusia stallion, and then the two of them rode off towards the Montez estate. With every step Naldo took, she drew closer to the house she had grown up in and a feeling of dread steadily took over. She knew her parents would be upset; there was no good way for this to end, and yet Caton insisted, and so she went, obedient for perhaps the first time in her life to anyone other than a ship's captain.

They rode up the long drive and Senona dismounted. Her companion followed her example, but she handed him Naldo's reins before he could follow.

"Stay here. I don't expect I'll be long."

Caton sighed but didn't argue. It was something she had to face on her own, and he understood that, however grudgingly.

The shocked look on Maria's face didn't shock Senona. Her old nurse had probably never expected to see her again, and yet there she was standing in the doorway.

"Senorita Senona, come with me," was her flustered answer as she struggled with how to react.

Senona was led, as if a guest, into the parlor to await her parents. She was told to wait, a stranger in her own home. She had to wonder if she had ever been more than that.

She didn't have to wait long. Marco Montez burst into the room, his eyes ablaze. "How dare you come back here? After you've shamed us, been with pirates, and who knows what else! How dare you?"

Senona didn't flinch as her father screamed at her. She kept her gaze steady and waited for him to run out of steam.

"Well? Answer me. Why did you come back? Did you see the error of your ways?"

Senona smirked. Errors? She didn't regret a second of the time that had passed since she had left home only a year ago.

"No," she answered calmly, smiling. "I came back because I thought you'd like to know that I'm back in the country, and I want to collect a few of my things."

No longer controlled by his emotions, his eyes turned cold and calculating. "You're not welcome here. Get your things and be gone. Never do I want to see you on this property again." He turned on his heel and walked out, not once looking back at his daughter. To him she was dead.

Senona went to her room and collected a few valuables she could sell and left the rest. Her father's reaction had hurt, but she had expected as much. She had to remain strong, though, had to appear as if it wasn't tearing her up inside that she couldn't be the daughter her parents wanted her to be. She was somewhat relieved her mother had opted to sit this one out. Senona had always thought she was the harsher of the two.

Caton was still waiting outside as she walked briskly from the house. She wordlessly grabbed the reins and mounted.

"That good?"

Senona sighed but didn't look at him. She struggled to hold her feelings in when all she wanted to do was run. "It went exactly as I had expected. Now I just need to find a place to live and work." Her voice was dead, lifeless in her attempt to keep out her rising emotions.

"What did they say?" His voice was full of sympathy that Senona didn't want.

"I'm never to set foot on this property again. But really, Caton, how is discussing this going to help? Right now my first priority is to find a place to sleep."

"I might be able to get you a job at the livery where I keep my horse."

"That will do. I have a few things I can sell to get me started in a tavern room."

She could tell Caton didn't approve but he said nothing, merely frowned and kept his mouth shut.

At the livery, Caton spoke with the owner. Senona watched as they whispered. Caton seemed to be arguing but in the end, they shook hands. She didn't know what Caton had said or if he had bribed the man, but it had worked. The means to the end really didn't matter to her.

* * *

Brant was in a foul mood. With Catherine always around, he had a constant feeling of guilt haunting him, and Brant didn't do guilt.

James and Johnny were both in a disgustingly good mood. Johnny had grown to like Senona very much in the short time he had known her, and had come to agree with James on the idea that Brant was much better off with her, and they knew they were very close to being granted their wish.

They had docked in Barcelona, after traveling the strait of Gibraltar into the Mediterranean Sea for the past week, and Catherine, who had been withdrawn, was now depressed.

Despite her current emotional state, she went with Brant to the Montez estate in search of the girl anyway. The butler politely led them into the parlor and informed them that Senora Montez would join them shortly.

A few moments passed, and then, Senora Carlotta Montez swept in, her elegance and pride casting a kind of superior air about her.

"I'm so pleased to see you, Catherine. And who might this be?

"This is my fiancé, Brant Foxton."

Carlotta looked at Catherine in shock "Fiancé? Is Brant Foxton not the one I was told helped Senona run away?"

Brant looked sharply at Catherine. So she had told her father after all.

"I am looking for your daughter."

Carlotta looked at Brant, trying to size him up and not succeeding. "She was here a few weeks ago, but Marco sent her away. I don't know where she is. I expect she got a job somewhere or left again."

"Where?" urged Brant, not at all in the mood to learn any information through casual conversation.

"I don't know. There are only so many things a woman can do for money," Carlotta replied snidely.

Brant looked at the woman in disgust. That she'd even suggest that of Senona made his stomach turn. She obviously didn't know her daughter very well. "Thank you for your time. I'll look for her myself."

Brant left the room, his rolling gait was relaxed from years at sea, but inside, he was seething. Catherine stayed behind a few moments to smooth things over with Senora Montez, but for all Brant cared, she could do with a little feather ruffling. Rich, pretentious snobs, every one of them. He had no respect for people who couldn't even accept their own daughter.

Brant had no idea where to start looking. Senona had been here at least three weeks ahead of him, and although he was certain she had started out here, she could be anywhere by now.

He waited impatiently for Catherine in the carriage. He was eager to begin his search and every moment wasted here, Senona's trail became colder and colder.

* * *

Senona looked up from the stall she was cleaning to see Caton leaning on the door, a goofy grin plastered on his face that made her want nothing more than to laugh with him at whatever joke he was privately enjoying, even if it was at her expense.

"What?" she asked with a laugh.

"Nothing. It's just that you went from a daughter of privilege, to pirate, to stable hand in about the span of a year. You truly are unpredictable, Senona Montez."

Senona smiled self-consciously. "Well, I never expected you to get on your parents' bad side."

"And yet I am still accepted in society. I know my place and you do not," he said with a chuckle.

"I choose not to have a place in this society."

Senona was still smiling, but Caton grew grim. "That's why you will always be stuck here," he said sadly, as if something had suddenly occurred to him, some great tragedy. Without another word he walked away to his waiting horse and rode off. Senona was left staring at his disappearing figure in shock and wondering what he possibly could have meant.

Senona was distracted all day. She didn't know why, but Caton's words had really struck a nerve. What was so bad about her choice of life? He had never expressed a dislike before. He had even helped her get a job, though she was still living in a tavern. Could it be that Caton truly disliked her as much as he did when he had dismissed her and their friendship years earlier? She could only confront him when he got back that afternoon. But he never came.

For nearly a week, Senona waited for him to return, but he never came. So she was stuck cleaning stalls and tacking horses and slowly what he had said slipped from her mind as she got into the routine of things. But somehow everything felt empty. She missed Sam, Sarah, James, and Johnny. Caton had been able to distract her from that for a time, but with that barrier gone, all the memories of the people she loved most came flooding back.

Senona wrote letters to them all to assure them that she was doing well and missed them. A couple times, as she wandered through Barcelona, she thought she heard someone call her name or she'd catch a glimpse of someone that reminded her of James or Johnny, but she always shook it off and went about her business. It was only her imagination.

* * *

Caton spent all week with Isidro. There were parties to go to almost every evening and plenty of skirts to chase. They would take strolls by the sea or go fishing. It was a relaxing life. Everything was back to the way it was supposed to be. Back to normal. And yet, Caton couldn't shake the thought of Senona. Why her? It made no sense. They were too different. It could never work, but he couldn't help finding himself wondering what it would be like. Her carefree, unrestrained way of living, almost autonomous, was a refreshing break from the masked charade of society, and at the same time, foreign and unsettling.

As they rode through the grounds Caton could sense Isidro watching him, examining and assessing.

"Caton, are you going to tell me what has you so troubled?"

"It's nothing, just a girl, and there are always more than enough of those," he answered offhandedly.

"Not that pirate girl I hope," Isidro teased.

Caton wrinkled his forehead in disapproval. "She isn't a pirate girl."

A chuckle escaped Isidro. "It is, isn't it? I thought it strange how passionately you spoke of her before, but now I see... You're in love with her."

"No, I can't be." But Caton's words were more for convincing himself than his friend.

"You're right; you can't be. It's far too inconvenient, and you have a reputation to uphold. What's her name anyway?"

"Senona Montez."

Isidro's smile vanished instantly. "Senona Montez? The little girl who used to follow us around as we ripped holes in our breeches?"

Caton nodded soberly. "I know, I know. So stupid of me to fall for her, but I didn't even know it was happening."

Isidro shook his head and laughed. Caton could tell his friend was a little shocked. Even he would never have thought he'd fall for the little girl who Isidro used to tease relentlessly, the same girl that Caton had so carelessly brushed off at her first ball. Never.

"You are like my brother, so I'm going to be honest with you. You haven't been yourself since you got back, and I blame her. So do what you must, because I want the old you back, even if that means marrying the girl!"

Caton laughed. "That won't happen. Something happened while she was abroad, and she has no room for me. She'll never admit to it though."

"Well, have a go at it anyway; otherwise, you're going to be miserable all your life wondering 'what if'. Maybe you can, but

I can't wait my whole life for the debonair Caton to wake up. Go home. Do what you have to do."

Isidro was being completely serious. This alone shocked Caton, but never in a million years would he have expected such a supportive reaction, and that alone was enough to convince him of what had to be done. He was going to see her. It was time to put his mind to rest.

* * *

Senona had given up expecting to see Caton walk into the stables after a week had passed, so when he actually did, she was shocked. It was like seeing a ghost. She saw him glance around, and she quickly went back to the job at hand, not wanting it to be apparent that she had just been staring.

It's not as though he were hard on the eyes. He was tall, muscled, had dark bronzed skin, his black hair was cropped short and his face clean-shaven except for his goatee. It was enough to make any girl swoon, and swoon they did.

Senona paused in her cleaning as she sensed a presence close by and looked up. There was Caton, with the same position and grin he had last week. She couldn't explain the strange flutter in her chest and so instead of attempting to decipher its meaning she grew angry.

"Caton Amador, how dare you show your stupid grinning face here after you left for a whole week without even a word of explanation!"

Caton grinned bigger than ever as she ranted, which only proved to infuriate her even more. Her language became more and more colorful, and he had to hold back a chuckle. Finally, when she had nothing more to say, she opted to just glare at him, and if looks could kill, then Caton was dying a most unpleasant death.

"I just came to see if you wanted to go for a ride with me, but since you're so angry, I think I'll go away before I have to endure any more verbal abuse."

"Oh," was all she said. "But I have work to do."

"I have already taken care of that, but as I said, I don't fancy being called a... well, never mind, but if you promise to have a better disposition, I suppose I could renew the offer." His eyes danced, and his smirk reflected his amusement.

"Where are we going?" she asked with a laugh.

"To visit a friend."

"I'm a mess."

"That has never stopped you before."

Senona couldn't help but laugh. "Okay, but I'm going to clean up first."

"And you promise to be nice?"

"I promise." She chuckled.

"You had better hurry up, I won't wait around forever."

Senona ran out of the livery and down the block to the tavern she was staying in. She couldn't explain the excitement she felt, but knowing Caton hadn't abandoned her brought a bit of happiness into her day.

She quickly sponge bathed and slipped on a full red and black skirt with a white blouse. She braided her hair and spritzed herself with some perfume to mask the overpowering smell of horses. She hurried back to the livery where Caton had already saddled Naldo and his stallion.

Caton paused when he saw her, staring unashamedly.

"What's wrong?"

"It's just been a while since I've seen you dressed like that."

"And even when I was in the past you never bothered to notice."

He didn't reply but Senona noticed a glimmer cross his face. What was it? Shame?

"Ready to go?" he asked nonchalantly, though feeling anything but.

"Of course."

They mounted and rode through the city towards the outskirts of Barcelona.

"So, where did you disappear to for a whole week?" Senona asked conversationally.

"To Isidro Amato's. I haven't seen him since before the voyage."

Senona laughed. "Isidro? You two were pathetic when you were younger."

Caton frowned. "Pathetic?"

"The two of you were always together, and a flock of girls was never far behind. It was sad."

"What makes you think that's changed?" he asked with a grin.

"Oh, I don't. Now I think you can't help it, and it's the girls that are pathetic."

Caton couldn't help it; he burst out laughing. "Are you implying that we are good looking?"

Senona looked at him square in the face, seemingly not at all ashamed or embarrassed. "I'm saying you are far too good-looking for your own good. It's as though you put a spell on them as they giggle and hang all over you, and yet they're still called nobility."

Caton smirked, amused by her boldness. "And what about you, Senona Montez? Do I put you under a spell?"

This time, Senona had the decency to blush, and it didn't go unnoticed by Caton. "No. I'm not like the other girls. I don't fall for womanizers."

Caton laughed but didn't contest the title. She was as far from being a normal girl as possible, which was what attracted Caton to her in the first place.

As they rode up to the Amato estate, two grooms took the horses from them. Caton offered his arm to Senona and led her up the steps to the house where Isidro met them at the door, as if he already knew they were coming.

"Back already, Caton?"

Caton smiled. "Can't stay away long. And I brought Senona. You remember her?"

Isidro shot her one of his heart-melting smiles that he used on all the girls. "Of course. Always causing trouble, weren't you?"

Senona grinned. "If you don't watch who you flash that smile to, you'll be causing a greater uproar than I ever did."

"She has you there," said Caton in amusement.

Isidro shrugged innocently. "Come, let's walk in the gardens. Really, Senona, why is it we stopped speaking all those years ago? I think you're great fun."

Senona felt a thrill of acceptance. These two men, figures from her past, suddenly seemed to overshadow her future. What would come of it only time would tell.

CHAPTER TWENTY-FOUR

"Really, Senona, you can live at my house. It's just next door to the livery and not nearly as dangerous as that tavern," insisted Caton.

Caton had been courting Senona for a week, and he had been trying to get her to leave the tavern since then.

"It wouldn't be right to impose on your parents like that. They don't like me, and they certainly don't want me living with them."

Caton sighed. They went through this at least once a day, and every day Senona won. "Then quit here and stay with Isidro. His family likes you, and we're out there often anyway."

Senona really couldn't argue with that, but she hated to be a charity case. "I'll think about it, but I promise nothing," she conceded half-heartedly.

Caton grinned from ear to ear. "Thank you. That's all I ask." He wrapped her in an embrace and softly kissed her.

Senona felt her heart flutter and smiled against his lips. She couldn't remember a time in her life when she had been happier. There were moments that came pretty close in Port Royale or on the *BlackFox*, but nothing quite like this. She felt whole and perfect when she was around Caton; the only thing that was missing was the true sense of home.

Caton broke the embrace, bringing Senona back to the cold harsh world, but still leaving his warmth surrounding her. "I'll see you later."

Senona swatted at him to shoo him away. She had errands to run for the livery and not much time left thanks to Caton. She walked quickly so that she would be back on time. Although Caton held a lot of sway at the livery, the owner still wanted a job done properly and Senona didn't feel right taking advantage of having certain connections.

Going about her business, she found herself moving with lightness in her step that she had never had before. She felt like dancing through the streets.

"Senona," said a voice she had tried to forget, and she plummeted back down to earth. She shuddered and dismissed it as imagination until the voice called out again, and she could no longer ignore it. Turning, she saw his face. The feeling that washed over her left her crippled, frozen in place. It was unexplainable, a mix of dread, joy, anger, and most of all a deep and utter hurt, as if her heart had been ripped out of her and torn into a million tiny pieces. Could she not just live her life in peace? It was beginning to feel like he'd haunt her forever.

She was about to turn around and leave him behind, out of her life once and for all, but she caught sight of James and Johnny walking up behind him. Their handsome faces brought a smile to her face, and at once, she changed her mind and headed in their direction, but not for Brant—for Johnny and James, her dear friends. Her brothers.

"Senona!" exclaimed James excitedly as he rushed forward and embraced her.

"James, I can t breathe," she said, laughing as James let her go, looking slightly embarrassed.

"What's this, Johnny? Don't I get a proper greeting?"

Johnny grinned and hugged her, being gentler than James but not at all with less meaning. "There really was no need to leave," he whispered and let her go.

And then there was Brant, standing right in front of her.

"Senona... I didn't think I'd actually find you... It's been weeks."

He looked so relieved to find her that Senona found she couldn't just walk away. "Why were you looking in the first place? Sam must have explained things to you. I don't want to see you."

Brant looked as though he had been stabbed in the gut. "What did I do?" he asked sincerely.

A feeling of disgust washed over Senona. "If you don't know, then perhaps you don't deserve Catherine."

James looked at his brother, shaking his head. "I used to admire you. Now I'm not sure what to think."

He touched Senona's arm. "Come on."

She had no trouble turning and walking away, but her heart hurt, and she trembled as she fought back tears. If it wasn't for James leading her by the arm, and Johnny following, she likely would have collapsed, overcome by emotions.

The boys kept her company and quickly cheered her up as Senona finished the last of her errands. Back at the livery, the boys stayed and helped her out, just happy to have another day with her. Senona laughed at a joke Johnny had made in his terrible Spanish that she had been trying to teach him before she had left.

"Johnny, I couldn't understand a word you said. What was that?" asked James between fits of laughter.

Johnny smiled—a smile that Senona was sure would melt hearts all over, like Caton, like Isidro, like Brant.

"Spanish," said Johnny defensively. "Senona understood."

"No, I didn't. That was the worst Spanish I have ever heard."

"I learned from the best," retorted Johnny good-naturedly.

"I never taught you that. You obviously never listened."

"Senona, my dear, you know he does not hear a thing you say. He's too enraptured by your beauty," teased James in nearly flawless Spanish.

This sent Senona into another fit of laughter while Johnny tried to get James to translate.

"Some things you are better off not knowing," said James.

When things had settled down, Senona had tears streaming down her face and her sides ached, but beneath all the joy, a question plagued her, and she couldn't bury it any longer.

"James, why did Brant come?"

James and Johnny both looked at Senona, startled. "Sam told him you left, and he flew into a rage. He was not too happy, that's for sure," explained James.

Senona frowned. "But Catherine. Poor Catherine."

Over the weeks, Senona had started to feel pity for her rival. She had mixed feelings about Catherine from the moment they had met, but after a couple weeks with Caton, her jealousy had all but vanished, and now she suddenly felt sorry for the woman who had left so much behind only to have Brant and Senona throw her into the middle of undecided love.

"She's downright depressed, but she insisted on coming. Brant didn't seem too happy about it," said Johnny only a bit too gleefully.

"Do you think I owe him an explanation?"

James looked at her steadily, his gaze intense and honest. "You owe him nothing, Senona. Any fool can see it's Brant causing all the hurt."

Senona looked from James to Johnny and then sighed. She saw the disappointment directed at Brant in James' eyes. She saw the struggle of loyalty in Johnny's face. What was going on was wrong. Before she came and interfered in their lives, there had never been animosity between the brothers. And she was sure Johnny had issues before, but he had always been loyal to his sister. Even when she had first met him, he had wanted things to work between Catherine and Brant, although his resolve was fading, but she had quickly persuaded him to turn on his sister. Yes, she had caused no small amount of trouble in the lives of the people she loved most.

"Nevertheless, I want to speak to him."

The boys nodded. "Just tell us when and where, and he'll be there," said James.

Senona thought for a moment. "The docks at dusk. Where he first met me."

* * *

Caton sank against the wall where he hid. He hadn't intended to eavesdrop, but when he had heard her laughing and saw the boys he knew that they were from where she had run from, which could only mean someone was looking and had found her.

He struggled with his emotions as he listened. So Brant was the one who had hurt her, the one whom she loved. Jealousy squeezed at his lungs, and he struggled for breath. It let him go suddenly, only for defeat to replace it when she had requested to see him.

Caton gathered his strength and left the livery undetected. His only choice was to follow her tonight or let things be. Part of him wanted to know exactly where she stood with this mysterious pirate, and yet, part of him was afraid of what he would learn. But he had promised himself that he would be completely honest with her. He had always said he wanted a real relationship with the woman he married, and up until a few minutes ago, he had truly felt that Senona was that woman. Yet, as his certainties crumbled, he refused to give up hope. He would not follow, but he hoped that she would be honest with him about it when she was ready.

* * *

Brant had been surprised when the boys had come up to him and gave him Senona's message. He had expected that he would need to persuade the boys to part with her location, and although he didn't have that, he did have the next best thing, a meeting. Of course, it was also possible that the only reason she wanted to see him was to yell and scream and tell him to stay away from her, but he would still have a chance to make his feelings known and that was all he needed. Just one chance and he knew she would come running back to him, of that he was certain.

Catherine walked into the cabin and looked him over. He was getting ready to go out, strapping on his cutlass and grabbing his hat from its perch.

"Where are you going?"

"For a walk."

Catherine looked stung by the lack of trust in his answer. She saw past his lies and, for a fleeting moment, Brant almost felt guilty about it. But guilt had no place in the life of a pirate. He took what he wanted without a second thought. That was who he was, and Catherine should know and expect that. That's what he was off to do now; take what he wanted.

* * *

James saw, perhaps better than anyone else, the changes that had come over his brother, and he blamed it entirely on Catherine. With Senona around, he was able to be himself, and now with Catherine, he had needed to change. He had become unhappy and was making bad choices.

He did not enjoy seeing Catherine in pain. James wasn't the type of person who enjoyed another person's suffering, but right now it seemed as if that was all there was. Brant's selfishness had caused too much harm already, and he hoped that Senona would end it.

But James was young and quick to blame Brant. Whether there was anyone else to blame or not didn't matter to him. It all lay on Brant's shoulders as far as he was concerned.

* * *

Senona waited impatiently at the docks. She looked around and saw the tavern where she had first met Old Richard and the docked ships moving to and fro as the waves struck their hulls. She took a moment to think back to the night she had led Naldo down this very dock and had fully expected to be waiting for Old Richard and instead got kidnapped by Matt and Brant.

Most memories were good, they had all been the start of a new life, a better life. She had grown so much since then. But right now, she wanted to get this done and over with, and she knew Brant wouldn't make things easy on her, but it was time for things to end.

Since being back in Spain, she had time to reflect on the things that had transpired and had come to see what a selfish person she truly was. All the grief she had caused her parents for the sake of a little freedom seemed trivial and juvenile now. The way she manipulated Brant just so she could have him for herself seemed cruel and wrong. She had thought about it and realized that it was time to put others before her. Catherine should have her life with Brant, and Senona knew, despite their differences, that it would work out okay if she would just stay out of the way.

Johnny would be able to find his way in life. Brant was a good role model, level-headed for the most part, and he needed to gain his respect and love back for his sister. James had to forgive his brother and see him the way he had before. All these lives Senona had ripped apart, and now it was her chance to fix what she could.

Brant walked up beside her and stood. He said nothing, just stood looking straight ahead to the Mediterranean Sea.

Senona allowed herself to look at him, his ever-present smirk remained plastered on his face, but the twinkle in his eye was missing, letting Senona know he wasn't happy. A part of her wanted to revel in the fact that she had been right, that Brant could never be happy with anyone but her, but she suppressed the feeling immediately, thinking of Caton.

"Why did you come to Spain?" she asked simply, not quite knowing how to start.

"Because I need you."

Senona tried to interrupt, but Brant quieted her. "No. You remember the day of the engagement ball? We went for that ride, and you told me that you wanted me back, but I said I wouldn't leave Catherine like that."

Senona nodded, wondering what exactly he was getting at. His voice was wistful, pleading for her to listen and so she did.

"Well, I realized that it isn't fair. Not to me, you... Not even Catherine. We have to be honest with ourselves, and that's what I'm doing."

"If you are being honest, then why did you bring Catherine? Shouldn't she be on a ship back to England?"

"She wouldn't leave me."

"Knowing you, you probably never were straight with her! You want to talk about fair, Brant? Let's talk about fair. It wasn't fair of me to judge my parents so harshly over the years, to have a love affair with you and to end it when I still felt so much. It wasn't fair that I tried my hardest to make you see the mistake I thought you were making with Catherine or that I stayed around as long as I did." There were tears streaming down her face as she released every thought and feeling that had been building up in the last month, her voice insistent and strong. "Brant, there is so much that isn't fair that I don't think you and I know what fairness is anymore. We are two people that are so self-absorbed that we can't even bring ourselves to care about the pain we cause others." She was begging him to understand. To see what she saw and feel what she felt. It would make everything so much easier.

Brant was silent, thoughtful.

"Don't you see, Senona? That's the only way people like you and I can survive."

"By hurting others?" She was appalled by Brant's answer. "I refuse to live like that."

He laughed. "It's a part of who you are. Don't deny it."

"It's a part of who I was. I can change. Humans are versatile creatures." Senona was angry now. Angry with Brant, angry with herself, mostly angry because she was afraid he might be right.

"Not that versatile. You and I, we're the way man is meant to be." Brant spoke calmly.

"No, Brant. We have taken that to the extreme. No longer are we humans, but selfish, heartless beings. We have become exactly what we hate, and we couldn't even see it."

"Then why? Why did you want to talk to me? What's the point?" he questioned, challenging her.

"Because I wanted to have a chance to fix everything that I broke."

"Some things can't be fixed, Senona." This time, his voice took on an air of solemnity. Senona knew he was talking about his relationship with Catherine, but she refused to believe it was true.

"You're wrong. Given the opportunity, anything living will heal."

"I don't want to heal. I want to be whole. You're the only one who can do that," he insisted.

Senona struggled with her tears. "What is whole, Brant? What do you consider to be whole?"

"Loving someone, being loved in return, being true to yourself, and finding happiness in all that," he answered easily, as if it was rehearsed.

Senona could only remember one other time when Brant was so serious, when he had lost his quartermaster, friend, and father figure, Karl.

"A heartless pirate? Never you, Brant. You care more for love than most. Perhaps that's why I loved you." She smiled sadly. "I want you to answer something honestly for me," her voice was soft, begging. Brant nodded slowly and Senona continued. "Were you true to yourself in London?"

"Yes," he said firmly. "There has never been a time that I wasn't."

"Were you happy?"

Brant thought. Had he been happy? He had never really considered it before now. But those moments with Catherine had been different. They had been reckless and beautiful... "Yes."

"Did you love Catherine? And didn't she love you in return?" Senona's voice trembled, afraid of the answer she would receive.

Brant flushed. "Yes. But—"

"No, you listen, Brant Foxton," she commanded. "You were whole. I imagine there were rough times, but you were whole, and I bet Catherine made you think of others. She made you a better person. And do you know when that all ended? When you came home and I was there to ruin everything."

"That means nothing, Senona. I love you and I love being with you."

"But I make you a worse person, and you do the same to me! We are too alike. We just encourage each other until we leave a path of destruction behind us!"

"Does it matter?" he asked. "I love you. What do I have to do to convince you of that?"

"Nothing you say or do will change my decision. I care for you, Brant, but I refuse to be the person I am when I'm around you." Senona was done. Her voice was quiet and defeated. She started to walk away, emotionally drained, but Brant grabbed her arm, pulling her to him and without warning kissed her hard. It wasn't the soft kiss she remembered but hard and demanding. Why? Why did it have to be like this?

"Now tell me you don't love me, and I will leave you alone." His voice was harsh, refusing to give up.

Senona just shook her head, tears welling up again.

"You say you want nothing to do with me? Then tell me you don't love me! A few simple words and you'll be free. Can't you say them?" Brant urged, pushed, insisted angrily, his eyes gleaming.

Senona was silent, unable to take that final plunge. The tears continued to flow, and Brant released her, smiling triumphantly. "I thought as much."

He was about to walk away, arrogant in his victory, but Senona's voice stopped him.

"I don't love you." It was only a whisper but Senona had said it.

Brant looked shocked. "What?"

"I don't love you anymore." This time, it was said with more strength than the first, and Senona saw Brant's arrogant, confident shell crack under her words.

He managed a chuckle and raised his eyebrows. "You're going to have to do better than that. Convince me!"

Senona shuddered. Why couldn't he just let it go? She searched for the strength she needed to sever that last, painful heart string. The memory of Caton gave her that strength.

"I don't love you anymore!" she said through pouring tears, shouting it loudly enough that Brant could not ignore her. Her voice had a biting bitterness to it. "I won't live like this anymore, Brant."

When she walked away this time, Brant didn't try to stop her.

CHAPTER TWENTY-FIVE

Catherine had been visiting Carlotta Montez as much as possible in the days following the *BlackFox*'s docking. She needed an escape from Brant.

He had been trying, that much could be said. He had been trying hard for the last week, but he never let it go. He never let her go, and he wasn't who he used to be. The very fact that he had to try spoke volumes in and of itself. He shouldn't have to try. He should just love her.

"Catherine, dear, what's wrong? Since you've been here you have been quite unlike yourself," Carlotta expressed, her voice not sounding as concerned as the words she said should warrant.

Catherine forced a smile and waved her hand. "It's nothing. I'm just being silly is all. Traveling has been hard on me."

"You know, there's a ball at the Amato's on Friday. Perhaps that would get your mind off whatever is bothering you."

Catherine smiled appreciatively. A good party always fixed everything in this world of money and privilege. "Thank you, but I wasn't invited, and I don't want to intrude."

"Nonsense! I know Maria Amato very well. I'll have her send you an invitation."

"Really, Carlotta, I don't want to be a nuisance. I'm sure Brant and I will be going home soon. He accomplished what he came for." The words were painful for Catherine to say, to admit out loud that Brant was here for Senona even after everything he had promised her.

Carlotta's smile vanished. "He found Senona, then?"

"He did, and as far as I know, she put his mind at ease," Catherine said with an unconcerned air, as if making Carlotta privy to the latest piece of gossip that didn't affect her but certainly piqued her interest. She had years of practice and was able to pull it off flawlessly. Catherine didn't know the details, but she was certain Senona had finally done the right thing and had sent him away, for that she was thankful, but it hurt that Brant still refused to leave.

"I see."

Carlotta, though she was more practiced than Catherine, seemed unable to hide her disdain for her own daughter. Catherine couldn't understand how she could be so cold to her only child. She knew well enough that Senona was not what the daughter of a don should be, but she could carry herself well enough in society, even if she did tend to shock people. To disdain your own child was unthinkable.

"I should be going. Perhaps I'll see you Thursday."

"I hope so, my dear. You're like a daughter to me."

Catherine cringed at the thought of taking Senona's rightful place but smiled gracefully as was expected of her and left.

She left the sanctuary of society, a place where everything was an act, and she didn't have to think about troubles and entered the real world. The world where, to survive, she had to pay attention to problems and even address them.

Catherine hated this moment, caught in limbo between the two worlds. It was torture to leave the act where everything was safe.

* * *

Senona resigned at the livery that morning, packed her things, and put on something that could pass for first class.

Presently she found herself walking to Caton's study. She knocked softly and was immediately answered with a, "come in."

"Senona!" exclaimed Caton in delight, somewhat surprised to see her. "Why aren't you at the livery?"

Senona smiled "You win. I'll stay at the Amato's."

"Isidro will be delighted, and Maria was very much looking forward to you staying with them."

Senona frowned. "You already told them?"

"I knew you would come around. Are you ready to go?"

Senona was a little taken aback. Things were happening so quickly. "Uh, yes. Naldo is waiting outside."

Caton and Senona rode in silence. She couldn't tell Caton the real reason she had decided to comply. After her confrontation with Brant, she was afraid he would come looking for her again now that he knew the general area she frequented. The last place he would think of looking for her would be living at a don's estate. She felt guilty keeping secrets from Caton, but she was afraid he would get the wrong impression if she told him. So she kept silent. It had already been dealt with anyway. Brant would give up and go home, go back to being the Brant she had fallen in love with. It was inevitable and in time, he would forget about her.

* * *

"Senona! My mother is so excited to see you, though I must say, your timing is impeccable; your mother just left," Isidro greeted them as they dismounted.

"My mother?" Senona asked, concerned.

"She was visiting. Don't worry; my mother said nothing of you staying here."

Senona breathed a sigh of relief and grabbed her bag of things from where it was tied behind the saddle.

"Do you want to settle in? Or have some tea perhaps?" asked Isidro, ever the perfect host.

Senona looked at Caton questioningly. "Maybe some tea. I'll have plenty of time to settle in later."

She could feel Caton's eyes on her all afternoon. Did he know something? She wanted nothing more than to confide in him but she couldn't. Not yet.

"Caton, are you planning on coming to the ball Friday?"

Senona looked sharply first at Caton and then Isidro. This was the first she had heard of a ball.

"Wouldn't miss it, it being your parents' anniversary and all."

Senona paled, Don and Senora Amato's anniversary would be a difficult thing to bow out of, especially since Caton would likely want her there at his side.

"Is the ball here?" she asked hesitantly, hoping it wouldn't be, though she knew it unlikely.

"Of course. My mother loves planning these things. You'll be free to do whatever you like all week as she'll be busy preparing." Isidro smiled, completely oblivious to the growing tension in Senona.

"Do you have a dress or will you need something made?" asked Caton cautiously, not quite so blind as Isidro.

"No, no that's fine. Sarah made me a new dress just before I left Port Royale."

"Oh, good! Then all you have to do is make an appearance," said Isidro happily, not seeing the glare Senona was directing at Caton.

"How lovely," she said, her voice laced with sarcasm.

* * *

As the afternoon wore on, Isidro left on some business, leaving Caton and Senona alone, much to Caton's chagrin. Senona was not happy with him and now he would have to face the music.

"Why didn't you tell me about this?" Her voice was calm but Caton saw the annoyance brewing in her eyes.

"I completely forgot." It was an honest answer, but he answered sheepishly, knowing it was a weak excuse.

"You know I don't like these things. Why didn't you warn me?"

"I honestly didn't think of it. I'm sorry."

"But don't you see? My mother and father will be there. Everyone will be there, and everything will be back to the way it was. Over the last year, things have changed so much and I don't want to go back, Caton. But now I can't avoid it." Her voice was frantic, no longer strong and confident. Her shell had fallen away in a moment of panic and Caton saw now how insecure she truly was. The woman he had thought was so strong was now reduced to a scared girl. It pained him to see her like this.

"Senona, it won't go back. Do you know why?" he asked, his voice reassuring. She shook her head, not looking any happier. "Because you're different. You've changed. You have learned how to carry yourself in these situations."

"But people will still whisper my name." Her eyes were wide and pleading.

Caton smiled and took her hand. "I thought you didn't care about them. What does it all matter? Didn't you enjoy causing scandal in Port Royale?"

"It's harder here, where I know everyone, and I know I don't belong. I wish people would accept me instead of whispering lies and hateful comments."

Caton smiled. "I have a secret," he said just above a whisper. He pulled her into his arms and whispered into her ear, "They whisper about everyone. It makes them feel mighty to make others feel small. It's what our society is all about; be all you can be. They whisper about me as well. I'm no stranger to the feeling, Senona. Not many people in the room are."

Senona forced a smile. "That doesn't make me want to go through it."

Caton was firmer this time. "Senona, you are an outspoken, beautiful woman, and you scare people." Senona frowned but Caton's eyes twinkled. "But over this last year, you have changed. You have learned how to handle yourself with tact and grace, but you haven't lost what makes you, you. The difference is you are mature enough to handle it, and that will truly terrify people. You and your ideas will catch on, and they know it. Even if it happens slowly, you threaten everything they know, a system that has worked for them all their lives. I can guarantee they will no longer be whispering, but openly talking. Don't be afraid of it, Senona. Embrace it. And if that speech doesn't do it for you, then think how wonderful it will be to see your parents' faces when they see you there. Reactions like theirs' will be worth more than all the money of Isidro's fat inheritance," he finished with a grin, holding Senona at arm's length, searching her face for a reaction.

Senona remained silent as Caton spoke. He didn't know what was going through her head, good or bad, until she laughed when he mentioned her parents.

"Well then, Senor Amador, are you prepared to be my escort?"

"I would have it no other way."

* * *

Catherine went through her trunk in search of something suitable to wear to the ball. Brant had not been happy when they had received the invitation, but he pulled out his nice clothes, which were much too similar to his every day clothes for Catherine's taste, and grudgingly agreed to go. With that battle won, the problem of finding a suitable outfit presented itself. She hadn't packed anything suitable, and so she sat there on the floor beside her trunk contemplating pleading sudden illness to get out of it. But the very thought made her blush in shame. She had gone to all the trouble of convincing Brant to go; she couldn't back out now.

Catherine was ready to cry. With her emotions on the rocky edge ever since leaving England, this seemingly trivial issue was the ounce to break the balance.

A timid knock sounded on the door, and Catherine took a long deep breath, getting a hold of her emotions and then called to come in.

"Ma'am, I was just going through some things we had in the hold and thought ye might find some use for this," said a respectful voice.

Catherine turned around to see Matthew. He held out some lavender fabric that, upon closer inspection, Catherine realized to be a dress.

She had known Matthew from when she first met Brant. He had been rescued from the same ship she was on and she helped nurse him back to health from an infected wound. He had seemed so young then, but now that he was older, the age gap seemed much less. He was not a little boy anymore. He was a man who had seen too much of the world.

"How did you know?" she asked.

Matt shuffled uncomfortably as he stood in the doorway. "Ach, it's nothing. Just overheard the cap'n talking and remembered we had this lying around."

"Hold it out; let me see it," she said with a smile.

Matt let it unfold so that Catherine could inspect it. It was made of the very richest lavender silk and lace, its cascading ruffles down the skirt and its thin waistline made it ideal for Catherine's slim build.

"This will do beautifully. Thank you so much, Matthew. You have no idea how much this means to me."

Matt smiled shyly. "Just helping out. But please, my friends call me Matt."

"Well then, Matt," said Catherine with a genuinely warm smile. "Could you send Johnny here? I'm going to need his help with this dress."

Matt nodded and left the cabin.

She quickly slipped into the appropriate petticoats and waited for Johnny to come. Perhaps tonight wouldn't be a disaster after all.

* * *

Senona nervously waited in her room by the large window overlooking the drive, waiting for Caton's carriage to arrive. She refused to spend any more time than was completely necessary among the guests.

It terrified her to be back here. She had run from all this, only to return, but Caton's words from only a few days ago echoed in her mind and gave her confidence.

"It's not so bad. What they think doesn't matter anyway. Just be yourself and don't care. Brant taught you that and Caton believes in you," she whispered to herself, attempting to work up courage.

With Brant she had never really been nervous, even with Sam she had been able to just let go and act naturally at those balls. But those people hadn't known her all her life. They weren't her parents and their friends.

Caton's carriage pulled up, and Senona took a deep breath in a feeble attempt to calm her nerves and turned to inspect herself in the full-length mirror. Beautiful. She didn't look as if she were wearing a mask. She could see her true self reflected, as she had been in Port Royale, and confidence enveloped her. Nothing had changed. No one controlled her just because she was home. And so, confidence found, Senona made her way to the ballroom where she met Caton at the base of the stairs.

"You look beautiful," he whispered as she gently took his arm.

"I wasn't sure if I should have put my hair up..." She had left it hanging freely.

Caton's hand strayed to stroke her hair. "Never change who you are, Senona."

Senona smiled and breathed deep, forcing her body to relax.

He led her onto the dance floor for a lively waltz, which had Senona smiling and laughing.

They didn't leave the dance floor for an hour, just danced and danced, completely oblivious of the disapproving glances shot their way at their loud and flirtatious behavior. From Caton it was expected, it was why everyone loved him. But from a woman, it was not to be tolerated.

Finally, when they could dance no more, they walked to the refreshment table where Isidro was busy wooing a group of young girls, probably just come out into society, who had gathered around him.

"Senona, my chica! You dance like an angel," said Isidro with a laugh and a wink.

"Thank you. With a partner like Caton, it's hard not to look clumsy; I do believe my toes are black and blue," she said teasingly.

"I would never step on a lady's toes!"

"Who said anything about stepping? You were stomping!"

The girls giggled at Caton as he waggled his eyebrows goofily.

"Well, when your toes have sufficiently recovered, would you allow me the pleasure of a dance?" questioned Isidro.

"Only if you promise to behave."

"I promise nothing." He winked, which caused the girls to giggle again.

Senona rolled her eyes, but she smiled. She was enjoying herself immensely.

"Senorita Catherine Marshall and Senor Brant Foxton," came the announcement from across the room.

Senona whirled around to face the entrance and gasped, "No!"

Caton looked as well and his face fell. "Are you okay, Senona?"

"Yes, fine. Startled is all," she said, distracted, her eyes not leaving Brant.

"Here, drink this," he said as he handed her a glass of red wine.

"Senona, I'm surprised to see you here. It's not really something you generally enjoy," said Brant as he approached her.

"I came with Caton." Her reply was short, cold. Her eyes sharp as daggers.

Brant's eyes flashed dangerously, and he smirked. "The boy you spared? Yes, I heard about that. I'm impressed, though, Senona, your voyage here was not easy, and from what I'm told, you handled yourself well. Duels!" he exclaimed.

Senona smiled, pleased by Brant's approval. "You taught me everything. I dare say I'm a different person than the girl who left here a year ago."

"Do you like that person?" he asked, hidden meaning lacing his words, making Senona uncomfortable.

"I like her right now," she shot back.

Brant smiled approvingly. "Miss Montez, would you honor me with the pleasure of a dance?"

"That depends."

"On what?"

"The same condition I have for anyone who wants to dance with me. You have to promise to behave like a gentleman."

Brant smirked. "Don't I always?"

Senona laughed and Caton felt a stab of jealousy. They bantered and teased so naturally that Caton couldn't help but feel like he came second, and he could only imagine how this Catherine felt. He clenched his fists as Brant led Senona onto the dance floor.

As soon as the set was over, Senona left Brant to be with Caton again. She loved dancing with Brant. She felt so free, but afterward, she was more than happy to retreat from his all too charming smile. Being close to Brant was dangerous ground, and the fact that he was being the perfect gentleman made her feel uneasy and distrust him all the more.

"Where's Isidro?" she asked upon accepting a glass of wine from Caton.

"Chasing after the affections of some unsuspecting woman, so don't worry about giving him a dance. Relax awhile."

Senona smiled. "I could use a rest. Let's go sit in the gardens."

They sat for an hour just talking and enjoying the cool night air as music gently drifted out to them. As they walked back into the ballroom, Senona caught Brant's eye and saw the mischievous glint. She returned it with a glare and turned away. He was with Catherine now, and she wasn't about to pull him away from her just for a little bit of excitement. Catherine looked happy with the attention Brant was paying her tonight, that was proof enough for Senona that they could work.

Caton had gone in search of more drinks, so she snuck a glance at Brant, but was startled to see he was no longer with Catherine. Senona tried to tell herself he wasn't up to anything, but she knew he was, and she likely wouldn't like it. The music changed and her gaze shot over to the orchestra where Brant stood, a smirk plastered on his smug face. He caught her gaze, sending a silent challenge. It was, once again, the Fandango. Apparently it was a favorite of his. Or he was trying to change the past. Either way, Senona was not pleased.

No, no, no, no. Someone else dance it, please, she prayed silently, but knew that the dance floor would remain empty. People were too curious about this newcomer.

Brant, tired of waiting, went to the center of the floor and began the dance. He was making a fool of himself. She let out an exasperated sigh. She couldn't just leave him alone, and it didn't look as if Catherine was about to go to his rescue. She made her way onto the floor and joined in. Brant's smirk infuriated her. It would serve him right if she had left him alone to be embarrassed and ridiculed.

"I don't know what you think you're up to, but you're acting childish," she said.

"Just trying to make you realize how right we are for each other."

"Is that why you brought your fiancée? Brant, just make it easier on all of us and give up. Make Catherine happy," she pleaded.

"I can't do that."

"You had better or I will have to leave again, and this time you won't find me."

"You'll change your mind."

They performed rest of the dance in silence, but a couple of times Senona caught Caton's eye, so full of hurt and rage, and her heart sank. She could only pray he wouldn't be foolish enough to challenge Brant. She'd seen Caton's sword skills, or lack thereof, and she knew he didn't stand a chance.

As soon as the dance was over, Senona fled the dance floor to Caton's side where she hoped to explain things before he did anything stupid, but Brant followed her.

"Caton I can explain..." she started, her voice pleading for him to listen.

"Who do you think you are?" Caton directed his glare behind her, pure hatred burning in his eyes.

Senona turned around to see Brant's reaction, but he only shrugged and smirked. "Just an old friend."

Senona saw the situation was well on its way to spiraling out of control, and she gently put her hand on Caton's arm, but he shook it off and took a step towards Brant.

"Caton, just let it go. He means nothing to me. Please, Caton, you know you can't win if it comes down to that," she begged, terrified.

"I mean nothing?" laughed Brant bitterly. "After all our history I don't really think I mean nothing. Have you told darling Caton about us?"

Senona could not believe the malice in which he spoke. This side of Brant, the jealous, spoiled, used to getting his way, Brant was something she had never seen before. "There's nothing to tell. I told you that night at the docks how it is. I don't love you anymore, Brant. Please accept that chapter of my life is over." She fought back tears but was firm in her resolve. She didn't need this from him. She didn't need this from anyone.

"It obviously isn't, since I'm still here."

"Not by my choice," she shot back.

Caton was still glaring at Brant. "Senor Foxton, leave the lady alone. I believe you have some explaining to do to your fiancée," cut in Caton icily.

Brant's eyes turned hard as steel as his attention was directed to Caton. "Don't tell me what to do, boy. You won't ever have anything with her like I did—the same connection. I wish you all the luck, because one day she will wake up to realize what a mistake she made, and she will come running back to me." He grinned maliciously and walked away.

Caton's eyes smoldered, but Senona grabbed his arm and led him away. She didn't even look at Brant. He didn't deserve the recognition.

CHAPTER TWENTY-SIX

As early morning dawned, Senona found herself riding with Caton down the countryside. Last night had been bad. Caton had been so close to challenging Brant to a duel. And Brant... well, she'd never seen him so angry, childish, and terrible.

"You know he's wrong," she said, trying to break the strained silence.

Caton refused to look at her; his eyes set on some unknown point in the distance. When he spoke, his voice was flat, as if he had accepted something he had no power over. "I'm not so certain he is."

Senona blinked away tears that threatened to overflow. "Don't you believe me? I love you. Only you. Sure, Brant and I have history, but that's the past. You are my future."

"Then why didn't you tell me about going to meet him?"

"I didn't want to upset you. My history with Brant is messy, and I didn't think it would be right to involve you. I had to deal with it on my own. I had hoped he would leave."

"Whatever you told him just made him try harder. I can't compete with him."

Senona looked at him, shocked. "You're right, you can't compete with him. You're better than him."

Caton smiled sadly. "Don't patronize me, Senona; I'm not sure I can take it."

"I'm not. In fact, you can challenge Brant the next time you see him."

Caton smiled genuinely. "Oh, so now you want me to die."

"Of course not! I'll train you. I can beat Brant if I try hard enough."

"Then why don't you fight him? You're supposed to be a progressive woman. Fight your own battles."

Senona laughed and pushed Naldo into a gallop, Caton close behind. For the time being, things were resolved, whether or not things would stay that way, only time would tell.

They ran until their horses had enough, and then they stopped and led them the rest of the way to the cliff's edge, overlooking the Mediterranean Sea. They let the horses go and sat, feet over the edge, talking.

"If you want to know, I'll tell you everything," Senona said softly.

Caton looked at her in surprise. "You'd do that?"

"If you want me to."

Caton just nodded in response, not sure if this was something he wanted to hear but committed to the idea that he should know to avoid any future situations like last night.

"He saved me, you know, in more ways than one; first from a pirate and from my parents, and perhaps most of all, from myself. I loved him for being there for me. For being my savior. But at the same time, he allowed me to realize I could save myself.

"He wouldn't give himself completely to me, and when I heard about Catherine, I realized why. Unwilling to only have a part of him, I let him go, fully expecting him to come back to me after Catherine gave him closure. That backfired and instead he brought her to his estate, engaged.

"I was hurt and upset, but I loved him, and even though I could see they were happy, I wasn't. So I set out to ruin things, and I nearly succeeded, until we danced the Fandango at their engagement ball. I thought then that I had won, and I didn't even care about the grief and shame I had caused Catherine. The only thing that mattered was that I had won."

Caton was frowning and shook his head. "What happened?"

Senona could tell he disapproved of the way she had acted, and she didn't blame him.

"Brant confessed his true feelings for her, and I realized I really hadn't won; I had only succeeded in causing a lot of grief, so I left. For the first few weeks, I was broken-hearted. Soon, what feelings I had for him began to slip away, and then I met you. You made me realize what a terrible person I had been, and I've changed." Senona paused, trying to get a feel for Caton's emotions.

"Brant followed me here. Apparently, he had every intention of marrying Catherine, but he wanted me around. I needed to clear things up, so I agreed to meet him, and it was then that I realized I didn't love him, though he tried his best to change my mind. So you see, you have nothing to worry about."

Through her whole story Caton had listened attentively, but when she finished, he just looked at her as if he wasn't sure how to respond, so they sat in silence watching the sun set over the ocean.

"It's beautiful out here," whispered Senona. Caton nodded and put his arm around her. She nestled her head on his shoulder and looked up at him.

"Caton?"

"Mmmhmm?"

"I love you."

Caton didn't seem shocked by the declaration, but she could feel him smiling. "I love you too, my *Corazon del Oceano.*"

"Ocean heart?"

"You are as unpredictable and as untamed as the ocean. I'm still trying to figure out if that's a good or bad thing."

Senona chuckled and closed her eyes, just breathing in the moment. She didn't want it to end.

* * *

Brant stood on deck, watching Catherine as she read. After the events of the night before, she was refusing to talk to him, and when she looked at him, her eyes were void of any emotion.

"What is wrong with you?"

Brant looked at James, who had come to lean on the rail next to him. "What?"

"What is wrong with you? You've changed since Catherine came back."

Brant smirked. "Changed? You want to talk about changed? Go look in a mirror."

James flushed. "I admit it was childish, but how else was I supposed to get through to you? Catherine is bad for you, and I was trying to make you realize that."

"Bad for me? That's not what Senona says," laughed Brant bitterly. "She says she's the one who is bad for me."

"You chased Senona away, and now she's in love with someone else, but whatever you did last night has even Catherine giving up on you. When you got engaged, I never thought anyone could break that, but you can't seem to make up your mind, and it's not right!"

Brant raised his eyebrows and snorted. "So you're rooting for Catherine now?"

James sighed. "Let's put it this way; you messed up royally with my first choice, and you were happy with Catherine until you started to lose your mind. Besides, you could certainly do worse. So let's leave and you can start fixing things. You owe Catherine that much," James finished.

"I don't owe anyone anything," said Brant bitterly.

"Brant!" James had enough. "I'm the younger one here, the child! Stop acting more childish than I do! It's not like you and I'm sick of it." James walked away, completely fed up, to where Johnny was waiting on the ramp.

"Where are you going?" Brant called.

"To visit Senona!" shouted James.

They walked away as Brant groaned and threw up his hands. How in the hell had he let things spiral so out of control? Senona, Catherine, and now even James had lost all respect for him. Brant sighed; the worst part was that his kid brother was right. He had thoroughly messed up with both the women he loved. He really did love them both; Senona just seemed simpler. He and Senona were two of a kind, and he knew life with her would be easy. When had he allowed things to become so confusing? Brant, who prided himself in quick decisions and an uncomplicated life, found himself in a tangled mess and he couldn't figure out where to start fixing things.

* * *

James and Johnny rode to the Amato estate. Senona had told them where she was staying, so they took that as an invitation and used her as an escape from Brant. They had handed the horses to a groom and now sat at a table in the garden where they waited.

"I'm sorry to keep you waiting, but Senona isn't here at the moment," said a tall, handsome Spanish man who appeared to be in his early twenties. He spoke in his native tongue, which left Johnny quite confused.

"Should we come back another time?" asked James, who had understood perfectly. He spoke in nearly flawless Spanish.

"No, no. I don't expect she'll be much longer. The sun is going down, and she said she'd be back for dinner."

"If it's no trouble."

"None at all. This is my home, and you are my welcome guests."

"Thank you, I'm James Foxton," he introduced himself with a smile.

"Isidro Amato."

Everything spoken up until this point was in Spanish, and even though Johnny was thoroughly confused he knew enough to introduce himself.

"And I'm Johnny Marshall, but I don't understand a damn thing you're saying, so please, someone tell me what is going on."

"I apologize. I didn't realize you don't speak Spanish; your friend speaks it so well," said Isidro in heavily accented English.

"Not a problem. So, where's Senona?"

"Out on a ride with Caton, but I expect her back soon."

"Oh, okay." Johnny grew silent.

"Foxton," said Isidro thoughtfully. "I met a Foxton last night."

"Brant, I presume. My brother, unfortunately. I hope he behaved."

Johnny chuckled. "Yeah right," he said, earning him a glare from James.

"I wasn't impressed. He harassed Senona and nearly had Caton challenging him, and Caton is not prone to violence."

James sighed. "I feared as much. He's had a tough time lately, not that that's any excuse, but he isn't usually like that."

Johnny and Isidro both looked at James disbelievingly. "Okay, he is rude and completely incorrigible, but he usually has a lot more honor. He likes to stir things up a bit but never intends to cause harm."

"He fully intended to cause harm last night," said Isidro bitterly.

"I'm very sorry to hear that. Senona and Caton aren't the only people he hurts these days."

"The woman he came with?" It was obvious how Isidro felt about Brant.

"My sister, Brant's fiancée," replied Johnny. "I'll admit, I think Brant and Senona make a more logical match, but I hate to see my sister hurt like this, especially since Senona told Brant there was no hope anymore."

Isidro nodded. It was dark now and servants were lighting candles on the terrace.

"You two seem to have pretty solid heads on your shoulders. Senona is lucky to have you."

James grinned. "Thank you."

"James! Johnny!" exclaimed Senona as she strode into the garden, Caton close behind.

"Senona! How are you?" asked James, standing up and giving her a hug.

"Furious at your brother, but other than that, I'm wonderful."

Johnny gave her a hug and winked. "Who's the friend?"

"This is Caton Amador." She was positively beaming as she introduced him to her friends, who were much more like brothers.

"Pleased to meet you, Caton," said Johnny with a smile, and then whispered to Senona, just loud enough for everyone to hear, "As long as I'm still first in your heart."

Senona laughed and playfully punched him. "Not in front of Caton!"

"Well, I imagine dinner is nearly ready. Would you care to join us?" Isidro invited.

James looked at Johnny and nodded. "Sure. We're still stuck on ship rations back on the *BlackFox.*"

It was only the five of them for dinner; Don and Senora Amato had gone somewhere else and wouldn't be back until late that night. For the most part, the conversation was light and playful, but eventually, Senona turned the conversation to more serious matters.

"How is Catherine holding up?"

"As well as can be expected. You know I used to look up to him, now I don't know what to think," said Johnny.

"I know. I feel somewhat responsible," Senona lamented.

"What?" asked James, shocked.

"Well, I tried to ruin things between them. I made Brant like this."

"We all tried to ruin things between them. No one made Brant like this. No one makes Brant do anything," said James.

"Besides, you told him how you feel, and he hasn't changed. Don't blame yourself," encouraged Caton, who had now fully forgiven her.

"I can't help but wonder what it would be like if I had never left home."

"It wouldn't be good," said Caton.

"I never would have found an inkling of my potential," added James.

"And I doubt I'd have ever left England," reminded Johnny.

"I wouldn't love you. Or at the very least wouldn't have noticed you," Caton put in; to Senona that was probably the most important.

"And I would likely still think you're that strange little girl in the corner who used to follow us around," laughed Isidro.

Senona smiled. "Thank you, but I think I've made a lot of things worse."

"Don't think that. It's not true. We're all better people for knowing you," continued Caton.

"Brant's not," she said quietly.

"Brant has always struggled with being a good person. If it wasn't you, it would have been someone else, and I doubt they'd feel as much remorse as you do," said James seriously.

Senona smiled again and nodded. "You know, we're all such different people, and yet you four are probably the people who matter most in my life. There was a time when Naldo was my only companion, and now I have more than friends; I have a family."

* * *

Isidro and Caton got along quite well with James and Johnny despite the large age gap, and Senona was just glad for an evening where her life seemed uncomplicated.

"It's getting late. Why don't you two stay for the night? We have plenty of rooms," suggested Isidro as the clock struck ten.

"Might be a good idea if you're sure it's not too much trouble," replied James.

"No trouble at all. I insist."

Johnny nodded his consent, and Isidro gave instructions to a maid for two rooms to be made ready.

"Johnny, you're from a respectable family, why are your parents allowing you to serve on a pirate ship?" asked Caton, leaving out the fact that Johnny's parents obviously gave their consent for Catherine to marry a pirate.

"I'm nothing but trouble at home. I wanted to join the navy, but my parents wouldn't hear of it, so I caused trouble until they had no other choice. Brant offered to allow me to serve on his ship for the legitimate runs, and besides all that, Brant has the king's protection. He's a Privateer."

"Will you continue to serve on the *BlackFox*?" asked Isidro.

"I don't know. I'm out from under my parents' thumb now, but I'd like to pursue a life at sea apart from my sister, so I really don't know."

"But you still want to sail," Caton stated.

"Of course; I love it. But I'm not sure the navy is the way to go."

"My father is a merchant, he has a shipping company. If you ever need help, I'll try and get you a position. Work hard and one day you could be a Captain."

Johnny grinned. "I might have to take you up on that."

"What about James? Any dreams?" inquired Isidro.

"Everyone has dreams. I'd like to get married, have a few children, and settle down on Foxton estate. But really, I just want to make a difference in someone's life," he grinned sheepishly at his seemingly insignificant dreams.

"If more people had that as a dream, as an ambition, then perhaps the world would be a happier place," said Caton.

"I have everything I've dreamed of. I sail, have close friends and a good life. So really, those are the only things that are missing."

"My dreams are to make a change in society's standards, to see people embrace who they truly are and not be ashamed of it or make others feel ashamed," said Senona.

Caton laughed. "Don't take on the world, Senona!" Then added more seriously, "You can get people thinking, but I doubt you'll be able to change things like that. I doubt that will ever disappear from society."

"You know, I never spoke to my parents last night," reflected Senona

"Is that a bad thing?" questioned Isidro.

"No, I'm just surprised is all."

"You don't need their approval," stated Caton.

"I know."

Senona snuggled into Caton as they sat on the couch and conversed with her two best friends, the man she loved, and Isidro late into the night. This, she thought, was the way life was meant to be.

* * *

Caton fiddled with the ring as he sat at his desk. A week ago he had told her he loved her and had purchased a ring the next day, but his heart still raced at the thought of what he was about to embark on.

Senona was spending the day with James and Johnny which, as much as Caton liked the two boys, made him uneasy since it meant Brant had not left yet. Without Brant gone, he didn't feel like Senona was completely his, so the ring sat in his jacket pocket until he felt right.

He stared at the ring. It was incredibly simple, a gold band with an ocean blue diamond. The blue diamond was full of flaws but the flaws just seemed to make it sparkle more brilliantly. It had reminded him of Senona, his *Corazon del Oceano*.

* * *

Senona was in the stables grooming Naldo when Caton walked in. He walked up behind her and put his arms around her, burying his face in her hair and breathing in the scent of roses.

"I love you," he whispered.

Senona sighed and leaned in, closing her eyes and feeling his heartbeat against her back. It was constant, rhythmic, and comforting. "I love you too."

They stood like that for a few minutes in perfect peace. "Senona?" he asked quietly as he fished in his pocket.

"Yes?"

"Will you marry me?"

The proposal was not eloquent or special but it served its purpose. He slipped the ring on her finger, and Senona could feel his heart beat faster against her back as he waited for her response.

She didn't turn around, just looked down at the ring and smiled. "Of course," she laughed. "Yes!"

Caton wanted to shout, but it would have ruined the moment. He hadn't been intending to propose, but with his arms around her like that, it felt so right and the absolution in her answer erased all traces of doubt he may have had.

"This is going to change things a bit, isn't it?" she asked.

"A bit, but it will be worth it."

CHAPTER TWENTY-SEVEN

News of Senona and Caton's engagement spread quickly through the upper class. With the lower class usually holding the title of gossipers, the upper class put them to shame on this scandal.

Senora Benita Amador, Caton's mother, was the worst for spreading the rumors; her disapproval of the whole situation abundantly clear to everyone she spoke to. Without the support of his parents, Caton and Senona hid at Isidro's where they were relatively safe from prying eyes and ears.

Caton would go to town early every morning for business but always returned in the evening. On one such day, he decided it was time to speak to his parents. He strode through his parents' house towards the parlor where they would be having coffee.

"Madre, Padre," started Caton as he walked in.

His mother raised her eyes in acknowledgment and bid him sit. Without a word, she snapped her fingers to the maid who hurried out and brought Caton coffee.

"So, Caton, you deigned your parents deserving of a visit?" asked his father, not looking up from his coffee and cake.

"Good to see you as well, Padre."

"And where is your fiancée?" questioned his mother, her voice harsh and disapproving.

"At the Amato's. I'm afraid my mother is too hostile, and I have no wish to subject her to that," bit Caton.

"I wonder why."

"I'd really like you to take the time to get to know her. She's not a bad person."

"Perhaps not, but she was cast out of society when she ran from her impending marriage to Senor Flamez, putting her family to shame."

"It's not that we don't like her, we just think it's bad for the family name," explained his mother, Benita.

"And for business," cut in his father, Cayo.

Caton frowned. "Of course, the business. I had hoped you would support me and be happy for me, but I suppose not. The business is more important than your son's happiness after all. I hope in time you can accept her into the family, but for now, I only ask that you stop gossiping. The worst of it comes from you, Mother, and it truly is shameful."

Benita, at least, had the decency to blush but refused to apologize and continued sipping her coffee.

Caton shook his head and finished the last of his coffee. "You'll receive a wedding invitation. I do hope you come," he said sadly, standing and walking out.

He left his home with a heavy heart. He had hoped his parents would accept her, but he had been sorely disappointed.

He had dinner that night with Isidro and Senona but said nothing of his visit with his parents. He didn't want to involve Senona with his family troubles; she had enough of her own as it was.

"I think we should look at buying a home of our own," said Caton as he sat alone with Senona that night.

"Can we? I'd be okay living with your parents."

"No, that's not right. We need a place of our own; a small house with a small staff and a stable for you."

Senona smiled. "Near a cliff's edge overlooking the ocean."

"If that's what you want, *Corazon del Oceano.*"

"Caton, I'd be happy with a shack."

Caton laughed. "You won't be getting a shack; I promise you that."

She frowned and sighed, struggling with how to continue. "I want to go see Brant again."

"What?" Caton was shocked, he didn't know what to say to that. He had thought they would leave Brant alone and eventually he would leave.

"James and Johnny stopped by today. Brant isn't planning on leaving, and he's still being terrible to Catherine," she explained.

"Please, just stay out of his life," pleaded Caton.

"I can't do that; I owe him too much. Please, Caton, you know where my heart lies."

Caton sat in silence as he thought about what she was asking. "Senona, you know I trust you; it's him I don't trust. I don't feel comfortable with the idea of you visiting him."

"I want to invite him to the wedding."

"Why?" Caton was at a loss. Had Senona completely lost her mind? The man seemed hell bent on ruining her life, and she wanted to invite him to the wedding? Sometimes he wished he knew how her mind worked, because she had just dropped two very large cannon balls on his lap, and he wasn't sure where they had come from or what he was to do with them.

"Because, as idiotically as he is acting, I care about him, and he's done a lot for me. I want him there."

Caton just shook his head and groaned. "Okay. If it means that much to you, then okay."

Senona kissed him. "Thank you. I knew you'd understand."

Caton chuckled. "More like I can't say no. Go talk to him, but be careful."

* * *

Senona walked down the docks towards the *BlackFox*. She remembered a night not long ago when she had first been abducted and taken aboard this ship. Brant had been looking out for her even though he had no idea who she was. That small action had changed her life drastically for the better, and she found herself smiling at memories of Karl's long talks with her, or sparring with Brant, feeling as if she belonged as she joined in the many jobs around the ship, and the way Brant would look at her when he thought she didn't notice, spending hours with James. It all meant so much to her, and she prayed she could make things right with Brant so she wouldn't have to lose it all.

"Senona!" exclaimed Matt as she walked on deck. Her face broke out into a grin, and she ran up to hug him.

"Oh, Matt, I've missed you! How have things been?"

"Not good. Cap'n hasn't been himself, and Lady Catherine is hurting."

"That's kind of why I'm here. They were happy together, weren't they?"

"They had some rough bits, but they love each other, or did, anyway. I don't know what went wrong."

"I do," said Senona softly. "Is Brant around?"

"Crow's nest. He used to go up there a lot when she first left all those years ago. Looks as though he's missing something, or someone, again."

Senona began to walk away but turned back to Matt. "I'm getting married in a week. If you're still here, I'd love for you to come."

Matt smiled. "I'd like that. Now go talk to the cap'n before he decides to throw himself off there."

She laughed and started climbing the rigging. At this point, she was a natural at climbing all over a ship, even during a storm, and climbing up to the crow's nest was done quickly and skillfully, though the dress and heels made it a little harder. She sat down and leaned on the mast, her back to Brant. They sat there for a time, both thinking, neither certain how to start.

"This has got to stop."

"You're engaged, aren't you?" His voice was flat, void of emotion, and it terrified Senona.

"Yes, and I want you to come to the wedding, but this has got to stop. Your crew needs you. James needs his older brother, Brant, and now you have to be a role model for Johnny as well. This isn't right."

Brant sighed. "What happened?"

"We lost our way for a time. I found mine; now it's time for you to find yours."

"How?" He sounded so helpless and lost that Senona was unsure how to respond. It was as if Brant had died and all there was left was a shell.

"You used to know exactly what to do. You controlled your life and went far because of that. It even got you Catherine back, and then I meddled, but that doesn't change how you feel about her, and we both know it. The only person you're fooling is yourself. Even Catherine knows you still love her despite the fact that you continue to hurt her. You're scared of losing this life. I brought that to your attention, and now you see me as your escape, but it isn't right. Please go back to her, Brant, and come to my wedding. I miss the old Brant."

"So do I," he said softly.

Senona sat a few minutes longer, then got up and climbed down. Brant sat and ran the conversation over and over in his head. He thought about the last year and everything that had happened. The ball where he had first seen Catherine again and what it had felt like to hold her in his arms, the moment of pure happiness when he had slipped that engagement ring on her finger, and then it dawned on him that Senona was right. He was only afraid, and although he still felt deeply for Senona, it was time to end Catherine's misery.

He climbed down and walked to his cabin where he knew she would be hiding with a book. He knocked softly and waited for a response, then walked in. She sat in the one chair in the cabin, curled up with a book in her lap.

"What are you reading?"

"Your journal," she answered simply, pain in her voice.

Brant didn't like that she had invaded his privacy, but he didn't let it show. "Why?"

"I'm trying to understand you. The way you used to write about me, that's how you write about her. Your whole journal flip-flops between us. What do you want from me, Brant?"

She had no tears left for him, but he could hear the pain in her voice, and it tore at his heart. "I want your forgiveness."

She looked up, startled. "What?"

"I've treated you terribly. I should treat the woman I love like a queen, but I've treated you like dirt. It's inexcusable. I'll understand if you want to go home, but if you can find it in your heart to forgive me, I'd love to have the honor of being your husband."

Catherine stared at him in shock, not entirely sure what to say.

"I'll go then..." Brant turned around to leave, but Catherine's voice stopped him

"Why? Why did you torture me?"

"I was scared that I would lose who I was with you. I was selfish. I didn't want to lose you, and I figured Senona could keep me on track. When she left, I felt the walls closing in on me, and I went after her because, in my terror and selfishness, I'd rather have her and hold onto myself than onto you and change. It's terrible, I know, but I swear to you it will never happen again."

Catherine nodded. "Your word doesn't mean much anymore, but I love you, and even though you hurt me worse than I ever thought I could be, I forgive you. What you told me in the garden kept me holding on. But if you ever do this again, I will leave you and will never look back."

Brant nodded and walked up to her, pulling her up out of her chair and embracing her. "It won't happen again. I love you, Catherine Anne Marshall."

* * *

Senona woke up late the next morning. With little to worry about anymore, she had slept well the night before and didn't wake up until noon. She got up feeling cheerful and refreshed and dressed in a simple pair of breeches and a blouse.

Since finding out Senona liked breeches, Caton had bought her a few more pairs so that she would be able to wear them more often, and although he would never admit it, he liked how she looked in them.

With only a week left before the wedding, Senona had to crack down on planning. Maria Amato had generously offered her time and expertise to help, and today they were supposed to go to a tailor and have a dress made.

She went to the kitchen and made a piece of toast, generously spreading butter all over it. Senona was never one for breakfast, so she hurried through it and went in search of Maria. She didn't have far to look. Maria was in the parlor entertaining a guest. Senona only intended to say hello and retreat to the stable.

"Senona, won't you say hello to your dear mother?"

Senona cringed at the sound of her mother's sickeningly sweet voice, feeling a sudden urge to run out of the room, but she knew it would disappoint Maria.

"I didn't know I had a mother. Now, if you'll excuse me." Senona was about to turn on her heel and leave but was once again stopped.

"My dear, your father was just angry. All that has changed. He's come around."

"I'm sure," Senona replied coldly.

"Senona, your mother came specifically to talk to you. Perhaps you should hear her out," urged Maria who, for all of her fondness of Senona, was eying her attire with disapproval.

Senona sighed and sat down, which Carlotta Montez took as an okay and began. "Your father and I are delighted to hear about your engagement and would like to throw you a ball. Maria and I have been talking and, although it's short notice, we believe we can have one at the end of the week and have the wedding a week later."

"The wedding is supposed to be this weekend," Senona said, sounding disappointed, as if it was entirely too bad that there would be no room for a ball in the strict schedule.

"Yes, dear, but if you're to have a ball, it's going to have to be postponed. What's another week?"

Senona sighed. She had been afraid of this; marry a man of good reputation and her parents would accept her back into the family, whether she wanted it or not.

"I'd have to talk to Caton, but I suppose it would be alright. After all, I wouldn't want to rob you of your last two weeks of control you have over me," was her cold reply, not at all happy about her mother's reappearance in her life.

"Dear, you have been out of my control since you learned you had a mind of your own. Balls are not so bad. I saw you enjoying the last one. That Fandango you did with the pirate was quite the spectacle. Perhaps you'd like to have a repeat of that little scene."

Senona had a biting tongue and a quick wit, but she had inherited it from her mother. No matter how harsh she was, her mother took it in stride and shot something right back.

"Brant is a friend and he's commissioned by the king of England. Do not call him a pirate," replied Senona in annoyance.

"Of course, dear. So, the ball?"

Senona put on an obviously fake smile. "Do whatever you wish, but I want a few invites to send out myself, I don't want only people you find suitable there, or it will be quite dull."

"Of course," her mother replied offhandedly. "Now I took the liberty of contacting my tailor. He'll be here in an hour to fit you for two new dresses."

"Fine," said Senona, bored. At this point, she didn't really care. Her mother had put her mind to taking over, and there wasn't a whole lot she could do. The wedding was just the wedding, whether her mother planned it or she did, it would all end the same.

"Now about floral arrangements—"

"Whatever you think is best, Madre. You can plan the whole thing and surprise me if you like."

Carlotta laughed. "Don't be silly! It's your wedding."

"No, it's not. The moment you walked back into my life you took that from me."

Carlotta's face grew grim. "You are an ungrateful child. I offer you the world and you throw it back in my face. How did you get Caton to propose? Did you seduce him and make him feel guilty when you got pregnant?"

Senona snorted her coffee in surprise. Her mother was usually more level headed than to come up with something as ridiculous as that. "I'm surprised that you think me even capable of seduction. You always drilled into my head that I was nothing to look at. Don't be so foolish, Madre. Besides, I've told you many times over, I'd only marry for love. Unlike some people, I don't back away from my principles."

Maria sat awkwardly and Senona felt a momentary twinge of embarrassment for involving her in family issues when she had been nothing but kind for the past few weeks.

"I don't know why I even try. I should have known you wouldn't appreciate my efforts." Carlotta got up to leave, but Senona stopped her. She knew how important it was to Caton that she made things right with her parents and, although he hadn't pushed the issue since her original attempt, she knew she still hoped she would be able to gain her parents' approval.

"Wait, Madre. Please. I'm sorry, you're right. You made an effort but you have to realize something; I'm still me and just because I'm marrying Caton, doesn't mean I've changed. I may have matured but I still have the same ideals and I'm not going to change that for you. If you wish to help with the wedding, that's fine, but you have to understand that I don't care overly much about the details. In fact, I would have no idea what to do."

Carlotta nodded. "What would you like to plan?"

"The dress," Senona said firmly. "The rest you can do whatever you like. I'm no good at these kinds of things anyway, but the dress I want to be my own."

As she conversed with her mother things remained tense, but the obvious effort by her mother touched Senona's heart. Perhaps Sam had been right, maybe she just hadn't been able to understand, but suddenly she felt the need to try.

"The engagement ball is short notice but it can be done. It will be held at home, and I'd really like you to stay there until the wedding; it would make things easier."

Senona felt ambushed but she smiled. "I'll think about it. How about I let you know at the ball?"

Carlotta frowned but nodded. "That's fine."

Senona was thankful when the tailor's arrival brought an end to her mother's endless and tiring details. There was only so much she could take and if it went on much longer all progress would be lost.

The tailor went about taking measurements and discussing ideas until Senona's head started to spin.

"I'm only going to need a wedding dress. I'd like to wear the one my friend made me for the ball."

The tailor, Senor Reyes, shook his head. "No, no that won't do. Your engagement ball requires a special dress."

Senona raised her eyebrows at her mother who sighed but complied with her daughter's silent request.

"Senor Reyes, I realize that a new dress would be the appropriate thing, but we have very little time and my daughter wishes to wear an old dress. It is her special day; I believe we can make an exception and give her what she wants."

Senona saw the obvious pain it caused her mother to say those words when it was against everything society expected from a family of their wealth and status, but Senor Reyes nodded and didn't argue the matter.

"Now, I believe we can make you a dress in the latest style. You would look very beautiful—"

Senona shook her head. "No. Just something simple. Please spare me the ruffles and lace. Ivory silk will do. I'm not overly particular about what you do, just nothing too extravagant or ruffly."

Senona tried not to laugh at the identical expressions of tight-lipped disapproval on both her mother and Senor Reyes' faces.

"As you wish. Then I believe I am finished here. I'll come by with some sketches tomorrow."

Carlotta nodded and thanked him as she saw him out. When her mother made no move to leave, Senona made the excuse of going riding and could only pray her mother would be gone when she got back. She appreciated the effort but knew if she had to take much more, she wouldn't last the two weeks until her wedding.

* * *

Caton was back in time for dinner and with news. He had found a nice house that he was certain Senona would like. She smiled as she listened to Caton enthusiastically describe it. She had said before that she didn't care what the house was like, but she agreed to go with him and see it after the dressmaker met with her tomorrow morning.

"I have some news as well," she started. "My mother came by today."

Caton looked surprised and wary, not entirely sure if this was a good thing or not.

"She wants to be included in the wedding plans. She agreed to respect my wishes and I agreed to make an effort, but she insisted on going about the wedding properly." Senona hesitated, reading Caton's reaction, but when she received no indication of annoyance she continued cautiously, "We are to have an engagement ball this weekend at my parents' estate and the wedding will be the weekend after."

Caton grinned. "That's wonderful! I knew they would accept you back eventually."

Senona frowned. "Personally, I think it's just because I'm engaged to you, but I'm willing to give it a try."

Caton stroked her hand and smiled at her adoringly. "I'm proud of you. You've told me about the way you used to be and I see that you've changed. You've matured into a beautiful young woman and I'm proud to call you my fiancée."

Senona smiled. "That means so much to me."

"Have you decided on a bridesmaid?"

Senona shook her head. "The only woman suited to the position is Sarah and she's in Port Royale."

"How about we leave that then? Do just us."

"What about Isidro?"

Caton chuckled. "He'll forgive me. I'll find something else for him to do."

Senona closed her eyes and sighed. "Whatever did I do to deserve someone like you?"

"I have no idea, Senorita Montez. I think I just took pity on you."

Senona's laugh was light and musical and seemed to come from deep within her soul. "Or perhaps you're just repaying me for saving your life."

Caton grinned his boyish grin that made Senona's, and any number of other girls' hearts flutter.

"Yes, that's definitely it." But Caton's face became solemn. "Though I could never repay you for saving my life. You do it again and again every single day."

* * *

Brant tried very hard all week to prove to Catherine how sorry he was, and upon receiving the invitation to Senona's engagement ball, he secretly contracted a dressmaker to make Catherine something new to wear to both the ball and wedding.

The day of the engagement ball was hectic. Brant had to get the dresses for Catherine since anyone else he could have trusted with the job was busy.

When Brant returned, Catherine was in his cabin getting ready. He knocked softly then let himself in. She wore the same lavender dress she had worn to the last ball.

She didn't notice him walk in, her back towards him, so he walked silently up to her and kissed the nape of her neck.

"You look gorgeous, Darling."

"Thank you."

"But that dress is not going to do."

Catherine sighed. "Well, it's going to have to because it's all I have."

"That is a shame. The fiancée of a rich pirate and you don't even have a new dress. What do you keep him around for?"

Catherine turned around. "Brant, you didn't!"

"What? What did I do?" he said, feigning innocence.

"Brant Foxton, don't play games with me."

Brant chuckled and directed her attention to the chair by the door. "One for tonight and one for the wedding. I hope you're pleased."

Catherine was positively beaming, she didn't even bother giving Brant an answer; she just rushed over to the dresses and pulled them out of their boxes for inspection. "Oh, Brant, they're amazing. Which one should I wear?"

"The blue will go so beautifully with your eyes."

"A sense of fashion as well. I'm impressed. Here, help me out of this one and I'll change."

Brant deftly unbuttoned the many tiny buttons in the back of her dress and then turned around to allow Catherine to change.

"Okay, you can help me button it up now."

Brant turned around, buttoned the dress, and stepped back to admire her. She spun around, did a couple waltz steps, and then curtsied. "What do you think?"

"Gorgeous. Absolutely beautiful. You are an angel."

* * *

Senona looked around as her parents' house filled with guests, all there to celebrate her impending marriage. She knew some people were there just to ogle, very few were there out of genuine care for the young couple, but she really couldn't care less, it was all for her mother anyway.

"You look terrified," chuckled Caton, as he took her hand in his and stroked it gently.

"The jackals look hungry tonight."

"Don't let them see your fear. Enjoy your party. Perhaps you would even like to give your fiancé a dance?"

Senona couldn't help but feel adoration for Caton grow inside of her and she was sure her feelings were apparent in her eyes. "You can have all the dances you want."

Caton led her down to the floor that was slowly filling up with dancers. The quadrille was a relatively new dance, but as younger people, they knew it well, and even Senona found herself stepping with a grace that she wouldn't have guessed she possessed a year ago. As the dance came to a close, the couples stepped back and clapped.

"What are you doing?" exclaimed Carlotta Montez as she pulled the couple off to the side. "You should be greeting your guests at the door. We haven't announced you yet."

Senona rolled her eyes. "I gave you your ball; now let us celebrate our way. Everyone knows why they're here; there is no need for any announcements.

Caton stood behind Senona, saying nothing, but his support was apparent.

"Fine." She brushed past them, back to the door to greet guests.

Senona laughed at the look on her mother's face. "It feels so good to know I don't have to listen to that spiteful woman."

"Congratulations, Senona Montez, you belong to yourself. Now if you'll excuse me, I see my parents have arrived."

"You don't want me to come?"

"No, I think it's best I greet them first and then bring them over to you. Unfortunately, I don't believe my parents' feelings about you have changed at all. Really, I'm surprised they came at all."

Senona nodded understandingly and watched Caton walk away, leaving her alone among the people who terrified her most. She walked around the outskirts of the dance floor, smiling, nodding, and thanking those who were polite enough to offer their congratulations. Her eyes wandered to the swirling fabric of the dancers monopolizing the center of the room. She passed through it all alone, reminiscing on how she used to do the same thing detachedly, as if she was in a dream. She saw Isidro dancing with a pretty girl of around sixteen and smiled. Was she the only one who had changed? Isidro still broke girls' hearts everywhere he went, her mother still tried to control, Brant was still arrogant and powerful, and Senona seemed to have done a lifetime of growing in only a year.

She glanced at the doorway to see Brant enter with Catherine on his arm, James, Johnny, and Matt all close behind. Her real family. She didn't approach or interfere as Brant led Catherine onto the dance floor, she just observed curiously, wondering if things were alright between them.

"Come, Senona, you are a new person. Show these people who you are," said Isidro as he came up behind her.

Senona turned and smiled. "Don't waste your time on me, Isidro. I am engaged and you have many young admirers wishing for a dance."

"But none as beautiful as you. Caton is caught up with his parents; don't prove people right by making them think that you need him. Shine all on your own."

"But I do need him," she confessed.

Isidro winked. "They don't need to know that. Come, it's a waltz and I know you love those."

Senona shook her head but smiled. She allowed Isidro to lead her onto the dance floor.

The rest of the evening was a blur. Caton rescued her from Isidro, and she danced with him, Johnny, James, and even Matt. She didn't know at what point she stopped caring about the people around her and started enjoying herself.

Senona watched Brant closely all night but she didn't approach him. She saw how happy Catherine was, and even Brant seemed to be at peace with himself. In the end, it was Catherine who approached her.

"Senona, we didn't part on very good terms but I know that you had something to do with Brant coming back to me and I just wanted to thank you."

Senona was shocked. "Thank me? I ruined everything to start with."

"Nevertheless, you fixed things and, for me, your good far overpowers any wrong you've done to me."

"Thank you, Catherine. You look beautiful tonight."

"Brant had the dress made for me."

"He certainly has good taste."

"Senona, dear, will you be staying the week here?" interrupted her mother.

Senona cringed, though her mother's voice wasn't shrill or hard on the ears, it still made her stomach turn and her head ache.

"Yes, but only until the wedding."

Carlotta was about to walk away but stopped. "Catherine, are you still staying on that dreadful ship?"

"Afraid so, Carlotta."

"You must stay here as our guest. I'm sure Senona would appreciate the female company."

Senona and Catherine looked at each other, Catherine lost and Senona almost pleading with her to say yes. She couldn't stand the thought of a week living with only her parents and Caton. Even having Brant in the house was more desirable.

"Let me talk to Brant."

Catherine made a quick retreat in search of Brant and Senona smiled at her mother, then walked over to James and Johnny, eager to escape.

"I need you to convince Catherine and Brant to accept my mother's invitation to stay here until the wedding. My mother insisted that Caton and I stay with them and I'm not sure I can last the week. I need friends around."

Johnny looked over at Catherine talking animatedly to Brant "She doesn't much enjoy the ship... James?"

"Brant will do anything for Catherine right now and I don't think I can really protest the idea of spending more time with you before we leave. But are you sure it's a good idea? Brant is just starting to turn around, and he and Caton aren't exactly friendly."

"I'm sure, and thank you. You may have just saved my marriage."

James laughed. "Glad to be of service."

Senona walked over to Caton who was getting drinks and informed him on the new developments.

Caton frowned. "Brant and Catherine are staying here? With us?"

Senona nodded. "I know that sounds like a terrible idea but it could be a really good thing. You can get to know Brant, I can get to know Catherine, and we can escape from my parents."

"Senona, what if—"

"No. Don't say anything. We'll just hope for the best."

Caton shook his head. He couldn't say no to Senona, but he didn't like the idea one bit. He put up with Brant because it was important to Senona, but he didn't want to be anywhere near the man, nor did he trust him. Senona was playing with fire.

CHAPTER TWENTY-EIGHT

Brant rolled out of bed to a bright sun and chirping birds. He groaned and blinked, slowly dressing in a loose fitting shirt, breeches, and knee-high leather boots.

Why he had agreed to stay here, at the Montez estate of all places, he didn't know. Especially since he and Catherine had just started working things out. He wasn't entirely sure this was the most appropriate time to put their relationship to the test.

Brant walked down the stairs, a jump in his step, and made his way to the kitchen where there was coffee being kept warm on the stove. He poured himself a cup and breathed in the warm, rich scent that awakened his senses and embraced his body.

He wandered through the house in search of some form of life. After the festivities from the night before, Brant found the house amazingly abandoned. Had he slept longer than he had originally thought? The sun wasn't that high but the house was cleaned up and no one could be found. Not even a single servant. Brant downed the rest of his coffee, put the cup back in the kitchen, and walked out to the stable. If Senona were anywhere, it would be there. Catherine was likely out with Carlotta, and as for everyone else, Brant had no idea.

As he approached the stables, he heard singing. It was a well-known British sailing song that he had heard Karl sing many a time, in fact, Brant was fairly certain Karl was the one who had taught it to Senona.

"Farewell and adieu unto you Spanish ladies, Farewell and adieu to you ladies of Spain; for we've received orders for to sail for old England, but we hope very soon we shall see you again." She sang the chorus and Brant whistled the tune as he walked in.

"English shanties now, eh?"

"It reminds me of Karl."

Brant smiled sadly. "Your father has a fine collection of horses."

"All the finest bloodlines in the country. Not quite your thoroughbreds, but they serve us well."

"He keeps mares."

"And one stallion for breeding. My father believes in the war traditions that mares are more loyal and so his riding stock is all mares."

"Andalusian?"

"All of them, except for Naldo. My father wouldn't mind if you wanted to take one for a ride. They get very little exercise."

Brant walked up and down the aisle visiting each mare. "I like this one," he said, indicating a pretty white mare.

"Sirena," Senona gave him her name. "Tack her up."

Brant disappeared into another room and came out with a brush, saddle, and bridle. As he brushed her, he was silent. Once they were riding along the road he spoke. "Where is everyone?"

"Here and there. Catherine and Carlotta are in town seeing to wedding plans, my father is off on business as usual, and Caton took James and Johnny with him to see to the house."

"House?"

"Caton purchased us a house last week. There are just a few preparations to take care of before we move in."

"You seem well suited to each other." Brant smiled, he seemed at ease with the idea that Senona had found someone else.

"We are. He makes me try to be a better person. If it wasn't for him I wouldn't be giving my parents a second chance."

Senona smiled as she thought about Caton. "Catherine is good for you. She'll be around when you're ready to settle down but she'll also stick by you through everything."

Brant nodded, a hint of a smile playing at his lips. "I've been such a fool. I didn't know myself the depths of my feelings for her and I hurt her. I don't even deserve her anymore. I'm not sure if I ever did." He spoke sadly but Senona could hear the love in his voice.

"Now we just have to keep from messing things up," she laughed.

"For us, that may prove difficult."

* * *

Caton walked through the house showing James and Johnny all the different rooms.

"Right now I only have one maid but the house is small and I doubt we'll need any more for some time."

James and Johnny looked around in amazement. They had both grown up in wealthy families, though James was more accustomed to a ship than the vast estate, and this house was by no means small. James had counted seven bedrooms, a dining room, parlor, den, study, library, kitchen, and servants' quarters. It was not large enough to host any large events such as had been held just last night at the Montez estate, but it was not small. For two people it was more than enough.

"It's beautiful. Has Senona seen it?" asked Johnny.

"Briefly, though she was more interested in the stable than the house," laughed Caton. He knew his fiancée well and had expected nothing different, which was why he had chosen a house that he liked rather than trying to get Senona to give her opinion on one.

"That's no surprise. This room is mine," said James as they walked into the room nearest the library.

Caton laughed. "Of course. And yours, Johnny?"

"The one overlooking the sea."

"And they will always be ready and waiting for you should you come visit us "

"I imagine that will be often enough. Brant often makes port near here," stated James.

"I'm sure Senona hopes so; you two are like brothers to her."

James walked into the library that was half-full of books and ran his hand along the hard leather spines. "You know, I'd like to think I've seen Senona at her happiest. At her greatest and her lowest. Caton, you put her at peace and that is not something I've ever seen in her. Senona means so much to me; at one time, I fully expected her to be my sister, and now she can only be one in my heart. Don't hurt her."

"Do you honestly think I ever could?"

Johnny walked into the room behind them. "She's more fragile than she appears, than she even knows."

"I know, and it's part of why I love her. You two are the dearest people in her life; she's lucky to have two brothers like you."

Caton finished the tour of the house and then asked the groom to have the horses tacked and brought out to them. They went to the Amador estate to join Isidro for lunch and ended up spending the rest of the afternoon there, arriving back at the Montez estate only just in time for dinner, but being a household accustomed to Senona, they started late anyway. Carlotta conversed with Catherine while Caton kept the boys busy. The only indication that there was any strain at the table was Senor Montez' deeply furrowed brow. Then she walked in. Her gait matched Brant's perfectly as she laughed at something he had said. Caton unconsciously clenched his jaw and found his eyes straying over to Catherine to gauge her reaction, which was similar to his.

Senona took her seat next to Caton and Brant sat next to Catherine. She made no attempt to apologize for being late; it was a normal thing for her. Brant, on the other hand, did, and Senor Montez nodded his head graciously and opened in a quick word of grace that Caton couldn't help but think was more for appearance and tradition than actual faith, but it was not his place to judge.

Caton attempted to appear nonchalant as Senona joked and laughed with Brant all throughout dinner, and he could see Catherine was struggling with it as well. Caton knew and trusted Senona better than to believe she could ever love Brant again, but still his jealous nature would spring up every time he saw them so happy together, and their history made it even harder.

Catherine seemed to be trying to ignore the fact that her fiancé was so comfortable with another beautiful woman. She laughed, smiled, and touched Brant constantly, as if in reminder that she was still there. Brant would turn to her, smile, and then continue talking with Senona.

Caton was relieved when dinner was over and everyone dispersed to do their own things for the evening. Caton and Senona left for an evening ride along the coast. They didn't broach the subject of Brant and Catherine; instead, they filled their conversation with discussion of their upcoming wedding. Senona had another dress fitting tomorrow, hopefully, the last, and Caton had to visit the tailors so they could fit him. They had decided not to have any wedding party, just them. It was the way it should be. Really, if they had their way, there wouldn't be any large fancy wedding that Carlotta was planning.

"You know, I almost dread it; all those people coming to stare and whisper about us, as if we're on display and not in a good way, either. Isn't it supposed to be our day?"

Caton shrugged. "It makes your madre happy and that's what we want, right? To at least have a civil relationship with your parents."

"I can't find it in me to forgive them; I just don't feel right fighting with them."

"Time heals all wounds. The wedding is only a week away, are you ready?"

"As ready as ever. I'm sure about this but I'm dreading all the fuss that is going to be involved in that single day."

"All you have to do is be there. Catherine and Carlotta are looking after everything."

"That's exactly what has me worried."

Caton frowned. "This wedding is going to be the biggest event to hit Barcelona in the last twenty years, isn't it?"

"With my madre and Catherine at the helm? It could be no less."

"I'm starting to realize why running away was so appealing to you," teased Caton.

Senona laughed and took off down the beach at a gallop, Caton in hot pursuit. At this moment in time, Senona knew she could spend the rest of her life with this man. This man who made her feel so alive, good, and whole.

* * *

"Senona, my dear, don't worry. It's just the dress will take a little longer than expected, but it will all be okay. We'll just have to postpone the wedding a few days," assured Carlotta.

Senona sighed. With her mother in charge, she shouldn't have been surprised with the delay; extravagance took time, but it was frustrating nonetheless. "A short little delay won't hurt any but if that dress isn't ready by next week Wednesday I'm getting married anyway," she threatened, and she meant it.

Carlotta paled but nodded. "The dress will be ready; I'll see to it."

Senona smiled and walked off, she knew Carlotta would do everything in her power to have the dress done. The shallowness of the ruling class was a constant that could be counted on.

With very little to do around the manor and with Brant and Catherine taking a day for themselves in town, Senona opted to go with Caton and the boys to see her house. After the news of her wedding's delay, she needed something to take her mind off things. And she had yet to tell Caton.

"Caton, it really is gorgeous"

"And just think, this Saturday night we will be living here."

Senona cringed and gave James and Johnny a look that they immediately understood meant to make themselves scarce. "About that, Caton... My madre talked to me today. She says we need to postpone the wedding just a few days."

"Postpone? Why?" he asked, his disappointment apparent.

"Apparently the dress won't be ready."

"Well you can't be a bride without a wedding dress," he said good-naturedly, not at all willing to let a slight delay ruin his good mood.

"You're okay with it, then?"

"I'm still going to marry you. Whether it's Saturday or next Thursday it makes no difference."

Senona hugged him. He was so much more understanding and patient than she was.

James and Johnny peeked around the doorway to see if it was safe to enter and then came strolling in.

"Delay in the wedding, huh?" asked Johnny.

"More time to work on our speech then," put in James.

"Speech? Who gave you two permission to make a speech?" asked Senona, feigning horror.

"Caton," they chorused.

Senona turned on Caton who shrugged. "I said no such thing. I know what's good for me."

Senona laughed. "No speeches. It's a wedding, not a social dinner."

"Too bad."

"Can we drink?" asked Johnny, who, after his first taste of rum decided he liked the stuff.

"Sure, just don't tell Catherine," said Senona with a wink.

"I wouldn't dream of it, especially since she just started liking you and all."

"Come on, let's have lunch. Carla is bound to have it ready now," suggested Caton.

The group made themselves comfortable in the cozy dining room as they ate soup and bread and drank coffee.

* * *

Brant and Catherine spent the day wandering through Barcelona and enjoying the sights. Barcelona was a center of art and architecture that Catherine found fascinating and even Brant could appreciate.

They walked along the outer wall of a cathedral. Everything was stone and somewhat dark and ominous. It gave Catherine the chills to see such cold beauty in the Gothic architecture.

"Brant, last night with Senona... Are we okay?" she asked, voicing her insecurities.

Brant looked at Catherine and raised his eyebrow, pulling her closer to him with his arm around her waist. "We're fine. I know, because of our history, that being friendly with Senona is not reassuring to you, but it's very hard not to be friends with her. I love you... But to be a stranger to her is impossible."

Catherine smiled with tight lips. "I understand. It's just hard for me to ignore or brush things off as nothing."

"Do you trust me?"

"I don't know, Brant. I really don't know if I can. You broke my trust and it's going to take some time to get it back."

"I guess I deserve that, but I promise you that I will do everything in my power to earn that trust."

"I know you want that, but my heart doesn't quite believe it yet. It just takes time, Brant."

* * *

"Madre, have you discovered when the wedding can be held?" asked Senona over dinner.

Carlotta smiled. "Tuesday, Dear. Does that work for you?"

Senona looked at Caton and nodded. "That's fine."

"Has the wedding been delayed?" asked Catherine.

"Yes. Terrible thing, really. I went to the dressmaker today and he said he couldn't have the dress done before Monday."

"Shame. But it gives us more time for preparations."

"Yes, more time for a big to-do," sighed Senona.

Brant smirked as Catherine and Carlotta completely ignored Senona. They were utterly oblivious to how unhappy the couple was about how things were working out, and it was their wedding.

As dinner came to an end, Brant followed Senona out of the dining room and to the stable. He hung back as she said goodbye to Caton, who was staying at his parents' house tonight due to a business meeting early the next morning.

"You could just tell them to stop," said Brant as he entered.

Senona spun around from where she was brushing Naldo and faced Brant. "I know, but I'm giving my mother this one last pleasure before I leave her life for good."

Brant smirked, amused. "I thought you had walked out of her life a year ago when you boarded my ship."

"Well, I walked back in. I didn't want to make more gossip than necessary with my wedding."

"So this one day that is supposed to be special for you and Caton is now turning into a Carlotta and Catherine festival."

"It keeps my mother busy, happy, and above all, out of my hair and Catherine is enjoying herself."

"In that case, I thank you for your sacrifice. How is Caton with all this?"

"He knows why I go with it and he understands but he's about as thrilled as I am."

Brant grabbed a brush and started grooming Sirena, who was in the stall across from Naldo. "I hope for your sake everything works out. You deserve a little happiness."

Senona laughed. "I have plenty of happiness, just not usually when my mother is around. Don't worry about me, Brant. I'm a big girl."

"I never said you weren't. You are more capable than most grown men I know."

Senona turned to look at Brant, an idea dawning on her and she smirked, her eyes full of mischief. "Brant, let's go out."

"Where?"

"Drinking! Let's go to a tavern down by the docks."

Brant laughed. "You do remember what happened last time you went drinking at a tavern?"

"Old Richard showed up." Neither one of them mentioned what else had happened that evening; it was something they were both trying to put behind them for the sake of their relationships. "I can look after myself now. Please, Brant," she pleaded.

He threw up his hands and walked into the tack room.

"Is that a yes?" she called after him.

He walked out of the room, Sirena's tack in his arms. "I suppose it is. Go get our swords, it's never a good idea to drink in a tavern with no means of defense."

Senona ran out of the stables and to the house where she quickly grabbed her sword and then stood in the hall outside Brant's room, looking first one way and then the other before tiptoeing in and grabbing his sword without a sound. She ran out of the house before anyone could stop her.

Brant was waiting with Sirena and Naldo tacked and ready to go. She tossed his sword to him, vaulted onto Naldo's back and took off at a gallop, Brant following close behind.

CHAPTER TWENTY-NINE

Brant slammed down the glass of rum he had just drunk and looked at Senona in challenge. She laughed at his attempt to keep a straight face as the strong amber liquid burned down his throat and settled uneasily in his stomach.

"Not at all impressed, Brant," she said as she shot back her glass of rum without so much as a cringe.

Brant frowned and stood up somewhat unsteadily. Shooting back five glasses of straight rum affected even Brant, a seasoned drinker. "I'll get us some more," he said and stumbled off in the direction of the bar.

Senona giggled as he fell against the counter and ordered two more drinks and then very carefully walked back, attempting not to spill and failing miserably. He set the glasses down on the table roughly, causing them to slosh over the rim.

"A toast!" he exclaimed drunkenly.

"To what?"

"Marriage! Loss of freedom! To Catherine and Caton!"

Senona giggled and raised her glass, clinking it unsteadily on Brant's, and then they both shot back the burning liquid.

"Brant, why haven't we done this before?" she asked, leaning on the table to rest her muddled mind.

"I don't really know, and now we are on the eve of eternal imprisonment. How does that make you feel?"

"Terrified." Senona's voice was quiet as her alcohol-dimmed mind started drifting towards sleep.

"No sleeping," urged Brant, who was slightly less drunk than Senona.

"I'm tired, Brant. I'm just going to rest for a little while."

"No, no we have to get home. Catherine and Caton won't be happy with us." Brant was still drunk, but the careless happiness that had overtaken the two of them only moments before had disappeared as he started to panic, thinking about how Catherine might react.

"No. Too tired," she mumbled.

Brant frowned but, knowing that it would be dangerous to even attempt to go home in the state he was in, settled into his chair and raised his hand for another rum, he wasn't even going to bother attempting a walk to the bar, and at this point he might as well drink himself into oblivion. He had messed up royally tonight, and there was no way to fix it.

* * *

Brant clutched his pounding head between his hands as he attempted to ease his headache and find the words to apologize to Catherine, who was sitting right across from him in the parlor.

"I'm sorry, Catherine, it was irresponsible of me."

She looked at him, tears threatening to spill over. "You said I could trust you, Brant, but you went with her and got completely drunk. What is wrong with you?"

"I don't know. It was just a bit of fun to ease the stress from the week and it got out of hand. All we did was drink."

"I know, but you were drunk! You passed out on a table in the middle of a tavern! I was worried about you last night. I didn't know where you had gone and when you didn't come back... What was I supposed to think when Senona was missing as well?"

"I don't know. Please, Catherine, it was just some drinks."

"Just some drinks? No brawling? No girls?"

"Just drinks. I wanted to get home but I was an idiot and drank too much."

Catherine searched his eyes, looking for the truth behind them. "I believe you and I forgive you, but dammit, Brant! You have to stop doing this to me!"

Brant attempted a grin but it was half-hearted and sadness lay behind it. "I don't deserve you. I do nothing but mess up, Catherine, and I don't know how to be a better person for you."

"I'm not expecting you to change for me. Just, please, put some thought into things before you jump head first into disaster."

Brant got up and crossed the room, pulling her into an embrace and breathing in the scent of lilacs that seemed to always envelop her.

"I love you, Catherine Marshall."

* * *

Senona nursed her hangover with a cup of coffee and toast. Her stomach rolled unappreciatively as the dry toast hit her stomach along with the acidic coffee.

She looked up as the clicking of heels she heard coming down the hall came to a stop right in front of her. The kitchen was always boiling hot at almost any time of year and today was no exception; it did nothing to help Senona's disposition. She said nothing to the woman standing in front of her. She wasn't in the mood to listen to yelling for pulling Brant away, yet again. Her head was pounding, her stomach wanted to reject everything in it, and she was sweating profusely. Now was not the time.

"How are you feeling?" asked Catherine, sounding genuinely friendly and concerned. Senona only groaned in reply.

A chair scraped on the hard stone floor and there was a rustle of fabric as Catherine took a seat. Those small noises grated on Senona's frayed nerves and she clenched her teeth.

"I'm not angry."

Senona looked up in surprise

"It was innocent enough and I've come to accept your relationship with Brant. I'm coming to you with a hand of friendship. We shouldn't be enemies, Senona."

"I, uh..."

"You were expecting I came here to express my anger over what happened last night. It wasn't your fault. Brant is like that sometimes, I know that, and you are so much alike. I really can't hate the fact that he finds good company with you."

"Then you don't see me as a threat anymore?"

"As I said at the ball, you gave him back to me, and I can't hate you for that."

Senona groaned. "I'm probably going to regret this, but will you be my bridesmaid for my wedding? I have no one else to ask, and Caton is understanding enough to have no one else standing at our sides, but I know he would like Isidro there."

Catherine smiled. "I'd be honored, if you will return the favor."

"Of course. Now if you don't mind, I have a hangover to nurse and I'm thinking this infernal heat is not helping it at all. I'm going to go take a ride and figure out how exactly I'm going to explain things to Caton."

"He'll understand."

"I hope you're right."

Senona downed the last of her coffee and made a face as it hit her stomach, but she took a deep breath and walked out of the kitchen into the clean, fresh air outside. It had an instant effect on her. Her stomach stopped turning though her head continued to pound. She saddled up Naldo and rode off at a steady walk down the road.

* * *

Caton had quickly forgiven Senona, even laughed at her and the misery she was in. He found it all quite amusing, which had Senona both miffed and relieved. It wasn't very nice that he was getting such enjoyment out of her misery.

By Saturday, the whole thing had blown over. Brant had to go back to the *BlackFox* to tend to a few things such as docking fees and checking up on his crew while Catherine went to tea with Carlotta at Benita Amador's.

Caton had freed up his day so that he would have some time for Senona. Brant, taking pity on them, dragged James and Johnny with him.

Senona decided to take advantage of this alone time to finally make good on her promise to teach Caton how to fight.

Senona's father was a great advocate of sparring so there were many weapons at their disposal. Senona and Caton had the drawing room cleared and the collection of weapons brought out. She turned a cutlass over a few times in her hand, slashed first one way, then the other, and lunged. Caton watched her curiously but said nothing.

"Good blade," she said and then tossed it to him, causing him to scramble out of the way in surprise. The cutlass fell with a loud clatter to the floor.

Senona turned to look, her eyebrow raised in question. "You're going to have to do better than that. Why didn't you catch it?"

Caton stared at Senona in shock. "Didn't anyone ever tell you it's dangerous to throw around sharp objects?"

"It's not if you catch it."

Caton shrugged sheepishly, picking the fallen sword off the floor and mimicking Senona actions, though somewhat less smoothly.

"This is going to take more work than I thought." Senona laughed good-naturedly.

"I told you I am quite the project."

"You weren't lying."

Caton shook his head and grinned.

"Okay, serious now," started Senona as she drew her cutlass. "We will begin with some simple sparring and follow the general rules of engagement."

Caton took a sloppy stance and Senona grimaced. "No! Like this." She demonstrated. Her body was poised and controlled, ready to spring.

Caton attempted to imitate, and although he looked significantly better, he still looked clumsy next to his skilled fiancée.

"Attack! Step! Parry! Step! Attack!" Senona sharply gave instructions as they sparred.

Caton had the right idea but he was clumsy and didn't know how to think ahead to the next step. Senona was beginning to think it was a miracle he had managed to stay alive long enough to reach her that fateful day on the merchant ship.

"Caton, you have to always be one step ahead of your opponent. If you step left and attack, how will I retaliate? You need to be ready to compensate for that before I even do it."

"I'm not a mind reader," Caton sighed, out of breath.

Senona immediately pushed him again. "Left! Parry! Left! Lunge!"

Caton clumsily followed directions until Senona put down her cutlass.

"Enough. Clearly we need to start a little less advanced."

Senona was not a patient teacher and Caton's struggles caused her annoyance to grow, though she tried to subdue it. He couldn't help it. However, her annoyance was clear in her voice.

Caton smiled in amusement, not taking it personally and pulled her into a hug. "Step by step, *Corazon del Oceano*. We'll try again tomorrow."

"Footwork tomorrow. Be prepared." She was still annoyed but Caton only smiled. If she didn't kill him by the end of this, he was sure their marriage would be a long and happy one, but first they had to last until the wedding.

* * *

"The footwork is like a dance. When dueling there is a leader and every step he makes influences his opponent's step, but the leader can change," Senona started out as she demonstrated a few quick left, right, back, lunge movements.

"It's also smooth like a dance. When you fight, imagine there is an orchestra playing that guides your movements."

"What if the music is slow?" Caton asked with a smirk, just trying to get on Senona's nerves.

"Then you die."

She took up a fighting stance but did not get a weapon. Caton, on the other hand, had a cutlass. He looked at her in question.

"Keep it. We're going to work on your feet, and I want to demonstrate how important it is. Just pretend I have a weapon."

Caton shrugged and took position.

Senona took the first step to the right, and Caton went to the left, slashing at Senona, who deftly made her next move and the sword whistled through the air harmlessly where she had been standing only a millisecond earlier. Caton tried again and again to hit her but was always just a step behind.

"Try and move at the same time as me. You have to be in the mind of your opponent," she panted out.

Caton pressed his lips together in a thin line of concentration. They danced around the drawing room as Caton slowly picked up speed and rhythm. They were both breathing hard but Senona did not allow him to quit. Not yet. He had to get the footwork.

But Senona was tiring, and Caton was getting better, quicker. He didn't even realize what he was doing; he expected it to miss. He slashed and she didn't move. Just threw up her arm to block as she fell back a step. The blade bit into her arm and caused her to gasp in pain and surprise. Caton threw down his cutlass and grabbed her arm, inspecting the deep slice.

"Are you okay?" his voice laced with concern and guilt.

Senona looked first at him and then at her arm and started to laugh.

"What's so funny?"

"You got it! You got me!"

"You had no weapon, Senona, and you're hurt."

"No, but you were moving with me! You got the footwork!"

"I sliced your arm!"

"That's amazing!"

Caton sighed. "Let's get that looked at."

He led her to the kitchen where he carefully washed out the cut and looked it over. Maria fussed behind him, clucking her tongue and shaking her head in concern.

"This is going to need some stitching."

Without a word, Maria left the room, hopefully in search of the supplies needed to perform the minor surgery.

Senona paled at the thought of a needle and thread going through her flesh and Caton chuckled, though still feeling terrible that he had hurt her.

"What? You laugh when you get sliced up by a sword but a little needle scares you?"

"I've been pricked one too many times," she said, looking a little green.

"I'm sorry, Senona, I thought you'd step away."

"Don't apologize, this is a good thing! It means you're catching on."

Maria came in with a needle and thread. "You hold her still so I don't poke her more than I have to," she said sternly.

"Caton, no! No needles. I really don't like needles. Please, Caton..." she pleaded as Maria dipped the needle in boiling water to sanitize it.

"You are afraid of nothing, Senona Montez, but a needle? I never would have thought," he scoffed in an attempt to bring her stubborn side into play.

"I know what you're doing, Caton Amador, and it's not going to work. Keep that damn needle away from me or it's going to end up in your eye," she threatened.

Maria rolled her eyes. "Just hold her arms, please."

Caton complied, and although Senona tried to pull away, he was much stronger and her arm didn't so much as budge. She was so intent on trying to escape his clutches that she didn't even feel the needle go into her skin.

"There. All done."

Senona looked at Maria in surprise, then to Caton, and fainted.

* * *

Senona could not believe she had fainted. One moment she had been ecstatic over the fact that Caton had gotten the better of her. And the next moment she was panicking and fainted, right there in Caton's arms. It was embarrassing and neither Caton nor Brant would ever let her live it down. In fact, on Sunday evening, that was all they talked about over dinner.

Her mother and Catherine showed some concern, but even her father managed a slight chuckle as Caton retold the story. Senona smiled bitterly and chewed aggressively at her steak, now if only they would forget all about it.

* * *

With only two days until the wedding, Senona found herself with more free time than she knew what to do with. Catherine and her mother were taking care of all the preparations, and Caton was busy getting their house ready, leaving Senona with James, Johnny, and Brant.

Senona filled her time teaching Johnny Spanish, talking philosophy with James—something he had taken a great interest in during his brief stint in England—and her daily ride and sparring sessions with Brant.

"Are you certain you don't want the life of a sailor? I could use a sword hand like you," said Brant as they sparred.

"Teach your boys."

"It doesn't come to them as it does to you. You're a natural."

"I don't think Caton would appreciate me working with you."

Brant frowned. "I think we're getting along okay. Don't you?"

Senona wrinkled her nose. Brant and Caton had been tolerating each other the whole previous week, but after Senona's episode with a needle just yesterday they had been getting along as if they were old friends.

"He's trying hard for me. With my mother taking over and the wedding being postponed, he's having a tough time."

"It will happen."

Senona sighed, dropping her cutlass and throwing her hands up in frustration. "All the preparations are done! It's just that dress and I don't even care about it! I just want to be married."

"She won't postpone it again. Two more days and you will be a married woman, which is something I never thought I'd see you as."

Senona frowned. "Why is that?"

"Never thought you'd want to have a man tie you down."

Senona laughed. "That's just it; Caton makes me feel freer than I ever have before."

"I'm starting to learn what that feels like."

The two of them sat in the middle of the drawing room floor as they talked.

"When is the big day? Have you decided yet?"

"Soon. But we're thinking low key. Just the two of us, James, Johnny, and you and Caton if you like."

"I already told Catherine I'd be honored, if it is at all possible to be there."

"Who knows, maybe we'll do it here."

"Come, let's go for a walk."

The two of them walked through Naldo's pasture enjoying the cool breeze coming off the Mediterranean Sea.

"Johnny mentioned something about staying here. He wants to serve on an Amador Company ship," said Brant.

Senona pressed her lips together; she was on dangerous ground. "Caton offered, but we would never dream of going through with it without Catherine's approval."

Brant was thoughtful. "I've been thinking of staying here. Getting a home and starting over."

"What?" Senona wasn't quite sure if she had heard correctly.

"Catherine loves it here, and with Johnny wanting to work for a company and James wanting to study, it just makes sense."

"Well, sure, but it's more dangerous for you here than in Port Royale. The king can't protect you here. You'll lose your privateer status."

Brant nodded. "I've been thinking about this for a little while, actually. What if I gave all that up?"

"Brant-" Senona said softly. That ship, that life. It was everything to Brant.

"I don't need to pirate. I can start a shipping company of my own."

"And Foxton estate?"

"Sam has been running it for the past few years. He can have it. I have enough money saved up to have a place built here."

"What does Catherine think?"

"I mentioned it to her yesterday. She loves the idea."

Senona shook her head. It was all so overwhelming. Brant Foxton was talking about giving up who he was, and he said it without any second thoughts.

"That's why I want you around," continued Brant. "Matt is a good quartermaster but not like Karl."

"No one will ever be able to replace Karl."

"No, but you know and understand me better than most people."

Senona didn't know what to say. It sounded wonderful. She loved being on the ship and she knew she could handle the position and with Brant going straight... "If I wasn't getting married, I'd say yes, but there are a lot more things to bring into consideration. I don't think this is the right time."

"Think about it."

Senona smiled. "I can promise you that much."

"Captain Foxton and First mate Montez—"

"Amador," corrected Senona.

"Sorry," chuckled Brant. "First mate Amador; terror of the high seas."

Senona laughed. "I thought you were giving up piracy."

"Oh, right." He winked. "Bringing supplies safely wherever they're needed."

"Now that's just downright blood-curdling."

"No pirate will dare mess with us."

Senona sighed. "But I can't... Caton..."

"And I have Catherine. Perhaps not now, but give it time and Caton will support you if it's what you want."

"It sounds so wonderful. Brant, you are cruel dangling this in front of me!"

"Couldn't resist, my dear. Couldn't resist."

CHAPTER THIRTY

Tuesday morning, Senona awoke to a dreary rain, but her spirits were high. She was getting married tomorrow! She would be out of her parents' control once and for all, and she could start her new life with Caton.

She dressed quickly and went downstairs to the dining room, a bounce in her step and a smile on her face. The only downside to all of this was spending the day with her mother and Catherine going over final preparations for the wedding.

Breakfast was a leisurely affair. No one was in any great hurry to go anywhere. The maid brought out round after round of tea, coffee, and freshly made toast with butter for the group of people. They didn't even bother leaving the breakfast table until nearly noon. Even Carlotta Montez was enjoyable company. Perhaps she was just feeling sentimental, but it was a welcome change.

Senona felt a little sad that the woman she saw today wasn't the mother who had raised her for seventeen years. If Carlotta Montez had been more like this, then maybe she never would have left, but as she thought about it, Senona realized if she never left she wouldn't have known Brant, James, or Johnny and it was very unlikely that she would have ended up with Caton.

All things happen for a reason, she thought with a faint smile playing over her lips.

Marcus Montez snapped his fingers for the servants to clear the table. He sat back comfortably in his chair, folded his arms over his stomach, and sighed.

"It is lovely to see so many happy people around my table. I don't believe I have ever seen my daughter so happy, and I thank you for making her so, Caton." He paused, took a deep breath, and continued. "Today we are all separate families but tomorrow, with the exception of Captain Foxton and Lady Marshall, we shall become one family."

Carlotta cleared her throat, but Marcus waved his hand in annoyance at her. "One moment, I'm not finished yet."

Carlotta glared at him but he took no heed. "Every father wishes for a son; I was blessed with a daughter. Some men may not see this as such a blessing, but I see this as an opportunity: I get to pick my son."

Senona caught Caton's eye and tried to hold back a laugh.

The only two people not smiling were Carlotta and Marcus; Marcus looking quite solemn and Carlotta glaring angrily at him. "Now, as I was saying, this is a joyous occasion and with this union tomorrow, I wish to express my blessing formally to these two young people and wish my daughter, and my soon-to-be son, much happiness and joy in this new life they are about to embark on together."

Carlotta cleared her throat angrily now at her husband.

"Yes, Dear, go ahead."

"Gracias," she said, not sounding at all thankful. "Now if you had only let me speak when I wanted to, perhaps we could have avoided this long-winded speech of yours. I got news last night that the wedding is not to be held tomorrow, there has been a problem with the church—"

"No, Madre, we are getting married tomorrow, even if it's outside," said Senona, suddenly realizing why her mother was being so agreeable. Carlotta had just wanted her in good spirits for this news.

"Well, my dear, there is nothing that can be done. It is simply not proper for you to be married outside of the church."

Senona was fuming and she shot an accusing glance at Catherine who had a bewildered look on her face. Caton saw the situation quickly turning ugly and he placed his hand in warning on Senona's arm. "Let's go for a ride, Senona," he said.

"I'll try and figure things out, Senona," urged Catherine.

Senona pushed back her chair angrily and left in a rustle of skirts. She didn't look at her mother but Caton stopped before following behind.

"You almost had your daughter back but now I think you may have lost her forever. You pushed her too far, Carlotta. Senona is strong, too strong to allow you to rule her. Learn to choose your battles."

* * *

Senona and Caton rode to the cliff's edge where he had first told her that he loved her. Before they had left, he had told Catherine and Brant where they were going and to come find them if they figured anything out.

Senona was obviously still angry as she galloped along the cliff's edge in an attempt to erase the thought of her mother and to feel freedom again. As they stopped, Senona took deep breaths, closing her eyes and emptying her mind of everything, just letting her surroundings fill her senses. She opened her eyes as Caton rode up beside her.

"It's not so much the wedding being postponed again, it's how my mother is controlling every aspect of my life without even consulting me. I never should have allowed her back into my life."

"I feel somewhat responsible for all this, pushing you back into a relationship with your parents."

"None of this is your fault, Caton. It was my choice and it was a bad one."

Caton didn't argue the fact. He sat there in silence and listened to the wind and the waves crashing against the cliff wall below. Neither one of them spoke. The horses pawed restlessly a few times and then would take a few steps, nibble at some grass, and start again. Their riders sat motionless on their backs, not caring what went on around them.

An hour later the sound of distant pounding hoofbeats drew nearer and came to a stop next to them. Brant and Catherine dismounted, leaving their horses to graze and Caton did the same. Only Senona remained on Naldo, drawing comfort from his warm living body and quivering muscles.

"Your mother won't budge. She is convinced you will come back for the wedding and that you're just upset," said Catherine.

Senona looked from Catherine to Brant and then to Caton. "Is she right, Caton? Are we going to go back?"

"No," he said firmly. "Your mother is done controlling your life and I stand behind you in cutting her out." He turned to Brant. "You're a captain."

Brant smirked. "Yes, I am. How very observant of you."

"Marry us. You, Catherine, James, Johnny, and Isidro... You're our family. Marry us today on your ship."

Senona looked at Caton and grinned. "It's perfect. Brant?"

Brant rolled his eyes but he was smiling. "Alright, you have convinced me. Collect everything you need. I'll get the *BlackFox* ready."

"I'll get the dress. You two go and get James, Johnny, and Isidro," said Catherine, walking over to the mare she had borrowed from the Montez stables.

The four of them rode off to their separate tasks. Senona felt elated, even happier than she had this morning. In fact, she couldn't imagine doing it any other way.

* * *

Brant shouted orders to his sailors in preparation for Senona and Caton. He expected Catherine to be here any second, and once everyone else got on board, he wanted to cast off. This wedding had to be perfect for Senona; she deserved it, and now was his chance to make things up to her.

Matt ran around relaying orders for Brant as he took a moment to get changed. Catherine arrived on the ship and breezed right into his cabin.

"They're going to be here any moment, Brant! Don't worry about getting changed!" she scolded as she searched around for a place to hang Senona's wedding dress. She opted for just laying it flat on Brant's bed and then chased him out of the cabin.

Caton, Senona, and the others were a bit longer as they had to go first to the Montez estate and then the Amato estate to fetch the boys and Isidro, but they made better time than expected and arrived shortly. They left the horses at the stables next to the Amador house until they returned.

Johnny and James raced each other to the ship, both eager for the wedding and to be back at sea, if only for a day.

The *BlackFox* cast off almost immediately after its passengers boarded. The crew was ready and waiting and things went smoothly and without a hitch. Brant didn't raise his voice once and he walked around the deck looking quite smug. It wasn't often a ship ran this well.

Catherine immediately whisked Senona off to Brant's cabin to get changed, leaving Caton with Isidro to wander the deck.

"So, this is where Senona became the woman she is now," mused Caton as he stroked the rail.

"You know I've never been to sea, but I imagine it would be a good place for epiphanies."

Caton scoffed. "I've been to sea. It's hard work, terrible food, and uncomfortable quarters. Nothing romantic or philosophical about it."

"But you, my friend, were working on the ship. I would be going as a paying passenger," replied Isidro. "I like my comfort too well to sacrifice it for any true experience of the sea."

Caton patted his friend on the back. "Leave it to you, Isidro, to see the real importance in life. Hard work might ruin those hands of yours."

Senona stepped out onto the deck all in white, but true to request, the dress was simple, the only ruffling being a few layers down the back of the skirt, which were done quite tastefully. Her hair cascaded freely down her back and blew in the cool sea breeze. Brant joined Caton and Isidro by the rail, admiring Senona.

"You think you're ready for this?" he asked Caton.

"More than ready."

Brant chuckled, his eyes twinkling. "Perhaps I phrased that badly. Do you think you can handle her?"

Caton smiled. "No one can, it's why I love her. She's her own person and she's just kind enough to be willing to spend the rest of her life with me. I won't ever be able, or ready, to handle her."

"Good. Then you understand."

They stood in silence as Senona walked over, Catherine walking just ahead.

"Can we do this on the upper deck? Nothing fancy, Brant." She looked pointedly at him in warning. "No speeches," she emphasized. "Just the vows."

Brant smirked but nodded. "As you wish."

The small party made their way to the upper deck and found places to lean along the rail, except for Brant, Senona, and Caton. Brant took his place just in front of them all and Caton and Senona stood side by side facing him.

It was nothing special. Nothing overly romantic for the storybooks. Senona and Caton repeated the vows word for word, after Brant. It was nothing spectacular but they said every word with such sincerity and love.

As they both said "I do", Brant shrugged and gestured for them to kiss, sealing their promise, to much applauding from all the crew.

Senona laughed and kissed Caton again.

"Hello, Senora Amador," he whispered against her lips.

Brant looked at Catherine who was smiling broadly and he winked at her. That would be them someday very soon. He walked over and put his arm around her, pulling her close.

"So, Miss Marshall, how would you like your wedding to be?"

"Large and expensive."

Brant looked at her in shock but he attempted to pull it together. "Well, if that's what you want—"

Catherine laughed and leaned in. "Of course not! A small wedding is fine, though maybe a little more traditional and formal than this one. I don't love pirate ships that much."

"Just the pirates that sail them," Brant teased.

"Sail ho!" came the shout from high above, interrupting the celebrating and bringing the crew rushing to the rail.

Brant prayed it wasn't a ship from the Spanish navy; he wasn't exactly on friendly terms with them.

James ran up with his eyeglass, knowing better than to wait for Brant to request it. Brant pulled it out and searched out the ship for colors or some sign of what its intentions were.

"Damn it!" he swore loudly, getting a look from Catherine. "Catherine, get below deck. Senona, you better change fast and find a weapon. Caton—" he paused. "You think you're ready to put that training to the test?"

Caton nodded but he didn't look too sure.

"Good. Matt, go get him something to fight with."

Brant turned around, about to shout orders to his crew, but they were already on the move, getting cannons ready but not rolling them out, waiting until they were sure they would need them.

"Remind me to give them a bonus," said Brant to James and Johnny, waiting for Brant to send them below deck with Catherine. Brant looked at them. "What are you still doing here? Go get some swords and then help out! You're on my crew, aren't you?"

"Yes, Sir!" they said in unison, sprinting off.

Senona came running back, wearing a pair of borrowed breeches and a shirt. "What're we looking at?"

"Spanish navy vessel. I'm hoping it's just sailing around looking pretty, but I doubt there's a naval officer in the Spanish Armada that doesn't know my ship."

"We're looking at a confrontation, then?"

"It's likely."

"Don't be afraid to surrender."

"Senona Amador, am I hearing you correctly? Surrendering is not an option!" He laughed.

Senona's voice remained solemn. "You have Catherine and two sixteen-year-old boys on this ship. There is no gold in this fight. If things get ugly, please surrender."

Brant nodded grimly. "I will, don't worry. Now go find that husband of yours. You may need to protect him."

Brant watched the ship carefully as it rolled its guns out and its colors flew high and proud. He could run up the white flag now, but that would do nothing but result in a search of the ship and perhaps his arrest, something that would not bode well in Spanish territory. He wasn't exactly well liked, and he doubted that even after spending the week with the Montez' that Marcus Montez would be overly eager to pull strings and get him out of prison. Helping his daughter run away was not something that he would easily forgive.

The first cannon exploded into the water near the starboard bow in warning and Brant cringed. "If they hit my ship, I will not be happy," he muttered, his hand on the hilt of his sword. "Keep those guns in!" he commanded as a couple of eager sailors started to roll out a cannon. "We do not want a battle on our hands!" But Brant knew they would get one. The only hope of escape would be a battle and a victory, and then he would have to run, ruining all his plans for settling in Spain.

He hadn't told Senona, but before he had even gone to her engagement ball, he had applied for merchant status and had received it only this past week, which was why he had brought it up. The papers were safely in his cabin and now he would have to give them up. They would not allow a known pirate ship to go, and after a sea battle in indisputable Spanish territory just off the coast, he could never return even if he managed to escape.

Another cannon shot burst into the water, closer this time, causing the ship to rock a bit. Brant once again held his hand up in warning to his crew. Right now they could just be trying to scare him, and Brant wasn't going to react. That's what they wanted. No, let them get close enough so that when he did react they would get it full force.

An hour they waited, tense and ready as the ship slowly drew closer and continued to fire warning shots. An hour until the ship drew close enough to do some damage and before they let off a shot that would potentially injure or kill some of his crew. Brant gave the signal to fire, and in a second the crew had every single cannon on the starboard side rolled out and fired. At least three hit their mark while others slammed into the water so close that the ship rocked, causing men to stumble or fall. Brant smiled and nodded his head at the commanding officer, who was now close enough to see him.

"Do not board!" Brant shouted to some of his men who were waiting eagerly at the rail. "We have no quarrel with them; we're just defending ourselves."

The Spaniards brought the fight to him, boarding, and soon Brant had a full out battle on his hands. He glanced around for Senona, who he saw fighting back to back with Caton, James guarding their left and Johnny their right, in the center of it all. Brant fought, a smirk on his face. Really, he wasn't worried, but the Spaniards were good, though not nearly as good as him.

He glanced around again at the state of his crew; a few injuries, nothing serious, but it would turn ugly very quickly if it wasn't brought to a stop.

* * *

Senona and Caton stood back-to-back, breathing heavily and surrounded by Spanish navy. James was to her left and Johnny to her right, holding their own against the Spaniards who came close enough, but they were careful not to kill anyone. Before the fighting had begun, Senona had talked to them. Neither had killed, nor even hurt anyone before, and Senona knew it wasn't the time for them to start killing, neither one of them was ready for it.

There was a brief break in fighting and Senona glanced over to the stairs leading to the hold. Catherine was standing there, frozen in fear.

"Not good. Not good at all." She was about to make her way over to Catherine to guard her, but Brant had noticed her about the same time Senona had and was heading over to her as quickly as he could.

"This isn't quite how I imagined our wedding," said Caton in a weak attempt at a joke.

Senona laughed. "I'd think there was something wrong with you if you did. Though somehow it seems fitting."

Caton grinned and touched her hand before running a man through.

"By order of his majesty, stand down!" came the loud booming voice of the commanding officer.

Everything seemed to halt instantly. His voice held a commanding presence and everyone felt inclined to listen to him. Senona found Brant and nodded; they couldn't win this fight with swords. She dropped her sword, and slowly the rest of the crew followed suit when they saw no argument from their captain.

Caton gripped Senona's hand and she squeezed it reassuringly. "This isn't good," he whispered.

"Never said it was."

"If Brant gets taken away..." Caton started but couldn't finish his sentence.

"He's a dead man. That's why we won't let it happen."

Senona once again looked at Brant and beckoned him over. He grabbed Catherine's arm and walked over to Senona.

"You spoke of ending all this... I'm guessing you looked after it before even mentioning it to me. Do you have papers?"

"In my cabin."

"Good. I may be able to get us out of this mess."

Brant nodded, he wasn't entirely sure it would do any good but it was worth a try. Maybe Senona would be able to get through to him.

Isidro walked over to Caton from where he had been fighting; through all the excitement, he had slipped everyone's minds. "What's happening now?"

"Senona has a plan."

"Senor! Senor! May I ask why you attacked this ship when it posed no threat to you?"

The captain turned to face Senona. "I would think that is apparent, Senorita."

"Well, humor me, Captain."

"This is a well-known pirate vessel. It has attacked several of our ships in the past."

Senona laughed. "You must be mistaken. This vessel is a merchant ship."

"Is that so?"

"Si, Captain. The papers are in the cabin; I've seen them myself. In fact, that is precisely why my husband and I are on this ship. We were having a meeting with Captain Foxton about working for the family company."

The captain looked over at Caton. "Senor Amador, I'm sorry, I did not recognize you, and Senor Amato."

Caton nodded. "You can hardly be expected to know every face in Spain, Captain. But please, could we sort this out quickly?"

The captain nodded and sent one of his officers off to search Brant's cabin for the papers.

Senona looked at Brant, worry shining in her eyes as she asked the silent question of whether or not his privateering papers were in there as well. Brant just shook his head 'no.' Senona knew he would have them on the ship in case of an attack by an English ship, but they were well hidden, most likely in a secret compartment somewhere.

The officer came out moments later, papers in hand. He passed them to the captain who carefully studied them. "These are, in fact, legitimate, but they were dated only a few days ago."

Brant stepped forward now. "I have the papers. When they were issued is not relevant. Do you have any further business on this ship or may Senor Amador and I continue with ours?"

The captain waved his hand. "Yes, yes we will leave. Look after your wounded, Senor Foxton. I'm sure we will be meeting again soon."

As the Spanish navy boarded their own ship, everyone seemed to breathe a collective sigh of relief.

Catherine hung onto Brant as the fear finally let her go and she collapsed against him, exhausted.

Caton just held Senona and breathed in her confidence and reassurance. Confrontation, death, and violence were nothing new to her. Even James and Johnny were shaken up. But as the hours moved on, cuts were tended to, and the day melted into night, things were forgotten and thoughts went back to the joyous occasion that had started the day; Caton and Senona's wedding.

They lit torches around the deck and brought out various instruments. Brant went into his own private stash of rum and brought out four large bottles for the whole crew to drink in celebration, it was the last of his stash, and he lamented it greatly, but he was feeling generous tonight and with every complaint he smiled and winked.

After a lot of drunken singing and dancing, and after Isidro was safely passed out in a corner, Senona and Caton found themselves alone at the bow of the ship. She leaned against him, his arms around her stomach and holding her close. She closed her eyes as she breathed in the salty sea air.

"This is the wedding I wanted."

"The people important to us, simple, a fight with the Spanish navy, Brant nearly being arrested, stitching and bandaging cuts and slices and a drunken party afterward. Perfect," Caton said, amused.

Senona laughed. "Well, when you put it that way it's pretty terrible. But take out the fighting and the bandaging, the people, the simplicity, even the drinking and dancing on a pirate ship is much better than anything my madre could have planned."

"I'm glad you're happy, Senora Amador."

Brant and Catherine joined them not too much later. Brant was staggering slightly and hoarding a bottle of the good stuff all to himself. "Here, Caton! This is the last bottle and it's your day."

Caton grinned and took a swig, handed it to Senona who did the same and then it went back to Brant after Catherine shook her head with a smile. She may be marrying a pirate but she still liked her fine wines and champagne.

Senona laughed as Brant sat down on the deck, leaning against the rail. "Maybe you should stop, Brant."

"No, I'm celebrating. I'm straightening my life out and building a house here for Catherine; I can drink until the bottle runs dry," and with those words he passed out.

Catherine gently pried the bottle from his limp hand and handed it to Caton. "Enjoy."

Caton nodded his thanks and walked away to check on Isidro.

Senona felt sorry for Catherine as Brant sat slumped against the rail passed out, but she was smiling, and it didn't look fake. "You know, I used to get upset when Brant would do things I considered inappropriate, but now I've stopped fighting it. He's still a boy at heart; soon enough he'll settle down."

Senona nodded. "He needs someone like you who can understand that and be patient with him. I can't condone a lot of things he does. I can't condone a lot of things I've done, but I must say I admire you for wanting to make him a better person while being willing to let him become that in his own time. I was lucky enough to find Caton."

"Or he's lucky enough to have found you. You have your faults, Senona, but you're a strong and good person and I'm honored to have fought you for a man and won."

"It seems we ended up with who we were meant to. If you'll excuse me I'm going to go collect my husband and find some place to sleep."

Catherine nodded and sat down beside Brant, leaning on him. Senona smiled and walked away, finding Caton lying on the upper deck staring at the stars. She lay down beside him and rested her head on his chest. Neither said a word; they just let the majesty of the night sky wash over them until they fell into a deep sleep

CHAPTER THIRTY-ONE

Senona and Caton walked hand in hand along the beach. They left the horses about a mile back, grazing on seagrass and weeds. The sun set over the water, and Caton pulled her into his arms and held her as the pink light washed over them while it slowly sank over the horizon.

"My *Corazon del Oceano*," he whispered into her ear.

They stood there enjoying the feeling of being close to each other and the serenity of the surrounding atmosphere.

"Who ever thought I would end up here with you?" Senona asked.

"Certainly not me," he laughed.

"I've messed up so much of my life and yet you love me and you'll never stop, no matter what I do. How many times does that happen to someone?"

"Once in a lifetime," he whispered. "It's what the stories are made of."

The sun set below the waterline and as the day closed, a new chapter of their life opened.

Betrayed by the Ocean

Christine Steendam

CHAPTER ONE

Spain- 1671

Brant stared at Catherine, her words not quite sinking in. His ears buzzed as if they were in the aftershock of a cannon firing. "What do you mean you're leaving?"

Catherine's eyes welled up with tears. "I got a letter from my parents. They're worried about the unrest between Spain and England and they want me to bring Johnny home. We leave tomorrow, and I won't be coming back."

Brant walked away, unable to look at Catherine. He looked out the window of the house he had built for her. It had been completed a month ago. She'd just moved in, and she had spent hundreds of doubloons on furnishing and decorating the house that was supposed to be their home.

He'd promised her the wedding she'd been asking for this coming spring. He'd given her everything she'd ever asked for, and now she was leaving.

"I don't understand," he said, still looking out the window. Unable to look at her tear streaked face—the sorrow that mocked him and his pain.

"This past year with you has been... an experience. We've been through a lot, and we've done our fair share of hurting each other—"

"And we moved past that, stronger than ever."

"No, we forgave and tried to forget, but didn't fix anything."

"I gave up my life for you!"

"I know."

"Everything you could ever ask for, it's here."

"Except you. I've ruined you, Brant. You're living life half asleep."

Now he turned to face her. He knew his eyes burned with anger, accusing and violent. He didn't care how much it hurt or scared her—it was her fault. "You wanted this. You wanted me to live a legitimate life."

"I know," she replied, her face falling, guilt written all over. "Brant, have you ever thought that maybe we just aren't meant to be together? You fought so hard for Senona, why didn't you fight like that for me?"

"You're bringing up Senona? We moved past this a long time ago. And I thought we moved past this sacrifice you think I'm making. I feel like we're stuck in a loop. I *love* you, Catherine. Why can't that be enough?"

She shook her head, tears streaming down her face, her eyes red and swollen. But she remained stalwart in her decision. "Johnny and I will be leaving tomorrow morning. I'd appreciate it if you didn't make this any harder than it already is."

Brant couldn't bring himself to say anything in return. He pressed his lips together tightly in an attempt to keep the tears that were burning his eyes and the back of his throat at bay.

Walking out of the house, he found his horse in the stables and saddled him quickly, all the while hoping that Catherine would change her mind, that she would run after him and tell him that she had made a mistake, she'd had a momentary lapse of judgment, and she loved him. That she'd bring Johnny home and return as soon as possible to *finally* marry him.

But no one came. The stable remained silent and empty apart from the four-legged animals confined to their stalls.

Mounting his horse, Brant rode away from his house and his life with Catherine.

In Barcelona, he stopped at the first tavern he saw and dismounted, tying his horse to a post outside. Walking in, he slammed a doubloon on the counter and took a seat.

"Rum, and keep them coming until the doubloon runs out."

The barkeep nodded and snatched up the dirty coin, simultaneously pouring the golden liquid into a foggy glass.

The second the liquid stopped pouring, Brant grabbed the glass, shooting the burning liquid back.

Placing the glass back down, it was quickly refilled. With the initial pain purged by the quick shot, he sipped at this drink. The tears he had been fighting earlier were gone now, and all he felt was anger and bitterness.

He'd given up so much for her, everything, and this was how she repaid him?

With each drink he finished, his anger increased. A doxy draped herself over his shoulder and whispered something in his ear, but he didn't hear. He pushed her off roughly.

"What's your problem?" she asked. Somehow she sounded less pathetic than her English counterparts, speaking in lilting Spanish.

"I'm not here for that."

"You're here for something, and it sure ain't cards. Who you drinking away? I can make it better."

Brant chuckled, but it sounded bitter even in his ears. "You can't make anything better. The only thing a woman is good for is ruining men. Go take your business elsewhere and leave me be."

The woman huffed and flounced away to find her next victim. The minute she was gone she was out of Brant's mind. But his thoughts returned to Catherine, and Senona; he'd only ever been betrayed by the women he had trusted. He'd been land bound too long. He needed to return to his first love, his mistress, the only thing that had never betrayed him; the ocean and his ship. They were the only constants in his life, and he had so foolishly put them aside, for what? For a chance at a normal life? To settle down and have a family? He should have known better, should have known he could never have those things.

Downing a few more drinks, Brant's vision began to swim and he leaned down on the bar top. He just needed to rest.

"Hey, you can't sleep here!" shouted the barkeep, shaking him roughly.

Brant blinked at him a few times before the words sunk in, and he nodded. Getting up, he walked unsteadily across the room, bumping into a few tables and chairs. He received angry glares and exclamations as he went, and then finally stumbled through the door and out into the street.

Unsure of where he was going, his feet moved aimlessly through the streets of Barcelona. He had no idea how far he walked. He briefly thought about his horse, and frowned, pausing in his stumbling walk. Where had he left that animal? He shrugged, unsure of what he was concerned about, and continued on his way. Somehow, he found himself in a familiar area of the merchant quarter, and he wove down the street towards the townhouse that Caton kept.

Making his way up the steps, he rang the bell and sat down with his back against the door. Then everything went black.

* * *

Brant woke up the next day with a pounding head and a churning stomach. He sat up slowly in the plush bed and looked around. How had he arrived at Caton's house, and in his own bed? Rubbing his eyes, he looked around. All he could remember was the dirty bar near the docks the night before, and way too many drinks.

Slowly climbing out of bed, he sat on the edge and waited for the room to stop spinning before he attempted to stand. He didn't bother searching for his boots, just walked out of his room in stocking feet in search of someone who could tell him what had happened.

"Good morning, Captain Foxton," came a much too familiar, feminine and mocking voice. She shouldn't be here.

She never came into the city. This house was for Caton when he worked in the city and for Brant when he was in port.

"Senona, I didn't expect to see you here."

She smiled and held up a cup of steaming coffee in invitation from where she sat at the dining room table.

Brant walked over and sat down, accepting the coffee.

"You going to tell me what happened last night?"

Brant shook his head and groaned. "Don't really want to talk about it."

"Then maybe you want to explain to me why Catherine stopped by this morning and asked me to check on you. The servants told me they found you passed out on the front step sometime after midnight, and had to drag you up to your bed." Her expression was that of disapproval, but was contradicted by her amused tone and dancing eyes.

Brant groaned again and sipped at his coffee. "I don't even remember leaving the tavern."

Senona reached for his hand, but he flinched and pulled away from her touch. He didn't want to open up to her, but there was something about Senona that had always made him feel at home, comfortable, despite the feelings that he still harbored for her—or maybe it was because of those feelings.

"She left me," he said. The words still didn't seem real.

"I don't understand. I know she left. But—"

"Neither do I. I thought we were in a good place, now suddenly she's leaving for England and not coming back."

"She didn't explain?"

"She said she was ruining me."

Senona's eyes no longer danced in amusement. Instead, they held pity, which only made him angry. She reached for his hand again, squeezing it in sympathy. "You haven't been yourself lately. Caton and I have noticed it as well."

"You're the one that told me I needed to be a better person. She did that for me."

Senona said nothing. Getting up slowly from her chair, she embraced her round, pregnant belly, and walked over to the window. She was six months along now, and the sight of her starting her family with Caton had Brant's chest tightening in painful jealousy. This was what he wanted. He was supposed to be starting his life with Catherine, starting a family. She wasn't supposed to walk away, not after everything they'd been through.

"Her ship left an hour ago," Senona said, staring out the window, refusing to meet his eyes.

Brant sighed. "So she's gone. I won't see her again." But he could. All he had to do was collect his crew and sail after her. She'd said that he had never fought for her— maybe that was her begging him to make some grand gesture.

Brant stood up, the realization bringing with it hope. "I have to go."

"Don't." Her tone told him she knew without him saying anything what he was going to do. "Let her go. These ups and downs have gone on too long with you two. You need to move on. It would have been easier for her to stay than to return home to all the questions and whispers. Don't you think if she had any hope, if she saw a future with you, she would have stayed? Don't you think the fact that you were willing to give up everything was gesture enough?"

She was right, and he hated it. He'd lost Senona and now he'd lost Catherine. It was as if the world was telling him he would always be alone, that there was no place for women in his life. He didn't deserve happiness.

He nodded slowly and sat back down. "I think I need something stronger than this."

Senona smiled slightly, but it was patronizing and not amused. "The last thing you need is more alcohol. And besides that, it's ten in the morning."

"What do I need then? You tell me, because right now I don't know. I don't think I've known what I needed for the last two years."

"Where were you the last time you were happy and at peace?"

"Sailing; I was my own master and answered to no one. I was a free man."

"What are you now?"

Brant sighed. "Trapped. I feel trapped by this business. I spend too much time on land, and when I'm at sea, I'm controlled by deadlines and destinations. I want to sail again just for the love of it."

Senona nodded. "Then do that."

"I have a business—"

"You have a partner. I'll talk to Caton. He'll contract another ship and you can leave for as long as you need."

"What about James?"

"He is happy here. You aren't his only family anymore, Brant. Caton and I are happy to step in. You need time to find yourself. You've been raising James since you were barely a man yourself."

"What's that supposed to mean?"

"It's supposed to mean that you have too much on your shoulders."

Senona was his constant, his rock, and she was right; he needed to get away. But not just from Spain. He needed to get away from her. If he needed to let Catherine go, he needed to let her go as well. Too long he'd been living in the past, holding onto something that wasn't there.

"Talk to Caton. I'm going to leave next week."

* * *

Brant stood on deck of the *BlackFox* as Matt, his quartermaster, shouted orders to the crew. He watched the activity around him and smiled. For the first time in a year, he felt good. This time he was sailing for himself. There were no deadlines. There was no destination. Brant was heading out to sea because he loved it. He had pulled out his letter of Marque, collecting dust in his cabin safe and read it over, reminding himself of the life he had once had—the life he was trying to get back to.

He'd talked with Caton a lot over the past week. They hadn't said anything to Senona, but they both knew that Brant didn't plan on returning. This life wasn't for him. And if he chose to return to his life as a privateer for the crown, there was no safe return to Spain.

He had transferred ownership of his house to James. Caton would act as his guardian until he turned eighteen next year, when he would receive the remainder of his inheritance and take over Brant's shares in the Amador-Foxton shipping company.

Brant smiled and placed his hat on his head. Looking towards the dock, he saw the approaching figure of a pregnant woman in breeches and a billowy white shirt that she'd left untucked. So, she'd come to bid him goodbye. He wondered when she'd make an appearance. She'd kept her distance ever since their initial talk, as if she knew he couldn't handle being around her. However, she had never missed a launching, and apparently, she wasn't about to break her tradition.

She waddled up the gangway, and Brant chuckled at the sight, trotting over to offer his arm.

"You shouldn't be here. This is no place for a lady, especially one in your condition."

He knew that she wouldn't appreciate the comment. She was a capable woman, as capable as any man on his crew, and she knew it. She hadn't taken kindly to her reduced capability through pregnancy, but she smiled graciously and seemed to accept that it was for the greater good.

"My condition? Give me a cutlass and I'll show you just how capable I am, Brant Foxton. If I were you, I'd keep your tongue tied if you don't wish to be shown up by a woman expecting a child."

Brant laughed, "Wouldn't that be a sight. Now, what brings you here this fine morning?"

"You didn't think I'd miss a launch, did you?"

Brant shook his head. "I guess not." But he had hoped. Goodbye wasn't something he was good at, especially when it came to saying goodbye to someone he loved as dearly as Senona.

"Take a turn around deck with me. We're almost ready to cast off."

Senona grasped his arm tightly as she moved beside him. She was slower than she used to be. Not nearly as steady or strong physically, but emotionally she was still an immobile rock.

"Where will you go?" she asked.

"I'll sail the high seas like I did before, and stay out as long as I can. I'll only make port long enough to repair and restock."

"The good old days have returned, then."

"I hope so."

"Will you be making any visits to Port Royale?"

"Sam?"

Senona nodded.

"I hope so. But that is no longer my home, and I don't want to intrude."

"You think Sam and Julie would consider your presence an intrusion? You are their friend."

"Senona..." he trailed off, unsure of how to appropriately put to words what he felt.

"You're cutting us out," she said, stopping and turning to face him.

"Senona..." he trailed off again. He didn't know how to confirm it when her eyes held so much pain and hurt just at the thought.

"You aren't just going back to the good old days. You're going back to when you had no friends, no family, and no ties to anyone but yourself and this ship."

It wasn't a question. She saw right through him. He should have known that she would. She always had been able to, which was why he had been avoiding her, and why he had hoped she wouldn't show up today. It would have been easier just to disappear and she could think that he was lost at sea, or dead. He never would have had to look in those wide, sad eyes and realize he was letting her down... again. Instead, she saw the truth of it; he was abandoning the people who loved him and called him family.

"I didn't know how to tell you."

"You could have just said it, Brant. You could have just said you'd be leaving and you weren't going to come back."

He nodded.

"Caton knows?"

He nodded again.

"That's why you've been avoiding me? That's why he has been skirting my questions all week?"

"I'm sorry."

Senona grabbed his hand and squeezed it tightly. "Do what you must, Brant Foxton. Sail away into the horizon and never return if that's what will make you happy. But know that there are people who love you and care about you. You've impacted our lives and you can't just erase yourself, even if you can erase us."

"Senona, please. I just need time to find myself again."

She nodded. "I know, and I understand. But that doesn't have to mean forever and I don't have to be happy about it."

Dropping his hand, she embraced him. Then she reached up, balancing on her toes, and planted a kiss on his cheek. She didn't say goodbye; she didn't say another word. She strode off the ship and didn't look back once.

Brant watched her until she was out of sight, and then turned back to his crew. Matt was standing nearby, evidently waiting for orders.

"Cast off," said Brant, walking towards the bow of the ship where he watched the open sea welcoming him home.

AVAILABLE NOW

ABOUT THE AUTHOR

Christine Steendam is the award-winning author of the Great Canadian Plains Series and the Ocean Series. She also flirts with sci-fi and comic book writing and is a yearly participant in NaNoWriMo.

Christine makes her home in Manitoba, Canada on a sprawling 15 acre ranch with her husband, two young sons, and a brood of animals including Guinness, her beloved chocolate quarter horse; Smokey, her mischievous pony; and her dogs, Beau and Marshall.

www.christinesteendam.com
kcsteendam@gmail.com

Other books by Christine Steendam

The Ocean Series
Owned by the Ocean
Heart Like an Ocean
Betrayed by the Ocean

The Great Canadian Plains Series
Unforgiving Plains
Ropes & Reins

Other Fiction
Shadows of the Unseen